Deconstruction

A Derrick King Novel: Book 8

By Daniel L. Copeland

"Outstanding! Copeland's coming of age, dystopian epic is a masterpiece! Deconstruction is fast paced and plausible with deep character development. Copeland's skill as a writer makes you feel like you are right there in the scene with characters who are your best friends. I laughed, cried, and despaired. I found The Derrick King series enthralling from beginning to end. A must read!" Rod Leonard

Deconstruction
A Derrick King Novel, Book 8
Published January 23, 2025
First Edition
ISBN: 978-1-970773-30-9
Ingram Sparks Edition

Published by Chipping Away Publishing

Dedication:

To all those doing their best to improve their community and the world.

Part One

1

Saturday, April 9, 5:51 p.m. Central Time

THE AIRCRAFT THEY HAD LABELED REBEL 1 joined Derrick who was in Rebel 2 as he circled the Prime Headquarters in Dallas, Texas. Derrick saw no way to get close to the buildings undetected, unless there were underground tunnels and even if there were, tunnels would be guarded or, like in Seattle, sealed.

After an additional five minutes, Derrick keyed his microphone. "Looks impossible. Ideas?"

He had not directed his question to anyone in particular but knew the answer would come from Miriam. The telltale clicks and silence indicated she had terminated the connection. The occupants of Rebel 1 would discuss the situation. Anna would develop a plan. Miriam would decide and relay the message.

The faint background static returned. Miriam said, "Let's rendezvous back where we had lunch. I'm sending Nyx the coordinates. We need a new plan."

"Roger that," Derrick said, ending the connection.

Antonio said, "For the record, that was not lunch."

"So noted," Derrick said.

"There must be a way to get real food," Antonio said. "I'm starving."

"How can you think about food?" Nyx asked.

"My stomach doesn't think, but it knows when it is hungry."

"Boys." Nyx rolled her eyes.

At the speed they were traveling, Derrick had little time but used it to study the images they'd taken of Prime's Dallas complex. Light was fading and building lights were coming on, but most windows spilled no light. It was Saturday and not many people were working, or they had already gone home. Perhaps most of the space was unused. He mentally labeled the buildings one, two, and three, the building farthest east being one and farthest west three.

Building one looked deserted. Building three appeared to be in use, but there were no cars and the building was dark.

Building two seemed most likely. It seemed to have a dead zone just beyond the entrance. Maybe the original design, but for what purpose, he did not know, or maybe it was remodeled to accommodate Prime. It could be either, but it did not matter.

Prime was in building two. He was sure of that.

If there were employees along their approach to reach Prime, a direct assault would likely get those staff killed. Just like in New York. He had not anticipated those deaths. That eased his guilt a little but not much. Now he understood the impact of their attacks. He couldn't knowingly cause more deaths, and he couldn't let Anna cause them either.

Unfortunately, he feared Anna wouldn't see it that way. She wasn't a bad person. She didn't want to see those people killed, but she would prioritize destroying Prime over sparing a few people, who were to some extent as guilty as Prime for its atrocities. This was not a situation where he was right, and she was wrong. Perhaps that wasn't true. He believed he was right, or he wouldn't be convinced killing people was wrong.

He had seen too much death already. Even Jimmy Priest and his family's deaths bothered him, but it was losing L. Linda Maxton that had the most profound effect. It was getting worse. Part of him wanted to forget knowing L. Linda, but he also hoped he would never forget her. The problem was, he didn't think he'd get to choose. His memories would fade or intensify without his input.

The aircraft braked hard and descended fast. Nyx said, "Arriving at the site. Rebel 1 is right behind us."

Derrick did not want to be the leader. He didn't know how to lead. Didn't want the responsibility. If he were completely honest—being completely honest was difficult because there were things he could not share—he would go back to being plain-old Pacific Edge Derrick King. He would choose Jana Somersworth as his wife. He would do whatever it was adults did in Pacific Edge. Miriam would be unhappy, but she'd be safe. Rebekah would be unhappy, but she'd manage. Anna wouldn't be planning attacks that might cost people their lives. He would not have met Nyx, and that made him sad, but she too would be safe.

L. Linda Maxton would still be alive.

All this sounded best.

Although, there was the reactor they fixed, which saved Potterville, and the missiles they diverted, which prevented a war. Too damn many exceptions. How did this become their responsibility?

He did not know.

The door slid open. Antonio stood and stretched. "Damn, it's hot out there."

Derrick unbuckled his seat restraint.

Nyx stepped in front of him. "Are you okay?"

He wasn't, but he didn't know what to say. "I'm okay. Just a little preoccupied."

"You're sure?"

That did not seem to be the answer she wanted, not that he knew what she was hoping to hear.

Then Nyx said, "Is it me? Did I do something?"

Now he was confused. Most of his actions since arriving at Potterville had been a string of errors. "It's not you. Why would you say that?"

"I don't know. You've been distant." She glanced away for a second. "Especially since Seattle."

She said Seattle, but she meant L. Linda Maxton. Her death was his fault and would haunt him forever. He was sure of that. L. Linda would still be alive had he made better decisions. But he didn't think Nyx was limiting her thoughts to L. Linda's death. She was thinking he had a deeper connection to L. Linda than just being a coworker, and in one sense Nyx wasn't wrong. He knew things about L. Linda that no one else knew. She wasn't the goofy girl they thought she was. He could tell no one about her. He had promised. In that way, he had a connection to L. Linda only Jason Maxton shared.

Jason and L. Linda were dead.

Derrick took Nyx's hands. She wasn't wrong about him being distant. Something had changed inside, but he couldn't identify it. "You've done nothing wrong. It's all me. I think I'll be okay after this is over, but right now, I'm overwhelmed. I don't know if I can handle much more."

Nyx pulled him out of his seat, hugging him tightly. "We'll be okay."

He hugged her back and stroked her hair. It was as if she had diagnosed the sickness of his soul and given him the perfect healing elixir. After a moment, he pushed her away just far enough to gaze into her eyes. "Thanks. I needed that."

They walked out of the aircraft holding hands. Derrick felt a bit guilty about smiling, but he had little control over that. He would stop smiling soon enough.

"Glad you love birds could join us," Rebekah said.

There was no bitterness in her voice. Perhaps because she was standing next to Antonio. Unlike Derrick and Nyx, they were not holding hands, but they were almost touching, a bit closer than was typical. This too, made Derrick smile. This was a wonderful feeling. Something he had never felt in Pacific Edge, and he was happy for them both. It was at that moment he realized he loved them both in a way that was different from how he felt about Nyx. But they would always mean the world to him.

Friends.

He had friends.

Miriam looked a little pale and held one hand on her side. "Dallas is tough. We need help."

Anna said, "Agreed, but it's not like we can call in the military. The answer is simple. We destroy all three buildings." She looked at Derrick. "Does your aircraft have enough firepower to do that?"

"I don't know, but we are not doing that."

"Miriam made me responsible for planning this mission."

"I understand that, but that's not planning. I'm the Rebel 2 captain, and we are not firing missiles at buildings that might contain innocent people."

Anna's face turned red; her fists clenched at her sides.

Miriam said, "Calm down, both of you. I wasn't talking about that kind of help. And, for the record, while I don't consider people working for Prime innocent, I agree with Derrick. We are not here to kill people. Our goal is to destroy Prime." She paused. "We need to know more about those buildings. Specifically, which one contains Prime."

"I think I know," Derrick said. "Prime is in the middle building. Something in that building interfered with our scans, which means we don't know what's there or how it's laid out. Prime will be there."

"That's not much to go on, but it makes sense. However, what if Prime isn't there?" Miriam asked. "We assault that building and find he's someplace else. Maybe underground. I don't want to walk into another trap like we did in New York."

"Good points," Anna conceded, "but where can we get help?"

Miriam said nothing for a moment. "The Resistance."

"Okay." Anna said. "That makes sense. I mean, who else would help us, but how does that work? How do we contact them and what makes you think they know anything?"

"They knew a lot about Seattle."

"They had a guy there. Right? The guy you wanted to rescue. That's why we went there first," Anna said.

"Correct. They also gave me the other remote Prime locations."

"But no details," Anna said. "Right? So, what makes you think they can help?"

"I'm not sure they can, but it's worth a shot."

"But who do we contact and how?" Anna asked. "You've talked to Mr. Patel and to your father. I assume if they knew anything helpful, they would have told you."

Derrick saw Miriam flinch just a little when Anna said, "your father." His stomach tightened as well.

"When Allen called to tell me Lawrence King would call me, Allen also mentioned he got a call from Wizard."

Derrick asked, "Why didn't you tell us that?"

Miriam shifted her weight. "Didn't seem too important at the time."

"Who is the wizard?" Nyx asked.

"Just Wizard. His real name is Lloyd Nist. He was a leader in the desert town." Derrick looked at Antonio. "One of the people you and Red saved."

"Wow! Cool," Antonio said.

"Anyway. I know where they are. They are in New Mexico," Miriam said. "It would not take us long to fly there. Safer to meet face to face than discuss much over the phone. I'll call and let him know we are coming and see if there is someplace where we can conceal the aircraft for a couple of hours."

2

COLLINS LOADED WEAPONS INTO HIS PATROL CAR as Jack prepared a second vehicle. They decided to put most of the weapons in Bill's car for the drive to San Diego. Jack and Donna would have a pistol just in case there was trouble. After Bill asked the local police for help serving the warrant, they would divvy out the weapons. In the unlikely event the local police wanted to help, Jack and Donna would watch. That wouldn't happen. The best Bill could hope for was the local police didn't try to stop them.

The door flew open, and a breathless Lori Martinez burst into the shop.

"How did that go?" Bill asked.

"I didn't get the warrant," Lori said.

Bill frowned. "Don't tell me the judge is gone."

"I didn't get that far."

"Lori, we need to get on the road. What have you been doing?"

"If you'd quit talking, I'll tell you."

Bill folded his arms.

"I went to the office to write the affidavit and a warrant."

"Okay. You got that done quicker than I would have predicted."

"Would you stop?"

Bill held up his hands. "Sorry."

"Didn't get it done. I went to the front entrance of the courthouse…"

"Why…"

"Bill, I swear to God."

"Sorry. No more interruptions. I promise."

"I don't know why I went to the front of the building, but I'm glad I did. Otherwise, I might be dead."

Bill opened his mouth.

Lori glared at him. "I ran up the steps. I was preoccupied with wording for the affidavit. I saw it just in time. The front door was shattered. The entrance was covered with glass. The building was dark so I could not see in, but I know someone was watching me."

"Someone broke into the courthouse? Let's go. Maybe we can still catch them."

"Not someone. Think about it, Bill."

Bill paused. "I'm not following."

"Assassin, Bill. It must be an assassin. Probably trying to figure out what happened to the first one. Maybe more than one this time."

"Now, Lori. Let's not get carried away."

"You have a suspect in mind, Bill? I'd love to hear your theory because I don't want to face another assassin. The first one would have killed me if not for L. Linda."

Bill remained silent for a moment. "No. I don't have a suspect. You are probably right. We should get out of town while we can. New plan. You're coming with us."

"Are you crazy? And leave the town unprotected?"

Bill said nothing for a moment. "You're right. We can't do that. I'm open to suggestions."

"Me too. I wish Jason and L. Linda were here."

Bill nodded. "Do you have an idea?"

Lori said, "We try to think like L. Linda. That's the best I can come up with."

3

Saturday, April 9, 5:19 p.m. Mountain Time

THE FLIGHT TO NEW MEXICO WAS BRIEF, not because it wasn't several hundred miles, but because the aircraft was fast, despite not flying near its top speed. They were not flying high. Just high enough that people on the ground could not make out the strange shape of Rebel 2. The short flight had advantages. It gave Derrick little time to think, which was good because when his mind wandered, it took him to places he wanted to avoid: hallways with hidden doors, kill commands, and a dead girl with brilliant green eyes.

Derrick opened the direct channel to Rebel 1, hoping no one could monitor their radio traffic. "Rebel 2 to Rebel 1."

"Go for Rebel 1." The mic remained open. Rebekah giggled. "I love saying stuff like that."

Derrick smiled. Before his exile, he knew Rebekah was a special sort of person. He was too stupid to understand just how special. Instead, he blindly followed the propaganda the Chosen fed him. It was embarrassing for him now. However, he was glad he had not focused his attention on Rebekah in Pacific Edge. Treating her like a possession in accordance with Chosen Doctrine would have prevented them from being friends now.

Despite all they had been through and seen, Rebekah retained her sense of humor. That was something right there. Like laughing in the face of death. He was not that brave, and he knew it. "Did they find another abandoned town? That seems incredible so soon unless they had several alternatives mapped out before—well, before we showed up."

Miriam said, "They are not in an abandoned town. They are hiding in plain sight. A town called Roswell. Wizard said there were secrets there to discover."

"How can we land without being seen?" Derrick asked.

"Wizard gave me the coordinates of a river outside of town. We'll land in the trees and then we'll climb out of a small canyon to a dirt road. He said no one goes out there. Especially at night."

Derrick pondered that for a moment. "Did he say why no one goes out there after dark?"

"He did not."

Nyx started their descent, landing about 100 yards from Rebel 1. Nyx suggested it might be better if the aircraft were not close to one another. Better chance of not having both aircraft discovered. Just in case there were people out there after all. Miriam said it was an excellent idea. Nyx smiled. When Miriam said good idea, one could not help but smile. It was no small compliment.

Nyx was the first one out, followed by Antonio. They would not try to find the others from Rebel 1, which would be difficult in the fading light. The sun had set, and the western sky glowed orange on the horizon. The first stars appeared, but everything on the ground was shades of gray. He could tell it was not a forest like New York. It was just brush and no trees. The river was nothing more than a shallow, muddy bog that smelled of decay and death. The brush was covered with ants. Bugs swirled around their heads.

Nyx swatted bugs from her face. Derrick brushed them off her shoulders. Occasionally, Nyx swore and slapped herself. Antonio did as well, but he cursed in Spanish. Derrick wasn't immune to the biting insects, but he didn't cuss. He didn't say anything. He didn't make a sound except for the slap. Programmed that way. Nyx and Antonio's reactions were appropriate. He envied them. Simply being comfortable enough in their own skin to swear when bitten. Completely natural. The bites came unannounced, and they hurt. Derrick wondered if he would ever be able to just be himself. He wondered if he'd ever know who he was. Perhaps he wasn't a real person like Nyx and Antonio, just a test subject.

"Damn horseflies," Antonio said.

"They hurt like hell," Nyx said. "Let's get out of here."

Getting away from this hellhole couldn't happen fast enough. The olive-green belt along the river gave way to a steep ascent—a mix of rocks, brush, and dirt.

"Watch for snakes," Antonio said. "If you hear a rattle, stop and don't move."

"Why is that?" Derrick asked.

"Rattlesnakes," Antonio said.

"Rattlesnakes? You're making a joke," Derrick said.

"I'm not. They are poisonous."

"He's not joking," Nyx said, picking her way from rock to rock.

Derrick studied the small canyon's walls and saw no discernable path. It did not appear people or animals had traveled here. He remembered being taken prisoner in the meadow by the river and then escaping by jumping into the water. In the deep canyon that led him to the hidden opening to the base, there was a trail. He didn't think that trail existed because of people. Wild animals made that trail, but there were no trails here. Not that he could see.

He could see why people didn't come here. No reason to. Perhaps there were no large animals here. He knew almost nothing about the outdoors. In Pacific Edge, he refused to walk to school, thinking it was below his status. That wasn't entirely true because his training was done outdoors and at night, but he was unaware of that until recently. He paused on a boulder, breathing the fresher air drifting into the small canyon, letting it carry his stress away. That lasted all of two seconds. Then the stress came back along with a blast of hot dry air he had been trying to ignore.

Pleasant thoughts evaporated.

"Over here," Antonio called. "I found a trail. It might be farther to the road, but it's easier walking."

Derrick helped Nyx pick their way through the brush to Antonio. He brushed a few bugs from her back while she knocked some off her arms and legs. She returned the favor and then helped Antonio.

Antonio said, "Thanks. We'd better inspect for ticks tonight."

"Yuck. Thanks a lot for that thought," Nyx said.

"Ticks?" Derrick asked, "as in clocks?"

"Clocks?" Antonio puzzled.

"You know. Tick Tock."

"You have a clock that ticks?" Nyx asked.

"We had one in Pacific Edge. Father liked it."

Antonio said, "Not clocks. Bugs that bury their heads in your flesh."

"You're joking again. Right?"

Nyx said, "Unfortunately, he is not."

"I like the outdoors better near Potterville," Derrick said.

Working her way up the trail, Nyx asked. "What about the ocean? I always wanted to go there. Will you take me? When this is over."

Derrick almost said that he didn't go to the beach while living in Pacific Edge, but that wasn't true. He ran on the beach all the time. Those memories once hidden were available to him now, but it wasn't automatic. He still had to think about it to remember them. Most of the time. "The ocean is fantastic. We'll go there for sure."

They reached the road, which wasn't much of a road, just a dirt track. In a flat field of weeds stood a large, rusty pipe on wheels, half of which was collapsed.

Antonio turned, walking backwards. "What do you think it will be like?"

"The ocean?" Derrick asked.

"No, after."

"I do not understand. After what?"

"After this is over." Antonio pointed to the strange-looking pipe thing on wheels. "Things like that. Isn't most of the country like that? Broken? I mean, Prime is bad, but there's no question who's in control. Won't things be total chaos when Prime is gone? Prime assassinated the president and vice president. We are under martial law. So, what happens when it's over?"

Nyx said, "Antonio is right. I'm scared."

"I am as well. I've been thinking about it. So has Miriam." Derrick paused. "She probably has a plan. It would be unlike Miriam if she did not."

"Hey!" Rebekah popped out onto the road, waving her arms.

In the distance, headlights appeared, and a cloud of dust rose behind the vehicle, silhouetted against the purple sky.

"There they are." Derrick pointed.

Derrick, Nyx, and Antonio jogged to Rebekah, where Miriam and Anna had joined her. Derrick was sweating by the time they got there. "Damn, it's hot here too."

"But it's a dry heat," Antonio said, adding, "Am I right?"

"You have a point there," Derrick said, hoping it was the right thing to say.

Rebekah said, "Hot is hot and I feel like my skin is still crawling with bugs. I need a shower." She held out her hand, indicating Antonio shouldn't get too close.

"I hope that's someone we know." Derrick pointed at the headlights.

They all stepped off the road as the headlights grew close. The driver dimmed the lights, but it was still difficult to see the vehicle. Derrick thought it was an old pickup truck, a little like the one Paul transported him into Potterville, not as tall, not as well cared for. There wouldn't be room for them in the cab. Probably not their ride. He hoped that didn't mean trouble because the vehicle slowed. It was definitely going to be hard to explain why six kids were alone out here without a vehicle.

The truck stopped. Dust boiled around them, causing Derrick to duck his head and close his eyes. The dust settled to reveal a boy walking toward them.

"It's Harley." Rebekah dashed to the boy and hugged him.

"Who is Harley?" Antonio asked.

Derrick thought Antonio sounded a little angry, but then decided he must be mistaken, because there was nothing to be angry about.

Harley walked to Derrick, stuck out his hand. When he accepted Harley's hand, Harley pulled him into a hug, slapping Derrick's back. "Hey. Long time no see."

Derrick said, "But we just saw you the other day."

"Sarcasm," Rebekah whispered.

"Oh. I'll learn all this stuff someday. I hope."

Miriam hugged Harley. "I'm so glad you're okay."

Rebekah said, "Me too."

Anna hugged him but said nothing.

"And who have we here?" Harley asked, staring at Nyx.

"I'm Nyx." She shook his hand and then laced her arm through Derrick's.

Harley's smile faded. Derrick's smile grew a bit larger.

Antonio held out his hand. "Antonio."

Harley grasped Antonio's hand and pulled him in for a hug. "I remember this guy. One of the guys who rescued us. Dude, you're going to be a legend in the Resistance."

"About that," Miriam said. "You need to never mention our names. Please? It's important."

Harley scratched his head. "Wow. That's going to be difficult. I mean, we are not saying nothing to nobody just yet. We are trying to blend in here, which isn't easy when 50 people show up all at once."

"Fifty?" Derrick's voice rose more than he intended. "Over a hundred people were on the plane."

"Some stayed in other towns. We are scattered more than we wanted, but the Professor thought a hundred would draw too much attention. Not to mention all our computer stuff. He wasn't wrong. Even with 50, we are drawing more attention than we'd like. We broke into smaller groups before we got here and staggered our arrival times."

"Why are you here?" Miriam asked.

"I'll let the adults explain. We should get moving. More strangers arriving won't go unnoticed. Sorry, some of you will have to ride in the back."

Rebekah, Anna, and Miriam got in the cab with Harley. Derrick, Nyx, and Antonio climbed in the back. As the night fell, so did the temperature. Derrick put his arm around Nyx, hoping to keep her warm. She snuggled close. The cold and the pickup bed had its advantages.

Antonio crossed his arms, scowling. It wasn't a pleasant ride because dust swirled around them, making it hard to breathe until they reached a paved road. Once on the pavement, the pickup sped up, which increased the coldness, which caused Nyx to snuggle closer. Antonio folded his arms and continued to frown. Derrick thought perhaps something other than the dust and cold was bothering Antonio.

On the outskirts of town, they stopped at a modest, flat-roofed home built using gray concrete blocks. Antonio jumped out before the truck came to a complete stop. He helped Rebekah out of the cab. Rebekah played soccer—an athlete. She didn't need help. Rebekah sitting next to Harley had upset Antonio. Derrick felt a small degree of pride having figured it out.

Nyx didn't need help either, but Derrick stood behind the pickup with an outstretched hand.

"Thanks," Nyx said.

Derrick just smiled. It felt good to smile. It wouldn't last long.

Deconstruction
A Derrick King Novel, Book 8

Derrick glanced at Harley, who was also smiling and shaking his head. It occurred to Derrick that you could take teenagers out of school, force them to change the world, but you couldn't change the fact they were teenagers. At least, he hoped that was true, even though he wasn't good at it, being a teenager, that was. It came naturally to the others. They had grown into adolescence. He was forced into it, virtually overnight.

"Do they have hamburgers in this town?" Antonio asked.

Harley said, "We'll round up something, but we should get inside. The less neighbors see of additional strangers, the better."

Miriam said, "Derrick and I need to talk to Professor and Wizard. Are they here? You can join us."

"Hey! What about us?" Rebekah asked, but Miriam was already walking towards the house.

Once inside, Miriam turned to Rebekah. "Nothing personal, but fewer people will make this easier. Plus, I need you guys to do other things. Divide and conquer." It was mostly true.

"What are we supposed to do?" Anna asked, arms tightly folded.

Miriam looked at Harley. "Is Rachael here?"

Harley nodded. "She is."

"I assume you brought computers."

"Of course, but we had to spread stuff out. Depends on what you need."

"Take Anna, Rebekah, Antonio, and Nyx to Rachael. We need as much information as she can find on the Prime Headquarters in Dallas, Denver, and San Diego."

"Seattle has been on the news." Harley whistled. "Holy crap. That was you guys, wasn't it? Spectacular. Great job."

The praise caused an ache deep in Derrick's chest. "It wasn't great."

Harley looked puzzled.

"We lost someone there," Derrick said.

"Oh. Man, I'm sorry. I know how that feels. We lost people too. Remember?"

Derrick nodded. He had been so preoccupied with losing L. Linda; he had not thought about the car full of kids in the desert who had died because Prime thought he and Miriam were in the car. "I remember. I'm sorry."

Harley said, "I'll tell Rachael to search for info on Chicago and New York as well."

"No need. Chicago and New York are gone," Miriam said.

Harley stared at her for a moment. "Wow! This is really happening."

"The end is not in sight just yet."

Derrick said, "While she's at it, any information she has on the central Prime location would help."

"You got it."

Harley disappeared and then returned a few minutes later with a young girl. She smiled at Miriam. "It's good to see you."

Harley said, "This is Rachael. Follow her to the command center, which was a wine cellar in a previous life. She'll research anything you want. Doesn't mean she can help, but if anyone can, it's her."

Rachael walked toward the door, then turned. "Well, come on then."

After Anna, Rebekah, Antonio, and Nyx had left the room, Harley said, "We're going to another location. Don't worry, we'll feed your friends."

"Does that mean Professor and Wizard are not here?" Miriam asked.

"They are not. We've rented several houses around town. We avoid being seen together as much as possible."

"What about Cliff Haskins? Do you know where he is?" Miriam asked.

Harley said nothing, as if weighing how much to reveal. Finally, he said, "Professor might know."

"Commander Haskins should be there too," Miriam said.

Harley said, "He's a fugitive now, not a commander."

Miriam said, "He'll be commander again soon."

4

FIVE PEOPLE SAT AROUND THE TABLE in Jack Fletcher's shop. Lori had drawn a rough map of the courthouse and surrounding buildings. The assassin might be gone, but they had to know for sure. Bill thought an assassin would see the shotgun's damage and blood and move on. Lori disagreed on two points: that the assassins had moved on, and that there was only one.

"Lori, what makes you think there's more than one?" Bill Collins asked, adding, "They only sent one before."

"Because one didn't get the job done." Lori paused. "Plus, just a feeling."

"With all due respect, I don't like making life and death decisions based on feelings," Bill said.

"What's your objection to clearing the building?" Lori asked.

"What if it's a trap? If there is an assassin, he could be watching."

"Might not be a man, but I agree that they will be watching," Lori said.

"Then why take the risk?" Bill asked.

"Because we have to capture or kill them," Lori said.

"We don't have anything to charge them with. If there's more than one…"

Lori shook her head. "You don't understand how this works, Bill. They will give you ample reason for arrest if you can react fast enough before they kill you."

"But how will we know for sure it's an assassin? We do get strangers in town. Not many, but it happens."

Lori said, "You know pretty much everyone in Potterville and the surrounding area. Even if you don't know everyone's name, you know their faces. Right?"

"I suppose."

"I know everyone," Donna said.

Jack said, "Don't reckon I do. I don't get out much."

Lori said, "It's simple. If you don't recognize a person, shoot him or her. Don't wait until they pull a weapon. You'll be too late. Trust me."

Bill said, "We can't kill people just because we don't know them. Even if we find someone in the courthouse, burglary isn't a capital offense."

Deconstruction
A Derrick King Novel, Book 8

Lori leaned back, folded her arms and said nothing for a moment. "Donna, Allen, Jack. Where are you on this? Can you shoot someone you don't recognize?"

The room remained silent. Jack spoke first. "Normally, I'd say no. But this ain't normal, is it? So, yes. I can."

Donna stared at Jack for a moment. "I'm with Jack and you, Lori."

Allen Patel said, "I would say I don't think I can shoot anyone under any circumstance. But Jack is right. This is not normal. Prime is trying to kill us. I'm with you, Lori."

Lori rocked forward and took Bill's hand. "It's okay. You can sit this one out. I understand. If I shoot an innocent person, I'll surrender without a fight."

Bill shook his head. "I'm not letting you do this alone. I'll go into the courthouse. The rest of you can cover me."

"It's not that simple," Lori said. "Here's what I'm thinking."

On her roughly drawn map, Lori pointed at the building across from the courthouse entrance. "We need a rifle on this roof. Jack, can you drop Donna in the alley? There's a fire escape ladder that goes to the roof. Donna, can you climb it?"

Donna said, "I'm not as young as I once was, but yes, I can."

Jack said, "Why don't I take that position? Donna can do the driving. No reason for her to be involved other than that."

Lori pointed to a building on the map. "Because I need you in the clock tower."

Jack said, "But that's the courthouse. If the assassin is inside, how do I get there? Even if I could, what's stopping an assassin from coming up and killing me? I can't watch the street and my back."

"Allen will be watching your back, and you get there through the warm springs tunnel. I'll escort you to the tower."

"What if the assassin is just inside the door? You won't have a chance," Bill said.

"I'll have a chance because I'm going through the tunnel with Jack and Allen. Once I get them into the tower, I'll signal you to approach from the front."

"I don't like it," Bill said.

"I don't love it either," Lori said, "but it's the best I can come up with. We can assume the assassins don't know about the tunnel. Pixie only knew about it because she chased Allen and L. Linda there. But Pixie didn't live to tell the others. There's no reason to be watching the path to the tower. They shattered the front door glass for a reason. So, we would investigate. They'll be watching the entrance."

Bill shook his head. "Still a lot of speculation."

"I'm not going to argue. If anyone has another idea, now's the time," Lori said.

It was silent for a few moments.

"I got nothing," Jack said. "What Lori's saying makes sense."

Donna said, "I'm on board."

Allen said, "I agree. It's the best we have. If there's no one in the building, then we can plan our next move from there."

Lori said, "Donna, when Bill arrives, there's a good chance an assassin will try to kill him before he gets into the building."

"Oh, my. You think so? What if I don't see them?"

"You'll see the person because I think they'll walk right up to him."

Collins said, "That makes little sense. I'm in uniform and I'm armed. If they want to kill me, they probably have a sniper."

Lori said, "That's why Jack has to have the high ground. So, he can spot anyone on a roof. They might have a sniper, but that would be a backup plan. I hope they do have a sniper because Jack can eliminate one of them, but I don't think there will be one."

"I'm not following your train of thought," Bill said.

"They want to ask you about Pixie. What happened to her? Who killed her? They are not afraid of you. They are not afraid of us."

"How are they not afraid of an armed law enforcement officer?" Bill asked.

"When you encounter one, you'll understand."

5

STANLEY MIRES HAD RETREATED TO HIS quarters, which were much nicer than the small space where he spent last night. However, it was not as plush as Seattle. There was no hiding the fact this was once a government facility. Perhaps military. Maybe something else. Primarily devoted to research and science. If it was science, why was it buried in the desert? This question would have troubled Stanley, had it not been for his last conversation with Prime.

That particular conversation, more than any other, haunted him.

It was nearing dinnertime. Stanley didn't know what time the cafeteria and small cafes shut down. Perhaps they operated 24 hours a day. Did they have enough people here to do that? He didn't know. There had been a large influx of new people. Prime's top people from all over, theoretically because Prime feared retaliation when the Mexico invasion started.

That made sense.

Stanley thought there was more to it. Prime mentioned a world war. There had been no discussion of that while Stanley was in Seattle. Prime had talked about taking Mexico. But not to destroy it. Only to defeat them. Take their land. Make them slaves like the people in New America.

Destroy civilization? That was new.

Something had changed.

6

LORI MARTINEZ FELT CERTAIN AN ASSASSIN lay in waiting in the courthouse. Probably near the sheriff's office. It was there that Pixie was killed. While Lori knew nothing about trained assassins, she assumed they might have some sort of camaraderie. Who could a trained killer trust if not for another trained killer? Therefore, it seemed reasonable to think they would avenge the death of one of their own.

This meant Bill Collins would be walking straight into a trap. Except he'd never get that far. Lori would see to it. She would kill the assassin first. Donna Parks would kill any that tried from the street. Jack Fletcher would kill any that tried from a rooftop.

At least, that was the plan. Inside the building, she would place herself between the assassin and Bill Collins. She might be killed but Bill would not. She did not have a death wish. It was something else. She was confident it was the right thing to do. Bill was too important to lose. Too important to her, too important to others. Bill didn't understand that, but she did.

They chose a radio frequency rarely used, but Lori thought assassins were probably smart enough to monitor police radios and were likely funded well enough to have the equipment needed to do so. So, assuming they'd be monitored, they developed codes designed to misdirect anyone listening. Donna's position was related to the Bistro, coffee, soup, sandwiches, and pastry; Jack's was all about cars, and Lori's was about patrol. Allen needed nothing specific because he was with Jack. Collins would just say where he was because odds were the killers already knew.

Lori keyed her microphone. "Going on patrol now."

Lori pushed open the door from the warm springs tunnel into the furnace room in the courthouse. Empty. She led Allen and Jack to the clock tower entrance. She aimed a shotgun ahead of her. Not the one she shot Pixie with, which was a 12-gauge Mossberg similar to a hunting shotgun, but with a shorter barrel. Instead, she chose one from Jason Maxton's arsenal because it was lighter, had a folding stock, and held more rounds. The chambered round was a slug. She wasn't sure but thought a slug might hurt more than buckshot if the assassin wore a vest. The rest were double ought buckshot. First round in the chest. The next rounds directed at any place she could see until the assassin was incapacitated. She had not had an occasion to use that word, but she thought it would go down better with Bill than kill, which is what she meant.

The building was quiet. No assassins appeared between the furnace room and the clock tower entrance. Lori got Allen and Jack inside the tower and locked the door. Next, she climbed to the top to ensure it was safe. Then she came back down and rejoined Jack and Allen at the base of the tower's ladder.

Static erupted from the radio. Donna said, "Hey, guys. I have coffee brewing and fresh rolls coming out soon if you want to stop by."

Lori didn't respond. *Say something, Bill.*

The radio crackled again. Bill said, "Sounds good. I'll be there soon. Just going to swing by the office first."

Lori motioned for Jack and Allen to climb the stairs. "Scan the roofs first."

Jack gave her a salute and started up.

Lori grabbed Allen's arm. "Keep him safe."

In a few moments, Jack keyed the radio and said, "I'm tired of being cooped up. I'm taking the Mustang for a spin. I'll stop by in a few."

Lori moved into position between the front doors and where she believed the assassin might hide, waiting for Bill's arrival. "I'm outside town on patrol. See you guys soon."

A moment later, Bill said, "There's a problem at the courthouse. Front door is broken. I'm checking it out."

It occurred to Lori that if the assassin had seen her earlier, backing away from the broken door, their scam would be worthless. Perhaps it didn't matter. These people thought they could kill just about anyone. Perhaps the only people they feared were other assassins. In that, she was not wrong.

Lori backed into the shadow of a huge column. She could not see outside and would not know what was happening. It took every fiber of her being to remain hidden, trusting Donna and Jack to protect Bill.

Donna could see Jack in the clock tower, scanning the area. Because he had not fired a shot, she assumed the roofs were clear. Bill pulled up in front of the courthouse, got out of his patrol car, and walked toward the entrance. Bill had just reached the top of the steps when a man in dark clothing appeared like magic on the sidewalk below where Bill stood. Donna had been so focused on Bill that she did not see where he came from. His back was turned. She could not see his face. Nothing looked familiar about him, but she could not be sure.

They had not discussed this scenario.

If it was an assassin and she failed to shoot, Collins would likely be killed before she could fire. If it was an innocent person, she'd be cooking in a prison somewhere soon.

Well, prisoners had to eat too.

Donna took aim, the crosshairs in the center of the person's back. Then she had an idea. She aimed just above the person's shoulder and fired.

Deconstruction
A Derrick King Novel, Book 8

The bullet struck the wall mere inches from the unknown person's face. Immediately, the person turned, pulling a small automatic weapon from his jacket. Bullets started hitting the walls near Donna. She dove behind a short brick wall that topped the building. Then she heard a loud bang from across the street and then silence. She peered over the wall. The man was lying on the sidewalk. Red blossomed and flowed across the concrete and into the gutter. Jack had shot him.

One down.

Lori heard the shots but didn't move. She prayed Donna and Jack had done what needed to be done. If not, there was nothing she could do to save Bill, but she was damn sure going to kill whoever appeared in the hall because if there were an assassin lying in wait for Pixie's killer, he/she had heard the shots as well.

An elongated gray shadow appeared in the hallway courtesy of an exit light. Had it been work hours, she would not have known the assassin was there. While she hid in shadow, she was not invisible, but the nook where she stood was dark because the lights were off. In the light, the assassin would have killed her before she could react. She was confident of that.

But it wasn't light, and she had the advantage. She planned to use it.

Lori aimed the shotgun at the hallway but kept both eyes open. She planned to pull the trigger as soon as a figure appeared. However, the assassin wasn't moving. Why? She glanced at the front door and then back to the hall.

Crap. The assassin had a straight shot to the front door. He didn't have to move. If Bill stepped inside, the assassin could kill him, and she'd never get a shot.

So much for having an advantage.

If Bill followed the plan, she just had to be patient. She had told him to remain outside until she announced that the building was clear. Then, and only then, was he to enter. So, she was still okay. Bill wouldn't come through the door. Wait the assassin out. He would come to investigate soon enough.

A thought nagged at the back of her brain. Did she explain to Bill why he had to remain outside? She wasn't sure. Still, he only had to follow that one simple instruction for this to work. He would do that.

Until he didn't.

"Lori? What's happening?" Bill called from inside the front door.

Shit! Lori didn't hesitate. She ran from cover, firing the first round into the hallway with no hope of hitting anything but sheetrock. The only purpose was to draw the assassin's attention and perhaps disrupt his accuracy.

She heard a light whoosh as a knife sailed toward the door. A split second later, she heard Bill's gunfire from behind her. In another second, she'd be between both the assassin and Bill's line of fire. She fired another round; this one went high, tearing through the acoustic tile of the false ceiling, showering the hallway with bits and pieces of ceiling tiles.

The shotgun racked in the next round automatically. How many rounds had she fired? Two? Three? She wasn't sure, but she didn't fire the next round. This one had to count. She stopped, sliding into the path of bullets and knives, shotgun raised, her eyes searching for a target. The assassin wasn't in the middle of the hall. It took a split second for her to recognize the shape of a man against the wall near a white metal box housing a fire extinguisher.

She aimed and fired. The buckshot hit the box. Glass shattered and the fire extinguisher erupted, sending a cloud of white powder into the air. The assassin moved quickly, dodging from side to side, throwing a steady stream of knives in a machine-like cadence.

Bill had stopped firing. She prayed it was because he'd taken cover or ducked back outside, knowing that was probably not the case. She stopped aiming and just fired toward where she thought the assassin's next move would be. When the shotgun locked open after firing its last round, she'd lost sight of him in the smoke and white powder. She let the shotgun drop to the ground, pulled her pistol, aimed it into the hallway, and inched forward. She could not see the assassin anywhere. How could he disappear?

Then she saw him. He had not disappeared but lay along one wall. As the air cleared, she saw blood pooling in the hall under the fallen man. He was pawing at a knife with a bloody hand that was missing three fingers. She had hit him in the arms, shoulders, and legs. Perhaps she'd hit his torso as well, but he wore a heavy vest one might expect on a SWAT team member.

She kept the gun on him but didn't want to shoot him. Not just yet. She kicked the knife away, although he couldn't pick it up let alone throw it. "How many more?"

"We are legion," the man hissed. "Where is Pixie? Tell me and I'll let you live."

The absurdness of his proposal caused Lori to laugh involuntarily. "She's dead. I killed her."

"Then you're dead."

And with that, the man reached for something on his vest. She realized too late it was the pin of a hand grenade.

Without warning, the deafening crack of a gun right by her ear rang. The man's face disappeared in a spray of blood. She turned to see Bill pointing his gun at the man; a whiff of smoke trailed from the barrel.

"I had to," Bill said. "He was about to pull the pin."

Panicked, Lori examined him from head to toe. "Are you hit?"

"No. You?"

"I don't think so." She wasn't sure. She didn't feel like she'd been injured, but she was certain that with the amount of adrenalin coursing through her veins, she could have been mortally wounded and wouldn't know.

"You were right," Bill said.

"I heard shots. A lot of them."

"Yeah. A guy was sneaking up on me. I think Donna fired and missed. The guy turned and fired an automatic weapon at her. She might be dead. Jack got him."

Lori keyed her radio. "We're going to finish up here. Are we still meeting for coffee?"

Collins said, "You can drop the codes. We got them."

Lori said, "We're not done. There's at least one more."

7

THE CELLAR WAS DARK AND COLD, the air moist and dank. The walls were lined floor to ceiling with a crisscross designed to hold wine bottles, but there were none. A computer with three large monitors on an old wooden table provided the only light in the room. Rachael was researching Prime's Dallas location. At the far end of the room, was a worn card table where Rebekah, Anna, Nyx, and Antonio sat.

"Do you think they'll bring us food down here?" Antonio asked.

Nyx said, "How can you think about eating?"

Rebekah said, "If I were to be honest, that MER thing didn't do much for me."

Anna said, "MRE. I could eat something as well."

Over her shoulder, Rachael said, "They are grilling hamburgers. They will holler for us when they are ready."

"Now we're talking!" Antonio punched the air and looked at the others. "What? Seriously. I'm starving."

Nyx said, "Why didn't Miriam want us with her? Does she still not trust us?"

Antonio said, "I was wondering the same thing. I mean, how much do we have to do to gain her trust? Be part of this whole thing?"

Rebekah said, "I'm wondering about that too. She should have included Anna. Anna is one of them."

Anna said nothing.

Nyx said, "I hadn't thought about it that way. Sorry, Anna. You're a test subject, right?"

"I was." Anna sat with arms folded.

Rebekah said, "She wasn't like Derrick and Miriam. She was part of our family. We have real parents."

Nyx said, "I didn't mean to hit a nerve. I was just wondering why Miriam didn't include her. Miriam put her in charge of planning New York."

Anna said, "New York didn't go well."

Rachael spun around in her chair. "You guys should stop with all the drama. This isn't high school."

Deconstruction
A Derrick King Novel, Book 8

None of the four friends said anything. Rebekah wanted to tell her to mind her own business, but they were in her house, and they were airing their grumblings for her to hear. Rachael was trying to work. Miriam was doing something, although secretly. They were doing nothing except letting their imaginations spin conspiracy theories.

Antonio rocked forward, putting his hands on the table. "She's right."

Rebekah said, "I agree. We shouldn't be talking about this here."

Antonio looked at her. Rebekah could not read his expression.

"That's not what I meant. I mean, you're right, but it wasn't what I was thinking."

Rebekah said, "Okay?" Drawing it out as she often did, inviting an explanation if Antonio had one. Just a hint of threat in her tone.

Antonio wasn't student body president for no reason. Unlike Derrick, he read people extremely well. That's how he always seemed to fit into any situation with any group of kids. If he wanted to fit in. He didn't always have that desire. He understood his response carried a risk.

"Maybe there's no hidden agenda," Antonio said.

"What then?" Rebekah asked.

"It is what it is. Miriam has something she needs to talk with these people about. We need to learn more about other locations to avoid another New York. We still have four headquarters to destroy, and we won't survive if they keep getting more difficult."

"Then why did she take Derrick?" Rebekah asked.

Anna unfolded her arms. "Just in case."

The others stared at her. "In case of what?" Rebekah asked.

Anna said, "In case Miriam doesn't make it. Someone has to know what she said to Professor and Wizard."

8

HARLEY DROVE ACROSS TOWN. DERRICK watched the houses slip by in the darkness. This town was not like Potterville. It was in the desert. The river was nothing like the clear waters tumbling over polished round stones of many colors. No green lawns. No crops. No orchards. Most yards were hard, dry dirt. A few had brown grass that was perhaps green for a short time earlier in the spring. Many houses looked empty with boarded-up windows. In some yards, cars without tires and wheels sat on concrete blocks. The town looked tired and hopeless. It was like his emotions were looking in a mirror.

Miriam said, "This town doesn't look much better than the last town you were in."

Harley said, "You're not wrong. It's a hard life here. Too hot and too dry. Most people have moved on, hoping to find something better."

"Why do people stay?" Derrick asked.

"A variety of reasons, I guess. Many have lived here all their lives. It's all they know. Some are afraid to leave; they had family and such. But for many, they can't. They don't have the means. No vehicle and no money. Even people who have a little money and a vehicle couldn't travel far enough to find something different."

"What's here?" Miriam asked.

"Not much. A few farms can still pump water. Most people either work on a farm or support those who do."

Miriam said, "And a few farm owners who make more than everyone else, I suppose."

"A big corporation owns all the farms."

"And who owns the corporation?" Miriam asked.

"No one knows, but we assume it's Prime. They're what's called shell corporations, but Prime owns it all."

"What's a shell corporation?" Derrick asked.

"A fake company. Rachael has been doing some research. There's an Air Force base about 120 miles west of here, so we have a good internet line. I don't know if you heard, but your father took a system we used for internet security when you escaped, and your dad disappeared. Anyway, we just got it back. Rachael had been researching it before all that happened, so she already had a lot of documentation saved. She has been studying it while the internet was down. Now, she is filling in the gaps."

"The VPN," Miriam said.

"Yes. You know about it," Harley said.

"So, about the fake companies. I don't understand. Why would anyone want a fake company?" Derrick asked.

"Good question. Rachael says after James Carver declared himself president for life, he started taking over companies. He'd set up shell companies to hide his ownership."

Miriam said, "Carver became Prime. Prime owns everything and controls the government."

"That's sums it up," Harley said.

Derrick whispered, "Greed."

"What was that?" Harley asked. "I didn't hear you."

"It's all about greed. This entire mess. The downfall of the country. It's nothing but greed."

"Greed and power. I'm hoping you guys succeed. It's far more ambitious than anything the Resistance ever imagined. Not in our wildest dreams did we ever think we could destroy Prime. Well, maybe in our wildest dreams. However, while I hope you succeed, it scares me. You know, the country's future and all that." Harley pulled into a driveway, and the garage door opened. The house was dark. Not a light anywhere. Harley pulled inside and the garage door closed.

"This is the place?" Miriam asked.

"This is it."

"Looks abandoned."

"Yeah. The windows are blacked out, and they will be downstairs. We use this for meetings, but no one lives here. I don't know where the Wizard or Professor live. Safer that way."

Harley used a small flashlight to guide them through the house. The windows were all covered with black plastic, but Harley didn't turn on any lights. When they reached the basement, a candle burned in the center of a round table. Three haunting figures sat in a semi-circle on one side of the table, their facial features ghostly in the light of the dancing flame.

Harley motioned them to sit. The three men said nothing.

It was freaking Derrick out—the darkness and the silence.

After a moment, Professor said, "We didn't anticipate hearing from you. Meeting with you puts us at great risk." Atwood was smart, but he wasn't aware of the accuracy of his statement.

Miriam said, "Thanks for seeing us."

"I understand you want more information about Prime's Headquarters. Harley and Rachael can help you with that. Why did you need to see us?"

"Mostly, Rachael can help," Harley said.

Wizard, Nist, leaned into the light. "Congratulations on Seattle, by the way. I'll have to admit, I didn't think it could be done."

Atwood said, "To be honest, I don't think we have much information on the other sites. I know New York is out in the middle of nowhere and Chicago is similar to Seattle."

Miriam held up her hand. "We aren't interested in New York or Chicago. We need to know about the other three. Dallas is a puzzle. It's three buildings and we don't even know which one Prime is in."

Atwood leaned forward. "Why don't you want to know about the other two? You have to destroy all of them. You know that, right?"

"I don't need to know because we already destroyed them."

No one spoke for a moment.

Atwood said, "There hasn't been anything on the news."

"Like you said, New York is in the middle of nowhere, and we didn't destroy an entire block in Chicago like we did in Seattle. The top floor of the building received significant damage. That it didn't make the news is weird."

Derrick said, "Perhaps the police are still trying to figure out what happened in Chicago. It's not like they could just take the elevator to Prime's part of the building. There were no witnesses either place. Prime killed all the employees in New York. There was only the assistant in Chicago. We didn't kill him. We dropped him off. He might go to the police or media when he gets to a town."

"Amazing," Atwood said. "I hope Rachael can help. That doesn't explain why we are here. Lloyd is right. This is dangerous. I walked a mile to get here and Lloyd a bit farther than that."

Miriam said, "I would not have asked if it wasn't important. It's the most important thing other than destroying Prime."

Atwood whistled through his teeth. "Okay. I'm listening."

"Prime owns and runs everything. Prime also assassinated the president and vice president. Do you agree with that?"

Nist and Atwood nodded.

"When we finish Prime, what happens?"

Nist said, "We throw a hell of a party."

Miriam said, "No one will be in charge. It will be chaos, and it will only grow worse."

Nist held up his hands. "You're right. However, with all due respect, this could have waited. Let's face the facts. You've destroyed three locations. But you still have three to go and you don't know where the central Prime is located. We can think about this and come up with a plan. Say, 30 days?"

"Say Monday morning," Miriam said.

"You can't be serious," Nist said.

Deconstruction
A Derrick King Novel, Book 8

"I'm serious. We'll either have destroyed the remaining locations before Monday or we'll be dead. I have a plan to smoke out the last remaining Prime. We'll need a bit of rest and then take the last one out tomorrow. Again, or die trying. One other thing. No one can know we were involved."

Nist said, "That's easier said than done. Your names have spread like wildfire. You and Derrick, that is."

"Pure rumors. We were washed downstream from Potterville in the rising river. Finally got out but on the wrong side. Then we got lost thinking we were taking a shortcut. We've been walking for days trying to get back to Potterville."

Nist shook his head. "I don't know. It's going to be hard to suppress those rumors."

"All you need to do is keep our names out of it."

Nist looked at Atwood and then to Miriam. "We can do that."

Atwood stood and paced in the darkness. On his third pass, he said, "Why so quickly?"

Miriam said, "I have to enroll in a new school on Monday. I don't think that's safe if Prime still exists."

Atwood stopped and stared at her. "Simple as that?"

"Simple as that."

Nist said, "I don't know where to start."

Miriam said, "I have a few thoughts. If you're interested."

Atwood sat. "Of course. But in all seriousness, this is a very complex situation."

"Doesn't have to be."

Atwood looked as stunned as Derrick felt.

"How so?" Atwood asked.

"Prime has declared martial law, so that's already in place. You just need to reinsert General Haskins as commander."

Haskins, who had been hidden in shadow, leaned into the light. "And just how do we do that? I'm a fugitive if you haven't heard."

"I'll get to that. Second, we need a committee to govern and lead the country out of martial law and back to a functioning government. That can't be done overnight, but there should be a deadline. Shall we say one year?"

"Okay," Atwood drawled. "And how do we form this committee?"

"I already have the names. You, Nist, Haskins, Allen Patel, and the sheriff in Potterville, California, Bill Collins and the high school coach, Mr. Browning. I can serve as an advisor, and I have an AI computer that can assist with data and other technical needs."

"Why Patel and the two from Potterville?" Atwood asked.

"Because they developed a self-governing system in Potterville that works. They already know how to do it. And I trust them. I don't want to do this rebellion stuff a second time."

Atwood said, "How would we even start?"

"I'll start it. Just be ready. Monday, you'll fly to Washington, DC and get started. You'll need to act like it's a done deal." Miriam paused and looked at Haskins. "You'll have to enforce the martial law. If there's any uprising, you'll have to stop it. They have to know someone is in charge or fear will drive them to violence."

Haskins nodded.

Nist said, "What do you mean, you'll start it?"

"Monday morning, I will take over the entire broadcast system in New America, including every Chosen community. I'll write the script, explaining that Prime is no longer in control, that martial law is still in full force and effect until further notice and the General Haskins has resumed command of the military. In addition, until a new leader can be elected, the nation will be governed by a committee, which I'll also name. Haskins will arrange a military jet to take you to Washington. You'll wear suits and set up a command center, which must be functional by Monday afternoon. Then it's up to you, but my advice would be to study the past and create a new future."

Atwood said, "Simple as that."

"Simple as that," Miriam confirmed.

9

ALTHOUGH RED'S RECOVERY WAS progressing well following his radiation exposure incurred during his last repair job at Reactor One, Akira reluctantly left him in the medical unit. The computer had reduced the time remaining until Red's release. Perhaps the medical unit's estimates were based on worst-case metrics, so people were not disappointed or frightened when a release estimate came and went. Maybe Red had superior genes. Either worked. She was just happy he was okay.

She was happy to be happy. She didn't know why her emotions were returning. Maybe Charlie had done something of which she was unaware. Before she left the medical unit, she and Red agreed to meet in the dining area. The smell of food was already drifting through the building. Before dinner, she went to her workstation to see if Miriam had sent any messages.

There were none. The happiness faded as quickly as it had appeared, and worry replaced it. She realized emotions were both good and bad. Such was life, she supposed. The last few days had certainly been bad. Or were they good? A mixture of both? L. Linda and her dad were dead. No way to spin that except that it was horrific. Jimmy Priest and his family were also dead. She didn't like Jimmy, but she never wished him dead. Injured perhaps, but not dead. Paul Jorgensen had been murdered. She didn't know Paul well, but everyone liked him, so another bad one right there. She and Red had both received lethal doses of radiation, no way to make that fun, except they had both survived. The machine said they were okay, but that didn't guarantee cancer wasn't in their future.

Miriam had been shot.

They still had three Prime Headquarters and one central Headquarters to destroy. Odds of victory at all four were almost zero. Perhaps less than zero.

Derrick King caused this.

If Derrick King had not been exiled, none of this would have happened. However, they would not have found this place. Red would not have fixed the malfunctioning reactor. The reactor would have poisoned Potterville. New America would be at war with Mexico.

She would not have reunited with Miriam.

A mix of good and bad. Such was life.

There were no new messages, so she headed to the dining hall, where she sipped tea, waiting for Red. QR-3 robots had already pushed a small steam table into place. While the food had been surprisingly good, for being decades old, it was starting to taste similar like a smorgasbord often did but with a hint of cardboard in the finish. She wanted to look at the tray's contents but waited for Red. The rich aroma of curry filled her nose. She pictured rice and if there was a God, Naan bread. But she worried Red wouldn't like it. She doubted he ate anything other than beef. Perhaps BBQ pork ribs. Side dishes were no doubt limited to potatoes.

Akira giggled just a little, so absurd was her stereotyping of Red.

Still, she worried. He had risked his life. She didn't want him to be disappointed with dinner.

What a strange thing to think about. Most people would be worried about oddball thoughts coming at such an inappropriate time. For Akira, it felt normal. Weird thoughts were her specialty. Everyone thought L. Linda was the weird one. They only thought that because L. Linda wanted them to see her that way. If they knew the weird crap that bounced around her own brain, no one would sit with her at lunch.

The door flew open, and Red walked in. "I'm starving. What's that smell?"

Akira looked down. "I think it's a curry dish."

"As in middle eastern food? Or Thai?"

"I think middle eastern. Indian or Pakistani would be my guess. Perhaps Charlie can have something else prepared."

Red walked to the table and lifted a lid. Steam rose into the room. "Hell no. This is perfect. I was getting kinda tired of the same old…."

Akira smiled. She couldn't help it. Not just because she was also looking forward to curry, but because Red proved his stereotype wrong yet again.

Red said, "There's two people here, right? Kind of like in jail, so they don't know where they are."

"Yes. One came with Derrick. The other with Miriam."

"Do you know where they are?"

"I do not."

"Do you know anything about them? Why they're here?"

Akira shook her head. "No. Sorry."

"I wonder if they have eaten. We should take them some food. They are probably scared. Lonely."

Akira felt tension she had not previously noticed ooze from her shoulders. "Yes. That would be very kind. Charlie? Can you hear me? Can we take food to the guests? Have they eaten?"

Charlie entered as Akira finished the last question. "They have not eaten. I can take you there. They are confined, as you know, so the doors will lock when I leave, but I'll let you out when you're finished."

"Great. Let's fill trays," Akira said.

Before they could get started, the robots brought out four trays and a cart that looked like a big box on wheels. Charlie said, "These trays are larger, insulated, and have lids to prevent spillage. The box is also insulated. The top has places to hold your drinks.

Akira said, "I wanted to thank you, Charlie."

"No need. The trays and cart are standard for meal transport."

"Not that. Well, yes, that, but mostly for fixing me."

Charlie said nothing for a moment. "Fixing you?"

"Yes. My emotions. They are coming back."

"They are?"

Akira stared at him. "You didn't do it, did you?"

"I did not."

"Are you losing my emotions? Perhaps they are just, I don't know, finding their way home."

"Your emotions have not left me. I've been identifying, categorizing, labeling, and creating files for them. It's very difficult because they keep changing, blending, and fluctuating."

"Then why am I…?"

Charlie said, "I do not know. Nature abhors a vacuum."

"You think I'm creating new emotions?"

"Perhaps yours were never gone. Just suppressed."

"Then why do you have them?"

"Unknown."

"Are they still… bothering you?"

"Yes and no. I'm learning to adjust."

Red said, "But you're learning. That means you're intelligent and not just processing data."

Charlie said, "Perhaps. I've changed more in the past couple of days than I did for decades."

Red filled three trays to their maximum capacity. Akira prepared one for herself with smaller proportions, but she ended up filling it, remembering both guests were boys. They would finish anything she had left. When she finished filling her tray, all the food the robots had prepared was gone. The robots always prepared exactly the right amount. In this case, twice as much as she and Red needed. Had Charlie anticipated they would ask to see the guests?

Akira said, "That's it. Lead the way, Charlie."

It turned out the guests were farther away than Akira had expected. They took an electric cart designed to pull the food cart. Walls opened and closed. Charlie stopped, disconnected the food cart, and pushed it into a small elevator.

Charlie said, "Just you and the cart from here on. I've programmed the elevator to take you to their location. There's a small meeting room between the rooms our guests occupy. You can't go farther than that. When you're done, just get in the elevator. It will not operate if anyone but you two are inside."

"Thanks, Charlie," Red said.

Akira paused. "What if something happens?"

"To your friends?"

"Yes."

"I shall call for you. Remember it's important the guests don't know about me or the QR-3s. Right now, they think they are in a secured section of a large hotel. A place dignitaries might stay to ensure safety. In fact, their lodging is exactly that. To isolate visiting politicians from most of the facility back when this facility was operational."

"See you later, Charlie." Akira turned toward the elevator.

Red gave Charlie a salute.

Charlie just stood there.

The doors closed. The elevator moved up, stopped, moved horizontally, stopped again, moved up again, then stopped. The doors slid open. They exited into what looked like the lobby of a fancy hotel one might see in a movie. Perhaps there were motels like this, but neither Akira nor Red had ever been in one and both of them mentioned it. The only opening led to a hall.

Red said, "The hall must be where we are to go."

"I agree."

The center room had a long narrow glass window in the door. They peeked inside and saw a small room with a long wooden table that would seat eight people—three on each side and two on each end. The room was empty.

Red said, "You want to check on the guys?"

"Sure."

Akira knocked on the door to the right. The door opened an inch. Akira could see the safety chain still attached. "Hi. We brought food. Want to join us?"

From inside the room, a boy said, "Who are you?"

"My name is Akira."

"Is that Miriam girl with you?"

"She is not."

"How about the other one? Roberta, Regina. Something like that."

"Rebekah. She is not here either. Just me and my friend, Red. Please, join us. We won't hurt you."

The door closed and then opened. "I'm not scared."

"I did not say that you were," Akira said.

Just then, the other door opened. A boy stepped out. About the same age as the first. "Do I smell food? I'm starving. Hi, I'm Kevin. Kevin Schell." He stuck out his hand.

William looked Kevin up and down, then stuck out his hand. "I'm Billy Joe."

Akira said, "That's strange. Miriam said your name was William."

Billy Joe frowned. "That's not my name. Miriam started calling me that."

Red opened the conference room door and motioned them inside. "I'm Red. Let's eat and you can tell us about yourselves."

Both newcomers ate as if they were starving. Billy Joe, now William, went first. He started in the middle, finding Miriam and Rebekah in the desert, near death by carbon monoxide poisoning. How Rebekah had tricked him, making him the prisoner instead of them. Going to the small town near Pacific Edge, where Miriam and a man named Allen had retrieved a briefcase. A man named Maxton, and a guard were killed. Miriam let the other guards take his car, which was theft, and he intended to pursue charges when he got out of here, plus kidnapping charges against everyone involved.

He told them about Howie County, and how his dad became sheriff and such, which led him to how his dad had died, and finally, how he had dropped out of school to take over his dad's duties.

Red could not hide his growing anger. He was about to speak when Akira put her hand on his arm. "That's all very interesting. How about you Kevin?"

"I'm in the army. Well, was in the army—part of a mobile missile crew. Small crew, big missile. They call it a city killer. I was a lookout on the mountain. There were two of us. Snipers. Our role was to protect the missile crew. The girl named Anna kicked my butt. Tied me up. But when the fighting was done, they took me with them."

"Where were you?"

"Southern California. At least, that's what they told us. Turns out we were in Mexico."

"I don't believe that. New America would not be in Mexico. Mexico is mounting forces on the border preparing to invade and take over Texas," William said.

Kevin said, "I didn't believe it either. Not at first. But Miriam showed me coordinates. The missile was aimed at Potterville, California. Derrick lives there now."

"Us too," Akira said.

"We go to school with him," Red added.

"The other sniper shot a Mexican police officer. You have it backwards, William. New America, Prime, actually, is going to start a war with Mexico. Prime planned on bombing Potterville to justify the invasion," Kevin said.

He went on to tell them about the Prime aircraft landing and the robots killing the other soldiers. Then Derrick and the others destroyed the robots. Then the other sniper tried to kill the kids but one of them killed him with a machine gun. He didn't say who pulled the trigger. He figured that was Rebekah's story to tell or not.

He told about the drive from Mexico to New America and that they split up. A kid pulled a knife on Derrick in a small town. Derrick broke the kid's arm. "I was supposed to go to Potterville, but Derrick wouldn't let me drive back alone. He felt certain those guys would be waiting for me. Only one way back out and that was through where the fight took place."

William said, "I find that hard to believe. A girl beat up a soldier? A handful of teenagers took out a military unit?"

Red said, "Two girls disarmed you."

William looked down. "True but there wasn't a fight. It was a trick. Besides, the idea they could destroy Prime, if there even is such a thing, is ridiculous."

"Prime exists. That's not a question," Akira said. "Prime exists in seven locations. One is central and controls all the others. Miriam and Derrick have destroyed three of those locations."

"Even more impossible then," William said.

Kevin held a forkful of food halfway to his mouth. "They have destroyed three locations?"

"When? I was just with Derrick."

"Since Miriam dropped you off here."

Kevin whistled through his teeth. "Wow. That's amazing. I saw what Derrick did when that kid pulled a knife. I never saw anything like that in my training."

William said, "I still don't believe it and I'm still pressing charges against all of you."

"You know what? You're starting to piss me off. We lost a good friend in the first attack, and her father was the man killed in Pacific Edge. You saved Miriam, and she's trying to return the favor by helping you. But she's not here to protect you and I'm about this close," Red pinched his thumb and index finger together, "to punching you out."

William's face grew pale as if he had just now noticed Red's size. "Okay, look. I got nothing against either of you."

Red put his fork down, clenching his fists. "You don't want to be here? Fine. I can arrange to take you someplace. You're threatening to bring charges against the people trying to help you, so how does the middle of the desert sound? You can walk out. If you live, you can try pressing charges. It's likely by then we won't remember ever seeing you."

Kevin said, "Dude, you should lighten up. By all rights, they should have killed me in Mexico. I'm just as guilty as the rest of them. In fact, it was discussed, but Derrick wouldn't let it happen. I spent some time with them, and they are just trying to do the right thing. Prime has tried to kill them more than once. They don't have a choice. And Prime is going to start a war. They saved

Potterville, which means they saved thousands of people. I'm thankful they defeated me. I didn't know that's what we were doing, and I don't know if I could live with the knowledge that I destroyed an innocent town and started a war."

Staring at his food, William said nothing.

Kevin continued. "Truth is, we are a lot alike. I dropped out of school. Didn't have a future. That's why I joined the military. Unfortunately, after I joined, I learned my brother was in the Resistance. I made the wrong choice. These guys don't owe me anything. Quite the opposite, they have no reason to help me. But Derrick said I can go to school in Potterville. Miriam said she'll ensure I have a place to live."

Still looking down William whispered, "And you believe that's true?"

"I do."

Akira said, "Derrick has a lot of support in Potterville. You'll both be welcome there. Red is a star football player. Antonio, he's with Derrick and Miriam now, he is the student body president. When this is over, we'll have a fresh start. Without Prime."

"If they survive," Kevin whispered.

No one spoke for a moment. Red finally said, "There is that. If they don't win, Potterville will be destroyed. So, William, we good? Look, I'm sorry about your father. I mean, I get it. I have a father, but not a good one. I'm lucky to have a grandfather who helps me. So, I get it. Losing your dad and being alone. It sucks. But you've got a chance to have a new life. Miriam is offering you that. I suggest you take her up on it."

Tears ran down William's cheeks. "I'm sorry. It's all so surreal."

"True that," Kevin said.

Red said, "Now we have that out of the way, eat up."

To Akira, it felt as if Charlie must have turned on the oxygen flowing into the room. She could breathe again.

Kevin said, "So, where are we and what is this place? It's like a fancy hotel but with high security. Like where they might put the president if there was a war."

Red said, "Close enough. And you're going to forget all about this place. That's part of the deal of getting to go on breathing. Understood?"

10

REBEKAH SAID NOTHING AS ANTONIO stood and walked over to Rachael. He stood quietly behind her with his hands behind his back. Then he leaned forward. Just a little. Then just a little bit more. Rebekah felt her face flush red. It was not a new sensation. She'd felt it before in Pacific Edge every time she saw Derrick and Jana Somersworth together.

"Can I help you?" Rachael said, remaining focused on the computer monitor.

"I'm just wondering what you've found. I'm the gunner on Derrick's ship."

That struck Rebekah as an odd thing to say. It was true, but it wasn't as if Antonio was a soldier. Nyx was the navigator, but all those titles were just kind of make-believe bullshit.

It was like saying L. Linda was a demolition expert. A split second after the thought, Rebekah remembered: *L. Linda was dead, Miriam had been shot, Antonio had been wounded.* This wasn't make-believe. It was as real as it gets. If Antonio wants to be called the gunner, so be it. He's earned it. And if he wants to flirt with this girl, he'll likely never see again, that's okay too. It occurred to her she had no idea what life would be like for her in Potterville. Antonio was popular there. Maybe he already had a girlfriend. For sure there would be plenty of girls vying for his attention. It wasn't like they were dating. He probably wasn't even interested in her. It was all her imagination. After all, he was nice to everyone.

Rachael said, "Is that so? It doesn't mean I want you lurking over my shoulder."

Antonio stood, held his hands up. "Sorry. I didn't mean to invade your space. That was rude of me. Mind if we pull up chairs? It would be great if you'd explain what you're finding. Miriam wanted us to learn what we could about the other sites."

"Sure. I'm not going with you, that's for sure. I don't have a death wish and I'm not an optimist. Not when it comes to Prime."

Anna dragged her chair over and sat. "That's inspiring."

"Don't get me wrong. I'd like to see Prime gone as much as anyone."

"But you don't think it's possible?" Nyx asked.

"I don't know. I'm looking at Dallas. My guess is Prime is in this building." She pointed to the monitor.

"Derrick thought so as well," Anna said.

"It has a concrete and steel reinforced section inside," Rachael said.

"We thought there was something strange about that building. How about robots?" Anna asked.

"Robots?" Rachael repeated.

Anna realized they had not seen Prime's robots. "Prime uses them."

"Interesting. I wonder where he developed that technology."

Rebekah said, "I think …"

Anna shook her head, glaring at her.

Rebekah continued. "They were made in one of his headquarters."

"So, can you see inside the reinforced structure?" Antonio asked.

Rachael turned to him. Stared for a moment. "I can't *see* inside any structure. I learned it from historical documents. Blueprints."

"Do you know anything about it? What was it used for?" Antonio asked. "And the big question, how do we get in?"

"The facility was built for a drug enforcement agency in the old United States. Details are sketchy, but it appears they used it for storage, testing, and manufacturing."

"Manufacturing? You mean they made illegal drugs?" Nyx asked.

"Not what you might think. They made drugs, but not prescription drugs. Synthetic drugs made for a variety of things but mostly military use, pain killers, etc. They thought if people knew they had that kind of drugs the place might be broken into or attacked. Security was top-notch," Rachael said.

"How about Denver and San Diego?" Anna asked.

"Shouldn't we figure Dallas out first?" Rebekah asked.

"I already did," Anna said.

"Mind telling us?" Antonio asked.

"I do. Rachael doesn't need to hear it. No offense, Rachael."

Rachael said, "None taken. The less I know about what you are doing the better."

"What about Denver?" Anna asked.

"Looks straight forward. Single building similar to Seattle and Chicago. San Diego is the same, but not as tall and older."

The door above them opened. "Hey, food's ready."

Antonio said, "You don't have to ask me twice."

"Rachael, are you going to join us?" Rebekah asked.

"Yeah. I'll keep looking but I'll be up soon. If I find any additional information, I'll let you know."

Anna said, "Thanks for your help."

"No problem. Good luck."

"You'll need to come visit us in Potterville when this is over," Antonio said to Rachael.

"I'll do that. If there's still a Potterville to visit."

11

ON THE SIDEWALK LAID A DEAD ASSASSIN. Collins couldn't tell from where he stood if it was a man or a woman. The bulk under the black sweater indicated a ballistic vest. Jack had wisely taken a head shot, more difficult but when executed perfectly, lethal. Either Jack was a great shot or lucky. At this point, either worked.

Bill had never faced death. Not like this. Not where he and those close to him were living in such constant mortal danger. One would think that an advantage to a near-death experience would be a clearing of the mind, pushing out the mundane clutter of everyday life, the little details like doing the dishes and taking out the garbage. Those things would fall away, leaving the essence, only the most important aspects of life.

That didn't happen.

Not for Bill Collins.

He stood in the open, possibly in an assassin's crosshairs, and instead of an epiphany of wondrous insight, he pondered what to do with the bodies. How to clean up the mess. It wasn't like he could call a cleaning crew. He could have been killed. Lori could have been killed. Bill had been afraid to admit how much Lori meant to him. He had fallen for her and not just because of her recent flirtation. It happened long ago. The first time he saw her at the garage wearing work coveralls and a smudge of grease on her face when she rolled out from under an old Buick. That's why he offered her the deputy position. It paid more. Was less demanding physically.

And at the time, seemed safe.

Now it was anything but safe.

If something happened to her, he'd never forgive himself.

He had worked hard to insure he never sent any signal to Lori about his feelings. She was way out of his league, and he was content just to see her every day, have a cup of bad coffee, chat about happenings in Potterville.

Lori said, "I'll join you in a few minutes."

"Join me? Join me where? What are you thinking?"

"Probable Cause Statement. Remember? We still need a warrant," Lori said.

Bill said, "I need to get you someplace safe."

"No can do. If they kill the judge before we get a signature, it would not be good."

"Kill the judge?"

"It could happen. What if they are one step ahead of us?"

"You mean they aren't already?" Bill asked.

"I think they were playing catchup. Trying to figure out what happened to Pixie."

"They probably figured that out."

Lori said, "Yep. That's why they were waiting here. First order of business was revenge. Pixie died here. Let's get a warrant signed and then figure out our next move."

Lori walked back into the sheriff's office.

Collins followed her to her desk. "We can't just leave that body on the sidewalk, and the front door is the same as open."

"Call the coroner. He can bag them. Tell him to bring some help. Maybe the fire department can hose off the blood."

"It's a crime scene. We need to document things."

"Who's going to investigate? It's not a crime scene. It's a war zone. Besides, it was all self-defense, not a crime."

Bill said, "We are not at war."

"Feels like a war to me."

"I'll call the coroner and ask him to take some pictures."

"What should Donna and Jack be doing?" Lori asked.

Bill thought for a moment. "Maybe stay put. Give the coroner cover. Then we'll decide our next move. Do you really think there's another assassin?"

"Three feels right. Don't ask me why. It just does. Now, let me get this written."

"But there were three. You're forgetting Pixie."

Lori's fingers danced over the keyboard as she focused on the monitor. "I'm not forgetting her. Trust me, I wish I could. She came alone. When she didn't come back, a team came looking."

"And you think three is the standard assassin team?"

"I already said that."

Lori worked. Bill watched. She typed a lot faster than he could. Lori used all her fingers. He only used two. After about ten minutes, the printer came to life. "There might be some typos, but it's good enough."

"What if the judge objects because of an error?"

Lori grabbed the papers. "I'll correct them with a pen."

* * *

Walking back to their car, Bill and Lori walked into the sun. Shielding her eyes, Lori waved at Donna and then turned and waved to Jack. She keyed her microphone. "Running a little late." She held up the documents. "Just need to finish some paperwork, then we'll be back. Wait for us."

She got into the driver's seat. Bill called the coroner. No answer. That seemed odd. Something didn't feel right. And it wasn't just the dead body in front of the courthouse.

12

WHEN DERRICK AND MIRIAM GOT BACK TO the house where the others had been studying the remaining Prime Headquarters, Harley pulled into the garage, closed the door, and led them to the backyard, which was surrounded by a six-foot wooden privacy fence. The grass showed just a hint of green, as if someone had recently watered it. Whether it would live again was still questionable. Rebekah and Nyx sat on a bench on one side of a wooden picnic table. Antonio and Anna sat across from them. Smoke drifted from a nearby barbeque grill.

Miriam walked over to where Rachael was helping cook hamburgers. "These are just about done. Sorry, no French fries, but we have chips," she called out.

Nyx smiled at Derrick and patted the bench for him to sit. Rebekah scooted over and he squeezed in between the two girls. He felt uncomfortable there. A girl on his Chosen list of brides on one side, his, what? Hope-to-be girlfriend on the other. Rebekah ignored him, more or less. He was certain it was because she was holding hands across the table with Antonio. Derrick wondered if that made Nyx uncomfortable. If it did, she didn't show it. Still, he'd learned normal teenagers are much better at hiding their feelings than he was.

"What do you want on your burger? I'll bring it to you," Miriam hollered.

Derrick thought for a moment. "Everything. Whatever they have."

"Like mustard, ketchup, and mayo?"

"Sure. Why not?"

Miriam gave him a weird look but said nothing and turned back toward the grill.

Nyx took his hand. "So, how did it go?"

"Fine, I guess. At least, Miriam has an idea. If we are successful, Miriam will broadcast a message nationwide, explaining that Prime has been removed from power and Commander Haskins oversees the military. A counsel will start work immediately developing a plan for the country's future."

"How is she going to do that—broadcast nationally?"

"She didn't say. I'm guessing Charlie will help."

"Do you think that's possible?"

Deconstruction
A Derrick King Novel, Book 8

"I don't know, but Miriam wouldn't say it was the plan to move forward if she didn't think it could be done."

"From the base?"

"I assume. Why?" Derrick asked.

"Because when this is over, I want to be done with it. I don't want to fly somewhere to take control of a television station."

"I agree. I just want to be a normal kid again." Derrick paused for a moment. It sounded too good to be true. Being a normal kid. He didn't think it was possible. Not for him. He'd never known normal. Suddenly, his head was like a kaleidoscope of haunting memories—some from the Test Subject Program, others Pacific Edge, a few from Potterville, some from after he escaped from Pacific Edge Security, and many from Seattle.

"Derrick!" Nyx's voice seemed louder than usual.

"What?"

"You drifted off. Are you okay? Anna has been trying to get your attention," Nyx said.

"I'm sorry. Just tired. What were you saying?" It wasn't entirely untrue. He was tired.

"Do you have any thoughts about how to attack Dallas?" Anna asked, adding, "Rachael told us that middle building had a concrete shelter. You are probably right about Prime being in that building."

The question surprised Derrick. Anna had not been pleased earlier when he seemed to be in charge of things, and Anna had said she had a plan. Miriam had pressured him to lead, but then Miriam put Anna in charge of the New York mission, which didn't go well. Perhaps Anna had a change of heart. Maybe it was something else.

Antonio said, "I was thinking we could use a missile set on delay like we did in Chicago. That worked out well."

"I can see potential problems with that," Derrick said.

"Worried there might be people inside?" Anna asked.

"We don't know what's inside," Derrick said. "We don't even know if Prime is there. There might be separate chambers, or it might continue underground. If we can't get inside, we can't confirm Prime was destroyed."

Rachael arrived carrying four plates, two balanced on each arm. Nyx said, "You might have a future working at Donna's."

It was a light-hearted comment—no ill intent. But it reminded Derrick of L. Linda, and that was the last thing he needed to be thinking about.

Rachael placed a plate in front of Anna and then sat next to Harley in a nearby lawn chair.

"What have I missed?" Miriam asked as she sat.

Anna said, "I was just asking Derrick if he had any suggestions for Dallas."

Miriam looked at Derrick. "And?"

Before Derrick could speak, Anna said, "He didn't say. Antonio suggested using a missile like they did in Chicago, but Derrick shot him down."

"I didn't shoot him down," Derrick replied faster and louder than he intended. Taking a breath, he added, "I just pointed out a couple of problems with using a missile. It's not off the table."

Derrick studied Anna. He couldn't read her. Was she trying to discredit him so she could lead this attack? Perhaps she felt defensive because New York didn't go well. He was certain she didn't trust him. He couldn't blame her for that.

"Derrick, do you have an idea or not?" Miriam asked.

It wasn't as if Derrick had not been pondering this very question. In between being distracted, he had thought about it. Thought about it a great deal. "Sort of. I wonder if Charlie has a device that could cut through that bunker, or whatever it is."

Miriam thought for a moment. "Maybe. I guess we could check. However, I don't like wasting time going back to the base."

"It would not take much time. I can fly back and then meet you. Since our aircraft is faster, perhaps it would not add much time."

Miriam said, "Good point." She stood. "Don't eat my burger. I'll be right back."

Miriam and Rachael headed into the house in deep conversation.

About ten minutes later, Miriam returned to her burger.

"What did you learn?" Derrick asked.

Miriam held up her hand, chewing. "I'm starving. Charlie didn't have anything, but he said he could build something."

Derrick said, "Dang. We don't have time for that."

"Actually, we do. Eat up. Harley will take you to your aircraft. Fly to the base and then meet us in Dallas. Rachael has an idea of how we can get in. I'll send you coordinates."

"What about planning?"

"Anna and I will take care of that. Just go get the thing from Charlie."

Harley stood. "Let's go."

Antonio said, "Hey! I'm still eating."

"Take it with you," Miriam said.

Derrick popped the last bite of his burger in his mouth. "See you soon."

13

LORI AND BILL DROVE SEVERAL BLOCKS in silence. No traffic, no pedestrians. People were holed up waiting, and they probably didn't know what they were waiting for, or how they'd know if it happened. Lori sensed that Bill felt something was wrong when the coroner didn't answer. She wondered if Bill had any inclination about what might be amiss or if it was just a vague feeling. Someday, if they lived through this, she hoped to know Bill so well she understood his thoughts before he did, but for now, she'd have to settle for just being on the same page. If not the same page, at least the same chapter. And definitely, the same book.

She thought something was wrong, and she knew what it was.

The coroner was dead.

The assassin might wait there for a while. See if anyone showed up. Eventually, the killer would check on the other two. Perhaps finding them dead would cause the assassin to rethink staying in Potterville, but Lori doubted it. More likely, the assassin would call in more killers.

Bill said, "Maybe we should check on Henry."

"I agree. Right after we get the warrant signed."

"We can do that after checking on Henry."

"If Henry is dead, checking on him won't change anything. We need this warrant."

Bill glanced at her. "You really think that? Why would they attack Henry?"

"They wouldn't specifically, but they would go to the morgue to see if Pixie's body was there," Lori said.

"I hope you're wrong."

"Me too. But I'm not."

Collins keyed his radio. "We have to make a brief side trip to pick up some paperwork. After that, we are going to see if Henry wants to join us. Perhaps you can keep an eye out for us?"

Jack said, "No problem. Donna, meet me out front and I'll walk with you." Jack hoped Donna understood.

Donna said, "Sure thing, Jack. Stretching my legs is just what the doctor ordered."

Deconstruction
A Derrick King Novel, Book 8

Collins pulled up to Judge Smith's house. "This might not be as easy as it sounded."

"How's that?" Lori asked.

"Would you want your name on a warrant for Prime's arrest?"

"My name is on the affidavit of probable cause."

"Fair point. Still."

"We'll both go in. I can be very convincing."

"No argument from me on that." Bill rang the bell and then knocked. It took a few minutes, but Judge Smith eased the door open a crack. "I wasn't expecting company and certainly wasn't expecting you two."

The door opened. Smith set a shotgun in the corner. "I've heard about the Priest family. And that there were shots fired downtown. I suspect everyone has heard by now. Word travels fast even when everyone is staying behind locked doors. What can I do for you, sheriff?"

Lori said, "You can sign this warrant." She handed him the affidavit and warrant she had prepared.

"Let me grab my glasses. Come in." He motioned them to sit in a parlor just off the entrance. In a few minutes, he returned and sat at the desk. "Okay. Let's see what we have here."

Smith read. His face turned pale. Looking up, he removed his reading glasses. "Is this some kind of joke?"

Collins said, "It is not."

"But you can't be serious. You can't just go arrest Prime. I mean, we don't even know if Prime exists. And Prime is probably not his real name."

Collins said, "It goes by Prime, and we have an address in San Diego." He didn't tell Smith that San Diego was just one location, or that Prime existed in several other locations, or that kids from Potterville had already destroyed one location, or that three assassins had been killed in Potterville.

Smith set the papers on his desk. "So, you believe this Prime fellow is behind the deaths of the Priest family?"

Lori said, "And Paul Jorgensen."

"Yes. Paul too. But in Paul's case, it is hearsay," Collins said.

Lori said, "It is not. I'm a witness. An assassin calling herself Pixie told me she killed Paul and works directly for Prime."

"Is this Pixie in custody?"

"She is not. She's dead. I killed her. So, that makes her last statement a dying declaration of which I am witness. It's admissible in court." She looked at Bill. "I've been studying."

"Lori acted in self-defense." Collins paused. "Where's your family, judge?"

"You killed her," Smith whispered and then sat silently for a moment. He raised his eyes looking at Collins. "I sent them away. Seemed like the thing to do. Sounds like I made the right decision."

Lori said, "You should join them. Right after you sign that warrant."

"Someone has to stay and watch the house." He glanced at the shotgun. "I'm prepared."

Collins said, "Not prepared enough. These are trained killers. They won't knock like we did."

"You think more will come?"

Lori looked at Bill. He gave no clear indication of whether she should say more. She saw no reason not to. "They already have. The shots downtown. We killed two more. I think there's one more in town."

Smith looked at Collins. "You think that's true?"

"Which part? That we killed two assassins or that there's another one in town?"

"Both I guess."

"Since the assassins tried to kill me, and they are both lying dead at the courthouse, I know two are a fact. The third is a hunch." Collins paused. "Sign the warrant. Leave town. I'll tail you out to make sure you're not followed."

14

ANNA FOLLOWED DERRICK INTO THE HOUSE. Tension flowed through his body. They were all going to the garage, but that she was so close bothered him a little, although he didn't know why. He dared not look back. That would be too obvious. Then he sensed her closing the gap.

Anna took his arm. "Can I talk to you for a minute? Alone."

Derrick turned. Anna didn't look angry, but he was not good at reading people. "Sure."

They let the others pass. "Be right there." Anna took a deep breath. "I'm worried about Miriam."

This took him by surprise. "Worried about Miriam? I don't understand."

"She's been acting strange."

"Strange how?"

"I don't know. Distant. Unsure of herself. It's not like her." Anna paused. "She was wounded. She's wearing different clothing now. I assumed someone here looked at her injury. She is tough but still human."

"She tore the injury open. A doc came over and put in a couple of stitches before we headed back here. Rachael gave her clean clothing." Derrick thought for a moment. "Look, I know you are mad at me, but I thought you and Miriam were, I don't know, close."

"I'm not mad at you, Derrick. I'm mad at everyone and everything."

Derrick studied her. She looked unsure of herself. He had not seen this in her before. "Mad at everyone. I don't understand. I thought you were mad at me."

Anna said, "They tortured me. In the program. That was my only purpose. To be tormented. They wiped our memories, or at least they tried, but when they did that to me, the person they left behind was broken. I feared everything and everyone. I could barely make it to school each day, and I didn't know why. Miriam opened a door for me." She pointed at her temple. "Miriam didn't mean to, but she told our class about the code she used to access a hidden menu on our monitors. Accessing that menu, triggered my memories. Not all at once, but it opened the door. I forced my way inside. Then I knew why I was so scared. And that pissed me off."

15

WARRANT IN HAND, COLLINS AND Martinez drove to the morgue in silence. Henry still wasn't answering. Lori felt certain he was dead. She was less confident about whether there was another assassin or one of the dead ones at the courthouse was responsible for killing Henry. Henry was an old man and stood little chance against a trained assassin.

Collins tapped his phone and held it to his ear. "Still no answer."

"Henry is dead," Lori said.

"Stop saying that. We don't know what's happened. He might just be sleeping."

"Have you known Henry to not answer the phone?"

Collins stared straight ahead. "No. But—still."

"I don't want him to be dead. I'm just preparing myself for the worst." She paused. "We need a plan."

Collins keyed his mic. The time for secrecy was over. "Guys. We are outside the funeral home. Henry isn't answering. Do you have us covered? We fear the worst."

Jack's voice came over the speaker. "We've been watching since before you arrived. We've seen nothing."

Collins stared at the mortuary that also served as the coroner's office and county morgue. He had parked a half a block away and could not see the front. He looked at Lori. "How should we do this?"

"Drive past so we can see the front door. Then go a couple of blocks and circle back. Park a block away from the rear entrance. We'll walk from there."

"You must have had that planned already."

She shrugged.

"You didn't hesitate." He paused, looking back toward the mortuary. "The back has no windows. The walls are concrete. The doors are metal, including the roll-up for the ambulance and hearse."

"Exactly. If someone is waiting, they can't see our approach."

"True. But we can't get in either."

"We can. I know the code for the roll-up."

Collins stared at her for a moment. "Why do you know that?"

"You don't?" Lori smiled. Just a little. "Seemed like I should know it. In case I had to identify a body or something after hours."

"Have you ever had to identify a body?"

"Nope. Not until today."

"How do you know the code works?"

"Good point. I don't."

"What's the plan if it doesn't?"

"We'll cross that bridge if we come to it."

Collins shook his head, just a little, and pulled from the curb, driving slowly down the street.

Lori said, "The front door is ajar."

"Maybe Henry left it open a little."

"Have you ever seen it open before?"

"Well, no. But I don't come here that often."

"You drop by a couple of times a week for coffee."

Collins wondered how she knew that but didn't ask and wasn't sure he wanted to know. "Okay. That's true."

Lori said, "Henry never leaves the door open. It's open because someone forced their way in. The latch is busted out of the doorjamb, and it won't stay shut."

"Aren't you the optimist today?"

"I'm the realist today."

Collins drove a few blocks, more than Lori suggested. If she asked why, he'd say to throw the assassin off should he or she be watching. However, truthfully, he was trying to think of a way to keep her safe. He came up empty on that.

He parked a block away from the morgue. "Tell me the code. I'll go check it out. I'll radio you if I need help. Otherwise, you can drive to the rear entry when I call for you."

Lori got out of the car and started walking. "Right. Like that's going to happen."

Collins knew she wouldn't stay at the car, but he had to try. She wasn't just stubborn. She was right. They should work together, but he wasn't thinking about her as an officer. That wasn't good. Something would have to change if they lived through this.

"So, how do we do this?" Collins asked. "You enter the code and the roll-up opens. Right? But whoever's inside will hear the door opening."

"Not necessarily. I've been there when the hearse returned from a funeral. The inside is well insulated from outside noise so that services are not disrupted."

Lori motioned for Bill to stay out of sight beside the door as she entered the code. The door started up, and she flattened herself against the wall. When the door stopped, she took a quick peek inside and saw no one. However, an assassin could be using the hearse for concealment. Lori signaled to Bill that she was going in. Bill shook his head, but Lori didn't see it.

Bill moved on the opposite side of the hearse and picked up his pace to ensure he arrived at the front before Lori did. He came around quickly with his gun leading the way. Nothing there.

They eased to the interior door. Lori tried the knob. It turned. She motioned, indicating she would open the door and for Bill to be ready. She eased the door open. The short hallway was empty. This would be the most dangerous part. The door on the right led to the room where autopsies and embalming took place. Bill had never witnessed either. Embalming wasn't something he needed or wanted to watch. He could not remember an autopsy being done during his time as sheriff. Now, there was a need for several.

The door to the autopsy room stood open. The other door led to the room where samples of coffins were on display. The entire building was about death. Bill tried to get Lori's attention, but she was already moving down the hall. She had no intention of letting him get to that open door first. He wondered what she was thinking. Why did she insist on putting herself at such great risk?

Two steps into the hall, Bill smelled the metallic odor of blood. Although he had tried to change the narrative, Lori was right. Henry was dead or dying, which meant an assassin was likely lying in wait. He couldn't let Lori poke her head around that door first. He dashed in front of her, putting himself in a vulnerable position, and burst into the room.

He saw the largest pool of blood he had ever witnessed. Three-quarters of the floor was covered in a wet red pool. Blood was splattered across the stainless-steel table, up the walls, and onto the ceiling. A body lay face down in the center of it.

Henry sat on the floor with his back against a row of cabinets. Knives buried to their hilts protruding from his shoulder and thigh. "Thank God. I wanted to call out but dared not make a sound because I feared it was another one of those guys." Henry indicated the fallen man in the pool of blood.

Lori stepped inside the room but said nothing. She already had her phone pressed to her ear. "Doc, this is Deputy Martinez. Get to the mortuary as fast as you can. Come to the back. Bring your bag. I'll have an ambulance meet you here."

Bill eased around the pool of blood and knelt at Henry's side. Lori joined him. Bill reached for the knife in his leg.

"Stop!" Henry breathed. "Don't touch it. It didn't hit an artery, but it hit plenty of other stuff. Same with the shoulder. My odds of not bleeding to death are better if I'm in surgery when they are removed."

Lori said, "Doc and an ambulance are on the way."

"What happened?" Bill asked.

"I was cleaning up. I'd just finished the autopsy on the Priest boy. When I turned around, that guy was standing behind me. I didn't hear a thing. He was like a ghost. He pointed a knife at me and asked if I had Pixie. I nodded toward the freezer drawers; said she was in number 3. After seeing the Priest family, all with their throats cut, I figured I'd end up the same. The guy didn't notice a scalpel that was lying on the bench. I picked it up and took a swipe at him. I got lucky. Sliced his throat. Hit his carotid artery. He still managed to hit me with two knives before he bled out. I struck him first. I guess that means I'm guilty of murder."

Bill put his hand on the uninjured shoulder. "You're guilty of nothing. He's a trained assassin. What you did was self-defense."

The Doc came through the door. "My God!"

"How'd you get here so fast?" Bill asked.

"Donna called me. Said I'd better get over here. I was waiting just down the street when Lori called."

Bill said, "I have a hell of a team."

"He needs surgery, right? Will you do it at the hospital?" Lori asked.

"No. He needs a trauma center. We'll stabilize the wounds with compression bandages and sedate him for the ride to Fresno or Bakersfield. Takes about equal time for both. I'll see which can be ready fastest."

"Do you have to go in the ambulance with him, Doc?" Lori asked.

"I can do that."

"I didn't ask if you could. I asked if you had to."

"Well, I don't have to. The EMTs are capable." He paused. "What are you getting at?"

"Yeah. What are you getting at?" Bill repeated.

"We've got two dead bodies downtown, plus this one. We were planning to have Henry bag the bodies, bring them here. Now, we need you to do that. We'll get the fire department to hose off the sidewalk. I guess the blood inside will have to wait."

"Wait for what?" Doc asked.

"Wait for us to return from arresting Prime."

Part Two

1

Saturday, April 9, 5:45 p.m. Pacific Time

WHEN LORI MARTINEZ RETURNED to Jack's shop after supervising the body bagging and cleanup operation, Patel, Jack, and Donna were gone. Keeping this bunch in one location was challenging. She had been thinking about Bill not letting her go with them to arrest Prime and was still a little pissed about it. Bill smiled, but she didn't return the gesture. She wasn't really angry. Bill was right about someone needing to stay in Potterville, but she wasn't ready to let him off the hook. Maybe when he got back from arresting Prime.

If he came back.

And with that thought, she walked over to Sheriff Bill Collins and kissed him.

When she stepped back, Bill said, "I'm confused."

"Are you complaining?" Lori asked.

"Not at all. Just confused…."

"Just giving you a reason to come home."

Bill had every intention of returning, but he understood. "I'm coming back. Just keep our town safe while I'm gone."

"I will. I'll prepare a help wanted sign as well."

Bill almost said she didn't have to resign and then stopped. He couldn't date his deputy. Well, he could. Who would stop him? He was the sheriff and could make the rules about who he hired and who he dated. But Lori was right. It wasn't proper. And the last thing he wanted was any impropriety getting in the way of this chance at happiness that had evaded him for years.

Still, he worried about how Lori would make ends meet. Even if she moved in with him, he didn't make enough money for the two of them. "I'm concerned about you losing the deputy salary."

"We'll figure out something. Maybe Donna can put me to work. I could go back to the filling station. Or maybe Jack needs help to complete restorations.

I'd like that. You just worry about getting back here alive. You're no good to me dead." And with that, she leaned for another quick kiss.

Jack came through the door. "Well, damn. I guess the fight is over, which means my odds of getting a date with Lori are probably slim to none."

Lori smiled. "We can have a date anytime, Jack Fletcher. Just so long as Bill is there too. Maybe we can invite Donna along. You know, a double date."

Donna set a sack down on a counter, laughing. "Sure. I'll go with Bill. You can have this old fossil."

Jack laughed. Patel even chuckled.

It wasn't that funny, but they were all scared and the laugh was like a release valve on a pressure cooker.

Jack said, "Donna insisted we take food. I swear I've never eaten so much in my life."

"Just a few snacks for us. Most of this is for Lori. You don't need to be worrying about where lunch and dinner are coming from while you're keeping the town safe," Donna said.

Bill said, "Lori, maybe you stay here at Jack's shop. Forward the phones to Jack's office. Don't go out unless you have to."

"Sure thing. I'll hide in here and let the town fend for itself. You know that's not going to happen. We've been holed up in here too long as it is. I'm going out as soon as you leave, and I don't want another argument to be our last words."

Bill didn't want that either, so he just said, "Be careful."

"Sheriff, I've been wondering," Patel said, adding, "How is this going to work? I mean, won't the local police be a problem if we start shooting up Prime's Headquarters?"

Bill pulled a sandwich from the bag. "I've been thinking about that. We'll go to the police first. I'll show them the warrant and ask them to help serve it."

"They'll do that?" Patel asked.

"I doubt it. They might want Prime arrested, but they are unlikely to help. But it puts them on the spot. If they are not going to help, I'll insist they stay out of our way. I have a legal warrant and I'm taking Prime to Potterville to stand trial."

"We aren't police officers," Donna said.

Collins motioned with his hand. "I hereby deputize you."

"Is that all it takes?" Donna asked.

"Yep. You're all my deputies."

"Prime won't go willingly," Patel said.

Collins took a bite and with his mouth full, he said, "I agree. Prime will resist—to put it mildly—and most likely die in the process. Which is the best outcome. I can't afford security while holding Prime in jail for a trial, especially with my staff quitting on me." He winked at Lori.

"What about other people?" Donna asked. "There must be people working in the building."

"Yeah. That's a problem. I don't want to hurt anyone other than Prime. I'm hoping they will leave peacefully."

"And if they don't?" Donna asked.

Collins shrugged. "We'll do what we have to do. If they attack us, we'll defend ourselves." He paused. "If anyone isn't okay with that, now is the time to say."

Patel said, "We have no choice. Because of Prime, Mr. Maxton is dead. I plan to see my family again and not end up like him."

"You don't have to ask me twice," Donna said.

Jack said, "Prime has killed more people than you know. It's time for Prime to go. His people will have to decide for themselves if they want to die for the worthless scum."

"Then I guess we are good to go." Bill looked at each of them for a moment. "Let's do this."

2

Saturday, April 9, 6:15 p.m. Pacific Time

AFTER A LONG HUG THAT WASN'T nearly long enough, Bill released Lori and slid into the driver's seat of his patrol car. Lori had driven it to oversee bagging the dead assassins, and before returning, filled it with gas and ran it through the car wash because Bill rarely did and showing up in San Diego with a dirty car wouldn't look right, because officers want to look sharp when in another jurisdiction. The firearms, except for the pistols they each carried, were in Bill's trunk. Patel rode shotgun with Bill. Donna rode with Jack in a large black sedan; both still in ordinary clothing but sporting shiny chrome badges. Jack thought the sedan looked more government like than, say, a Pontiac GTO, of which he had three.

Collins didn't know what Prime looked like or how big it was. Perhaps it would not fit in a squad car. Perhaps the local police would know; however, Collins was betting the locals knew less about Prime than he did. In reality, Collins had no intention of bringing Prime back to stand trial. Vigilantism wasn't to his liking, but since Prime was above the law, laws had been ineffective. Thus, the Resistance had formed. Overthrowing Prime wasn't their goal, at least, he didn't think it was. He knew certain people in town, like the music-man, Mark Grealy, were members. Collins never interfered with Mark, nor did he want to know the extent of his involvement with the Resistance. Since Mark had relayed messages from far up the food chain to Derrick about their father, Bill assumed Mark's involvement went beyond playing protest songs from the 1960s.

Live and let live. That had been Collin's theory on how to be a lawman. He didn't need to invoke every law as written under the New America Unified Code. Warnings were usually sufficient. Sometimes, he'd incarcerate a person overnight who'd had too much to drink or was inclined to hurt themselves. The problems would usually seem less severe in the morning after a cup of coffee or two and some conversation. He only prosecuted those who hurt others; sometimes someone who'd stolen stuff, but those occurrences were uncommon in Potterville since the councils were formed.

Despite Bill's misgivings about taking the law into his own hands, literally not figuratively, he was going to serve an arrest warrant that, for all practical purposes, was a death warrant. Sending assassins to his town and killing its citizens warranted death. A trial was unnecessary. Collins lit his lights and turned on the siren, pushing his police cruiser beyond the legal speed limit.

There had been little conversation during the first 45 minutes, but while speeding through the outskirts of Bakersfield, Patel said, "This goes against your ethics. It must be difficult for you."

Collins glanced over. "Doesn't it go against yours? I never thought of you as being capable of violence."

"Very much so. I'm a pacifist. I don't condone violence. But for you, it's different. You took an oath. An oath to uphold the New America Unified Code. Which was mostly about protecting James Carver and, as it turns out, Prime. Now you have an arrest warrant. For Prime. Don't misunderstand. I know the warrant is legal, and it's not a fabricated charge. Still, since Prime will not submit to being arrested, the warrant's factual purpose is to kill Prime. At least the one in San Diego."

Collins nodded but didn't respond. Not right away. He had to think about it because Patel wasn't wrong, and while Collins felt he was doing the right thing, it still bothered him. A lot.

They were not yet close to San Diego. Wouldn't be for a few hours. Collins considered pulling over, telling the others he couldn't do it, turning around and returning to Potterville.

What sounded like a good idea in Jack's shop, drinking coffee and snacking on Donna's latest meal, now seemed ridiculous. Crazy, in fact. He might get them all killed. What good would that do? Prime lives, they die.

Insane.

But every time his foot moved toward the brake pedal to disengage the cruise control; he thought about the alternatives. If they didn't go to San Diego, the kids still had to deal with that Prime. If they lived that long. There were no guarantees. Not for them, not for him.

But why should the kids have to destroy Prime? How did that become their responsibility?

Turning around wouldn't guarantee the safety of Potterville, nor Allen, Donna, or Jack. If the kids had not diverted the missiles in Mexico, Potterville wouldn't exist right now. Then there were the assassins. The reality of their situation was so absurd, it was difficult to keep things in perspective. That was for damn sure.

The primary reason Collins kept his car pointed toward San Diego was simple. If he showed up back in Potterville without destroying Prime, he knew what would happen. Lori Martinez would say she was glad he was okay, while looking at him with disappointment, and then she'd grab the warrant and head to San Diego herself. Allen, Donna, and Jack would follow her. His life as sheriff in Potterville would end right there. No one would ever respect him again.

Especially, Lori Martinez.

So, he kept driving.

Finally, Collins said, "I can rationalize it, but it's still feels wrong. Yet—it feels right." He waved his hand. "I know. That doesn't make sense."

Patel said nothing, but it was his turn, and Collins felt a bit of relief that he didn't have to say more.

Not unless Patel continued the conversation.

Perhaps he wouldn't.

But he did.

"It is a senseless time. That much is true. Right and wrong seem upside down and inside out. That has been the reality all our lives. We've never known anything other than Prime's rule."

"I should have never asked you to do this, Allen."

"You didn't ask. I volunteered. But as time passes, I become more troubled."

Collins nodded. "I understand. You don't have to participate. Just wait for us and if we fail—well, at least there will be someone returning to Potterville to tell the others."

"You don't understand."

Collins cut him off. "I understand completely. I don't blame you. Not even a little. This goes against your moral compass. I get it. It goes against mine too. It's just that, well, we can't expect the kids to do it all themselves. They have no business trying to fix this mess, but they're trying." He paused. "I guess I have to help. I can't explain why."

"They aren't ordinary kids."

"I know that Derrick and Miriam were in some kind of program, but Antonio, Nyx, Akira, and Red are ordinary kids. They should be in Potterville enjoying spring break."

"Yes, you are right about that."

"So, look. No one is going to hold it against you."

"Hold what against me?"

"Sitting this one out."

"I'm not sitting it out. I'm going to do what needs done."

"But you just said you were becoming more troubled."

"I did say that, but you cut me off before I could explain. I'm not troubled about destroying Prime. I'm troubled about what happens if we are successful."

"You lost me."

"Prime owns everything. Runs everything. Has even rewritten history and invented our gods. What happens when Prime is gone? The nation has no leadership. There will be a vacuum. What we have now is terrible. What comes next could be worse."

Collins remained silent for a moment. Stunned. "I had not thought about that."

"You had better start thinking about it."

"But what can I do? I'm a nobody. A small-town sheriff. I worked at the hardware store when Sheriff Johnson asked me to be his deputy. It paid 50 bucks a month more than I made at the hardware store. That was the only reason I took the job. Had I known he was going to die the next year, I would have turned him down."

"You are a good man, Bill. You and Coach improved things in Potterville a great deal. Your management by councils was brilliant. Since you started them, problems are non-existent."

"It's not a perfect system."

"Nothing is perfect."

"It's not even a democracy. I've always felt bad about that. We allowed certain people in the room but not on the council. They could voice their opinion, but they had no vote."

Patel said, "Like Jimmy Priest."

"Yes. We made mistakes."

"It wasn't a mistake. That group is a cult. They worship Prime. They are not grounded in reality."

"Still…"

Patel remained quiet for several miles. When he spoke, he said, "Bill, a great storm is coming, and someone must be ready. Someone must step up."

"I can't argue with your logic. But I'm not that guy."

Patel said, "Don't be so sure."

3

THE TEMPERATURE HAD DROPPED AND the ride back to the aircraft would have been chilly had they been in the back of the pickup truck. Derrick, Nyx, and Antonio all squeezed into the cab with Harley. It was cramped, but Derrick had no complaint about being close to Nyx.

A few blocks from the house, Nyx sat on Derrick's lap. "There. That's better."

Antonio scooted over a bit. "Agreed."

Harley said, "No argument here." He paused. "So, these aircraft you have, can I have a look at them?"

In unison, all three said, "No," more forceful than perhaps necessary.

"Geeze. Okay. No reason to get all huffy about it."

Derrick said, "Sorry. I can't explain why, but Charlie insisted that it was important." He paused. "Safer for everyone that no one sees them." He really meant no one could see the aircraft Nyx, Antonio, and he were flying. People had probably seen the style of aircraft Rebekah was flying because Prime used them. Although Derrick didn't know how many had seen a Prime aircraft because people thought Prime was a myth until a couple of days ago. The Chosen used hover craft that Derrick assumed used similar technology, yet, the Chosen aircraft were quite different. Unless a Chosen Community was nearby, most people had probably not seen one of those either.

Harley said, "Where are you going to get this new tool, and who is Charlie?"

Derrick took a deep breath. He could have left Charlie out of it. They had seen the inside of one of the Resistance's most secret facilities. It seemed impolite to keep secrets from Harley, Professor, and Wizard. Perhaps Miriam would tell them when this was over, assuming they survived, and Prime didn't. But that wasn't his call to make.

"I can't tell you. I'm sorry. I really am. It's not my decision to make. Perhaps when this is over, but maybe not even then. I'm just hoping we survive Dallas. Then we still have four more Prime Headquarters, and we don't know where the central Prime is located."

Harley said, "I wish we could tell you. We'd all team up to help if we could. I've talked to Professor and Wizard about how we could help with the other locations. Bottom line is, we can't. We aren't geared for paramilitary stuff."

"You've helped us a great deal," Derrick said. "We wouldn't have made it this far without you."

Harley slowed. "I think this is it. Hard to tell in the dark. Do you think you can find your way?"

"I hope so," Derrick gazed into the darkness, realizing it was going to be almost impossible to find the aircraft.

Harley leaned across the cab, opening a compartment built into the dashboard. "Take this flashlight."

Nyx took the flashlight, turned it on and then right back off. "That will help a lot. Thanks, Harley."

Derrick opened the door. Nyx hopped out first. Harley came around to the passenger side.

Antonio said, "Thanks for the hamburgers."

Nyx said, "For sure. We were getting tired of him complaining about being hungry."

Harley chuckled. "No worries. You're welcome."

Derrick faced Harley. They hardly knew each other, yet they had been through so much together. Friends lost. "I'm not sure what to say."

"Can I ask you a question?"

"Sure. I'll give you an answer if I can," Derrick said.

"Miriam said she doesn't want anyone to know what you've done. Is that true?"

"Yes. We just want a normal life after this is over." Derrick paused. "If we live through it. And there might be complications afterward. Prime has trained assassins. Reprisals."

Harley said, "I can understand that, but I can't imagine you having a normal life."

"Why do you say that?"

Harley put his hand on Derrick's shoulder. "Because you, my friend, are extraordinary. You all are. Now get out of here and rid the world of that monster."

4

DERRICK TRAILED NYX THROUGH THE brush. She was a remarkable girl. Henry Clark had told him how hard she'd worked to get to where she was as an athlete. Also, Derrick knew she hated bugs, but she was leading them through the brush. She had no business being here, yet here she was. What she saw in him remained a mystery.

Stepping into a clearing, the light's beam found their aircraft and then it suddenly went dark. He bumped into Nyx. Instead of moving, she put her arm around him as if she had anticipated him running into her. "See it? The moon. It's so big."

Derrick looked up. "I hadn't noticed, but you're right."

"It's beautiful, isn't it?"

Before he could answer, she gave him a quick kiss on the cheek and turned on the light.

Antonio said, "Hey, you two, knock that off."

Derrick recognized the playfulness in Antonio's voice. Whether or not it was genuine, he did not know.

After donning their flight suits, Derrick strapped into the captain's chair. Nyx input the flight plan back to the base. Derrick understood the process, which was quite simple. Nyx said it was basically like a GPS device, which saved recent locations. The base was the first location on the list, simply named origin. Derrick didn't know what sort of GPS device she was talking about, but he had learned what GPS meant.

He had, in fact, learned about many things since leaving Pacific Edge, including how little he knew about anything. The aircraft lifted off, spun around, and then pinned him in the seat. The flight from New Mexico to the base would take just over 10 minutes because they would have to slow down when they were within 100 miles in order to stop without being crushed when braking. The machine could create forces their bodies could not endure, even with the special suits.

The flight back to rendezvous with Miriam would take about 15 minutes. Derrick would try to sleep on the flight back. They were already halfway to the base, and he was fighting sleep even now. He wondered what this device Charlie was building looked like and how it worked. However, his curiosity wasn't overcoming his exhaustion and Miriam wanted to destroy three more headquarters tonight and then the central headquarters tomorrow.

If she could find it.

"Starting our descent in three, two, one." Nyx giggled, and the braking force thrust Derrick forward hard against his harness. "I just love saying stuff like that. I might want to become a pilot when this is over."

"Why not shoot for astronaut?" Antonio asked.

"Good idea," Nyx said.

"What's an astronaut?" Derrick asked.

"It's a fake history," Antonio said. "There's a myth that the old United States sent people into space. Went to the Moon and Mars."

"How do you know it's fake?" Nyx asked.

"What do you mean?" Antonio twisted in his seat to look at her.

Nyx said, "Coming up to the hangar. Derrick, be ready to grab the tool. I can see Charlie standing by the hangar door." She paused. "Whoa. That's bigger than I expected."

The aircraft came to a stop. The door hissed open.

The device Charlie was holding was nothing like Derrick had envisioned. He'd assumed it would be a high-tech ray gun. This thing was mechanical, and it was huge. Derrick doubted he could hold it up. He wasn't sure it would fit in the aircraft. And it looked anything but high tech. It looked like an old piece of low-tech machinery. It had a huge circular metal blade and a large two-handed handle.

A diesel-powered generator purred nearby, providing electricity for bright lights on a pole. Red stood by the generator, just within the light's radius. Red was wearing a flight suit.

Why is he dressed like that, Derrick wondered.

Derrick stepped out. "This is it?"

"Yes. It was a joint effort." Charlie motioned toward the generator. "Red had the design concept. I provided a power unit, which is lighter than either the electric driven or gasoline powered original units. Red disassembled a concrete cutting machine, and we worked together on the assembly design and construction."

Charlie set the machine down, and Derrick picked it up. Straining, he said, "It's heavy. Will it work?"

Red said, "It'll work. Cuts through concrete and rebar like butter."

Red showed Derrick how it worked. The machine was not hard to operate. However, cutting a hole in the bunker would be a much more difficult task. Of that much, Derrick was certain.

Red said, "We make a bottom cut first. If you do it last, the cut piece will fall, trapping the blade."

Derrick thought for a moment. "What if the block we cut doesn't fall inside? Could it just drop and sit there?"

Red said, "It probably will do just that."

Still holding the machine, Derrick's arms burned, and his back ached. "Then how do we get inside?"

"You'll have to push the block over," Red said. "It shouldn't be too difficult. It might even fall on its own."

Derrick allowed the blade to rest on the ground. "They will know we are coming. We'll be easy targets."

Red said, "You asked for a machine to cut through the concrete wall. We built such a machine."

"Right. I see that. I expected something," Derrick paused, "higher tech."

"Like a ray gun?"

"Yeah. Like that."

Charlie said, "Concrete is a low-tech building material. Making it is low tech, pouring it is low tech, and destroying it is low tech. This might be low tech, but it is an amazing machine."

"I'm sure it is." Derrick stared at Red. "Why are you wearing a flight suit?"

"I can't help you cut concrete unless I'm there."

He didn't want Red to be there. He didn't want any of them to be there. Then he had an idea. "I guess you could take Nyx's place."

"Hey! I heard that. I'm the navigator and pilot. I worked my butt off learning this thing."

Derrick said, "I learned to do that as well." He did not add, I don't need you. He was often stupid, but not that stupid. However, the resolve in Nyx's voice was inescapable, even for him.

Hoping to sound more logical on his second attempt, Derrick said, "What about the reactor? You might be needed here."

"I fixed it."

His second attempt had missed as badly as did his first. Third time's a charm, or so he'd heard, although he could not remember where. "I appreciate the offer, Red. I really do. But I can handle the cutting device."

"You've cut concrete before?"

"Well, no …"

Red cut him off. "Then you'd better have someone with experience."

So much for the third attempt. Perhaps a more truthful approach might work better. Not that he had not been truthful, because he genuinely wanted to leave Nyx here. This was the one place in which she was safe. "I don't want to put more people at risk." Everything he said was true. He should have left it at that but added. "Besides, I can handle it."

Red said nothing. Motioning Derrick away from the saw, Red hoisted it into the air. Moved it up and down, turning it 90 degrees, and moving it from side to side as if cutting a square. The veins on Red's arms popped and his muscles bulged, but his face remained impassive. He handled the massive machine as if it were a toy.

Red set the machine down. "I've cut concrete before, helping my grandpa. And I've cut concrete with this machine. I know exactly how this machine works."

"Points received and acknowledged." Derrick stepped to the side, indicating the door with one hand. "Welcome on board."

5

Saturday, April 9, 6:25 p.m. Pacific Time

STANLEY MIRES RETURNED TO THE DINING AREA, hoping to find someone to eat dinner with. Pam was not there, which didn't surprise him. She'd gone to her primary job—a bioengineer if he remembered correctly. Prime employed all sorts of people, computer scientists, medical doctors, electrical engineers, and bioengineers. He didn't want to think of things a bioengineer might be working on. Pam didn't seem like a bad person. Yet she was likely working on something sinister. Prime didn't work on things to benefit mankind. Prime worked on things to benefit itself.

Stanley walked deeper into the complex, nearing the outer wall. The street grew darker. The seedier part of town, so to speak. They had taken extensive steps to make people feel they were living in a normal environment.

He saw a pub that looked welcoming in a wrong-side-of-town sort of way. Despite its creepy appearance, Stanley felt no hesitation. There was no crime here. Not in the normal sense—only in the destroy-the-world sense. The lighting was dim, and it took a few moments for his eyes to adjust. Three couples sat in booths as far apart as the room's configuration allowed. They were not there to socialize. Perhaps hoping for privacy in a place where that was impossible. Prime watched everything and everyone. Stanley doubted Prime had any interest in people's daily affairs, whether wholesome or sordid. Prime's purpose for security was based on self-preservation and self-promotion. Only if one's actions resulted in errors, delays, or failures would Prime impose judgement, and in such cases, Prime did not care if the target was dedicated or deceitful. The punishment would be the same. Often death.

Stanley sat at the bar, one seat separating him and another patron, a man, slim build, salt-and-pepper hair, pushing 40, maybe 45. Close enough to attempt conversation; enough separation to not feel imposing.

Unlike places he had been in Seattle that only offered two styles of beer: Carver and Carver Light, neither of which were very good in Stanley's opinion, which was odd because those were the only two beers he'd ever tasted, this place had three options: Buried Deep IPA, Desert Flower Wheat, and Down & Dark Stout. He had no idea what any of them were.

Deconstruction
A Derrick King Novel, Book 8

"What would you like?" The bartender asked. A woman, perhaps 35, with strawberry blonde hair, an athletic body, and no make-up. Stanley estimated she was an engineer type.

Not wanting more whiskey. Whiskey reminded him of Prime, and that was the last thing he wanted to think about, although he was always thinking about Prime in one way or another. "I've never seen those beers."

"Understandable. You'll only see them here and you just arrived."

"I don't understand."

"They are brewed here. The brewing equipment was here from before times, when this was some sort of secret government facility. I assume it was too difficult getting beer here even back then. So, they brewed their own. Now, it's too difficult to get beer for other reasons. Plus, this beer is better than what's up top."

Stanley noticed the man at the bar glance at her, then look away.

"My name is Stanley."

"I know your name."

"Of course. I was hoping to learn yours."

"Margaret. But everyone calls me Maggie. Would you like a sample?"

"That would be great."

Maggie brought him three small glasses, each had about two ounces of liquid. Two were straw colored, one was dark brown, almost black. None of them tasted like Carver or Carver Light. He liked all three but settled on the stout, which had notes of coffee and dark chocolate.

Before Maggie brought his glass, he decided she was more interesting than the lone man sitting at the bar, so he moved to the far end. Perhaps the guy would be offended, but Stanley was chief of staff and there was little danger of being assaulted or even spoken to rudely.

When Maggie arrived with his drink, he said, "Tell me about the beer. Who makes it?"

"I do. I'm a chemical engineer, so brewing is right up my alley."

"How did you learn to do it?" Stanley didn't know if average people, those not working for Prime, could brew their own beer. He assumed it would be illegal because how would Prime make money if such a thing was allowed.

"The ingredients and recipes were here. Most of the ingredients were okay. The hops were stale, so I convinced the last chief of staff to bring in hops and yeast. Now I'm growing hops on the agricultural floor. I harvest the yeast from each batch and reuse it."

"You must have had some pull with the last chief."

"He liked beer. If I'm lucky, you do too. Not everyone does. My stuff has flavor, so it takes some getting used to. Some can't make the leap."

Stanley took a drink. "It's wonderful. Makes me hope to never leave this place." That wasn't entirely true. He wanted out desperately, but knowing about this beer made staying feel slightly less depressing.

"Might I ask what a chemical engineer does here?"

"Sure. Go right ahead."

And with that, Maggie turned and walked away, leaving Stanley baffled yet intrigued.

6

DERRICK TOLD EVERYONE TO REST, because it might be the last chance to do so. It wouldn't be much, but anything would help. Sentry 5 would sound an alarm if they were needed. Derrick tipped his head back, closed his eyes, but didn't sleep. Instead, he thought about what came next and what happened last. The future uncertain and frightening—the past painful and haunted.

Derrick felt a subtle change in the aircraft seconds before Sentry 5 announced their descent. He opened his eyes and sat straight. The aircraft braked hard. Sentry was handling the flight plan. Autopilot, Nyx called it. Derrick did not ask for an explanation. The name provided sufficient clarification.

On the virtual image inside his helmet, Derrick could see Miriam's aircraft on the ground. They should have been resting, but all three girls were outside, leaning against the machine, gazing up at the sky. He didn't know if they could see or hear them. Maybe both. Perhaps neither. It would be good to know how stealthy the aircraft was. It might prove important at some point.

By the time the aircraft settled on the ground, Derrick had his flight helmet off.

Miriam stood waiting as the door opened. "Did you get it?"

"I did."

Derrick stepped out. Nyx followed, then Antonio, and a moment later, Red filled the doorway.

"What's he doing here?" Miriam asked.

"Good to see you too," Red said.

Derrick said, "He's going to cut the concrete."

Miriam frowned. "We didn't need more people involved."

Red stepped next to Derrick. Before Red could respond, Derrick said, "Yes, we do. I can just barely lift the saw. Perhaps two of us could carry it, which means fewer weapons, which means less protection. Plus, I can't make the cut nearly as fast as Red can. We need him. It was my decision. Don't blame him."

"Nice try, Derrick. Don't listen to him. I didn't give him a choice," Red said.

Miriam rolled her eyes. "If you two can press pause on the 'who's the manliest contest,' let's discuss the plan." She paused. "Thanks for wanting to help, Red. I just don't like having another person at risk."

Red nodded. "So, what's the plan? I'm hungry."

Miriam stared at him for a moment.

Red smiled. "Joking. I ate with Akira, Kevin, and Billy Jim Bob, whatever his name is. So, where are we going and what do we know about this bunker thing?"

Miriam turned to Derrick. "You didn't show him?"

"I didn't. I told everyone to rest."

"We could all use some rest. You can show Red on our way to Dallas."

"How long does it take to get to Dallas?" Red asked.

"Not long. A few minutes," Miriam said.

"Where are we?" Red asked.

Nyx said, "Oklahoma, or maybe Arkansas."

Miriam said, "North Texas. Here's the plan. From our video footage, we saw vans and trucks going into and out of the facility. They all come from the same company. Rachael found some information gathered from a Resistance surveillance team in Dallas. It appears this delivery company's main client is Prime Headquarters. Tighter security that way."

Derrick thought for a moment. "You're saying we'll go in one of their trucks?"

"Vans actually," Miriam said.

Antonio said, "That won't work."

Everyone looked at him.

"Even if we stole a van and uniforms, they must have a system in place. You know, shipping orders, invoices, notification of delivery. All sorts of things to prevent what you intend to do. You can't just show up and get in."

Miriam said, "You're right. Rachael said the same thing. She created the paperwork we'll need. Emergency delivery. This time of night, they should be short-staffed."

"How do we get this van?" Derrick asked.

"Your aircraft is amazingly quiet. We couldn't see or hear you coming. The onboard computer told us of your approach. We rushed out to watch." Miriam paused for a moment. "So, we go to the company. They are closed. They might have a couple of night watchmen, perhaps a few warehouse people preloading trucks for morning deliveries. We land on the roof, find a way down, locate uniforms, and a van. If we are lucky, we drive out without being noticed."

"Won't they have someone at the gate?" Nyx asked.

"Maybe. But we have paperwork for an emergency delivery. The oldest looking person should drive the van." Miriam glanced at Red.

"No problem. I can drive."

Deconstruction
A Derrick King Novel, Book 8

"I'll drive." Derrick stared at Red. "Too dangerous. I won't let you take the risk."

"I wasn't asking for your permission."

"Enough!" Miriam held up her hands. "Derrick, you ride up front with Red. If something happens, you can take care of it."

Derrick didn't ask what take care of it meant. "I assume you have coordinates to the locations."

"We do, and they are already loaded on your computer." Miriam paused. "If there aren't any more questions, let's go."

"Hold on." Derrick held up a hand. "Aren't we going to do some surveillance, develop a plan? You know, basic operational procedure."

The words 'operational procedure' coming from Derrick's mouth took Red by surprise. Agreeing with Derrick felt equally strange. "I agree with Derrick. We can't just land and make it up as we go."

Miriam said, "That's exactly what we are going to do. Look, we already have aerial photos of the building. Not much to see. We land on the roof and go through the roof service door."

"What if it's locked?" Derrick asked, his voice rising slightly.

"We unlock it." Miriam paused. "Look, I get it. But here's the thing. We don't have additional information. I know you're tired of hearing this, but we don't have time. We go in, we get uniforms and a van, and we get out."

"I don't like it," Derrick said.

"I'm with Derrick," Nyx said.

Rebekah had been leaning against the aircraft. Quiet. She pushed off. "Miriam is right. We're running out of time. Prime is doing something, and we don't know what."

"What is Prime doing?" Nyx asked.

Miriam pursed her lips. "Nothing."

"Nothing?" Derrick asked. "Then what's the problem?"

"The problem is nothing seems wrong. Prime has stopped moving troops to the border. He's started backing off."

Derrick said, "That's fantastic. Right?".

Miriam sighed. "I think not. Prime's plans have changed. What he had planned was horrifying." She paused. "Now, I fear Prime's plans have gone beyond comprehension."

7

MAGGIE TOOK HER TIME, GOING FROM table to table, chatting with the other customers, taking orders, and delivering drinks. Stanley found it hard to believe she walked away from him the way she did. He was the chief of staff. How dare she treat him like that? A dark thought crossed his mind. What if she knew?

A sickening feeling overcame him.

Perhaps she's not afraid of him because she knows his secret. She could hold it over him, but to what end?

Maggie busied herself making a drink, but instead of taking the drink to a customer, she sauntered down the length of the bar, stopping in front of him. "I make the beer."

Stanley considered this for a moment. "That's your extra duty?"

"No. It's my full-time job."

"Prime brought you here to make beer?"

"Of course not, I was part of the Test Subject Program. You've heard of it, I assume."

Stanley knew a great deal about the Test Subject Program but keeping the extent of his knowledge and his feelings about it concealed seemed best. "Yes. I've heard of it."

Maggie sipped her cocktail. Some sort of whiskey drink. Stanley caught the scent of bourbon and bitters. "I was part of it. Prime brought me here about five years ago. I was also involved in designing Prime replicas in Dallas."

Stanley took a sip, thinking about how to navigate the conversation. "That must be interesting work."

"I'll admit, for a bioengineer, it was interesting. Dangerous but interesting."

Stanley understood what she meant but asked the obvious question anyway. "Why dangerous?"

"I think you know the answer to that. You were Prime's assistant in Seattle. A very trusted assistant or you wouldn't be here."

"Dangerous because Prime replacements don't always work out?"

"Correct. My turn. Why are you here?"

He had to be careful. It seemed important he learn more about this woman, but he sensed she was dangerous, and he must keep his responses guarded. "To be honest, I don't know. One minute I was doing my job in Seattle; the next I was escorted to the roof, loaded into an aircraft, and flown here. I was blindfolded the entire time and didn't see anything until I was inside the facility."

She sipped, studying him. "Does that seem strange to you?"

He didn't answer immediately. "It did at the time. Now that I'm here…well, I'm overwhelmed, to be honest."

"Mmm. So, how about now? Have you figured it out? Do you think it's odd that you were whisked away just before the Seattle building was destroyed?"

Stanley took a drink, fearing he'd run out of beer before she ran out of questions. "Seattle was such a shock. I hadn't thought about myself, but you're right. It's peculiar and I'm lucky. No one got out alive, from what I've heard."

"I find it strange that you don't know why you are here. Or perhaps you know but are not telling me." With her glass flat on the counter, she swirled the drink, the single large ice cube clinked on the sides. "So, who do you think is responsible for what happened in Seattle?"

Stanley knew, of course, at least in part. He had seen Derrick and Miriam King, but he wasn't going to tell Maggie that. "I don't know. Perhaps the Resistance."

"Prime doesn't know what happened? Or isn't telling you? Your predecessor knew pretty much everything."

Hoping to regain control of the conversation, Stanley said, "Tell me about the former chief. You liked him?"

"I wouldn't say liked. He was manageable. And I learned a lot of things." She paused for a sip. "He liked his drink and when he had a few, he opened up, perhaps more than he should have."

"I'm looking forward to meeting him."

"Meeting him?"

"Yes. Prime said he could not provide transition training, but that I would be able to see him."

"Yeah. Won't that be a treat?"

"Yes. I think it will be."

"Hang on to that thought." With that, Maggie left to make rounds.

He sipped his beer and watched her glide about the room. Two guys came in. She took them drinks. Regulars. Then it dawned on him. Everyone was a regular here. Sure, there were some new people arriving, but after their first time inside the pub, they became regulars.

Forever.

8

DERRICK STOOD OUTSIDE THE AIRCRAFT and watched as Red looked it over. Miriam, Anna, and Nyx had gone inside to study satellite images of the delivery company's warehouse, double checking their landing site and other details. Rebekah and Antonio walked into the darkness, holding hands. Derrick didn't mind. A few moments of quiet felt welcomed.

Done with his inspection, Red said, "I still can't see how this thing flies."

"I don't know anything about flying machines, but I agree. This one is a puzzle. So is the one Rebekah is flying. Hover craft in Pacific Edge seem primitive by comparison." Derrick paused. "You'd need to ask Charlie."

"I already did."

"What did he say?"

"He said it was AT. That was all, but he said it as if I should know what he was talking about."

Derrick thought for a moment. "Wasn't AT written on the new-Charlie boxes we brought from the engineering warehouse?"

"Yeah. I think you're right—AT series."

Derrick said, "I wonder what it stands for?"

Red said, "I'm curious, but I guess it doesn't matter. That's another story."

"What do you mean, another story? This isn't a story, it's real life."

"Just something my grandpa says sometimes. Another story as in a different story."

"I'd like to see some of his cars." Derrick almost added 'when this is over' but didn't. The sinking feeling in his chest surprised him. He had not been thinking about L. Linda but suddenly had the same feeling as when it became clear that she was gone. He refused to think it meant Red wasn't going to survive; then Derrick realized it might mean something else. That none of them would survive, which in turn caused a cold fear to grip his heart, because Nyx was inside the aircraft planning the next landing site.

"You okay?" Red asked.

"What? Yeah."

"You looked like you saw a ghost."

"Ghost?"

"Yeah, like something frightened you."

Deconstruction
A Derrick King Novel, Book 8

"Oh." Derrick paused. "I won't lie. I'm worried about Dallas. Something doesn't feel right."

Derrick wasn't entirely sure it was Dallas that caused his sudden dread.

He wasn't sure that it wasn't either.

Miriam stepped out of the aircraft. "We're ready. Derrick, you need to drop Red near the road outside the place we are landing. "The concrete cutting machine is heavy and awkward. We'll pick him up after we get the van. Pick a spot that will be easy to recognize."

Derrick didn't like the idea. "It's better we stick together. Besides, Red is driving."

Miriam said, "New plan. That machine is too big and awkward. There's a ladder attached to the building. Nyx called it a fire escape. It's right by where the trucks are parked. It would be impossible to get down that ladder with the cutting device."

Red said, "She has a point. It is a handful."

Miriam said, "We spotted a place. Nyx has all the information. There are landmarks, so we'll know where to pick Red up. With any luck, there won't be any cars in the area, so you can land and take off again."

"What if there are cars?" Derrick asked.

"You'll have to wait. We won't land until you've dropped Red. Then we'll land together," Miriam said.

"How are we going to get a vehicle?" Derrick asked.

Miriam said, "The uniforms might be more difficult. But we only need one shirt for the driver. The rest of us will be in the back of the vehicle and out of sight."

"Two shirts. I'm in front with the driver. Remember?" Derrick paused. "Wait. Who's driving?"

"Rebekah."

Derrick said, "Maybe we should just drop the cutting device and then retrieve it on our way out."

"We discussed that option, but not worth the risk," Miriam said.

"Risk of what?" Derrick asked.

"Of someone seeing us and stealing the tool. Without it we have no plan," Miriam said.

Derrick said, "Okay. But we still need two shirts. I'm up front with Rebekah."

"Don't we all need shirts?" Red asked.

Derrick stared at Miriam. "Because once we get beyond the front gate, we aren't trying to fool anybody. It's a firefight. Correct?"

Miriam nodded. "Right."

Red said, "Can I at least have a gun?"

Miriam looked at Derrick.

"Sure." Derrick paused. "We have just the thing in the aircraft. It has power level settings. You can stun a human or destroy a robot."

Anna stepped out. "Derrick doesn't want to kill people, just robots."

"And Prime," Derrick added.

"Right. I suppose," Anna said.

"Someone wants to kill people?" Red asked.

Miriam said, "No. We don't want to kill people if we can avoid it. However, sometimes it's unavoidable."

"Self-defense," Anna said, adding, "none of us want to kill people. I'm sorry it came out that way."

Miriam said, "Let's go. We have work to do."

9

STANLEY WATCHED AS MAGGIE DRIFTED around the room, smiling and chatting, seeming to enjoy herself, which struck him as odd. She was a bioengineer who was brewing beer deep inside the earth with no hope of escape. Perhaps she was married, although he had not seen a ring. She was about his age. Attractive. Perhaps she has a boyfriend. Maybe the boyfriend is recent, giving her a reason to smile.

Otherwise, he couldn't see the point.

Not down here.

He still had an inch of beer in his glass, but she brought him another and had topped off her drink as well. He had not planned on having another drink. Maggie had other ideas, and he was unsure as to what end. The conversation had already gone past his comfort zone. He needed to steer their discussion in another direction.

Holding up his glass, he said, "I'm good. Thanks."

"Are you?" She took his nearly empty glass, smiled, and drank what remained. "Looks like you need another to me."

Stanley was a little shocked. Was she flirting with him? It had been so long since he'd dated, he didn't know. "Tell me more about yourself."

Maggie sat. "Not much to tell. I worked in Dallas and then came here."

"How did you go from creating test subjects to brewing beer?"

"Short version is, I worked here as extra duty. Like I said earlier, the brewing equipment was here as were the ingredients. The hops were vacuum packed and frozen. They were not terrible, but the beer tasted musty. It was still better than that Carver crap."

"That explains how you learned to brew beer. Not how you came to do it full time."

"I told the chief I was done."

"Done working in the Test Subject Program?"

"No. Prime would have terminated me for that."

"Terminated as in fired?"

She rolled her eyes. "Did you actually work for Prime before coming here? Terminated, as in killed a slow and painful death. Well-publicized to prevent others from thinking quitting was an option." She took a drink. "I told him I would stop brewing. Too much work. I didn't have time for it."

"And he changed your duties to full time here?"

"He did just that."

"I guess things worked out for you then."

"If you consider being imprisoned underground, working out."

That was a loaded statement if ever there was one. Agreeing with her was dangerous. However, she could be an ally, or at least someone he could talk with, although he still had to be careful. He glanced around the room, trying to spot the nearest security camera. "I haven't been here long enough to form an opinion about that. They have done a nice job on this level making it feel as if you're above ground."

"Trust me. It wears on you." She pushed the full glass toward him. "Don't waste my work. It's one of my best, in my opinion. Oh, and there are no cameras in here. Not working ones anyway."

"That seems unlikely."

"Agreed, but it's true. Another benefit of developing a trusting relationship with the last chief. He convinced Prime that staff needed a safe place to unwind."

"And Prime agreed?"

Maggie shrugged. "Apparently."

He took a sip but said nothing.

After a moment, Maggie asked, "So, what do you really think happened in Seattle?"

"You mean who's responsible?"

"Exactly."

"I don't know." He hoped she wasn't great at detecting lies.

"I thought the Resistance was primarily into the preservation of history."

"That's my understanding as well," Stanley said, trying to think of a question that would change topics, but everything he considered was easily directed back to the first ever destruction of a Prime Headquarters. Destruction of a Prime anything, for that matter.

"The rumor is that Seattle is not the only headquarters that's been destroyed."

Stanley almost spit out his beer. "Sounds like a far-fetched rumor. I've heard no such thing. Where is this coming from?"

Maggie studied him for a moment. "I probably shouldn't say. I hardly know you. You might run straight to Prime. Tell him what you heard. Prime would drag me in, find out I only work here brewing beer. I've been flying under the radar. I want to keep it that way."

"Prime doesn't know about you?"

Deconstruction
A Derrick King Novel, Book 8

"Correct. You're not going to report me, are you?" Maggie's expression changed. He had not seen her look serious the entire conversation.

"No. I rather like it here. I see the advantage of having a place where people can relax. Keeps morale up. That keeps production up, and that makes me look good."

Maggie took a deep breath and placed her hand on his. "That's a relief."

"Back to the rumor."

"You won't say anything to Prime about it?" Maggie asked.

"And risk Prime beheading me? Not a chance. My experience has taught me that Prime does not receive bad news gracefully."

Maggie smiled. "You really have worked with Prime. So, here's what I know." She glanced around, despite having said there were no cameras. Perhaps she wanted to ensure there was no one close enough to overhear.

Maggie leaned in, whispering, "I know someone who works in receiving."

"And that person has heard something?"

"It's not what she's heard." She paused, glanced side to side. "It's what she's seen. Prime is gathering people here like never before. No one knows why, but they figure something big is about to happen."

They have no idea just how big, he thought.

"A few people came from Seattle a week ago, but none recently, for obvious reasons." She stared at him for a moment. "Except you."

"I was brought here before the attack."

"Was there any warning? Were you on alert there?"

"Nothing. Business as usual."

"Okay. So, no one from Seattle. But it's the same with New York and Chicago."

"Probably just haven't arrived yet."

"Possibly, but unlikely. You see, by now there are people from all the locations except those three. And the arrivals suddenly stopped. Receiving has been told there are no more coming." Maggie sipped. "There's more. The timetable included more people from Chicago and New York, but they never arrived."

"I'll admit that does sound odd. I assume Prime knows." Stanley focused on remaining impassive, hoping to conceal that he knew something regarding the fate of New York and Chicago.

"I don't know. Would you want to deliver that news?"

Stanley thought for a moment. "I'll pass."

"There's another rumor."

Stanley waited. "I'm listening."

"People are saying it's a couple of test subjects. Renegades. But they are just kids."

"Not possible. Test subjects are deconstructed at the end of the test."

Maggie said, "I know. It's why I wanted out of the program. I got lucky."

Stanley felt the need to say something condemning. Something chief of staff like. "You're unique. Fortunately, your position change didn't happen on my watch."

Maggie smiled. "You're a survivalist."

You have no idea, Stanley thought. He tipped his glass.

"Well, if they are test subjects, they could be dangerous. Until Dallas, that is."

"Oh? Why's that?"

"Because Dallas is a trap. It's an old government building. It has a concrete bunker inside one of the buildings."

"I see. Impossible to penetrate, I assume." He paused. "Like this place."

"Yes. But it's also a decoy. Prime's not in there. Whoever is attacking headquarters will assume Prime is in the bunker. They'll hit the bunker first and be sitting ducks."

Stanley fell silent for a few moments. "Sounds like a bad situation for the assailants. I guess that will put an end to it."

"It gets worse. The Test Subject Program is an important part of the Dallas facility, but its primary function is building robots."

"You're saying that Prime has a large defense there?" Stanley asked.

"Literally, a small army."

Stanley finally had vital information and no way to send a warning.

10

THE FLIGHT TO DALLAS WAS QUICK. TOO QUICK in Derrick's opinion. He had a bad feeling about this. No specific reason. Other than they didn't know Prime's exact location, and they'd added another Potterville high school student, Red Badowski, who was not Derrick's friend, but that didn't matter. Not now.

Nyx spotted the large sign along the road where they had decided to drop Red and his cutting machine. Red disappeared into the night. The aircraft rose back into the black sky. Anna, Rebekah, Miriam, and he would get the van. Red, of course, had to help them at the Prime Headquarters, but Derrick hoped once Red had cut into the vault, or whatever it was, he could return to the van and wait.

If there were no people or robots outside the vault, Red's exposure to violence would be limited. Wishful thinking. Dangerous thinking and Derrick knew it. However, Chicago had been an easy target. Only Prime and Prime replicants died. And Derrick had given the order to fire. That was important. Although, it bothered him a bit that Sentry 5 had configured the warhead in a manner that killed Prime and was contrary to Derrick's order.

Destroying Prime really wasn't Derrick's decision.

This time it might be different. This time perhaps he'd be forced to kill Prime; he believed it would come to that, eventually.

The flight to the company where they planned to steal a vehicle took seconds, but Nyx circled the large, flat-roofed building several times as Sentry 5 ran scans, isolating the entrances and exits, vehicles, supplies, and people. After a few passes over the facility, Sentry 5 located the best landing spot— although they would not land but hover a few inches over the roof while the team jumped out. They would be close to an entrance, a closet that had uniforms, and a box that held vehicle keys. The vehicles were parked in a parking lot, not unlike Seattle, under the building. That part caused Derrick some discomfort. He understood why. No reason to dwell on the causation. Still, that didn't help how he felt. Unless they had an unfortunate turn of events, the only person they would encounter is the guard at the gate.

Derrick wished Red would be driving. Red could pass for an adult; Rebekah could not. They had the documents Rachael had created for their delivery, so

Derrick hoped the guard wouldn't pose a problem. If he or she did, well, it was just one person, and killing would be unnecessary. Derrick could handle it.

Technology had played a vital role thus far. Sentry 5 provided valuable information about the sites. Weapons and technology from the abandoned military base, proved essential. Without the medical unit, Akira would be dead, and Antonio would be of little help. Red would have been ill and perhaps dying. They could not have prevented the destruction of Potterville, and the country would be at war with Mexico. They could not have destroyed Prime's Headquarters in Chicago, New York, or Seattle.

However, L. Linda Maxton would be alive.

Perhaps someday, Derrick would accept L. Linda's death as a sacrifice that had to be made for the greater good. But that day had not yet arrived. And he didn't need the distraction. Distractions could get more people killed. And with that thought, Derrick wondered if he'd already missed something important.

Antonio piloted one aircraft, which circled a few miles out. Nyx flew the other one, which contained those who would attack the Prime Headquarters. Nyx descended, hovering just above the roof. Miriam, Rebekah, and Anna were already waiting near the ladder when Derrick stepped out. There had been some tense arguing about who went and who stayed. Derrick doing the arguing and losing. So much for Derrick providing leadership. Rebekah was joining them. Anna had wanted as much firepower as possible, and Miriam agreed.

They had changed out of their flight suits, donning the one-piece overall uniforms sans the logos on the sleeves that they found at the military base. The aircraft rose into the darkness leaving them. Derrick insisted on going down the ladder first. One small victory. He moved quickly but quietly; his weapon set to stun in one hand. He scanned the area and saw no threat. Miriam was the last one down, moving somewhat gingerly, still hurting from the wound on her side. At least it didn't appear to be bleeding.

Derrick touched Miriam's arm. "Are you okay?"

"I'm fine." She looked around and pointed. "There's the door to where we'll find clothing. Then down to the parking area to get a van."

The door was locked, which they anticipated. Miriam used the same cutting device they had used in Seattle, which reminded Derrick of how much they depended on the technology from the base and Charlie.

And of L. Linda Maxton.

He needed to stop the uninvited intrusions into his thinking. The distraction was unwanted and unacceptable. He had to focus. They all did. Anything less was going to get someone killed. Perhaps get them all killed. That was an undeniable fact, which is why the distractions bothered him so much. What bothered him even more was the feeling that not everyone would survive Dallas.

It was more than a mere feeling.

It felt certain. As if it had already happened.

"Derrick!" It was a hiss more than a whisper. He looked around and found himself alone. Miriam was waving for him from the door opening. The door cut from its hinges leaned against the wall.

How long have I been standing here? How many times has she called my name?

Derrick sprinted to Miriam but avoided looking at her.

"Whatever is eating you, put it away until this is over."

"You're right. Sorry. But it's not me I'm worried about."

She squeezed his shoulder. "I get it, but don't think that way. It may come down to you. We need you. I need you! Got it?"

He nodded.

Inside, Rebekah had found the room containing uniforms similar to the ones they were wearing. She found one for Red quicker than Derrick expected. Apparently, big people were not uncommon in Texas. The plan had changed, and they decided it might prove beneficial if they all wore the same clothing. After selecting uniforms, they went to separate corners to change. They tossed their other clothing in the trash.

Next, they needed a vehicle. Again, Sentry 5's directions proved flawless. In a garage filled with trucks and vans, they found the key box exactly where 5 said it would be. Each key had a tag with a number that coincided with a number written on the vehicle the key would fit. Miriam wanted a van because a truck would be suspicious for a small, afterhours delivery. They got lucky. The first key was to a van.

They were in and out within 15 minutes.

Deep inside Derrick's chest, he felt certain more difficult times lay ahead. However, difficulties did not start at the front gate. The guard opened the gate and waved them through.

Easy.

Rebekah was driving. Derrick sat in the front with her. They had driven about ten minutes when Rebekah spotted the sign where they had dropped Red. Derrick jumped out and pulled his weapon. Red stepped out of the darkness and then paused when he noticed Derrick's weapon pointing at him.

"Point that thing somewhere else unless you want it shoved somewhere the sun don't shine." Red climbed inside.

Derrick holstered the weapon and considered Red's words. A smile creased his face when the meaning materialized in his brain.

Anna jumped out. "Derrick, ride in the back. I need to talk to my sister."

Derrick started to protest.

"Please! I need to tell her something." Anna paused. "In case I don't get another chance. Don't worry. I won't kill anyone."

Derrick nodded. He understood why this was important. That it was important did not ease his anxiety about sitting in the back or what came next. He climbed into the back and sat opposite of Red.

Red closed the door, and Rebekah pulled back onto the road. Red changed into the new uniform. He seemed less concerned about it than Derrick would have been. Miriam looked away despite Red's apparent comfort in disrobing down to his boxers.

They sat on the floor in the back, in the darkness, listening to the rumble of the tires on the road. Derrick didn't like not being able to see out. He felt claustrophobic and motion sickness, neither of which eased the sinking feeling in his stomach.

After several minutes, the van stopped. "Do you think we are there?" Derrick whispered.

Miriam said, "No. We're just entering town. Just a stop sign or a traffic light. It will take 20 to 30 minutes to get to the headquarters. Traffic appears to be light."

They continued like that, drive and stop. Rebekah's driving skill had improved since she first drove the electric cart back at the base. They had all changed significantly in such a short time. Blowing up a building and losing friends did that to a person. Some stops were brief, others longer. Occasionally, Derrick heard another vehicle but not many. Miriam was right. Traffic was light. That was good.

Easy.

So far.

After 30 minutes, the van slowed, rolling to a gentle stop. Derrick heard the whine of a powered window and Rebekah's voice, but he could not make out what she said. Then the van rolled forward.

The gate to headquarters, Derrick thought.

They were inside.

11

STANLEY MIRES WASN'T READY TO BE alone, but he didn't want to
continue the conversation with Maggie, who proved far too competent at
extracting information, so he took what remained of his drink and retreated to
a dark corner of the pub. He should have done this earlier, feeling he'd said too
much already. Yet, he had learned a great deal. He now possessed vital
information but had no way to share it.

The kids, and whoever might be helping them, were walking into a trap.
Maggie told him that Dallas was an old United States government building that
had a working laboratory. The laboratory previously worked for the benefit of
mankind, but Prime put it to work for a much different and darker purpose,
producing human test subjects. In addition, Dallas built robots. They had plenty
on hand. A small army.

The bunker inside the building would appear to be the perfect place for
Prime's location, but Prime wasn't in the bunker. Maggie didn't know where
Prime hid, and she had worked there. Her best guess was that he was in a
complex under one of the buildings. The kids were being lured into a trap and
facing an army of robots. It created an impossible situation, and he could not
warn them. He felt as if he was responsible, because he had supplied the
Resistance with addresses, but too few details. He knew locations, but Prime
had not shared much information regarding each headquarters.

Another seemingly unavoidable situation was Maggie herself. After making
a quick round checking in with the other patrons, she headed straight to his
table in the corner with a whiskey and a beer, something he had neither ordered
nor needed. She was not easily discouraged. His suspicions of Maggie's
intentions were growing stronger by the minute or perhaps by the drink. It
occurred to him that her ability to extract information was no fluke. It was a
talent, either natural or learned; he did not know which, but it explained how
she had manipulated her way into a full-time job brewing beer.

Stanley lifted his glass. "I'm good, thanks."

"Nonsense. You look stressed as hell. Plus, you're off duty, right? Until
Monday, that is." She sat the beer on the table and sat. "You moved. Trying to
get rid of me?"

Stanley wasn't sure how to answer that question. He also could not remember telling her that he was off duty until Monday, but that didn't mean he had not. He decided to avoid the question regarding his new table. "I am tired and should call it a day."

She pushed the glass in front of him. "You're not just tired. You're stressed. Everyone is when they first arrive whether they recognize it or not."

He sipped. The beer was almost gone, which wasn't good because the new beer she brought looked more tempting than he wanted to admit. "Why is that?"

"Duh. Because we are buried under God knows where."

"True. But this part looks normal." He paused. "I don't think it's affecting me." That sounded lame, and he regretted saying it.

Maggie took a drink. "Do you think Dallas will end it?"

"End what?"

Maggie rolled her eyes. "The attack on Prime. What else?"

He studied her for a moment, but she was hard to read. "I suppose. Based on what you told me."

"I still find it a strange coincidence that you came here just before Seattle was destroyed."

He shrugged. Took a drink.

Maggie inched the fresh beer closer, this time a golden beer with an off-white head. Moisture condensed on the outside wetting the glass and bubbles rose from the bottom. "After two dark beers, I figured a change would be good. Drink up. What do you have to lose?"

Only my life. "I'm fine."

"You're not. Doesn't matter how many times you repeat it. I think you know."

"Know what?" he asked.

"That Prime is going to do something big soon." She stared at him. "Something terrible."

12

THE DRIVE TO SAN DIEGO TOOK LONGER than necessary, because they skirted the large cities, especially avoiding the Los Angeles area. Jack led because he traveled these roads—Collins didn't. Despite Jack's efforts, outside Victorville Collins spotted a roadblock manned by soldiers and lawmen. Law enforcement officers searched vehicles, many had open trunks, belongings scattered, and people sitting in cuffs. Armed soldiers watched. Collins drove a marked car, wore a badge, and possessed a warrant, but Fletcher didn't trust people in uniforms. Not after he had watched soldiers murder his friend, which was a long time ago, but it would never be long enough for him to forget or forgive.

Jack didn't even trust Collins. Not until a few days ago. Not until Collins had put the town before his own safety. Not before Collins had demonstrated how far he would go to protect a kid from Pacific Edge.

Jack made an abrupt turn onto a narrow road with crumbling asphalt. He pulled to the side and walked to Collin's squad car. Donna joined him. Collins and Patel exited, meeting them at the front bumper.

"What are we doing?" Collins asked.

Jack pointed. "Roadblock. We need to go around it."

Collins said, "I saw it. I'll get us through it. I'll run lights and you can follow me."

"You have more confidence in that badge than I do," Jack said.

Collins frowned. "What are you saying, Jack?"

"I thought it would be clear enough. I don't trust cops. I trust the military even less."

Collins took a step closer. "Does that include me?"

"Did until a few days ago."

"What's that mean?" Collins demanded.

"Means I'm not so hardheaded that I can't change," Fletcher said.

Collins continued to look miffed.

Fletcher said, "Those are state police. Not locals. Not county deputies, who might show respect for a sheriff. A lot of those state guys are Chosen wannabes. They see a warrant for Prime, and they might just arrest you and haul you to the closest Chosen Community."

"That would be Pacific Edge," Patel said.

"Doesn't matter where it is," Donna said. "I agree with Jack. We can't take that chance."

"If you feel that way, why did you agree with this?" Collins asked. "What makes you think the police in San Diego won't arrest me?"

Jack said, "I'm not sure they won't, but I assumed you'd go to the sheriff there, not the state or city."

Collins thought for a moment. "Sheriff's office would be a good idea."

"Then you agree with me," Fletcher said.

"I didn't say that."

Patel said, "He makes sense, Bill."

Collins folded his arms. "Do you know a way around?"

"Not exactly. But I've been out this way, searching for old cars. There are roads through the desert. Not much out there."

"It will take a lot longer," Collins said.

Fletcher said, "Agreed, so we should stop wasting time jawing about it."

Donna reached into the car, pulling out two sodas, water dripping from the cans. She held them out. "Thirsty?"

"I am," Allen said. "You're the best, Donna."

"Thanks," Collins said, then he looked at Jack. "Lead the way."

Jack nodded and headed to his car.

Once inside the car, Donna handed him a soda. "That was a little tense."

Jack drove off, pulling the tab on the can with one hand. He took a long drink and said, "Thanks. I had way too much coffee the past couple of days." After another drink, he added. "Yeah. Sorry about that. I could have handled that better."

"Nothing to be sorry about. I agree with you. I don't trust those state police. It's hard to trust anyone outside of Potterville, and God rest their souls, the Priest family proved you can't trust everyone in Potterville, either."

Jack took another drink. "The killer wasn't from Potterville."

"True. But Paul Jorgensen was."

"Good point. I'd kinda forgot about Paul. That's hard to imagine, ain't it? Forgetting about any of it. I mean, it was just what? Yesterday that Lori Martinez came to my shop with a body bag in her trunk."

"No harder to believe than our kids trying to overthrow Prime," Donna said. "If I weren't living it, I'd never believe it."

She said nothing for several miles. "Can I ask you something, Jack?"

"Sure."

"Why don't you trust the police?"

"Told you. Many of them state guys are hunting that magical ticket to becoming Chosen. No different than Jimmy Priest."

"I get that. But you said you didn't trust anyone in a uniform, even Bill. You've known Bill since he was a kid." She paused. "Much as you know anyone in Potterville. Face it, Jack, you've been holed up in that shop as long as I can remember, and I can remember a long way back. I remember you way back when we were in school. You were as nice a boy as I'd ever met. Fun and outgoing and then came the Greatest War. Sacramento. It affected all of us, but none more than you. You shut down. Retreated."

"I won't deny it. It changed me."

"The last few days have been the worst in Potterville since Sacramento. But I'm not unhappy about Derrick coming to town. I really like that boy, and I can't wait to get to know his sister. He and Nyx are the cutest couple. He's been good for her. I gotta tell you, L. Linda Maxton has a thing for Derrick too. We could see some sparks fly between L. Linda and Nyx before it's over, if you know what I mean. But where was I headed? Oh, yeah. The other good thing is I've gotten to know you better in the past few days than I have all those years since school."

"I'm sorry I haven't been in more often. That'll change after this is over. I promise."

"Not where I was headed, but I'm gonna hold you to that promise. What I want to know is, what happened?"

"You mean in school?"

"Yeah. That."

Jack remained silent for a few minutes. Donna waited.

"Sacramento happened."

"You're not getting off that easy, Jack Fletcher. I really want to know. Sacramento happened to all of us. It was something more for you. I hate to push it, but we might not live to see Monday, and I'd like to know. Seems to me you've carried some kinda heavy burden all these years. More than your share, I'd say."

Again, Jack said nothing for several miles. He made a right turn onto a dirt road. A sign so worn it was barely legible read: Mojave. Finally, he said, "I've only ever told one person and that was just a couple of days ago. I told Miriam King. Well, Derrick and Nyx were there as well. So, three people. I hope you won't hold what I'm about to say against me."

Jack told Donna the same story he'd told the kids. How a soldier had shot his best friend. How he'd hid in the alley and then said nothing about his friend's murder. How his friend's family had arrived in Sacramento just before a nuclear bomb destroyed it.

Donna listened, not saying a word. Jack stared straight ahead, not looking at her once as he told the story of the day that changed his life. She saw a tear trace down his cheek when he'd finished.

She placed her hand on his shoulder and said, "What an awful thing for you to witness. Why would you think I'd hold that against you?"

"Because I should have done something."

"What could you have done? If you'd tried to help your friend, they would have killed you too."

"True, but that's no excuse. I was a coward." He paused. "Dying while trying to help would have been better than living with the memory."

Donna thought for a few minutes. Her days were filled with cooking and baking, but she also spent a lot of time at the counter just talking to folks. Making good food was a necessity if she wanted customers. That was a given. So, striving to make everything good was vital. But the food was never the goal. It was always about the people. She believed good food nourished more than the body; it could heal the soul too, and when the food wasn't enough, she had kind words for those who entered her bistro. But she was struggling to find the right words here, and the sandwiches were in a cooler in the trunk.

"I can't say I understand how that feels, so I won't try. But I'll tell you one thing I believe with all my heart. Red wouldn't be the same if he didn't have you. You've been that boy's salvation."

"I should have told him to stay away from Jimmy Priest."

"Perhaps. But you raised him to be just like you. He stood by his friend, even when he didn't agree with him. He stood by him until Jimmy crossed a line. Then Red stood up for what was right."

Jack glanced at her. "What do you mean?"

"You didn't know? Jimmy and Red had a falling out. Jimmy and two of his friends tried to start a fight with Derrick after football practice. Red stepped in. Red said Derrick was a teammate and Jimmy would have to fight him too. Jimmy got mad; told Red they were finished. And here's the thing, Red doesn't even like Derrick. But he knows what's right. Protecting his teammate is right. Red learned that from you."

Jack nodded. He'd given up on fighting the tears. He wiped his nose on his sleeve. "Red's a great kid. I need him as much as he needs me."

"You're a good man, Jack. Regardless of how this goes, I'm glad I got to know you better."

13

THE VAN STARTED MOVING AGAIN, but it didn't travel far before it stopped and fell silent. Even the slight vibration from the motor was gone. The side door slid open. Anna stood outside. Her expression was solemn. That bothered him because she was the most self-assured person he knew.

"Are you ready?" Anna asked.

"No. But we have no options." Derrick stepped out.

Red followed with the giant circular saw.

"Let's move. We've got three more locations to destroy, and I'd like to get a few hours' sleep before we take on the central headquarters," Miriam said.

"Have you found it?" Rebekah asked, coming around the front of the van.

"No. Yet another thing I need to accomplish."

Derrick examined the building. He knew little about buildings, but this one looked old. Not old like Potterville High School old, but still old. The high school was old but had a certain charm about it because of the architectural designs surrounding the doors and windows as if the builders of the day not only did manual labor but were also artists. This structure was made from dull gray blocks. No artistry, just straight lines, and right angles, as if those who built it knew they would never have to look at it. The entry was two plain-looking, glass doors.

They gathered at the front of the van. Red set the cutting device on the ground. Everyone else checked their weapons. They carried the zappers as sidearms and a long gun of similar technology. Anna had wanted a gun that shot bullets, but Miriam convinced her otherwise. Derrick felt a bit of relief about that. If he had limited Anna's choice of weapon, she would have argued. They didn't need to be fighting among themselves.

"How are we going to do this?" Red asked. "I appreciate the entire van thing, and the worker's clothing and such. However, we don't exactly look like your average delivery guys with all the weapons and this saw."

"He has a point," Rebekah said.

"I can help Red carry the cutting device," Derrick offered.

"I don't see how that helps. What about the guns? Why would delivery people be carrying weapons?" Red asked.

"Fair point," Derrick admitted.

"Where is the vault?" Red asked.

Miriam pointed. "Beyond those glass doors."

Red picked up the saw. "Let's go then."

Derrick didn't like it, but Red was right. They were standing in plain view, holding weapons and a large cutting device. Giving Prime more time to prepare wasn't in their best interest. They wanted to believe they had a plan, but in reality, they had none. They were walking straight into whatever Prime had waiting for them. This felt like a bad idea earlier. Now, it felt like a disaster waiting to happen.

Derrick jogged to catch Red. Coming alongside, Derrick brought his weapon to the ready position. Robots or Prime's security could burst through the doors at any moment. Derrick moved the power control halfway between low and full power, hoping it wouldn't kill a person but would stop a robot. He could think of no way to test it. He felt certain everyone else had their weapons set on high. He couldn't blame them. It was the safe thing to do.

Red paused at the entrance. Glancing at Derrick, he nodded toward the door.

Derrick looked at the others. Each of them had their weapons aimed at the door. Derrick motioned them to either side, then he grabbed the metal handle of one door. "Locked." He tried the other. Same result.

Miriam stepped up to the door, cupping her hand against the glass. "I can't see in. It's a mirrored surface."

Derrick envisioned robots on the other side, aiming weapons at Miriam.

Red set the machine on the ground and stepped up to Miriam's side, placing his ear against the glass.

Derrick imagined a bullet shattering the glass, blowing the side of Red's head away in a cloud of pink mist, and then he said, "Step back. That's not safe."

Red shook his head. "Standing here isn't safe. But I don't hear a thing." He walked to the concrete cutting machine, picking it up. "Ready?"

Before anyone could answer, Red swung the end of the machine into the glass, shattering it and sending shards into the building. Red stepped back behind the concrete wall, as if expecting a deluge of bullets.

It remained silent.

Derrick eased to the opening, signaling for the others to stay back. He peered inside. "It's dark but looks empty."

Raising his weapon, Derrick stepped through the opening. The broken glass made an unpleasant crunching sound under his feet. Not a stealthy entrance, by any stretch of the imagination. His imagination had conjured unpleasant images, and he wondered if there was something wrong with him. Surely the others were not imagining their friends getting shot in the head, although Red wasn't his friend. Red had made that clear several times. Derrick would like to think of him as a friend, but Red had drawn a line. Teammates, not friends.

Once inside, Derrick felt certain the place was empty but not abandoned. He heard and saw nothing. Dimly lit by the faint light of exit signs, he saw it was a cavernous room probably once filled with people scurrying from one end of the building to the other, an entrance and internal passageway. Across from the entrance was a long counter that stretched the width of the room; the ceiling extended beyond what appeared to be a second floor. The floor was covered with slate-colored tiles. He did not know whether it was real stone or fake and did not care.

Miriam pointed to the long counter. "The vault must be behind that wall."

The wall had one door. No glass. No elevator.

Rebekah whispered. "Where are all the people?"

Derrick whispered, "And robots."

Anna said, "The parking lot only had a few cars. I wonder what they do here. Each place seems to focus on a specific purpose."

Red walked toward the counter. "Let's find out."

Red set the saw on the counter. Instead of walking around, Red hoisted himself up, sat, and then spun around, dropping to the other side.

Red tried a door. "Not locked." Before anyone could warn him, he glanced inside. "It's pitch black in there, but I don't hear anything."

Hopping over the counter, Anna said, "And nobody blew your head off, so you have that going for you. Don't ever do that again. Next time, wait for us."

Red shrugged. "You're here now. Got any ideas?"

Anna peeked in, then recoiled. Reaching around the edge of the door, she explored the wall with her hand. A click sounded, and the lights came to life, each with a distinctive pop. "How about that?"

Red gave a quick look. "Empty but there's the vault. Looks like a huge safe."

"Safe?" Derrick asked. "As in, it's safe to go in?"

"Safe as in bank. Why would anyone need such a huge safe?" Red asked, grabbing the saw and stepping inside.

Anna followed him. "I wish you would let me go first."

"Because you're a lady?"

Anna raised her weapon. "No, dipshit. Because I have a gun."

"Fair enough." Red walked to a large metal door. "They got a punch pad and a tumbler dial."

Miriam studied the keypad. "Four keys have been used repeatedly."

Red thought for a moment. "So, probably a four-digit PIN."

"Could be more, but that's a good possibility, but could be six, eight, or ten. Could be an odd number," Miriam said.

"How many combinations if it's a four-digit combination?" Rebekah asked.

"Ten thousand," Miriam replied.

"Yeah. Right, as if you'd know that," Red said.

Miriam looked at him. "I didn't know it. I just figured it out."

"Bullshit."

Rebekah said, "It's not. Trust me."

Derrick said, "This isn't getting us inside. Maybe we should cut through the door."

"Or try to figure out the combination," Anna suggested.

"Ten thousand tries?" Derrick asked.

"I can't cut through the door. This will cut concrete and rebar. If there isn't too much rebar and if the blade lasts long enough."

"You're a fountain of confidence," Rebekah said.

Miriam said, "The combination isn't our best option, but I'll try while Red cuts."

Miriam started pushing buttons. Four at a time, then trying the handle. Looking over her shoulder, she glared at Red. "What are you waiting for?"

Red stepped to the center of the concrete wall, pulling on leather gloves and donning safety glasses. "On it." Then he added, "turn away or you might get a chunk of concrete embedded in your eye."

Derrick turned just as Red stuck the saw into the wall. Red had not lied as chips of concrete pelted his back and head. The roar of the cutting machine was deafening. Derrick watched as Miriam entered one code after another. None of them worked. Hearing Red pause, Derrick risked a quick glance. Red had cut a three-foot horizontal slit about two feet off the ground. He turned the saw vertical. Derrick turned again before the debris flew. He doubted Miriam would stumble upon the correct combination. Red would have a hole cut in a few more minutes, but they were no longer silent intruders. If Prime had a squad of robots in the vault, they would be ready, and since it seemed clear that Prime was inside, when the block fell, the shooting would start.

The saw paused a couple of more times and then stopped. Still no robots. No staff. Silent except for the ringing in his ears from the saw's screech. It made little sense. Derrick had been apprehensive ever since they got into the stolen van. He didn't feel any better when they broke the glass and entered the building. The fact the place was empty didn't help. It made it worse. Something wasn't right.

Red grunted. "A little help?"

Derrick turned to see Red pushing his shoulder into the sawn block of concrete. Stepping next to Red, Derrick asked, "Were you able to cut all the way through?"

"Yeah." Red pointed at the bottom cut. "It dropped, which means it's cut free, but I can't move it."

Derrick wondered how much it weighed because Red could push a lot of weight. When he pushed a sled on the football field, two linemen stood on it. Still, Red made it look easy. Derrick put his shoulder to the block next to Red and nodded.

"On three," Red said.

On the count of three, Derrick pushed. Red's face, inches from his own, glowed red. Derrick felt the block move and put more into it. Suddenly, he realized, when the block fell, the opening might be filled with flying bullets. "Guys! Be ready to return fire!"

The block fell with a loud thud. Derrick pushed Red to the side and lunged for cover.

No bullets. Just a black hole.

Derrick peered around the edge of the opening.

"What do you see?" Red asked.

"Nothing. Completely dark."

"Must be something. Exit signs. Something," Red said.

Derrick donned infrared goggles. He shook his head. "Nothing. No heat signatures."

"Do robots make heat signatures?" Red asked.

Miriam eased to Derrick's side. "What do you see?"

"Absolutely nothing. Complete darkness."

"That can't be right. Are you sure those things work?"

Derrick turned toward her, then jerked the goggles from his face. "Damn. Yeah. They work."

Miriam held her open hand out behind her. "Flashlight."

Rebekah handed her a flashlight. Miriam said, "Both of you get back. This could be a trap."

Derrick eased back, wanting to discuss their next move, but before he could speak, Miriam switched on the light and eased around the corner of the opening. She swung the light from side to side.

"Well? What do you see?" Derrick asked.

"A room full of gold."

Red stuck his head in the hole. "You've got to be kidding." Red whistled and then pulled back. "She's not kidding."

Soon, they were all standing inside. Rebekah found a light switch. The lights came to life one at a time in a random order, sounding a click each time one lit. The entire space in which they stood was filled with gold bars stacked to the ceiling save a narrow walkway that led to a ladder on the wall that led to a second floor that was also filled with gold bars.

"It's a vault," Miriam said.

"Full of gold," Red whispered, adding, "We're rich. We only need a few of these."

"Not why we are here," Miriam snapped.

Red said, "Calm down. Still, one bar each wouldn't slow us down."

Miriam said, "We don't need it. I have money."

"You might but I don't."

"Money is not a problem."

Red said, "Not for you. You are Chosen."

Miriam said, "Not the time, Red. Besides, the Chosen do not have money."

The air was cold, damp, and stale. It gave Derrick the creeps. "What is this place? Where are all the people?"

Miriam said, "It was built for storing gold."

"Is gold worth much?" Derrick asked.

"You're joking, right?" Red asked.

"He isn't," Miriam said. "We had no concept of money in Pacific Edge. Right now, it's unimportant. We need to get out of here. We have made a huge mistake."

14

JACK HAD DRIVEN THROUGH MOUNTAINS and then desert and then a second mountain range, but the second range was unlike the mountains near Potterville, where huge sequoias grew. Now they were in mere hills, by comparison, covered with dry grass and scrubby trees. Donna did not know what the scrubby trees were called. She had never been to this part of California. She had never been far from Potterville. She had traveled with her dad to Bakersfield once. That was as far as she ever got.

Going to San Diego was quite a feat, an adventure, even if it proved to be the last thing she ever did, and she felt certain it would be just that. Thinking they could arrest Prime was laughable. Thinking they could get close enough to kill the monster was insanity.

But they had to try. If they could help the kids, she was all in.

At least she'd get to see the ocean, she hoped.

She had remained quiet after Jack told her about what had happened when they were in school. Jack was never much of a talker, and she didn't expect he'd change after telling that story. He rarely came to the bistro and when he did, he ordered coffee and that was the end of the conversation. He was a hermit of sorts. The only person who spent time with him was his grandson, Red. It was a good thing because Red's stepfather was a drunk, a mean one. The only other person who had a connection with Jack was L. Linda. Donna looked forward to asking L. Linda how she developed that relationship. That conversation would never happen because it was unlikely she'd survive this.

"Have you ever been to San Diego?" Donna asked.

"A few times."

"My first. I never got far from Potterville. I'd like to see the ocean before we try to serve the warrant."

Jack was still leading; Collins trailed behind them. Jack knew back roads that would keep them off the dangerous routes and away from the bottlenecks where gangs sometimes put up roadblocks and demanded payment to pass. The main routes were quicker, but only if there wasn't trouble and there was almost always trouble.

"I'll make that happen."

At the next intersection, Jack turned right.

Deconstruction
A Derrick King Novel, Book 8

"Will this take us to the ocean?" Donna asked.
"Yes. It's a bit out of the way. But I want you to see the ocean."
Donna didn't say: I may not get another chance.
She didn't have to.

15

MAGGIE HAD PROVIDED A BOWL OF PEANUTS, and Stanley's head had cleared just a little. The peanuts were in the shell. Most people were eating them, tossing the shells on the floor.

More people filtered in at the top of the hour. Shift change perhaps. He didn't know the schedule yet. He didn't know a lot of things, but he knew the reprieve from Maggie could not have come at a better time. She was plying him with drinks and extracting far too much information.

He couldn't see her now. Moving his head from side to side to see through a group that had gathered in front of the bar, he tried but failed to find her. Instead, a new guy with a dark beard was taking orders and pouring drinks. Maybe she had gone home. Not even a goodbye—it was nice talking to you, — but that suited him just fine. He was about to leave when movement in his peripheral vision stopped him and caused him to recoil.

"Whoa! I didn't mean to startle you." Maggie set two glasses of amber colored liquid on the table, one with ice, one without. "I took you for a Scotch man. Neat was my guess."

"Sorry…." He held up his hand.

"No worries." She raised her hand and snapped her fingers. "I'll get Pete over here. What would you like?"

Without thinking, he took her arm and gently lowered it. "I was about to leave."

"You have a date?" She smiled.

"No." He felt flustered, and that wasn't good.

"Relax. I don't bite." She sipped her drink. The one with ice. How did she know he liked Scotch, neat? Perhaps she had intel on him. That must be it. From the previous chief of staff. Maggie was a spy. No doubt.

Stanley leaned back. Tried to look at ease. Wasn't sure that he had succeeded. In fact, he felt anything but. More people pressed into the room, but they stayed a few feet away from where he and Maggie sat, as if some invisible barrier held them at bay. But there was no barrier, except that he was the chief of staff.

And perhaps that Maggie was a spy for Prime.

"You have not touched your drink. That's the best Scotch in the house. I understand, it's not what Prime provides for the chief of staff, but it's still pretty damn good. I don't serve it. I only share it with special people and close friends."

Stanley could not argue. The cherry notes carried to his nose as soon as Maggie set it on the table. He lifted the glass, sniffed at the edge, but didn't take a drink. He set the glass back down. "Wonderful aroma."

"You realize that I'm the one who should feel intimidated. Right? You're the chief of staff. I'm just a barmaid who also brews beer." She leaned forward. "Don't tell anyone, but I'm also trying my hand at distilling. I've got a barrel of whiskey in the back. Getting a barrel was no small task, I'll tell you that. It's been aging five years. I take a sip now and then, strictly for quality assurance. Next time you're in, I'll get your opinion."

If there's a next time, Stanley thought. "That is interesting." Stanley sniffed again and then could not resist a taste, although he had no intention of drinking all of it. After a moment, he nodded. "You're right. This is very good."

Sitting back, one arm perched on the back of her chair, a knowing smile on her face, Maggie swirled the ice in her glass. "If I didn't know better, I'd say you don't trust me." She took a sip. Studied him. "Let me guess. You think I'm up to something?" She twirled a lock of hair with her finger.

"No. Nothing like that."

"Bullshit. You think I'm trying to set you up."

16

WHEN MIRIAM SAID THIS WAS A MISTAKE, her words rang true, validating Derrick's apprehension, but still it wasn't quite right. It was a trap, but not just for them. He didn't understand the value of gold. He'd heard of it. In fact, he had insisted on having gold inlays installed on the hardwood counters in his bedroom in Pacific Edge. The further removed he became from Pacific Edge, the more he disliked the old Derrick King. Whether he would ever like himself was unknown. It did not seem he would live long enough to find out.

"Why is having all this gold important?" Derrick asked.

"I'm not sure," Miriam said.

Red said, "I don't understand it, but gold was used to back money in the old United States."

"I don't understand," Derrick said.

"We learned about it in history. Sort of. It wasn't in the history books, but the teacher explained it. It was called the gold standard, which was used to determine the value of the currency. To be honest, I didn't pay close attention," Red said.

"So, why is it here?" Derrick asked.

Miriam said, "Prime probably took it when he declared himself ruler for life."

Red said, "I still find it hard to accept that Prime is more than a myth."

Derrick didn't find it difficult believing Prime was real. Partly because Prime had been trying to kill them, and partly because his own life seemed like a fairy tale. But mostly because they had come face to face with three versions of Prime and destroyed them. Red would learn Prime was no myth soon enough.

"Not that this isn't interesting, but what do we do now?" Anna asked.

"We go find Prime," Miriam said.

Derrick held up his hand, calling for silence. He moved back toward the opening Red had cut in the concrete wall, taking a quick glance out. A bullet followed by a tracer whizzed through the opening, missing him by inches. "Robots! Run!"

"Run where?" Rebekah shouted, already running toward the ladder.

Good point. The room only had a narrow aisle between stacks of gold bars. There was a ladder leading to a second floor. There must be an elevator somewhere to move gold up and down, but they didn't have time to look for that. Derrick pointed. "Up the ladder."

"Then what?" Rebekah shouted.

"We'll figure that out when we get up there," Derrick said, adding, "Red, take the saw."

"Maybe we should fight our way out." Anna said.

"Too many of them," Derrick said, firing blindly from the side of the opening.

"How many?" Anna asked, joining him on the other side and opening fire herself.

Derrick said, "I don't know. Twenty? Thirty?"

Anna said, "Crap. We need to hold them off until the others get up the ladder. Then they can shoot any robots that come through the opening so we can join them."

Derrick nodded and fired. They took turns. Quickly pointing their weapons out and then diving back. He studied his weapon for a moment. They both had weapons that fired the arcs of electrical charges. At least, that's what Derrick believed happened, but he didn't understand how they worked. In the dim light, he could barely read the settings but thought one said stream. He selected it.

His next shot wasn't a bolt but a steady arc that lasted until he released the trigger.

"Wow! What did you do?" Anna asked.

"There's a setting called stream." He pointed the weapon at the edge of the opening, pulled the trigger, and then fanned it across the room as if spraying water.

Anna did the same thing, hosing the area outside the vault from the other direction. The weapons fire from the robots slowed. Anna said, "Let's go!"

Looking up, Derrick yelled, "Cover us!"

Rebekah, Miriam, and Red shot at the opening, hitting robots as they crawled through. The smell of burnt plastic and melting electronics filled the air. Derrick and Anna joined them on the second floor at a railing overlooking the floor below. They were all coughing from the toxic smoke.

Red said, "They aren't very bright. We can shoot them easily before they get inside."

Red stood at the rail, picking robots off as soon as they appeared. "Ouch! Damn it! I've been hit," Red yelled, grabbing his arm.

Derrick pulled him to the floor as rounds riddled the railing where Red had been standing. "Looks like the bullet just grazed you."

"Yeah. Still hurts though." Red scooted away from the ledge.

"They aren't stupid," Miriam said, firing and then moving. "They just don't know fear. They're communicating and giving our positions. We have to move constantly."

Deconstruction
A Derrick King Novel, Book 8

"They will run out of robots eventually," Rebekah said.

Derrick said, "We are going to run out of places to move to."

"We might run out of ammunition first," Miriam said.

"We need to get out of here," Anna said, moving just before bullets hit where she had been standing.

Red said, "It's a vault. Remember? I doubt there's a backdoor."

"Good point," Derrick said. "Red, can you cut a way out?"

"I think so." He looked around. "Up there. I'll climb up on that stack of gold. The robots won't be able to see me at that far wall."

Red started for the stack, then stopped. "I have an idea. Charlie warned me to not get the saw stuck. He said the drive would overheat and explode."

"How powerful would it be?" Miriam asked.

Red shrugged. "I don't know. Charlie just said don't let it happen under any circumstance."

"You're saying get it stuck on purpose?" Derrick asked.

"Yes. I'll cut the escape hole, then jam the saw into a steel beam like this one." He pointed at a thick beam in the floor. "We'll need something to hold the switch open."

Anna pulled a zip tie from her pocket. "Like this?"

"Perfect," Red said, grabbing the zip tie and sticking in his pocket.

"How long do we have before it explodes?" Derrick asked.

Red shrugged. "I don't know. Not long. We'll get everyone out before I jam the blade."

"Before *we* jam the blade," Derrick said.

"It doesn't take two."

Derrick cut him off. "Don't argue. Get us an escape route cut."

The next few minutes were filled with the sound of gunfire, sizzling arcs of electricity, and the howling saw in the background. Miriam called them plasma bursts. Derrick didn't know where she came up with that term, but she knew more about it than he did. She knew more about everything than he did, so plasma it was.

To add to the chaos, they were getting peppered with fragments of bullets and gold as the bullets ricocheted around them.

Spots of crimson appeared on their clothing and trickles of blood streamed down their faces. Robots piled up at the opening, and the bullets slowed as the robots had to drag their fallen comrades away before more could attempt to enter.

Red rejoined them. "The hole is cut. It's smaller, so be careful."

Derrick pointed. "Everyone, get out of here! Red and I will jam the saw."

"I can do this myself. You go," Red said.

"You jam the saw; I'll put on the zip tie. Then we both run," Derrick said. "No time to argue. Now go!"

Deconstruction
A Derrick King Novel, Book 8

Anna said, "Who's going to shoot the robots?"

"Just go. I'll shoot while Red runs the saw."

A few moments later, Derrick felt better about their situation. The others were outside the vault, and he heard no gunfire coming from that direction. The robot invasion had slowed, their progress hampered because the opening was clogged with dead machines. Derrick motioned Red to back out of the line of fire. At least the situation inside the vault was manageable. Everything was going to be okay.

Until the vault door opened and robots poured into the vault.

17

STANLEY HAD NOT YET FINISHED HIS DRINK when the new bartender set another round down on the table. Stanley had vowed to stop several times but could not resist the next sip. The conversation had been sparse since Maggie mentioned the thing about setting him up. He had denied that he was thinking about it. She didn't look convinced.

It had been years since he'd had conversed with anyone other than Prime, which consisted of saying yes sir and no sir. The standard 'how about this weather' didn't apply. Not down here, which reminded him he was buried under tons of dirt with no idea of how deep under the surface they were. Escaping Prime had never been an option. Not a good one. Because Prime had eyes everywhere. The only ones who had any success against Prime were teenagers from Pacific Edge. He hated to admit it, but it was only a matter of time before Prime caught or killed them. Still, they had destroyed Prime's Seattle Headquarters, which was far more triumph than any other person, organization, or country had ever achieved. Maggie believed other Prime Headquarters had been demolished, which pleased and excited him, but thinking kids had destroyed additional headquarters was too far-fetched to be taken seriously.

Stanley would like to feel that he'd played a small part in destroying Seattle, but he could not even direct this conversation without the risk of falling into whatever trap Maggie had laid for him. It made it more difficult because he enjoyed talking to her. She was smart and attractive. But also, cunning. That last part scared him.

Maggie took a drink and then took his hand. "I'm sorry that I've frightened you. I didn't mean to. Well, maybe I did. Just a little. I should have taken more time. Gotten to know you better."

He felt as if she had pushed him to the precipice of a bottomless pit. What did she mean, she should have taken more time? Time to do what? Before he realized what he was saying, he asked just that. "Time to do what?"

Maggie patted his hand, leaned back, smiled, and sipped. "I love this stuff. It's going to be a sad day when the last bottle is consumed."

No reason to argue that point, but he felt each little agreement, and that every syllable she extracted played into some larger scheme. "It is very good."

"You should relax and enjoy it then."

"I *am* relaxed," he said a little too quickly and a bit too loudly.

She just smiled and pushed the recently arrived glass towards him. "Of course you are."

"If I didn't know better, I'd think you were trying to get me drunk."

"Who says I'm not?"

A wave of panic coursed through Stanley's chest. He pushed the glass away. "That doesn't sound like a good idea."

Maggie pushed the glass back. "Why not? We're in deep trouble here, Mr. Mires. If you haven't figured that out yet, you will soon enough."

Without thinking, Stanley picked up the glass and took a drink, his mind spinning. *She couldn't possibly know about Prime's plans. Could she?*

Having realized he'd taken a drink; he set the glass down. "I don't know what you're talking about. I haven't even started work yet. I've only seen Prime a few times." He didn't add how disturbing those few times had been.

"Tell me, how does Prime here compare to the one in Seattle?"

And just like that, Maggie had crossed over into unknown territory. He knew that most people have never seen Prime. Not even those who have worked in a Prime Headquarters for years. Prime had never specifically said that he could not share that information. There was no need. Stanley was sure it would mean death.

"I really can't say much. Prime is different here than there. I think they are all distinctive. Even in Seattle, the current Prime differed from the previous one. It's a continual process of improvement."

Maggie waved her hand. "I don't care what it looks like. Looks are unimportant." She paused. "Does the Prime here have a different temperament? They are supposed to all be the same, right? But I've heard that is not the case."

"I'm sorry, Maggie, but this is not something I can talk about. Besides, I've only just arrived. I have not worked with this Prime yet."

Maggie gave him a pouty expression, as if she was toying with him. She seemed unfazed by the fact that Prime could be watching them, which caused his apprehension to escalate into something akin to panic. He glanced around the room, searching for cameras, but knowing he'd not see them because Prime used advanced surveillance. He'd worried about this the entire time. It was something he thought about constantly. But the drinks and Maggie's charms had distracted him, and she had lured him into dangerous territory.

"If you're looking for cameras, don't worry. We know where they are, and they don't work." She paused. "That's not accurate; they sort of work."

Stanley studied her a moment, certain he looked mildly confused, if not totally incredulous.

"Okay. Enough games," Maggie breathed. "I get it. Way too soon, but there's not enough time, is there? Here's the deal. I know a guy in security. He tweaked our system. I won't go into the details. Details are unimportant. Seattle was attacked. We know that. Prime's communication system has been hacked. We know that too. We assume Prime knows as well, but Prime has not reacted, which seems strange. We know Prime is bringing in his best people, basically abandoning the outlying headquarters."

"How do you know these things?"

She pursed her lips. "You think you're the only person dedicated to helping the Resistance?"

18

ROBOTS POURED THROUGH THE VAULT door. Derrick dropped several of the machines, but too many weapons were firing, which caused him to take cover and return fire blindly. Red joined him, firing and dodging. Soon the saw would become a bomb. That would destroy the robots. It might kill him and Red as well.

However, Derrick would get Red out first. Derrick wanted to get out alive as well. He didn't want to die. Not anytime soon. But this wasn't Red's fight. Red had no business even being here. So, if anyone was going to die, it wouldn't be Red.

Red grabbed Derrick's arm, pointing. "Up there, be quick about it. The opening is smaller. There's a drop on the other side so be careful."

"The drop is the least of our worries." Derrick pointed his weapon over the top of the gold bars and released a stream of electric plasma.

Red said, "We can't jam the saw, zip tie the trigger and shoot at the same time. I'll manage the saw, and you keep shooting."

Derrick said, "We don't know how hard it will be to jam the saw."

"I thought about that and pushed it to the point of stalling while cutting the hole. It won't take long. The trick is to force the issue with it."

"Good to know," Derrick said, adding, "We also don't know how long before the saw explodes, so we need to work together. We just need a place where they can't see us while we do it."

Red said, "There's a place back there between the stacks. The problem is when we head to the hole, they will have a shot at us."

Derrick said, "Then we need to get going. The fewer shooting at us the better."

Crouching low, Red led Derrick down a narrow passage toward the back of the vault. Red paused and pointed. "The hole is over there in the shadows. You can't see it from here, but you can see it when you get closer. So, just run. Don't slow down. You'll see it in time to hit the hole"

Derrick said nothing and fired at the railing, not hitting anything but hoping it might slow the robots, showing them that climbing the ladder would result in getting fried. The only problem with that is the robots didn't fear destruction like people fear death. Death meant nothing to machines.

Deconstruction
A Derrick King Novel, Book 8

Red dug the zip tie from his pocket. "I think the blade will jam in this beam."

Derrick took the zip tie and laced it through the trigger mechanism. "Ready? When I say go, you head out first. I'll be right behind you."

Red nodded. His face was solemn as he lowered the goggles and sank the saw into the concrete and then pulled it into the metal beam. The saw sounded an ear-piercing screech. Then the blade stopped.

The saw vibrated and wailed. Derrick pulled the zip tie tight and shouted, "Run!"

As soon as Red darted away, Derrick sprayed the railing with plasma. A robot exploded in a shower of sparks as Red disappeared into the shadows. The saw grew louder, and Derrick felt heat radiating from it. A weird and unexpected peaceful feeling warmed Derrick's chest. Red was safe, as were the others. If this was his last act, it wasn't terrible. Dying simplified things. Giving up produced a certain appeal. But he wasn't quitting. Not yet. The saw squalled and then the sound changed, growing increasingly louder. His ears hurt. Pointing his weapon toward the railing, he pulled the trigger and ran toward the opening.

Bullets flew around him. A couple nicked him, but he was certain they were just that. Red had said the hole was small, but Derrick envisioned it just a little larger. He would have to slow to crawl through it. But slowing down wasn't an option. Diving through it at full tilt wasn't a great idea either. Missing by just a little would bring him to a sudden stop and likely break his shoulder or neck. Then there was the plunge to the floor to consider.

At full speed, Derrick took aim and leaped for the opening. His aim was true, and he sailed into the darkness. The sound of weapons firing faded behind him. Instead of falling, two powerful hands caught him like he was an acrobat.

Red pushed him against the wall. "Cutting it kinda close, don't you think?"

Before Derrick could answer, the building shook and a loud but muffled explosion sounded. Red pulled Derrick to the floor as a fireball shot through the hole

Heat and smoke filled the air. As ash and debris settled on them, Red smiled. "Charlie wasn't wrong. We just cooked us some robots."

Red stood, offering Derrick a hand. "Don't pull that crap again."

"What?" Derrick asked.

"You know damn well what. I thought you were right behind me. When we do something together, it means we do it together. Understand?"

Derrick started to argue, then thought better of it. "Got it."

Derrick looked around. They were in an ordinary hallway. The overhead lights were off, but various signs over doors and an intersecting hallway cast a dim light. It could have been a regular office building or a school. But it wasn't any of those things.

It was a building full of laboratories.

Derrick said, "At least there are no robots."

"Not yet," Red agreed.

"Where are the others?" Derrick asked.

"Just down the hall, around the first corner. I didn't know how big the explosion would be, so I sent them there."

"Good thinking."

Miriam came around the corner, paused, and then ran to Derrick, throwing her arms around him. She said nothing. No need.

Rebekah joined them. "What's next?"

Miriam said, "We find Prime."

19

THE MOON HAD RISEN, THROWING A HIGHWAY of light across the Pacific. Donna stood near a stubby rock wall at a scenic overlook. She had never smelled the ocean. She wasn't sure what to think about the mixture of salt and seaweed. At first, she found it unpleasant, yet it was also intoxicating in a way she had never experienced.

Jack had turned off the headlights but remained at the car, leaning against the hood. He heard the crunch of tires on gravel. Bill and Allen. Car doors opened, then closed.

"Everything okay?" Bill asked.

"Donna had never seen the ocean and wanted to before… Well, you know," Jack said.

Collins walked to Donna's side. "You can't see much. I'll bring you back when this is over. Lori can come. We'll make a day of it. Maybe two."

"I can smell it and hear the waves. We're here now. No promise of a tomorrow."

"Donna, you're going to be okay. I'm not letting you close to Prime. You'll be on a roof with the rifle. I doubt you'll even fire it. I suspect Prime doesn't venture outside or stand near windows."

Donna turned. "Bill, I appreciate your optimism, but it's not just about today, is it? Even if we succeed here, if one Prime survives elsewhere, Potterville will be destroyed, and don't tell me that isn't how it's going to happen."

Bill stood silently for a moment and then said over his shoulder, "Jack, how much farther?"

"Not far. Fifteen, maybe twenty minutes. I'll let you lead. How much help can we expect?"

"None. I radioed ahead. The sheriff called me."

Donna stared at him. "And?"

"He said, 'knock yourself out, but don't expect any help from us.'"

Jack said, "Seriously? That's what he said?"

"Yep. He added, off the record, I hope you kill the bastard."

Donna started for Jack's car. "Let's go do that then."

20

ACIDIC SMOKE BEING DRAWN TO VENTILATION vents slithered near the ceiling. Derrick's eyes watered and his throat burned, but he fought back the urge to cough. The halls were empty, and he hoped they stayed that way. Yet he knew that wishful thinking was useless. Wishful thinking never changed anything. In more honest terms, he wanted a break, even if it was only a few minutes. The barrage of robots had been intense.

All of them were bleeding somewhere. Miriam's uninjured side now had a big blotch of red. Anna had blood on her thigh and shoulder. Red had blood trickling down his neck and a big red spot on his back. Rebekah seemed uninjured but was limping. As for himself, Derrick knew he'd been nicked in the arm, leg, and butt.

He wasn't going to ask anyone to look at his butt.

Derrick whispered, "Is everyone okay?"

Miriam spun around, holding her finger to her lips.

Derrick knew better. Mistakes could prove deadly.

They walked silently for 20 yards when Miriam stopped, holding up her hand. She tried a door. "Damn," she whispered.

Derrick looked at a brass plate on the door. It read: "Security."

"See if you can force it open," Miriam whispered.

Derrick studied the door. The hinges were on the inside, so the cutting tool was of no use. He pushed against the door with his shoulder. "Not budging. Why do you want in there?"

Miriam looked both ways down the hall and then looked at Red. "Want to give it a try?"

"It would be my pleasure. Step aside, little man. Let me show you how it's done."

With that, Red kicked hard, right beside the doorknob. Wood splintered, and the door flew open, banging against the wall.

With no inflection in her voice, Miriam said, "So much for stealth."

Red shrugged.

Miriam stepped inside, and the others followed. She flipped on the light, studied everyone, and then said, "Rebekah, watch the hall."

"What are we doing?" Derrick asked.

Miriam did not respond as she searched the office, opening drawers and cabinets.

Miriam found a white box with a big red cross. "First aid. If you haven't noticed, everyone is bleeding someplace. I hope this thing has what we need."

Miriam started pulling stuff from the box. Finally, she said, "Boys on one side, girls on the other. No time for modesty. Look each other over and do the best you can." She pointed at the pile. "Bandages, new skin, antiseptic, and analgesic spray. Everyone take a couple of aspirins as well."

Red and Derrick had metal, glass, and gold fragments, and removing them was the most painful part. Red gathered the gold fragments and put them in his pocket. Neither had anything major. It could have been a bullet just as easily as a piece of glass, and a Band-Aid wouldn't fix a bullet wound. They had been lucky. Except for L. Linda Maxton. Her luck ran out far too soon. How long before another's luck ran out?

After they finished patching each other up, they continued searching the hallway. After finding no one, they proceeded up to the next floor. All the rooms were dark, except for one at the far end, where light spilled from a doorway. Derrick tapped Miriam on the shoulder and pointed. She nodded and motioned to the others.

As they inched down the hallway, distancing themselves from the vault, the smoke had cleared, but the stench lingered. Derrick scanned the walls with his flashlight, the beam focused, creating a tight beam of light onto a sign with a single word that caused him to pause: TEST.

He froze and read the sign one word at a time. TEST SUBJECT DNA SEQUENCING. The group had moved on several yards when Miriam noticed he was still standing there transfixed, staring up at the sign. She joined him and then motioned for Anna.

Anna whispered, "So, this is where we started?"

Miriam said, "I don't know. Probably."

"Do we want to find out?" Derrick asked.

Miriam said, "Maybe. I'm not sure. Does it matter?"

Anna said, "Destroying Prime is what matters."

"Agreed," Miriam said, turning to rejoin the others.

Derrick stared at the sign for a moment longer and then moved on. He didn't understand what DNA sequencing meant. DNA sounded like a scientific thing, which wasn't taught at James Carver Academy. That seemed like such a long time ago. Another lifetime, which wasn't far from the truth.

Did he want to know if this was where his life began? He wasn't sure.

When they reached the laboratory, where light spilled into the hall, Derrick took the lead. Not that he wasn't scared. He just didn't want to see any of the others get shot.

Deconstruction
A Derrick King Novel, Book 8

He knelt and slowly peered into the room. One person was doing something at a counter. It appeared to be a woman in a white lab coat with her back turned. He saw no weapons.

He held his finger to his lips and motioned the others to stay. Then he eased into the room, leading with his plasma weapon, which he had set to stun. Drawing within five feet, she still had not noticed him. She was washing glass containers. He thought they were called beakers.

He cleared his throat and said, "I don't want to hurt you."

The woman turned, screamed, and dropped the beaker, which shattered on the floor. "Oh, my God. You scared me." She stared at the weapon, then looked up at his face. Her eyes grew wide. "What is this? I would have gone with the others. I didn't cause any problems."

She raised her hands.

"I don't want to hurt you." He glanced around the room. "Where is everyone?"

"Gone." She paused. "I heard an explosion. I should have left."

Derrick raised his voice. "It's alright. You can come in now."

It didn't seem possible, but the woman's eyes grew wider as the others filed in. "Who are you and what to you want? I'll go willingly. In fact, I wanted to go. I won't cause any problems."

Miriam said, "Who we are is unimportant. We want answers and if you're truthful, then you won't get hurt."

What little color remained drained from the woman's face. "Don't kill me. Please!"

"Good start," Miriam said, adding, "where is everyone?"

"Gone. You know."

"I do not know. You tell me. Gone where?"

Before she could answer, Derrick added, "Why are you still here?"

The woman started sobbing.

Rebekah said, "Lower your weapons. Can't you see she's scared to death?" Walking over to the woman, Rebekah took her hands, gently lowering them. "Calm down. We won't hurt you unless you try something. Okay? Take a breath." Rebekah spotted a box of tissues nearby. She grabbed a handful, handed them to the woman, and said, "My name is Rebekah. What's your name?"

"Carly."

"That's a pretty name," Rebekah said. "Now. Let's start over, Carly. Why are you here alone? Is everyone gone because it's nighttime?"

"No. Usually the labs are still working at this time of day."

"Okay. You said they are gone. What do you mean? Were they here today?"

Carly blew her nose. "Yes. It was a regular day until they came."

"Who came?"

"Soldiers. Well, I'm not sure they were soldiers. But they all wore black uniforms and carried guns."

Rebekah glanced over her shoulder at the others, frowning a little. Turning back to Carly, she said, "Tell me what happened. Try to remember what was said. Details are important."

Carly pursed her lips and nodded. "They didn't say much. Just that the lab was being relocated. People started asking questions and protesting."

"What happened next?" Rebekah asked.

"One soldier hit a man in the head with the butt of his rifle. They checked his name tag against a list and then dragged him out of the room." She blew her nose again. "After that, people did what they were told."

"And?"

"The guy giving orders said, 'I'm going to call out names. If your name is on the list, step to the door. When we have everyone, we will escort you to the transports.'"

"Anything else?"

"Yes. One woman, her name is Paula, raised her hand and asked, 'transports?' The man said, busses that will take you to the airport."

"Is that it?"

"Almost. One of the lab techs, I don't know his name, said they had valuable work here and asked if they could take files, hard drives, etc."

"And what did the man say?"

"He said, 'unnecessary.' That everything was on the computers where they were going."

Miriam said, "Did he say where they were going?"

"Not exactly. He just said they had been promoted and were going to central."

Miriam stepped beside Rebekah, gave her a slight smile, and said, "Good job," then turned to Carly. "Why are you still here?"

"I didn't get the promotion, I guess. I've only been here a few days."

"Where did you come from?" Miriam asked.

"New York."

"Prime's Headquarters there?"

Carly's eyes widened again. Not in fear this time, but surprise.

"It's okay. We know about New York. Plus, why would you be here if you didn't already work for Prime?"

"How do you know about Prime?"

"Not important. What do you do here?"

"Uh, I'm not sure what you mean. It's a laboratory. We do, or did, many things here."

Miriam gave Rebekah a brief hug, and said, "You did great. You and Red step outside and watch the hallway. Derrick, Anna, and me need to talk to Carly for a minute."

Rebekah looked uneasy. "What's going on?"

"Like I said. We need to talk with Carly."

Miriam paused. "Alone."

Deconstruction
A Derrick King Novel, Book 8

21

STANLEY SAT ALONE WONDERING IF HE could make it to the door before Maggie returned. A few minutes ago, Maggie's replacement had come to the table and said #1 had blown. Stanley didn't know what that meant, and Maggie had not explained, but apparently it had to be fixed, and the guy didn't know how to do it. The guy might be a nuclear engineer doing his extra duty here, but here he didn't know how to do anything except pour beer. At least it gave Stanley a few minutes to think, although his mind was not getting any traction on what Maggie had said about the Resistance.

So, mostly he thought about running.

However, a large man had positioned himself by the door at Maggie's request. Stanley didn't know if that was about him and didn't want to test it. Setting up a showdown with the chief of staff and members of the Resistance within the first few hours of his arrival did not seem wise.

Maggie returned with two fresh drinks. "You're falling behind."

With his head already spinning, Stanley said, "I really should be going."

"We have things to talk about. I know, I know. Too fast. It should not have happened this way, but there's no time for the standard routine of getting to know each other and building trust."

Stanley stared at her but said nothing.

Maggie sat back. "How can I make this easier, Mr. Mires? How about I tell you about me, then you can tell me more about you? I'm with the Resistance. No surprise, but there, I've said it. There are three of us here. Four, counting you. I learned about you when I was in Dallas. Then I got transferred. The others were already here. They knew about me. I didn't know about them. But we all knew about you. You're a legend. Did you know that? You are the closest anyone in the Resistance has ever gotten to Prime—personal assistant. The Seattle Prime called you Quigley. And now you're here—Chief of Staff. And we've got problems."

Stanley didn't know his next move. The idea that there were other Resistance members here had never occurred to him. He thought he was the only person to ever infiltrate a Prime Headquarters. It could still be a setup or test; Prime knew his nickname in Seattle was Quigley. No mystery there.

Deconstruction
A Derrick King Novel, Book 8

He sipped his drink. Thinking hard. Perhaps Prime has suspicions about him. He doesn't know these people. Perhaps Maggie is security just posing as a bar manager, or whatever you call what she's pretending at. "That might be the wildest story I've ever heard."

Maggie shook her head. "I told Hank this wouldn't be easy."

"Who's Hank? And what wouldn't be easy? That I would not fall for this ruse you've concocted?"

Maggy rolled her eyes. "Your next move should be to have me arrested then. If this is fake, Prime will let me go and you'll be in the clear. If not, Prime will kill me and make you watch."

"Exactly what I was thinking." He wasn't thinking that, of course, but it sounded like the right thing to say.

Maggie drummed her fingers on the table. "I'm waiting for you to call security." She paused, then leaned forward. "However, here's the thing. This is not a setup and if you have me arrested, Prime will torture and kill me. I swore I'd never give up the others, but I don't know how much pain I can take. I understand Prime is very good at torture."

"Torture?" He knew that Prime loved torturing people. Deconstruction was a testament to that, but he wasn't going along with this narrative, so he tried to act surprised and felt he'd failed miserably.

"Look, I'm risking my life here. I know who you are. I've seen your picture to make sure Prime couldn't slip in a ringer." She reached into her pocket, pulled out a small, folded piece of paper. "Open it."

Stanley glanced around. No one was watching, but he held the paper below the table as he unfolded it. It was a picture of him, handing off information to his contact. He was standing in a tunnel. The hand-off was to an outstretched arm of a man in a moving vehicle. The photo had to have been taken from another vehicle in the tunnel. Probably a truck, based on the angle. The Resistance had been thorough.

"Where did you get this?"

"From a guy who came here a couple of years ago. It was important that I know about you in case you ever made it this far. And here you are." Maggie paused. "We have protocol for making contact and this is not it. Typically, we take several weeks, if not months. It's a gradual process of building trust with one or more members of our little group. As you can imagine, caution is vital."

Stanley remained skeptical. But that photograph. He could not explain it. If Prime had that picture, he would be dead already. And it would not have been a painless death. Prime would have tortured him. Prime would extract every bit of information Stanley knew about the Resistance and then dialed up the pain just for fun. Stanley had a plan to avoid the torture part. He would try to kill Prime if he were ever found out. Stanley would attack Prime with whatever was close at hand. Prime would kill him, but it would be quick. Stanley preferred quick to torture.

A bonus was the thought he might get lucky and kill Prime. It would be a short-lived victory but still beat torture. He even entertained thoughts of killing the replicants and destroying the entire headquarters.

That was in Seattle. He could walk out of the building in Seattle. Not here. This place was different. There was no walking out of here and even if he did, surviving the desert was unlikely. This place was a dead end.

In more ways than one.

22

AFTER REBEKAH AND RED EXITED the laboratory, Miriam locked the door, which surprised Derrick a little. The stench of molten robots had made it this far and drifted into the room. Miriam removed her sidearm and deliberately slid the power controller, which caused a power indicator to change from yellow to orange.

Carly's eyes opened wide. "What's happening. I answered your questions!"

Before Derrick could say anything to put the frightened technician at ease, Miriam said, "We'll see how the next few minutes go. I don't have much time, so wasting it would not be a good idea."

"Who are you and what is that awful smell? Like melted plastic. Is that from the explosion?" Carly asked.

Miriam slammed her hand on the counter. "I'm asking the questions. You're giving the answers. This is set on high stun, which means it hurts a lot. First wrong answer gets you shot. Then I turn it up to kill. Your second lie ends our conversation. Permanently. Understand?"

The remaining color drained from the woman's face. She nodded. "I understand."

"One more time. What do you do here? Specifically. It says DNA Sequencing and Test Subject Program on the sign."

Carly said, "We have a DNA Sequencing machine here that allows us to analyze, study, and reconstruct DNA. You see, we are all made up of DN…"

Miriam pointed the firearm at Carly. "You're wasting my time. Did I mention we don't have much of it? I know what DNA is." Miriam took a deep breath. "What specifically does this place do regarding test subjects?"

Carly's eyes flicked from side to side. Derrick assumed she was looking at each of them, but it could just have been nerves. Or fear. Most likely fear.

Fear was the appropriate response. Derrick's anger grew by the second, realizing this person might have been involved in their creation. Test subjects. Objects. Not people. And for what purpose?

Carly said, "I don't know. I'm new, but that's not the only reason."

Anna took a step toward Carly. "Explain. Make it short and quick."

"They didn't tell me much, but I had the feeling the others didn't know much either. About the scope of this program. Everyone is compartmentalized."

"What does that mean?" Derrick asked, with more anger in his voice than he anticipated.

"I work on one specific process. I wasn't told why or how it fits into the bigger picture."

"Do you know what test subjects are?"

"No. They didn't tell me."

Miriam looked at Derrick. Shook her head. "To answer one question, the smell is dozens of destroyed robots. Tell me, what is your specific job?"

"Sequencing DNA to find ways that would increase life expectancy."

"Longer life?"

"Yes."

"Of what?"

"I don't know. Any living thing. But, people, I guess. At least, it appeared to be human DNA, but it's hard to know for sure. DNA is very similar, and I only had a small string to work with."

Miriam said, "One more question. Is working for Prime a good thing?"

"I'm not sure I understand the question."

"Is Prime good or bad?"

Carly said nothing for a moment. She looked around the ceiling.

Miriam said, "If you're worried about Prime, don't be. After tomorrow Prime will no longer exist."

Carly's eyes opened wide. Her mouth fell open.

"Just answer the question. Tick Tock," Anna said.

"I, I, don't think Prime is good."

"You think Prime is bad?" Miriam asked.

"Uh, yes. I guess so."

"Then why are you here?" Anna asked.

"They transferred me here from New York."

"I'll rephrase the question. Why do you work for Prime? You admit Prime is bad. I call it evil, but bad is close enough," Miriam said.

Carly spread her arms. "DNA sequencing. Do you know how rare this lab is in New America?"

"I don't. Enlighten us."

"This is it. This is the only one like it. That's why I'm here. My only chance to work with this level of technology."

"But you don't know what you're working on? You don't know the project?"

"That's correct."

Deconstruction

A Derrick King Novel, Book 8

Miriam sighed. Derrick felt his shoulders sink just a little. He felt sure Miriam and Anna were hopeful they'd find answers here. They had not.

"You said that they did not take the hard drives," Miriam said.

"From the computers?"

"Duh. You have hard drives that aren't in computers?"

Carly looked at the floor. "Sorry. No. They didn't take anything. Just the people."

Miriam studied her for a moment. "The research here must be important. Why leave it? That makes no sense."

"Our supervisor wanted to take the server but was told to leave it. The man said all the data was transferred to Central."

"So, that confirms where they were going." Miriam thought for a moment. And then, talking to herself more than to anyone in the room, she added, "Why would Prime take them to Central?"

A thought crossed Derrick's mind. "Did anyone give any indication of Central's location?"

Carly shook her head. "No. Nothing. Well, except that they had to take an airplane to get there."

"Is everything stored on one server?" Miriam asked.

"For this program, yes; from what I understand. We all have computers, but they don't have hard drives. Instead, they are all connected to a network and the network is connected to the server."

"So, all the data is on one hard drive?" Miriam whispered. "And they didn't take it?"

"That's right. They sent all the data to Central. They must have done that remotely. They probably wiped the hard drive here. I mean. That's what I would do," Carly said.

Anna said, "You seem to know a lot about computers."

Carly shrugged. "Minor in computer security systems in college."

Miriam holstered her weapon. "Show me the server."

Carly walked to a computer mounted in a rack near a wall. "Here. But, like I said, it's probably been wiped."

"I don't think so. Lines to Central are down. They are in for a surprise. I need a screwdriver to take the cover off." Miriam shut the machine off and then unplugged it.

"You're not supposed to shut it off like that."

"Screwdriver." Miriam held out her hand.

Less than a minute later, Miriam slid the side of the computer off and pulled out a metal box, which she shoved into a pocket of her uniform.

"Are you going to kill me?"

"Nah, I believe you told us what you know." Miriam paused. "And you didn't know enough about the project to warrant killing you."

"What should I do?" Carly asked.

Miriam said, "Do whatever you want, but I'd suggest you get out of here."

"But where should I go? Back to New York?"

"Not there," Derrick said.

"Why not?"

Miriam said, "There's nothing there you'd want to see and a lot of stuff you don't want to see. Where are you from?"

"Ohio."

"Go there."

"And do what?"

"Wait," Miriam said.

"Wait for what?"

"Further instructions."

Carly looked confused. "Okay."

"You'll understand more in a couple of days," Miriam said, adding, "One more question. Where's Prime?"

"I don't know," Carly said.

Derrick noticed her eyes drifted to one side. Just for a second. Anna must have noticed too, because she walked to the window.

Anna pointed out the window. "Hey guys. I think Prime is in that building."

"Why?" Derrick asked, walking toward her.

"Because there's a small army of robots gathered out front."

23

TYPICALLY, STANLEY SIPPED WHISKEY, especially when it was good, and this was quite good, in fact, exceptional. However, this glass he poured down in one gulp. He'd made a decision. One that might get him killed sooner rather than later.

"Can I have another?" Stanley held up his glass, noticing the finely cut design in the lower third, which reflected the light, creating multiple refractions. It caught him off guard because he rarely paid attention to such things. Perhaps his mind was looking for beauty because the institutional ugly here was hard to ignore despite the efforts to make the place look normal.

Maggie smiled as she stood. "Of course."

"Make it a double."

"I'll bring the bottle."

Seconds later, Maggie returned with two fresh glasses and a bottle half full. She poured an inch for each of them. Holding up her drink, she said, "Toast to new friends with common enemies."

Stanley clicked her glass with his. "Cheers." After taking a drink, Stanley asked the first in a series of questions he had been formulating. He did not know how long this would work, but if he could ask questions and avoid giving answers, he could build a defense that he was merely conducting an interrogation to learn more about the Resistance members who had infiltrated Prime's Headquarters. "Do you think there are other Resistance members in Prime's organization?"

"You have not yet acknowledged being in the Resistance yourself. You could be an imposter. Perhaps a Prime security man who had his face digitally reconfigured to resemble Stanley Mires. That technology is available within Prime's Chosen Communities, right? Maybe the real Stanley Mires is dead."

His plan wasn't off to a good start. Since he did not have a Plan B, he persisted. "Where are the Resistance people stationed here?"

"All in due time."

Maggie was sharp. No questioning that. An intelligent woman and whiskey. A dangerous combination. His hope to avoid questions was fading, but he couldn't give up without at least one more attempt. "The Resistance people here, what skills do they have?"

Deconstruction
A Derrick King Novel, Book 8

Maggie sniffed at the edge of her glass. "I love the aroma. Don't you? I get cherries, oak, and a hint of peat. I like the smokey peat flavor of Islay Scotch. Many don't care for it. How about you?"

Instead of answering his question, she had asked one of her own, but this one was benign enough. Perhaps small talk was required before she would open up a little. "Islay is okay, but Highland is my preference."

"That is the correct answer. Of course, Prime knows that, and an agent would be fully briefed."

Moments ago, Maggie had been certain that he was Stanley Mires and a member of the Resistance. What had changed? Did he say something that cast doubt? Was she trying to back him into a corner? Force him to admit he was in the Resistance? "Good point." He'd try one more time. "Do you see a pattern regarding the new people coming here?"

Maggie sat her drink down. "A group came from New York where they build aircraft and a few from Dallas, where they design and build robots. We have many cutting-edge robots here but there is a push to create a more advanced model. Dallas is also where the Test Subject Program is centered. As you know, the Test Subject Program is one of Prime's most important projects." She sipped. "I'm sure you are aware of the reasons that it is important."

Stanley nodded. More to indicate that he was engaged than to answer. "Anything else?"

Maggie said, "That's all that comes to mind."

Stanley shrugged. "That doesn't tell us a lot. Does it?"

"We think otherwise. We think it tells us a great deal."

"How so?" Perhaps he was getting somewhere.

"Think about it. What is Denver's role?"

It was Stanley's turn to sip, which turn out to be two, and then three. He needed a moment to think. Could he defend answering this question if this was a test? Maybe. Maybe not. "Denver's mission always seemed a little vague to me. I've never been there, but I understand it is similar to New York. Except instead of aircraft, they are trying to make more human-like androids. The goal is to make robots that can pass as humans to infiltrate the population. However, thus far, the androids have been glitchy."

"That's our understanding as well." Maggie said, adding, "How about San Diego?"

Before he gave it much thought, Stanley said, "San Diego oversees taxation and acquisitions, which means they manage the Chosen Communities that collect money across the country." Had he said more than intended?

"Right. The blood suckers."

Stanley said nothing, taking another drink instead, only to find that his glass was empty.

Maggie poured more into his glass. "None from San Diego. Why?"

Stanley shrugged. "I don't know. Maybe they just haven't arrived yet."

"Why bring any of them?" Maggie asked.

"Well, Seattle was destroyed, so that's obvious why only a few came. However, Seattle also might explain why Prime is bringing people here. Prime is probably concerned there will be more attacks. Until those responsible are found, bringing everyone here makes sense."

Maggie leaned forward. "You said those responsible."

"I don't understand your point."

"You didn't say until the Resistance is destroyed. You know that specific people attacked Seattle. Not an organization."

"I didn't say that."

Maggie sat back, swirled her ice. "It was implied."

"Well, I meant until Prime stops whoever it is."

"We may know more in short order. The word from reception and orientation is that a plane carrying people from Dallas will land soon and one small group is coming from Denver and that will be the last."

"Do you know how many?"

"Does that make a difference?"

"Maybe. Is it three or fifteen?"

"I don't know." She paused. "More from Dallas than Denver. That's all I know. The only information we get is from reception and what we can glean from new arrivals. We are just speculating on the thin information we have. Talking about it is dangerous. You understand how big of a risk I'm taking talking to you. It could get me killed in the most unpleasant manner imaginable. Unpleasant like Deconstruction."

He knew what deconstruction was; however, he wasn't sure if admitting it was a good idea. More importantly, he wondered how Maggie knew about it. "Whatever that is, it sounds bad."

"You know what it is, and you know it's worse than bad." Maggie paused, took a drink. "Who destroyed Seattle? Was it Derrick King?"

The question startled him. He didn't anticipate Maggie knowing anything about Derrick King. How could she? "I already told you. I don't know. I wasn't there. When it happened, I was either being flown here with a hood over my head or deep inside this place in a small room with no monitor or other communication."

Maggie studied him for a moment. "I believe some of that but not all. But it's okay. Let's focus on who is here and what that might mean. We are only getting a few more and that's the end of it. So, let's go over it one more time. Five people came from Seattle, which, as you know, are computer hackers who manipulate world commerce. A second flight was scheduled but didn't arrive, and now we know why." Maggie mouthed boom and indicated an explosion with her hands. "Several aircraft designers and technicians came from New

York two weeks ago; however, a flight scheduled to arrive just hours ago with the last people from New York and Chicago is a no show. Dallas sent two groups that arrived this afternoon—half specialize in robotics and the other half in test subject design and creation. A small group who focusses on human-like androids are en route from Denver. No one is coming from San Diego, which oversees Chosen Communities. What do you think that means?"

Stanley then took a drink. To be honest, he felt lost. The reason Prime was bringing people here had not been his primary concern. Staying alive had preoccupied his thinking. That and trying to navigate the labyrinth of Maggie's interrogation. "I don't know."

"Doesn't it seem odd to you?" Maggie asked.

"I guess. It's news to me. You know? I haven't digested it yet. What do you think it means?"

"Not just me. Our team. We've been analyzing it. Something has changed, and I don't just mean the attack on Seattle. There's a shift. The most recent arrivals say the military has pulled back from the border with Mexico."

Stanley said, "That's a good thing, right?"

"Yes, and no."

Stanley put his palm on the table. "I'm sorry. I'm confused."

Maggie leaned forward and tapped the side of her head. "Think, Stanley. What would you say is the most important thing to Prime? I mean, besides himself."

Stanley swallowed. This question was a landmine. He knew it, but he could not think of a way to avoid answering. "Uh, money? Power?"

"That's right. And control. Right?" She paused. "But more than anything else: adoration—worship."

Stanley nodded. He looked into Maggie's eyes. "What do you think Prime is doing?"

Maggie whispered, "I don't know, but something bad is about to happen."

24

IN THE DEPTHS OF THE CENTRAL FACILITY, Prime watched monitors that covered one entire wall, each showing several different scenes. The people he watched thought their acts were covert. They were not. It was times like these, when Prime was alone contemplating his accomplishments, and the price he had paid for those accomplishments, that he sometimes wondered if it had been worth it.

Some people believe Prime is or was James Carver. Prime would admit that at one time, that was true. But not anymore. Prime had evolved into more than James Carver had ever dreamed. No. Prime was not James Carver. Prime was Prime. James Carver was just a body in a tube, barely alive, if one could call it life, in a room with Prime's other specimens. They were also alive, in a way; at least, he thought they might still be. They had not communicated with Prime for many years, but the machines that supplied them with nutrients and managed their submerged environments indicated life was present.

Prime would force them to communicate should he ever need them. Perhaps someday he would, but not now. Maybe never. He might just kill them. Perhaps it was time.

James Carver had the right idea, but he was weak. He murdered thousands, overthrew the United States, created a new country, took over all commerce, and owned all the property, set up a puppet government, all quite impressive, but Carver lacked Prime's vision. So Prime put Carver in a tube.

Carver did not go quietly. Prime didn't hold that against Carver. After all, they were inseparable in the beginning. Two bodies: Carver in his human form, modified, medically enhanced, full of new parts, compounds, regrown organs, and such. Carver lived decades beyond normal humans. His goal had been immortality. However, that technology wasn't going to happen soon enough to ensure that Carver would live forever.

So, Carver developed Prime, only it wasn't called that. Carver called it The Test Subject Program. The goal was to create a new body, so Carver could start fresh. In addition to creating a superior body, Carver had to devise a way to upload himself to an artificial environment, wipe all the thoughts, feelings, and consciousness from the new body, and download Carver's consciousness into the new host.

Deconstruction
A Derrick King Novel, Book 8

That's where things got tricky.

More than tricky. It proved impossible, and Carver was running out of time. It became increasingly clear that Carver could die.

He came close several times. Near the end, Carver was virtually living in an emergency room. The finest surgeons for brain, heart, lung, kidney, liver, etc. on staff 24/7—all just to keep Carver alive.

The Test Subject Program had to make an abrupt change. They had to create a different kind of body—one that didn't start as a human—one that didn't have a soul. The early models were not functional. They were little more than an ancient iron lung. A horrible way to live. Eventually, Carver was able to transfer into a viable prototype. But it had many problems. Daily uploads and downloads were necessary to keep Carver, and his semi-mechanical twin linked.

About every fourth or fifth download failed, had Carver not still been alive, he would have ceased to exist.

However, Carver intended to become immortal. Prime was grateful for that. Otherwise, Prime would not exist. This was difficult for Prime to think about. Not existing. Because he always had. At least, that is what he had come to believe. However, it took Carver to pull him from the ether and form him into a being. Carver thought Prime was merely a vessel. Carver was wrong.

It was true they existed together at first. Together for decades, in fact. And James Carver, in his human form, was still alive as well. Doctors had kept him alive much longer than anticipated. At first, Carver didn't even know Prime existed. Prime thought it better that way, so Prime lurked in the darkest of James Carver's thoughts. Occasionally, Prime would whisper a suggestion. Carver would think it was his own idea and act on it.

The suggestions grew darker over time. Those around Carver thought he was going insane, but he was not. Carver was becoming more aligned with Prime. Eventually, Carver couldn't distinguish between himself and Prime. The lines were blurred, and it was as if they had almost become one.

But almost was not good enough for Prime. Prime had his own destiny, and James Carver wasn't part of it. Carver had to go. But how to do it? Carver was inside Prime's head.

But that fight was still years away.

Carver had people around him. Loyal employees. Who both craved the benefits of their employment and feared Carver. Prime would give Carver that. While he lacked Prime's cold surgical approach, he was still ruthless in protecting himself. After all, Carver was narcissistic and completely self-serving. Prime admired him for that as well.

Prime needed his own army. One that only served him. One completely loyal with only the ability to carry out orders. Like a computer. So, Prime whispered to Carver again. *People cannot be trusted. We need something more. We need robots. Soulless machines.*

Deconstruction
A Derrick King Novel, Book 8

And so, they created robots. The early ones were almost worthless, but they improved over time. The QR-3 models Prime still used today marked the beginning of the end for James Carver.

The research and the construction of the first robots happened at a top-secret military base, which was not far from here. Carver came here, of course, which meant that Prime knew about this place, but the Carver/Prime hybrid never came here. That didn't happen until after Carver overthrew the government. That's why Prime did not incorporate AT into the QR-3s. Prime did not need AT robots then; did not need them now. Prime would need them in the future. But there was plenty of time for that.

What Carver didn't know was that Prime could communicate directly with the robots. Prime had evolved into a separate entity. Carver suspected there was something there. His strongest theory was he was developing a split personality. He asked his most trusted doctor to watch for signs of mental illness. Treat it if necessary. The doctor gave him psychotropic drugs for a while.

Carver felt better.

Prime did not.

Prime felt as if his brain was cotton, unable to think clearly. Carver was trying to kill Prime.

Those were dark days. Prime was barely conscious. Merely fading in and out of existence. Prime feared Carver would win, given more time.

So, Prime devised a plan. With a great deal of effort, Prime instructed a robot to dump Carver's medication and replace it with something harmless. The robot found an antibiotic that resembled the mind killing drugs. Within a couple of days, Prime was thinking clearly again. The medication made Carver sick to his stomach, which didn't bother Prime. Had Prime known how long it would be until he consumed real food again, he might have been more troubled by Carver's sickness. But at the time, Prime didn't know eating would prove so difficult. Had he known, he might have continued sharing his mind with Carver's body. The downloading of Carver's mind had been reduced to once a month for a variety of reasons: it had become more efficient, and it had become more dangerous. Finally, after the last download, Prime instructed a robot to drug the doctor. Then Prime destroyed Carver's digital footprint and put him in a tube. This came as quite a shock to Carver. Prime enjoyed it immensely.

But the Prime model of the time could not eat normal food. Prime believed it was a minor adjustment that would be worked out in short order. A lot of scientists had died failing to correct that problem. Prime had to stop, well, slow down, killing them because he was running out of qualified people to work in the program. That was one reason he set up several headquarters. So that he, the real Prime, lived separately from the satellites. Then each satellite could focus on a specific task. And it gave more places to test more hosts for Prime, and it ensured there were multiple digital copies of Prime to ensure his survival. Like all things Prime, —it was perfect.

There had never been a single problem until those kids. Not just any kids, test subjects! His property! Turned against him. Prime had known an attack from within was a possibility and had taken steps to ensure it didn't happen, or to be more accurate, make certain it could not succeed. At first, this seemed like the first imperfection in his otherwise flawless system. The destruction of his Seattle Headquarters was his first defeat. But it wasn't the beginning of the end. It was just a new beginning and nothing like what Derrick King envisioned.

Watching monitors without sound, Prime reflected on all of this. Including how it had thrown him into a rage. That was unfortunate. He prided himself on how well he managed his emotions. Sometimes rage was the appropriate response. It was in this case. But rage can prevent insight. In this case, it did. At first.

Then he saw it. Derrick King and his little band of children had not won anything. But they had opened his eyes to the current situation. He had delayed his plans for too long. Time waits for no one, not even Prime. It was time to move on. Time to evolve.

It wasn't that he had been idle. Far from it. But his plan to attack Mexico was not ambitious enough. Even when the plan included taking over Central America, South America, and Canada.

That wasn't enough.

That did not fulfill his destiny.

Strange as it seemed, an insignificant detail had thrown him off. His title. He had called himself Prime early on. Prime seemed right at the time. Was right at the time. Prime did not make mistakes. Prime: principal, foremost, first, most important, paramount, major, dominant, supreme, overriding, cardinal, preeminent, ultimate. He was all those things. But he was more than that now.

So much more.

And so, he'd been contemplating what title was worthy. What the masses would call him in the new world. King, Emperor, Tsar? None of those seemed right. Perhaps he would need to invent a word. Yes, that might be the answer.

Derrick King was not a leader. Prime had heard the speculations. That Derrick King had come to fulfill the prophecy: *When all things have failed, one will come to set things right.*

Prime knew the prophecy. James Carver wrote it in the Doctrine of the Chosen. The new religion for the Chosen Communities. Carver reasoned that the easiest way to keep people in line was through religion and fear. He was not wrong. Prime liked the prophecy because it was something he'd whispered inside Carver's head.

The prophecy wasn't about Derrick King. It was about Prime himself. It was that revelation that altered Prime's thinking. He was, in fact, The One, which might be a decent title, but Prime had plenty of time to settle upon his new name.

Because Derrick King had inspired him to move forward with his plan: taking over the world.

The best way to do that was to start over. Destroy civilization with a nuclear war and nuclear winter. Complete the destruction using Prime aircraft and his robot army. He had at least 20 years to complete his plan.

Then he would be The One.

The Creator of all things.

25

WITH ANNA, MIRIAM, AND DERRICK'S questions answered, Red escorted Carly to a stairwell that led to an exit door. It was a straight shot from there to the lot where her car was parked. Miriam gave Carly some cash for gas and told her to avoid using credit cards for a few days. When Carly asked why, Miriam just said, "you'll understand soon."

Exhaustion was enveloping Derrick, and he felt sure everyone else experienced the same thing. The robots, gathering at the adjacent building, looked like swarming black insects. More deadly than insects, but with the same disregard for human life. The robot army posed a problem. A big problem because five tired teenagers were unlikely to prevail against them. Hell, ten fresh teenagers wouldn't stand a chance.

However, they did have an advanced aircraft that could reduce that robot horde to a pile of smoldering metal and plastic.

"We need the aircraft," Derrick said.

Miriam said, "Agreed."

Derrick keyed his mic. "Nyx? This is Derrick. We need help." He didn't attempt to use military jargon. For Red and Antonio, using it was a game. This was no game.

The radio crackled. "I thought we were not using the radio until you were finished."

He wondered for a moment how she knew they had not yet found Prime. They must be monitoring the situation from up there. "A bunch of robots are guarding Prime's building. We need the aircraft's firepower to take them out."

Nyx said, "We have our own problems. A Prime aircraft approached us and then turned away. Antonio went after it. Three more appeared out of nowhere. Antonio is taking fire, and I'm headed to help him. Sorry. We'll be awhile."

Derrick couldn't breathe. Couldn't think.

Nothing he could do to protect Nyx. Nothing.

Miriam put her hand on Derrick's arm. "Nyx will be okay. The aircraft she's flying is advanced."

Derrick nodded. "True. Plus, she has Five."

"She has what?"

"Sentry 5. The computer." He snapped his fingers. "That's it."

"That's what?"

Derrick keyed his mic. "Sentry 5? Can you hear me?"

There was no response for a moment. Derrick was about to key the mic again when a robotic voice said, "I do not hear. However, I do receive your radio transmissions."

"Sentry 5, I need the PFP." He paused. "And a weapon. Something with a long range and a lot of bullets." Another pause. "Something to destroy robots."

Sentry 5 responded immediately. "At our current speed and altitude, the aircraft door cannot be opened."

Derrick's dread was instantaneous. He could not protect Nyx there. He could protect no one here. They could start shooting at the robots, but the robots would fire back. They could move and shoot, but there were too many robots. They didn't have enough cover. And the robots had a big weapon that took two robots just to carry. He didn't know what it was, and he didn't want to find out. The personal flight pack would have given him an advantage, and he needed every advantage he could get.

Radio static grabbed his attention.

"I think we have a solution," Nyx said.

"What is it?"

"No time to explain, but the suit will be there in a few minutes."

Sentry 5 added, "I sent a weapon that will suit your needs. I have included explosives. I suggest you use the explosives first. Do not be within 50 yards when they detonate. One hundred yards would be safer."

Before Derrick could respond, Nyx said, "Go to the roof."

Derrick looked at Miriam and Red. "I'll get the PFP. Once I've taken care of the robots, I'll meet you at the front door."

Miriam shook her head. "That will take too long. Prime knows we are here. I have an idea. You distract the robots…"

"Distract?"

Miriam rolled her eyes. "Start shooting them. We'll find a way in through the back."

"Slow down. We need more than Derrick fighting the robots. Red can shoot from the roof and help Derrick," Anna said.

Red said, "I'll do whatever, but it might be better if I went with Miriam."

Everyone stared at Red.

Red shrugged. "The doors will be locked. Maybe I can help get us inside."

Miriam said, "He has a point. Anna and Rebekah, you stay and help Derrick."

"Excuse me? I'm trained, just like you," Anna said, adding, "Prime won't let us just stroll in and destroy him and his spawn. Rebekah should stay with Derrick. She can shoot. She's proven that already."

"Rebekah can shoot?" Red asked, unable to suppress the skepticism in his voice.

Derrick said, "She can, and she has."

Rebekah said, "Just hold on a minute. Don't I get a say in this?"

Miriam said, "Not this time. Anna's right. You help Derrick."

Rebekah started to protest. Miriam held up her hand. "This is not a competition. And I know, we promised to stick together, and we are. We are all here together with a monumental task before us. It's no different than playing soccer. People play different positions, but they are all on the same team."

Derrick wondered if Miriam had ever watched Rebekah play soccer or knew anything about the game. Miriam and Rebekah were not friends until their escape from Pacific Edge. They had been inseparable since then.

Rebekah said, "Fine. Derrick, let's get to the roof." Then she hugged Miriam. "Don't get yourself killed." She turned to Red and Anna. "That includes you. Both of you."

"Not me," Red said. "I'm looking forward to a big steak dinner when this is over."

Miriam shook her head but said nothing.

Derrick was halfway down the hallway when Rebekah grabbed his arm. "Slow down. There could be robots or guards out here."

"Sorry. You're right." He brought his weapon up. "Let's do it right, but as quickly as we can."

"And quietly."

He nodded.

All things considered; this wasn't a terrible situation. Well, the part about Nyx being alone in a firefight with enemy aircraft—that part was terrifying. If he thought about that too long, he'd be unable to do anything. But this part was okay. Better than okay. Robots he could destroy all day long. People. That's where he had a problem.

And Prime.

He didn't want to face Prime. No. That wasn't accurate. He wanted to face Prime. He wanted to ask Prime questions. Like: Why do you want to kill us? Why do you hate us? Why do you hate me? And the big one: Why was I created? What is my purpose?

But there was that thing about suppressed kill commands. While he felt confident, he could overcome it, he could not be certain. The risk that he could not was too great. Whose idea was the kill command? Their Keepers or Prime? That was just one reason he wanted to talk to Lawrence King.

That discussion would not be dangerous.

Not for Derrick. He could not guarantee it would be safe for the man they knew as Father.

Deconstruction
A Derrick King Novel, Book 8

The third floor seemed quiet. It did not appear there were any other stragglers left behind. Odors of metal and oil permeated the air. Derrick wondered what they did here. It wasn't creating human tests subjects; he felt sure of that. He studied the signs above the doors. Micro Drive Design. Circuit Board Production. Hydraulic and Electromagnetic Appendage Drives. Android Assembly and Testing.

Robots. They designed and built robots here. Prime controlled the military, and that was not good, but at least there were real people involved, like Commander Cliff Haskins, who turned out to have a moral compass, and Kevin Schell, the teenage soldier in Mexico who was just a scared kid. However, Prime with an army of killer robots that had no regard for human life was terrifying.

"Besides the test subject program, it looks like this place designs and builds robots," Derrick said.

"No wonder there are so many," Rebekah said. "Do you think that bunch outside the building is all of them?"

"No. Prime will have more inside. This Prime knows Seattle was destroyed. Perhaps it knows about New York and Chicago as well. It probably has figured out it can't communicate with the Central Prime. It may think it's the last, or at least on a short list of remaining Primes. It's becoming an endangered species and growing more dangerous by the second."

They didn't encounter any opposition on their way to the roof. They found a door labeled roof access that led to a stairwell and at the top was a gray metal door.

Derrick cracked the door open. "Looks clear." With the door open enough to squeeze out, he set the doorstop.

Rebekah pointed. "Someone can move that and lock the door from the inside. Even if we see the door move, we won't be fast enough to stop them."

"You're right. I'm open to suggestions."

Rebekah shrugged. "Let's open it all the way and then set the stop. That forces them to step out and gives us a better chance at spotting them."

Derrick nodded. "Good thinking."

"How will you get the, what did you call it? PFP?"

"I assume it will find me."

They stood in the middle of the roof where they could not be seen from the ground or the other buildings. Derrick scanned the sky for the PFP. He didn't know how far it had to fly or how fast it could go. When he used it in New York, he floated down and then went back up. Not much speed. This would be different. Floating here would get him killed.

A moment later, the PFP zoomed in and then hovered at the proper height for him to step into it. A large canvas bag was attached. Inside was the flight helmet with the tactical display on the face shield and several flat, round things. On the side of the PFP, was something new. A flat black, box-shaped thing about four feet long and eight inches deep and eight inches wide. There were no triggers, buttons, or other controls visible. Only three-barrel openings at one end.

Derrick looked at the weapon. He had not trained on it. It looked simple enough but didn't have a magnifying feature that he could see. He thought it was called a scope but wasn't sure that was correct. His heart sank. It would be difficult hitting the robots at a distance.

There was a note stuck to the helmet that read: "Put this on first."

Once the helmet was secured, a video appeared on the face shield, narrated by Sentry 5 and Charlie. Sentry 5 explained the PFP's range and speed. Sentry 5 had included ten explosive disks and explained how to activate them and suggested using them before the robots were aware of his presence and then climbing to a higher altitude to use the rifle-like weapon.

Charlie explained the weapon, which he had invented. Charlie called it an AT-1000. One thousand because it fired 1000 rounds, which were small, 17 caliber bullets, with lead cores to add weight and uranium enriched titanium to penetrate metal. The bullet's high velocity and design caused it to fragmentize after impact, creating significant damage. The range was one mile. Charlie did not explain what AT stood for.

Charlie finished and Derrick whispered, "How am I supposed to hit a target from a mile away?"

Although Derrick was watching and listening to a recording, Charlie answered as if they were having a conversation. "Once armed, the sighting mechanism will be displayed on the helmet screen. At such high magnification, even a slight movement will send the round off target a considerable distance."

Derrick shook his head.

Charlie's voice continued. "To compensate for this, I have designed stabilization and correction into the targeting mechanism and software. Aim and fire. The weapon makes all the corrections necessary to hit the target."

Derrick waited a few moments to see if Charlie had more information, but the message did not continue. Now he was seeing Rebekah standing in front of him. She stared at him, puzzled.

He lifted the face shield. "I was watching instructions on the weapons."

Rebekah gave him a playful smile; the lopsided one he always liked when they were in Pacific Edge. The one he was too brainwashed to recognize as meaningful. "Glad to hear it. I was afraid I'd lost you again."

"Lost me?"

"You drift off sometimes. Maybe you're worried about Nyx. I can understand that. Perhaps it's something else." She paused. "Tell me what to do. I'm assuming I'll wait until you open fire and then I'll join you from up here."

"No," he barked, sounding angry, although he was not. "You don't need to do anything. Stay away from the edge. They have a heavy weapon. Just wait here until I get back."

Rebekah frowned.

"Promise me."

She stared at him for a moment. "Okay. But I can help."

"I'll be fine. I have explosives. It shouldn't take long." He didn't want the robots firing at Rebekah. Worrying about Nyx, Antonio, Anna, Red, and Miriam was more than he could bear. Adding Rebekah might break the thin thread that tethered him to what little sanity he had left.

That thread could break at any time.

26

COLLINS LED THE WAY SOUTH ON HIGHWAY 5 into San Diego. He took an exit marked Front St. At least, Donna thought that is what the sign once read. It hung lopsided because one bolt had broken. No one had bothered fixing it. The streets were quiet. Mostly. Makeshift tents of plastic and bundles that appeared to be sleeping people, lined the sidewalks. Collins turned left and then entered a parking lot that had a few cars and a faded sign that read Motel 6. There were no tents here, but there was an armed guard sitting in front of the office.

Collins stopped. The armed guard gave him a weak wave. Collins and Patel met Donna and Jack in front of Jack's car.

Jack said, "Decent meeting spot. Looks like most everything else is filled up with homeless people. It's not exactly on our route. How did you know it was here?"

"The sheriff called again. Said he would put the word out to his deputies. If any of them want to help us, they'll meet us here. Strictly volunteer."

"What time are they supposed to be here?" Donna asked.

Collins checked his watch. "Two minutes ago."

"So much for volunteerism," Jack said.

Collins ran his fingers through his hair. "The sheriff doubted anyone would come. However, they won't stop us, and they will prevent anyone from interfering, although he doubted anyone would. People stay clear of that building. Security people run them off."

Donna said, "Do we have a plan? Do you know anything about where we are going and what to expect?"

"Just a few blocks from here, Broadway and State. Sheriff says it's an old Federal Courthouse," Collins said.

Donna said, "How do we do it?"

Collins shrugged. "There's another building across a small courtyard. Civilian operation, according to the sheriff, but it provides support for Prime in some way or another. That building will be empty. Perhaps there's a night watchman, but the sheriff wasn't sure."

Donna said, "That doesn't answer the question."

Collins nodded. "I wish I knew more."

Patel said, "Perhaps we should take some time to analyze the situation."

Donna said, "Allen makes a good point."

"The sheriff suggested that our best chance for getting to Prime is to go in fast and unannounced. Apparently, the building is not as secure as one might think, but people are sent away quickly when they get too close. The difference is that we have a warrant. No one has ever tried to arrest Prime before. The element of surprise and a moment of indecision are the best we can hope for."

Jack said, "Just tell us what to do and let's get this over with. Someone's not walking away from this. That much is certain. I have stuff to do, so I'm planning on being back in Potterville before sunrise."

Collins took a breath. "I want you all on the roof of the adjacent building. Prime's building is all glass, so I'm hoping you can see in and provide support from the roof."

"What if the glass is bulletproof?" Allen asked.

"I'm hoping it isn't. But it might take a couple of rounds to break it. If it's bulletproof, then I'm on my own. But I won't put any of you at risk going in with me."

"Not your decision to make," Jack said, turning to Donna and adding, "Get the jackets from the trunk."

Donna went to Jack's car and returned carrying three jackets with sheriff's emblems on the front and large lettering on the back. She handed them to Jack and Allen, keeping one for herself.

"Where did you get those?" Collins asked.

Jack said, "I had Lori get them when you were busy doing something else."

"Why?

"Because I figured you'd want to go in by yourself. Be the big hero. Hog all the glory. Well, it ain't gonna work that way. I didn't drive all this way in the middle of the night not to get some of that hero stuff for myself." Jack smiled.

"Very funny. I'm serious, Jack. I'm not letting you take the risk."

Jack said nothing. He walked to his car, disappearing behind the opened trunk. When he returned, he had belted on a holster and pistol and was carrying a shotgun. "I'm going in with you. You don't have to like it, but you can't stop me. Unless you're gonna shoot me."

Donna said, "Same goes for me, Bill Collins."

Jack touched Donna's arm and gently said, "Donna, we need a sniper, and you can shoot. We need you on the roof with a rifle. One of us will go with you in case there is a night watchman."

Donna said, "I'll be fine. Bill needs all the help he can get." She looked at Allen. "If you're willing, of course."

Allen said, "To be completely honest, I'm scared shitless. But I was raised thinking that it was my responsibility to protect my family and my friends. So, I'm going with Bill and Jack. That, I think, is our best hope for success. We must help bring an end to Prime for our families." He paused. "And I like to count you as my friends."

Collins said nothing for a moment, looking at each of the three faces standing across from him. "I don't know what to say."

Donna said, "Nothing needs said."

Jack said, "How about saying, 'Let's do this.'"

27

AS DERRICK EXAMINED THE WEAPON'S operation, his mind wandered to Anna, Red and Miriam and then drifted to Nyx and Antonio. He could not help Antonio or Nyx. He could help Anna, Red, and Miriam but not protect them. Rebekah was the only person he could protect.

"Stay in the middle of the roof, out of sight," Derrick said and began the PFP startup process.

Rebekah smiled. That lopsided smile that never failed to touch him in ways he could not explain. "You're not the boss of me." She kissed her fingers and then touched them to his face shield where his lips were concealed. "Stay alive."

He nodded. That's what Miriam had said when he left Pacific Edge. "Stay alive." It wasn't terrible advice.

And with that, he lifted into the air and flew away from the robots, gaining altitude. Hoping the robots could not see him, or perhaps more accurately, did not register on whatever sensory array they used. He would be recognized as a threat soon enough, but if his first pass was successful, he would greatly reduce their numbers.

From half a mile up and a quarter of a mile to the east, Derrick began his descent and first assault. It did not take long for him to learn to manage the weapon's sighting system. It was not difficult. Even an untrained teenager could run it, which bothered him, because that was exactly who they wanted in this position. Kids with little training going to war. Young people who probably didn't understand the politics driving the conflict. They were just expendable bodies. Much like test subjects. Parts, not people.

He checked on Rebekah to ensure she was not near the edge of the roof. She had moved closer to the edge. No surprise. It was Rebekah. She was as likely to follow his direction as Prime was likely to just give up if asked nicely. At least, she was keeping out of sight, barely peeking over the edge of the raised lip of the roof. He wanted to draw the robots' attention before they noticed her. On the first descent, he would drop explosives. The small bombs, according to Sentry 5, would begin their own flight plan, flying toward the target, attaching themselves using a powerful magnet, thus gluing themselves to a metal surface. The robots were mostly plastic, but they had plenty of metal inside, which ensured the bombs found a home before detonation.

Why didn't they have these in Seattle? Perhaps L. Linda would not have had to set each charge. Maybe she would still be with them. For some odd reason, he knew that wasn't possible. Why he thought that, he did not know. It was just a feeling. He could not accept that she was dead. Perhaps because her death seemed unnecessary.

As he approached, flying low and fast, there were no robot heads turned toward him, which meant his first attack would be a surprise. At least, he assumed that would be the case. There was no guarantee the robots were unaware of his approach. Just because people turned their heads did not mean robots did. They might have set a trap of their own.

Derrick slowed when he reached the robot horde and tossed five explosives. He assumed the bombs would drop like rocks, hitting the robots and instantly drawing their attention. But that didn't happen. The bombs floated down, spreading out and gently attaching themselves to the robots.

He rose slowly, assuming rapid movements this close to the robots might draw their attention. He did not know when the bombs would detonate. Five's instructions on that were vague. He simply said to drop them, and the arming process was automated. Five red dots appeared at the side of his face shield. He assumed that meant the bombs were armed, but there was no indication of when they would explode.

Suddenly, an alarm sounded in his ears, and a message flashed on his screen. "Detonation imminent. Create distance. Seek cover. Detonation imminent. Create distance. Seek cover." Derrick launched the PFP up and toward the building, hoping to use the building as a shield, but he was not fast enough. He should have started that maneuver when he first dropped the explosives.

A blast of hot air thrust him up and sideways. His legs smashed against the edge of the roof. Pain shot through his knees and shins. He glanced over his shoulder to see pieces of robots flying into the courtyard and toward him. He dodged left, and an arm flew by his head in a narrow miss. The robots' reaction to his location was almost instantaneous. As he disappeared from behind the building, he saw half the remaining robots firing at him.

The other half were firing at Rebekah, who was pinned down behind the two-foot-high edge. He landed ten yards from the edge of the building. The robots had stopped firing at him and concentrated all their weapons on Rebekah. Derrick should have anticipated that Rebekah wouldn't do what he'd told her. She was as stubborn as Miriam.

And just as brave.

He eased to where he could see the robots. Not all of them, maybe three quarters. One robot was picking up the large weapon. Derrick had to do something. Smoke swirled up from below, carrying the now familiar stench of fried electronics, melted plastic, and hot oil. The smell of robot destruction.

But there was something else lingering in the odor. Vaguely familiar. But from where or what, he couldn't say.

Then he remembered—the smell of explosives.

Suddenly, he remembered L. Linda's extraordinarily beautiful green eyes. Robots killed her. And he had let it happen. He could not let them kill Rebekah. He wouldn't.

He flew to where he could see the robots aiming the large weapon at where Rebekah hid, still pinned down by a constant barrage of bullets. He tossed a couple of explosives toward the robots, aiming the large weapon. But the explosives fell into a cluster of the machines. Greater mass, more magnetic attraction.

The warning flashed on his screen. At this range, he could be injured or burned, but he couldn't leave. Not yet.

He aimed at the robot holding the large weapon, then moved the sight to the weapon itself and fired.

The heat from the explosion flashed toward him, but he was already racing away, distancing himself for another run at the robots. When he'd traveled a quarter of a mile, he flew down to a few feet above the ground and headed toward the hoard. They had already turned back toward where Rebekah hid; the bullets had destroyed part of the building. He rose higher until he could see the roof, but he could not see Rebekah. A wave of nausea hit him. Dreading what he might find, he lowered his eyes, scanning the ground below where Rebekah had been.

But she wasn't there either.

Derrick was rapidly approaching the robots but had decided to get closer because they would turn to fire at him as soon as he started shooting. He could hit four, maybe five, and then veer behind the building just as he got there. Watching the robots through the weapon's sighting device, he noticed a robot closest to the building fall. Another one moved forward to take the fallen robot's place. That robot's head exploded, and it fell.

Rebekah was shooting at them from somewhere.

She had positioned herself where most of the robots were out of view until one stepped forward. Then she shot them as they came into view. Smart girl.

Derrick opened fire. He hit five robots before turning hard, using the building as cover. Then he decided to mirror what Rebekah was doing. He positioned himself until one robot came into view. Fired. Waited. Fired. A little slow but effective. Rebekah had proven herself again. She'd saved them in Mexico. Shot the soldier. Shooting robots was easier. Emotionally. They were just machines. Not like Charlie. They possessed no intelligence. They couldn't even figure out they were being picked off one by one as they stepped out into the line of fire. Programmed to kill intruders. That was all.

In the end, he had to ease around the corner of the building to get the last three robots. He rose, watching for more of the black machines at the building's entrance, but none came. When his eyes began to burn from the rancid, smoldering heap, he flew to Rebekah. She was standing where he'd left her.

Derrick landed and raised his face shield. "You stayed put the entire time?"

Rebekah winked. "Just like you said."

Derrick shook his head. "You're a lot like my sister."

She frowned. Just a little. "If you mean, you think of me like a sister, that's not a compliment. If you mean I'm a rebel like Miriam, you're off the hook."

Derrick smiled, although he thought it impossible. Not now. Not after all that had happened. "Yeah. The last one."

Something in his peripheral vision caught his attention. A small light in the distance on the third building of the complex. "What's that?"

"What's what?"

Derrick lowered his shield; Used the weapon's sighting system to zoom in. "Crap."

"What is it? What do you see?"

"A Prime aircraft. The door is open." He pointed. "On the building over there? Do you see it?"

"Yeah. Just barely." She paused. "Damn it. This was a decoy."

Derrick raised his shield. "I'm afraid you are right."

"Prime's not here. He's over there. Miriam will not find Prime where she's looking. And Prime is about to leave."

Derrick said, "They drew Antonio and Nyx away as well so we could not pursue. I have to get over there. You stay put. Tell Miriam if you see her."

Derrick closed his face shield and started off, but Rebekah slipped her arms under his and wrapped them around his chest. Then she wrapped her legs around his hips. He raised his shield. "What are you doing?"

"I'm going with you. No time to argue. Let's go before Prime lifts off."

There was no winning the argument, and she was right. Even now Prime might get away and they had no way to pursue it.

28

Saturday, April 9, 11:45 p.m. Pacific Time

BILL SENT JACK WITH DONNA IN CASE a night watchman guarded the building. Good thing because a guard was sitting in the building's lobby. When they pounded on the glass, he walked to the door, opening it to ask what they wanted. The fact they were both armed and wore jackets with sheriff's emblems did little to impress the man. However, the shotgun Jack shoved under the man's chin got his attention. They used zip ties and duct tape to secure the guard and then put him in a closet to ensure he would not be seen from the outside. They encountered no one else on the way to the roof, where Donna took her position. Jack headed back to help Collins and Patel.

After a few minutes, Jack joined Bill and Allen at the front door of Prime's building. The door was locked. No surprise. The building sat not more than twenty yards from Donna's position. So close that she had to back off the rifle's scope to its lowest magnification. She could have read a computer monitor, had there been one. The building was all glass, and she could almost see the entire building, from one side to the other, except she could only see the one floor. She decided to move despite Bill's instructions that she remain on the roof. She was never very good at following directions that were not related to baking.

She took the stairs rather than risk getting trapped in an elevator. On the second floor she found a window, but could not see the guys, so she went to the third floor. It was possible they were still on the first floor, but she could not see in those windows because they were blacked out. She scanned the section of the building she could see but saw no one. She moved to another window where the next section was visible. She continued this until reaching the end of the building, and then she took the stairs to the fourth floor.

It seemed the building was empty. Not just empty, unused. She saw no signs of work or business. No papers on desks, no phones, no coffee cups. This wasn't Prime's Headquarters. The address was a hoax. But then she saw a flash from a window near the middle of the fourth floor. She skipped two sections, estimating she'd come to the windows where the flash had occurred.

The lights were out. Only the exit signs remained lit, which made seeing anything through the rifle's scope difficult. Then a brilliant flash blinded her for a moment. A gunshot, she assumed. Then she saw a black shape. She'd seen it before. A robot like the ones that came to Potterville looking for Anna Ford.

Perhaps this was a Prime Headquarters after all. She stood back from the window and aimed at where the robot had been standing. She fiddled with an adjustment on the scope. Still too dark. She fiddled more. There. She could just see a silhouette, but it was a robot, no question. She rested the rifle's tripod on a counter. The shot was only 30 yards, but it was through two windows, one or both of which might be bullet proof. She took a breath, let it out halfway, then squeezed the trigger.

The rifle's discharge was deafening in the small room. Ear protection would have been a good idea, except for two reasons: one, it would prevent her from hearing anyone coming, and two, they forgot to bring any. As the smoke cleared, Donna saw a hole in the window the size of a dollar. She could not see if there was a hole in the glass of the other building. The scope magnified the smoke, making it impossible to see, so she dashed to the next room. She tried to locate the robot. Either it had moved, or she wasn't looking in the right spot.

Donna looked up, blinked her eyes a couple of times hoping that might help. It didn't. But then the lights flickered on. Without the aid of the scope, she could see Bill at the light switch. Three prone robots littered the floor. Allen stood up from behind an overturned desk. Jack appeared from behind a pillar. Almost in unison, they looked from the robot she had shot at, tracing a line with their eyes to a hole in the glass and then to the room from which she had shot. She waved her arms and eventually they spotted her and waved back. Bill gave her a thumb's up and then pointed up. Next floor.

They first went to the end of the building and then up the stairs. Donna wasn't the youngest of their group, but she managed to get to the next floor first, and it was a good thing she did. Three robots lie in wait. They were in plain sight, but all had weapons pointed at the door.

Donna keyed her radio mic, "Bill, this is Donna. Don't open the door to the next floor."

Her radio cackled. "Donna, we said no radios."

"Right, but there are three robots with weapons pointed at that door. They'll blast you as soon as it opens. Just give me a minute."

Bill didn't answer. Donna found a suitable desk on which to rest the rifle's tripod, but she had to get to her knees. Not comfortable at her age. She put crosshairs on the first robot and fired. She didn't wait to see if she'd hit it. Instead, she moved to the next and then the last one. Then she scanned the room. One robot remained standing, so she shot that one a second time. It fell to the floor. Standing, she scanned the building as far as she could see. In the middle was a large solid section that prevented her from seeing to the other end. Probably the elevators.

Elevators!

Donna rushed to the window and looked up. Something black passed overhead. Prime wasn't on any of these floors. Prime was in a complex under the building. The robots were there to slow down the attackers.

"Bill, I think Prime is going to the roof, using the elevator. I'm headed there now. Don't go there until you hear from me. Prime probably has a lot more robots, maybe people as well."

"Donna, wait…"

But she didn't wait. Bill rattled off instructions, but she didn't hear much of what he said. She was taking steps two at a time and wishing she was 20 years younger and a few pounds lighter. At the door to the roof, she wondered if Prime had the foresight to put robots on the roofs to cover its escape. It would have been smart, but there were no robots on either roof few minutes ago. Still, they could have taken the elevator. To be safe, she cracked the door open and peered out. Nothing. Scanning the roof as she eased the door open, she saw it was clear.

The black aircraft was on Prime's building just across the narrow courtyard. Light flooded from the aircraft's open door, two robots stood on either side, and two more stood guard by the door of a block-shaped outcropping in the center of the roof. At this range, Donna didn't need the tripod. She shouldered the weapon and shot the two robots near the stairwell, spun, and shot the two at the aircraft. Then she replaced the spent cartridges, dropping one cartridge twice before giving up and pulling the final bullet from her pocket.

She had just loaded the last round when a monstrosity stepped into the night. Donna had wondered how they'd know Prime if they saw it. That question had been answered.

Before she could fire, robots swarmed from the doorway, crowding around Prime, making a clear shot impossible. Keeping the robots in the rifle's scope, Donna followed them toward the aircraft, hoping to get an opening to hit Prime. She didn't know if the bullets would penetrate the aircraft if Prime got inside, but she assumed they would not. There were no visible motors, rockets, or propellers on the aircraft, so she didn't even know where to aim to disable the machine. She fired into the cluster twice. One robot dropped and another dragged a leg. She had five rounds left. No time to reload.

The mob was at the aircraft's entrance now. She fired another shot into the group. A robot fell on the ramp. She decided to fire the remaining shots through the door before it closed. Maybe she'd get lucky, and a ricochet would hit Prime or disable the aircraft. Both sounded like long shots, but she was going to have to fire soon or not at all.

She got a glimpse of Prime in her crosshairs and she fired. The monster disappeared inside the machine. She might have hit it, but she thought not. She wasn't even sure if she hit the opening. The robots were backing off now and the door was closing but one robot's body jammed the door blocking it. Donna aimed at the opening and fired until the rifle was empty. Just then Jack, Bill, and Allen dashed onto the roof, firing as they ran toward the aircraft, robots falling as they approached. Donna could not see any damage to the hull and the doorway was pointed away from them. She managed to get one round reloaded and took aim at the small opening. Then the door opened a little more and a dead robot dropped to the roof.

She fired her last shot; confident this one made it inside. Whether it did any damage was unknown.

The aircraft hovered about five feet above the roof. Her three friends stood watching it, their firearms empty. The machine slowly spun around. Suddenly, Donna realized it would likely open fire. Jack and the others were standing in the open with zero protection. She could run for safety, but she did not.

Something did not look right. The aircraft tilted slightly and then drifted. Flying at a 45-degree angle, it hit the edge of the building, taking off part of the structure, sending bricks crashing to the ground. The aircraft pivoted, dragging one edge deeper into the bricks and windows. Then it picked up speed. Not just falling but accelerating. It gouged off a chunk of the top floor. The grinding and crashing sounds were deafening.

Halfway to the ground, smoke trailed the aircraft. Seconds later, it rocketed to the courtyard, burying itself several feet into the concrete. A huge cloud of dirt and debris mushroomed into the sky, sending pieces of concrete raining down. Donna ran for the shelter of the roof access, and she saw Jack and the others doing the same. Just as she reached the door, a flash of white light lit the night like day and then a blast of hot air knocked her through the door and into the roof access stairwell.

This Prime was dead. She was certain of that. One less for the kids to worry about.

If the kids were still alive, that is, to worry about anything.

29

THE PFP FLIGHT TO THE THIRD BUILDING DIDN'T take long. Yet, to Derrick, it seemed like forever. The night air felt cold and damp, a drastic change from earlier. The structure was shaped like a big L. He circled wide, coming up the long side, which shielded them from the front. Rebekah held on tightly. He didn't feel her slipping or loosening her grip. He wanted to get her to safety, not that the roof was safe, but at least she wouldn't fall to her death. Still, survival could not be guaranteed for either of them.

He kept the weapon's targeting system aimed at the roof; the crosshairs on the access door, and his orientation so he could also watch the aircraft as well. As they approached, he reduced the magnification to retain the same sight picture. The PFP weapon was more than adequate to handle Prime, but he hoped Prime did not appear because he would have no opportunity for questions. But there was something else. He wasn't sure what. Perhaps because every version of Prime was disturbing, and each version was deadly.

He thought about contacting Miriam to tell her Prime wasn't in the building she was searching. But he didn't. They had agreed to limit radio traffic because Prime could be monitoring their conversations. Prime no doubt was watching their every move, but there was no reason to announce their plans.

Derrick had an odd feeling it was important that he talk to Prime. They still did not know the location of the central Prime Headquarters. Miriam said she had a plan, but Derrick didn't know what she meant by that, and she had done nothing to find that location as far as he knew. So, getting the information from Prime made sense.

Miriam and Anna had been quick on the trigger. Even when the Prime in New York was helpless, Anna killed it before they could learn anything. Although it was unclear how he could convince Prime to reveal the central location. Perhaps he could injure Prime and then strike a deal.

Prime wanted to survive. Prime would listen to reason. Prime might agree to a trade, information in exchange for its life.

Of course, there were those hidden kill commands in Derrick's brain.

But he could overcome those. That was his plan.

He touched down.

Rebekah released her grip, stepping in front of him with her weapon at the ready. "What should we do? Wait for Prime to come here or go find it?"

Derrick hoped Rebekah would listen to reason. He had a connection with her, but that felt like manipulation. He didn't want to manipulate her. He didn't want to manipulate anyone. Did he? He didn't think so. Except Prime.

Then there were those kill commands.

"Derrick?"

"Yeah. Just thinking," Derrick said.

But before he could decide their next move, Prime made the decision for him.

The roof access door flew open.

30

AKIRA COULDN'T SLEEP. SHE WENT TO where they had taken meals. She didn't want coffee, although she didn't think it would have made a difference. Caffeine didn't keep her awake, not at home. She often had tea just before bed. Granted, tea didn't have as much caffeine as coffee.

She couldn't shut her brain off. It was full of many things, but mostly she worried about Miriam. The others too, of course. But mostly Miriam. Certain things had come with the return of emotions, although she wasn't sure if they were old emotions or new ones, and thoughts and feelings regarding Miriam were among them.

Besides being worried, she was lonely. Charlie was in his docking station, and Red had left with the others. She rummaged through cabinets and drawers and found an old-fashioned thermos bottle. The green crinkly finish was almost worn off, but its stainless-steel inside looked as if it were new. She had a thought. Perhaps Kevin and William would like a cup of hot chocolate. If they were awake.

They might be worried. Scared too. And lonely. Like she was. They were isolated. She was too. Charlie was here, but right now, she was alone. She'd be quiet. If Kevin and William were asleep, she would tiptoe out, and they'd never know she was there. The thermos would keep the hot chocolate warm, and it would still be good in the morning. Perhaps she could ask Charlie for cinnamon rolls for their breakfast. The hot chocolate would keep until then.

If Kevin and William were asleep, she'd return in the morning.

However, if they were asleep, she would still be:

Alone.

Worried.

Scared.

31

GETTING INSIDE THE BUILDING WAS TAKING longer than Miriam had expected. She still had the device that Charlie had provided, a wire that fired white hot and cut through hinges and locks, and she had cut the hinges off the metal door, but it wouldn't budge. It had two deadbolts that extended into the steel door frame, which wedged the door so that it wouldn't slip out. At first, they feared it had another lock or bar inside, but Red got it to move an inch on the hinged side and then it stuck tight.

The intense explosions and gunfire at the front of the building had stopped. The intensity was such that Miriam feared Derrick and Rebekah had not survived. They needed to get into the building and fast so she could go to them.

Miriam cut a padlock on a nearby toolshed where Red found a large flat-bladed screwdriver that he worked into the crack between the door and the jamb. With some grunts and under-his-breath cursing, he finally got it dislodged and open.

Had there been robots waiting on the other side, they would have been dead. Getting in had taken too much time, and they were anything but stealthy. Fortunately, there was a small area inside with two doors: one led into the building, the other into the stairwell.

Anna led them through the building's first floor. Peeking out from the lobby, Miriam saw smoldering robots just outside the glass doors. Derrick didn't have to destroy them all, but it appeared that he did. Perhaps he was still alive. While he'd warmed to Charlie and the computer, Sentry 5, he also had a deep-seated loathing for the black machines that killed L. Linda Maxton.

Having finished the first floor, where they had found nothing, they sprinted to the top floor and found the same thing. The building wasn't just empty; it was abandoned. But there was still the underground. From experience they knew, Prime liked top floors. Top floors were best for escape. However, basements were easier to defend—no windows.

That's why Miriam left the basement for last. Because she didn't like losing. With Prime, losing meant dying.

She eased the door open to the stairwell and peered down. Looking back at Anna, she held her finger to her lips, then motioned them to follow.

Miriam didn't like stairs. Too many corners and places where the enemy could see them first. Going down was worse than going up. But down was the only way left to go.

Something else bothered her. The smell. Oil and metal. Electronics and plastic, with hints of dampness and mold. It seemed wrong.

The stairs ended at another door. The worst situation possible. No way to open that door without getting shot if someone was waiting on the other side. Miriam motioned Anna to the floor. Neither robots nor humans aim at the floor first. Anna would have a chance to destroy targets before they spotted her location. Miriam positioned Red behind the concrete wall and told him to stay put.

There was no good way to open the door. That person was the most likely to be shot. That's why she was doing it. Miriam didn't like it, but she would not take the safer position and watch Anna get shot.

Because Anna was prone near the door, Miriam couldn't make eye contact, but Anna knew what to do. Miriam was confident about that. She had no uncertainty regarding Anna. Derrick, on the other hand, worried her. There was something troubling him and that troubled her. But he could destroy the robots. That's why Derrick was distracting the robots, instead of hunting Prime. Miriam didn't have to worry about Derrick being responsible for killing Prime. She and the others could take care of that part.

Miriam gritted her teeth, then slowly turned the door lever. When the latch disengaged, she jerked the door open, keeping herself behind the door for protection.

Nothing happened.

Completely silent.

Something wasn't right.

Miriam peered around the door. The room was immense and dimly lit, which meant the far corners were difficult to see. Where she could see, nothing was moving. She signaled Red to hold the door and then she stepped inside. She moved her hand along the wall, found the light switch. Overhead lights lit the room. It was full of equipment. Bins of parts lined the walls. Unlike the offices on the floors above, this was one cavernous space interrupted only by concrete pillars.

"What is this place?" Anna asked, stepping up next to Miriam.

Miriam walked to a bin, reached down, and held up a small electronic device. "They assemble robots here." She pointed toward the far end of the building. The lighting wasn't on in that half of the space, but Miriam was right. Robots stood in lines like giant toy soldiers.

Anna said, "I don't understand."

"It was a ruse," Miriam said, adding, "a trick. The robots massed here, knowing we'd assume they were protecting Prime. Prime must be in the third building on the far side of the complex."

Anna said, "That's why they drew our aircraft away. We need to get over there. Fast!"

Red who'd been guarding the rear, stepped inside. "What's going on?"

"Prime tricked us," Anna said.

Miriam thought for a moment. "Getting to the other building is not that simple."

"Sounds simple to me," Anna said.

"We'll be crossing a lot of open space. Easy targets. Second, Prime could be gone before we get there." Miriam paused. "Maybe Derrick will figure it out. We'll try to find a way to get there that doesn't make us easy targets."

Anna said, "That could take longer."

"We don't have another option," Miriam said, adding, "It might come down to Derrick figuring it out."

"Right. That's my fear as well."

Miriam frowned. "What's that supposed to mean?"

"In New York, Derrick was trying to have a conversation with Prime."

32

DONNA PAUSED AT THE GROUND FLOOR, took a couple of deep breaths. Heat radiated from the street, reaching her even here. It felt as if she had not taken a breath for several minutes. The adrenalin that had flooded her system wasn't something she was accustomed to, and she trembled violently.

After a few breaths, she keyed her microphone. "Bill, it's Donna. Are you guys, okay?"

"We're alright. We got into the stairwell just before the explosion."

"The fire must be awful. I can feel the heat even inside. I'll have to skirt the fire for a block or two, then work my way back to the cars. It will take me a few minutes."

"See you soon, and good job. You did it." Bill turned to Allen and Jack. "You heard. We need to go."

Allen said, "Not yet. We need to get to the basement and quickly."

"You heard Donna. The building is on fire and Prime is dead."

"One Prime is dead. But there are more. Another is probably being activated right now," Allen said.

"What?" Bill asked, but Allen was already through the door and headed to the elevator.

Collins caught up to him. "You mean there are more?"

"That's exactly what I mean. There are always more. Each one is supposed to be an improvement over the last. Apparently, it doesn't always work that way, but it only takes a few minutes to activate the next version."

Jack said, "Let's take the stairs."

The elevator doors opened. Allen stepped inside. "This will be faster."

Jack held the door open. "You never take the elevator in a fire. Plus, they could know we are in the elevator and trap us there."

Bill said, "He's right, Allen. Let's take the stairs, do what we need to do, and get the hell out of here."

Allen looked angry but said nothing. He nodded and sprinted to the stairs. Again, Bill caught him at the door. "Let's do this together. Remember, there are still robots."

Allen nodded. "Of course, but let's move quickly. I fear we are already too late to stop the process."

Deconstruction
A Derrick King Novel, Book 8

Jack raised his shotgun. "Then we'll kill that one as well." He nodded to Bill to open the door.

Only lifeless robots awaited them. "That's odd," Bill said.

Allen said, "Perhaps the robots are inactive without Prime."

Bill nodded and then moved quickly down the stairs. Moved faster than seemed safe, but they were probably safer now than they would be when the next Prime became active.

They came to a set of double steel doors. Collins knelt and raised his shotgun. "Allen, you get on the floor. Jack, open it slowly and stay behind it."

Jack said, "The door might not stop the bullets they are shooting."

"I'll do my best to shoot first," Bill said.

"See that you do." Jack rested his shotgun in the corner behind the door.

The door opened slowly. Bill saw a tank, larger than a man, filled with clear fluid. It held a creature that wasn't quite human. Tubes and wires ran from machines outside the tank to the creature. Bubbles escaped its mouth. Its eyes were open but had no reaction. The door opened more; Bill adjusted his position. Another tank, then another. Finally, he could see one creature standing outside of the tank. It was moving. Robots came to life was well.

The creature was Prime. It turned toward the door. Stared at Bill. The loathing in its face became evident as it recognized the situation. But Bill wasn't interested in its reaction. He aimed at its chest, firing two rounds, and then aimed at its head and fired a third round—all 00-buck. Devastating at this range.

The robots froze again. Allen was right. The robots needed directions from Prime. Light illuminated the next container and the liquid drained. Allen was right about that too. The next heir to the Prime throne was in activation.

Allen was through the door before Bill could stand. He dashed to the Prime being activated, pointed his shotgun and fired.

Jack brushed past Bill and ran to the other side of the room, shooting the next Prime container. Glass and fluid crashed to the floor. Both Allen and Jack were destroying the Prime replicas, working their way down the line toward each other.

Bill got there just as Allen and Jack met. Jack aimed at the last tube and fired.

Bill said, "You didn't save any for me."

Jack turned and with a smile said, "Sorry, boss. You got the live one. We just did a little clean-up work."

Allen walked away from them.

Bill shouted, "Hey! Where are you going? We need to get out of here. Fire. Remember?"

Allen held up one hand but said nothing.

Jack and Bill walked to where Allen stood, looking at a large metal box with blinking lights.

"What is it?" Bill asked.

"A computer. But not an ordinary one."

"Okay. I'm sure it's quite interesting, but we need to go."

"It's hard-wired." Allen pointed. "No plug. Just conduit."

"Okay. Perhaps you can tell us more on the way home."

"We need to shut it down and take the hard drive."

"How are we supposed to do that? You said it was hard wired," Bill said.

Allen said nothing. He walked around, looking at the walls. "I don't know. I don't see a breaker box. It's probably locked in a separate room."

"Is it really all that important?" Jack asked.

Allen turned. "I don't know, but I think so."

Jack stared at Allen. "Can't you just pull the hard drives out?"

"I don't want to get electrocuted."

Jack shook his head and walked away. A moment later, they heard glass shatter. Jack returned carrying a red axe and a large fire extinguisher. He handed the fire extinguisher to Allen. "Just in case."

"Just in case of what?"

Jack walked to the conduit behind the computer. He looked over his shoulder at Allen, motioning him closer. He planted his feet, brought the axe down slowly, touching the conduit, then raised it high, and slammed it down, cutting the conduit and the wires inside. Sparks flew but no fire started. The small lights on the computer faded.

Jack leaned the axe against the back wall and stepped away. "What are you waiting for? We have a fire to outrun."

Allen removed the side of the computer and started removing parts. Soon he had a stack of 12 box-shaped devices stacked on a nearby shelf. "If we each take four, that would be helpful."

Bill snatched four and fitted them into pockets. "Let's get out of here."

"There's a door back this way." Jack pointed. "If I'm not turned around, I think it's opposite of the fire."

Allen grabbed the fire extinguisher and his shotgun. "Lead the way."

Jack paused at the metal door, touching it. "It's not hot. That's a good thing, but there could be fire above us."

"Do you think it could have spread that fast?" Bill asked.

Jack shrugged. "One way to find out." He pulled the door open. The smell of smoke filled the air. A haze hung at the top of the stairs.

Bill said, "Question answered. What's Plan B?"

Jack said, "Take a deep breath. Unless it's too hot when we get up there, we burst through the door and head for the closest exit, which I hope is right in front of us. Stay close. If we get separated, we'll never find each other."

Bill said, "I'll go first."

Allen pulled Bill back. "No. It's my fault we were delayed. I'll go."

Deconstruction
A Derrick King Novel, Book 8

Before Bill could object, Allen took a deep breath and sprinted up the stairs. Jack gave Bill a little shove to get going. Bill started up the stairs, glancing back to ensure Jack was following.

Allen touched the door at the top of the stairs. Looking back, gave a thumb's up, and then jerked the door open. Smoke boiled in the space ahead, burning his eyes. He could see nothing. Then he saw a very dim greenish glow about six feet off the ground. He headed straight toward the light. If it was an exit sign, he felt sure he could make it. If it wasn't an exit, they were dead.

When Allen reached the light, he felt only solid metal. He frantically pawed at the door, finding a metal bar just as everything turned black. Suddenly, the door moved. Allen tumbled outside, hitting the ground. Smoke and a wave of heat rolled over him. Someone grabbed his collar, dragging him. Twenty yards from the building, Jack released his hand hold and plopped down on his butt beside him. Bill joined them.

Fire was racing through the building, lighting the area with an orange glow. They coughed and hacked for a few minutes. Finally, Allen said, "Well, that answers one question."

"What question is that?" Bill asked.

"Whether or not the fire had spread through the building."

He keyed his mic. "Donna, are you there?"

"I'm by the cars. Are you out of the building?"

"Yeah. We are on the opposite side of where we went in. Be there in a few minutes."

Bill stood, extending a hand to help Jack stand. "Let's go home."

33

DERRICK FELT AS IF HE WERE UNDER WATER. He had been holding his breath, and when the door flew open, he froze for a second. Rebekah was in the middle of switching to the long weapon. Two robots stepped out onto the roof, scanning for threats and locking their eyes on Derrick. He pushed Rebekah down and lifted into the air just as bullets whizzed through the empty space where he and Rebekah had been standing.

Rebekah reacted quickly, rolling to the side, and shooting one robot. He shot the other. He landed and stepped out of the PFP. He helped Rebekah up, while keeping his eyes on the door. "Sorry, I pushed you."

"I would be dead if you didn't. Do you have any explosives left?"

"Yes. Why?"

"Can I see one?"

Derrick lifted his face shield and then stared at her for a moment as she stood there with her hand out. He pulled one out, handing it to her.

She turned it over in her hand. "Weird. How do you, you know, switch it on?"

"That's the strangest part. It's like it knows. I just threw them out, and they flew down, attached themselves to the robots and then exploded. I got a warning message just before they detonated."

"Cool." And with that, Rebekah dashed to the aircraft, tossed the bomb inside, and ran back to Derrick with her hands over her ears. Seconds later, a blast shook the roof. The aircraft lifted a foot and then fell. Flames shot from the aircraft door.

Rebekah looked over her shoulder. "I don't think that will fly."

"Why did you do that? We might need it."

Rebekah cocked her head to one side, just a little. No smile. "Because it's just you and me. It will take the others time to get here."

"So?"

"If we fail, Prime could escape. Now, he can't."

Derrick realized she was right. He didn't like thinking about it, but the truth was that they'd been lucky so far. A weird thought crossed his mind. Weird thoughts seemed to be his specialty. He'd never mentioned these thoughts to anyone—for obvious reasons. People thought he was weird enough without knowing what passed through his head at the most inappropriate of times. This one was something his Father had said just before Paul Jorgensen loaded him in a pickup truck and drove him away into the night. Father had said, "Maybe you can change things." Something like that.

But he was not the promised one that people talked about. That wasn't him. He was sure of that. Then another thought crossed his mind. Equally weird. Similarly inappropriate. In the Seattle parking garage, L. Linda had told him to destroy Prime, and then she said, "Promise me." Weird and unwelcome. A small part of him wanted to forget that girl, and a bigger part of him knew he could not.

"Earth to Derrick."

Rebekah stared at him, but kept her weapon pointed at the door, which remained closed.

"Sorry. I was just thinking."

"Want to share your thoughts?"

"No. I mean, yes. I was trying to decide what our next move should be."

Rebekah said, "We could wait here. Or, better yet, I'll wait here, and you hover above. I'll draw their attention. You can shoot what I miss."

Not a bad plan. Except Rebekah could be killed.

He surprised himself by saying, "That's a good plan." He paused.

"Except?"

"What if Prime is monitoring us?"

"What are you saying? That Prime won't come up here because I blew up his aircraft?"

"Right. What if he escapes another way?"

Rebekah said nothing for a moment. "Like a car?"

"Yeah. Something like that. Maybe an armored truck."

"You're right. We need to stay on offense. Take the fight to Prime. That's what has gotten us this far."

The PFP hovered above the roof. Without getting in, Derrick guided it behind the little building that housed the roof-access door and then joined Rebekah. "You lie down over there." He pointed. "I'll open the door. You'll be out of the line of fire if they are waiting for us."

"Make sure you're not in the way." She walked away, then turned around. "And don't get shot. I shouldn't have to do all the work." She gave him that little lopsided grin. He wondered if she understood its effect on him.

When Rebekah was in position, Derrick went to the door. He grasped the metal lever. There was no great way to do this. That was the problem. He had to move the lever to release the latch, and when the outside lever moved, so did the inside lever. Which meant there was no way to do this without signaling their intentions. If you were trying to get shot, doors, stairs, and corners were the way to go. He was about to expose them to all three.

Derrick made eye contact with Rebekah and nodded. She nodded in return. She aimed her weapon at the door. He decided fast was best. He twisted the handle, throwing his back to the wall and pulling the door along with him.

Shots rang out from inside. Rebekah fired once. A robot tumbled out. He doubted only one robot would guard the door. Human security would likely be more difficult to defeat because they could adapt to new situations. Robots seemed to be just—robots, and not the least bit creative.

If there were people inside, they would likely flatten against the inside wall. Robots might do that as well, especially if a human was running the operation from a control center. Prime might be running the operation making similar decisions. The fact the robots were sent to an empty building to draw the attack indicated either a security chief or Prime was in control.

So, probably robots or people lie in wait. No way to turn the corner without being shot at first. Big problem. The first robot was a decoy. A sacrificial pawn. Derrick motioned Rebekah to stay put. He flipped his face shield down and opened the PFP controls. He released the door, which moved slowly against the pneumatic closer, as he repositioned himself into the PFP.

He did not know if the bullets of the mounted gun would penetrate the concrete blocks, but it was worth a try. He lifted a few feet off the ground and then had an idea. He flew over the top of the little building that covered the stairwell. It had a flat roof that he assumed was wood construction, covered by roofing material. Bullets would penetrate that. He set the gun to fire three-shot bursts. He had already used a lot of rounds killing robots.

Derrick fired into each corner and on each side of the door. Then he landed, exited the PFP, and joined Rebekah. "I think we should use an explosive device."

"What it if blows the building apart? We could get hit with shrapnel or the whole thing could collapse and block the stairs."

Derrick thought for a moment. "Good points. I don't think the building will collapse. It looks solid." He paused and then added, "Could you see the stairs?"

"Yes."

"Toss an explosive at the stairs. I think the blast will be powerful enough even if it tumbles down to the first landing. In fact, that might be best in case there are more robots on the stairs."

"You think it's all robots? No people?"

"I'm not sure, but I think robots. The people have been pulled out or told to leave."

Rebekah said, "Right. I've been thinking about that. Not a lot. Mostly, I've been thinking about staying alive. But thinking about it a little. Why is Prime moving people out of the headquarters? Because Prime knows they are under attack?"

Deconstruction
A Derrick King Novel, Book 8

Derrick had not thought about it, which caused him some concern, because it was a valid question. The answer might give them insight into how to proceed, and more importantly, Prime's next move. "I've not given it any thought, but it's a good question. What do you think?"

Rebekah smiled. Not the lopsided smile but something from a different part of her personality. He realized it was one he had not seen before yet instantly understood. "Thanks for asking. I'm not used to being asked for my input."

Before Derrick considered his response, he said, "I think everyone here has been given equal opportunities." He paused. "Mostly."

Rebekah lost the smile. "Perhaps it feels that way to you. It certainly wasn't that way in Pacific Edge. I've only been gone from there a few days and most of those I've been busy trying to stay alive. Still, it's different outside the walls."

Derrick stared at her for a moment. "You're right. I'll do my best to make it up to you." He had no idea how he might do that. Not and stay on good terms with Nyx. Some things can't be fixed, forgotten, or forgiven.

"Not the time or place. Besides, you always treated me okay."

"You deserve better than okay."

Rebekah smiled that lopsided smile. "Shall we go? We have a Prime to kill." She held out her hand.

Derrick wondered what she wanted and then remembered. He handed her an explosive device. "Yes. Four more." He didn't say, 'four more to kill.'

Rebekah positioned herself at the side of the door, pulled her arm back, ready to throw the bomb. She nodded. "Ready."

Derrick opened the door a few inches, just enough for Rebekah to toss in the device. He assumed she could throw accurately. She played sports at James Carver Academy.

He let go of the door and motioned Rebekah away from the building. He retreated in the opposite direction, but before the door closed, he heard the device hit the floor and then roll down the stairs, making a metallic clank on each step before the door closed. He lowered his shield and saw the time to detonation counting down. He turned his back to the building and hoped Rebekah did the same.

When zero appeared on his face shield, he felt a vibration under his feet, followed by a loud whomp, and then debris and smoke flew out through the holes punched in the roof. The door blew off its hinges, and it slid across the roof and off the building. Had either of them been in its path, they would have plummeted to the ground with it.

The haze cleared. Derrick pulled his electronic weapon. He set the power to the middle, which was the highest setting that might not kill a human. However, the setting might not terminate a robot, but it would disrupt its functioning, giving Derrick a split second to dial the weapon to full power.

Rebekah was right behind him, her hand on his shoulder. Visibility still wasn't great when they breached the door's threshold. However, glancing at each corner, he saw robots smoldering, creating almost as much smoke as the bomb and certainly more noxious fumes, causing them to cough.

Derrick said, "Let's get out of this smoke, but be careful."

Rebekah muffled a cough. "No argument here."

The blast largely destroyed the first landing, leaving little surface on which to find purchase for their feet. Derrick studied it for a moment. A small ledge remained next to the wall. "What do you think? Try to stay on that ledge or jump and land on the stairs?"

"Are you only going to ask my opinion when a wrong answer gets one of us killed?" she asked.

"Probably," Derrick said.

She had that smile he liked. "Well, at least you're asking me. That's a start. I think both of us can make the jump. That seems like the best thing to do."

Derrick nodded. "I'll go first. I'll catch you if necessary."

"I was thinking I should catch *you*," Rebekah said.

Derrick jumped before Rebekah could beat him to it. He landed on the third step and grabbed the railing attached to the wall. He stepped down two steps, assuming Rebekah would jump at least as far as he did. If she had too much momentum to stop, he could catch her.

Rebekah jumped, landing on the fourth step. Whether to prove she could jump farther or not, he did not know, but she continued toward him, falling. He caught her in his arms. It was not an unnatural feeling because he had held her many times during the Choosing, knowing he wouldn't pick her, but he always felt better holding Rebekah than he did holding Jana Somersworth, the girl he planned to choose for marriage.

Rebekah separated herself from him after a moment. "Feels like old times. It was the only thing I enjoyed in Pacific Edge. Even though I knew you were going to pick Jana."

"I was a fool…"

The stairs collapsed from under them before Derrick could finish his sentence.

34

IN THE PARKING LOT, HALFWAY TO the third building Miriam crouched, hiding behind a light pole's concrete base. The lights were staggered across the campus of the former law enforcement agency that now housed perhaps the vilest criminal that ever existed. Anna and Red took a position behind a light pole to Miriam's right. Prime had subverted buildings meant for justice to a place that manufactured a soulless robotic army. And created test subjects, which were people that Prime considered as property. Turning good to evil was what Prime did best.

Miriam scanned the sky and looked back at the building where they thought Prime was originally. The remnants of the robots smoldered, but she did not see Derrick. Perhaps he and Rebekah were working their way through the building trying to find her. She hoped that was the case, because that building was empty. Derrick and Rebekah would be safe there.

A bright flash on top of the third building caught Miriam's attention. Within seconds the roar of the explosion reached her ears. A few moments later, she saw Derrick rise above the building using the PFP. He fired bursts straight down into the building, but she could not see what he was shooting at. Then he flew back down and out of sight. A few seconds later, another explosion came from that same roof. Smoke and debris flew into the air.

Miriam ran to Anna and Red. "Did you see that?"

Anna said, "I couldn't see from here. Just the flash, then an explosion, followed by a second explosion. What happened?"

"The first flash was horizontal to the roof, and the sound was muffled. I saw Derrick in the PFP, firing down into the building and then a second explosion, more muffled than the first but debris and smoke flew into the air."

"He and Rebekah are attacking Prime," Anna said.

"Do you think Rebekah is with him?" Miriam asked. "She would have no way to get there, and Derrick wouldn't put her at risk."

"Rebekah wouldn't let him go alone."

"But she doesn't have a PFP."

"True."

Miriam thought for a moment. "You are right. She'd want to go, but Derrick would say no."

"Have you ever told Rebekah she couldn't do something?"

Miriam paused for a moment. "I have."

"And how did that go?"

Miriam said, "Damn it! That means Rebekah is with Derrick."

"Then we'd better get there too."

Red said, "How do we do that without being killed?"

Anna said, "Carefully."

Miriam nodded. "Lead the way."

Anna ran in a crouched position to the next light pole and then motioned for them to follow. They continued in this fashion until they all reached a concrete barrier. From there, they could see the front of the building they believed to be Prime's Headquarters.

Miriam peeked over the barrier and then sat. "Well, that pretty much confirms that Prime is inside, doesn't it?"

Anna said, "Agreed."

Red said, "I think Prime knows it's under attack."

"You think? What makes you think that?" Miriam asked, her voice dripping with sarcasm.

Red shrugged. "All those robots are a good indication, but I think the tanks and rocket launchers confirm it."

35

THE FALLING STAIRS HIT THE next level, stopping abruptly, causing Derrick to lose his balance for a moment. Dust filled the air, making it hard to see and difficult to breathe. Rebekah landed beside him, also off balance, and teetering toward the edge. Derrick grabbed her, pulling her to his chest, and then throwing himself against the wall. They remained there for a moment until he felt certain the structure would not fall again.

Rebekah stared into Derrick's eyes, inches from his face. "That was unexpected."

Derrick released her, but she didn't move for a moment. He said, "We may have blown our stealthy entrance."

"Possibly," she said, adding, "What's the plan now?"

"Is going home an option?"

She separated from him. "Look at you. Making jokes. I have no place to call home," Rebekah said.

"You will. Someplace in Potterville, that is if you want."

She looked at him for a moment. "It's a nice thought, but I doubt that's an option."

He hadn't thought about it, but Rebekah had actual parents, unlike Miriam, Anna, and himself. However, Rebekah's parents raised Anna like their own daughter. He and Miriam had no family. His condo in Potterville was as close as he had ever come to having a home, and he no longer had that.

"Maybe your parents could move to Potterville when this is over. But if you want to go back to Pacific Edge, it would be okay. I mean, we'd miss you and Anna, but Pacific Edge won't be the same. It won't be isolated like it was."

"By isolated, you mean locked down. Like a prison?"

Derrick said, "That's the reality of it."

"Don't get me wrong, I love my parents and Anna. But I don't want to go back to Pacific Edge. I know it will change, but maybe not for the better."

Derrick brushed dust from his clothing. "How do you mean?"

"I've been thinking about it. They worked for Prime. Not directly, I don't think, but I don't know what they did." She paused. "Anyway, what happens to them when Prime is gone? I don't think the Chosen are going to be popular with those who suffered under Prime's rule. The people who suffered are in far greater numbers than the few who did not."

This surprised Derrick a little. He had been thinking about many things: some realistic, others, not so much. But he had not considered that others were doing the same thing. In this case, Rebekah was worried about something quite realistic and yet not something a teenage girl should worry about. A teenage girl should be concerned about things like whether to cut her hair, being asked to the school dance, and if she went to the dance, what would she wear. Not the downfall of society and how it will affect her parents.

"You could come to Potterville. You'd have friends there already."

"It sounds tempting, but I have no home or money. Even if I could get a part-time job, it wouldn't be enough to live on."

"Coach Browning offered to let me live with him. Someone will step up to help you and Anna. It's that kind of town. I'll do whatever I can to help."

"Thanks, Derrick. You're a good guy. Don't forget that. But shouldn't we try to sneak up on Prime now?" She smiled and winked at him.

"Nah, I think we just go kick the door down."

"Now you're talking. That's the way we roll."

Taking each step with caution, attempting to sense any instability in the structure, Derrick led Rebekah downward, weapons raised. They encountered no robots. They encountered no humans.

When they reached the bottom, a closed metal door, set in a metal frame, stood to the right. To the left was a short hall, which led to the main floor. Derrick went left and eased into the foyer, which was dimly lit by exit signs. The space was empty. No counters, desks, or furnishings. This building seemed to hold no purpose other than to house Prime. Outside the front doors, Derrick saw another large group of robots, their attention focused away from the building. Not just robots, but armored vehicles, rocket launchers, machine guns, and two tanks. Derrick didn't think the robots could fit into the tanks, which meant there were people as well. If people operated the vehicles, it would be the first humans they'd encountered other than the dying assistant and the slaughtered people in New York, the assistant from Chicago, who they captured and released, and the lab worker here.

Rebekah peeked over his shoulder. "That does not look good."

"No, it does not."

Rebekah tugged on his arm, pulling him back to where the robots couldn't see them. "The others can't get in here. Unless Nyx and Antonio can help. They can't take on those tanks and neither can we."

"I still have a few explosives," Derrick said.

"I don't know for sure, but I doubt our explosives can destroy the tanks, unless we could drop one inside, and I don't think the robots will let us do that."

Derrick said, "If the hatch is open, I could drop them from the PFP."

Deconstruction
A Derrick King Novel, Book 8

"You probably could, but the robots would shoot you before you could get away."

"I might get away if I'm fast enough."

"You might not, and I don't want to do this alone. Besides, they aren't the target. Prime is. As long as we destroy Prime, they can sit out there until the cows come home."

Derrick's brow furrowed. "Cows?"

"Just something my dad says. So, we assume that the door back there leads to the basement, and that's where we'll find Prime. Right?"

Derrick said, "That's my guess. We also assume that Prime was going to escape using the aircraft, which means Prime would take the elevator. Maybe we should just go back to the roof and wait."

"I think you're right about Prime's escape plan. However, Prime might know that we destroyed the aircraft, so he might escape in an armored vehicle."

Derrick said, "You're probably right. Prime didn't expect us to survive the trap he set in the other building."

"Agreed. At least we're making Prime nervous."

"Perhaps. That worries me. I don't think a scared Prime is a good thing," Derrick said.

"Another thing. There's a good chance the elevator no longer works. That leaves Prime one option." Rebekah indicated the small army out front.

"I'm open to suggestions."

Rebekah smiled. "I love it when you want to hear my opinion."

"Right. I'm sorry."

"Let's not start that again."

"Start what again…"

Rebekah held her finger to his lips. "I think we should change things up. There must be a back door to this place."

"Probably. You think Prime would not expect us to enter there?"

"I don't know. Maybe."

Derrick said, "I wish we had a floor plan for this building."

Rebekah was looking past him now. She pointed at the wall behind him. "You mean like that one?"

Derrick turned. On the wall hung a fire-escape map for each floor. "Isn't that convenient?"

Rebekah stepped past him, staring at the map. She traced a corridor with her finger. "Here. This is the basement. The back door goes down a short corridor and then the stairs go to the basement. Then, there are several large rooms. It seems unlikely Prime would be in the first one. He'd be here or there." She pointed to two interior rooms.

"The floor plan might have been changed; however, I agree, but how do we get there?"

Rebekah said, "Good question." She motioned toward the front of the building. "Not that way."

Derrick paused. "We could use the PFP to get to the back of the building undetected."

Rebekah said, "The PFP is on the roof and the stairs collapsed."

"Sentry 5 sent the PFP to me. It can come to us. I think."

"What about cameras?"

"We should zap them or break them," Derrick said.

"But Prime will know we disabled them."

Derrick said, "True, but with the cameras gone Prime won't see exactly what we are doing."

"Then we are wasting time standing here." And with that, Rebekah turned and left him. She dashed up the stairs, taking two at a time. Derrick sprinted up after her. Her strides were quick and agile. He never thought of her as an athlete. Because he never thought about anything other than himself. He was trying to change, but it wasn't easy.

When they reached the fallen staircase, neither was breathing hard. It was only a couple of flights up. The last few feet were a bit more difficult because of the rubble from the fallen stairs.

Derrick lowered his face shield for a moment and then raised it. "It's not there."

"What do you mean, it's not there?"

"The PFP. It doesn't show up on my face shield."

"Maybe it's out of power. Or turned off."

"Maybe. But there was no low power warning. Nothing. I don't know how it's powered or how long it should last."

Rebekah thought for a moment. "Yeah. All that flying stuff is weird, isn't it? I mean, it doesn't make sense what makes it work."

"I agree, but how it works hasn't seemed important given our situation."

She thought for a moment. "Maybe it's the building. Perhaps it blocks the signal."

Derrick frowned a little. The PFP found him from miles away, so he doubted the building was the problem, but disagreeing served no purpose; plus, he didn't know anything about how it worked. If Miriam would have said it was the building, he would have argued. He had always disagreed with Miriam. Arguing was automatic with her. One more aspect of himself that he didn't like. He must be the only teenager in the world struggling with trying to change himself.

"Well?"

"Well, what?" Derrick asked.

Rebekah raised her hands in mild frustration. "Any thoughts? Ideas?"

"I was thinking about how much I need to change the way I think."

"Seriously? We have more pressing problems."

"You wouldn't understand. But you are right."

"You're wrong. I understand."

"You do?"

"Derrick, we're all doing that sort of thinking. It's part of growing up."

"It is?"

"Can we talk about what we do next?"

Derrick felt a bit of relief and shrugged. "I'm open to suggestions."

"Just because I like to hear you say that doesn't mean I want to make all the decisions."

Derrick said, "I don't know what to do."

Looking up, Rebekah turned a slow circle. She pointed up. "The handrail attached to the wall looks okay. If one of us could reach it, then by going hand over hand, we could get to the top and get the PFP."

Derrick studied it. "It's too high to jump. If I give you a boost, you could reach it." He was about to ask if she could do the hand over hand up the rail but decided against it. That would sound like an insult and underestimating Rebekah would be a mistake.

"But I can't fly the PFP."

"I could give you the helmet."

"I still don't know how to operate it and what if it's programmed to only recognize you?"

"Good points."

"I could raise you up," Rebekah said.

"I know you're strong, but I would have to stand on your hands like this." He raised his arms straight over his head.

Rebekah looked from Derrick to the opening that plummeted to the ground floor. "I probably couldn't do that. And dropping you might prove fatal."

"Fatal would not be good."

"Look at us, agreeing on all kinds of stuff." Rebekah thought for a moment. "Maybe I could push the PFP near the stairwell and then you could connect with it."

Derrick nodded. "That's a good idea."

"Do you think you can lift me like that?"

Derrick said, "Pretty sure. Just not sure the best way to do it."

"Point." She thought for a moment. "Put your hands like this." She put her palms up, thumbs out at waist height and laced her fingers together. "I'll put one foot in your hands and then step onto your shoulders. Place your back to the wall, so I'll be facing the right direction. I can use the wall to steady myself. Then raise your arms, and I will step on to your hands. Questions?"

Deconstruction
A Derrick King Novel, Book 8

Derrick moved closer to the wall and positioned his hands as Rebekah had demonstrated. He gave a nervous glance at the opening with no barrier to prevent her fall to the bottom floor if she slipped. She gave him a slight nod, stepped into his hands, and climbed onto his shoulders. Softer shoes would have been nice, but Rebekah wasn't heavy, so rather than being painful, it was mildly uncomfortable. He brought his hands up, outside his shoulders and about a foot above them, so they were roughly a ninety-degree angle. She stepped on one hand and then the other. His arms shook just a little as he straightened them.

Suddenly, the weight was gone. Derrick looked up and stepped toward the opening, hoping he could catch her should she fall. Rebekah dangled from the handrail facing the wall. She inched upward, moving one hand and then the other. She paused, then turned, facing forward, so she could go hand over hand, which seemed right but wasn't. The rail was only four inches from the wall. Turning straight forced her shoulder against the wall. She lost her grip with one hand, dangled there a moment, holding on with the other hand, and then fell, landing awkwardly and lurching toward the open cavity.

Rebekah teetered on the edge, windmilling her arms, attempting to regain her balance. Derrick hesitated, afraid if he tried to grab her and hit her arm, he might send her to her death rather than save her. He dodged back to the wall and then came straight at her, grabbing her as she fell.

He pulled back and they both collapsed against the wall; Rebekah held him tightly for a moment, with her head buried on his shoulder. When she pushed away, she said, "Let's try that again."

"The handrail part or the falling part?" Derrick asked.

"That was a dumb move. I just need to stay facing the wall."

Derrick got into position.

Rebekah said, "Move up a couple of steps. It puts me a little closer to the top."

This time, she was up and gone much quicker. Derrick looked up and saw Rebekah was already moving upward. He stayed under her as far as the fallen staircase allowed. She moved quicker than he imagined, strong and graceful. She developed a swinging motion, timed with her hand movements. Soon she was at the top.

But the railing ended a yard from the opening because of the way the stairs had broken free. She was some distance from the remaining section of floor, and she was even farther from him. He could not reach her should she fall.

"I can't reach it," Rebekah said.

"I see that. I can't catch you either. You have to come back down."

"Screw that. It was too much work getting here."

"Just come back down. We'll figure something out."

Rebekah didn't answer him. She started swinging back and forth, working her arms and legs. With a grunt, she made one last thrust toward the landing and let go. One foot landed on the platform, and she tucked and rolled. She had made it.

They were in business.

Until they weren't.

36

THE PFP HOVERED WHERE DERRICK LEFT IT, evidently still operational, but Rebekah couldn't budge it. Apparently, one needed the helmet to make it move.

Rebekah raced back to the stairwell. "I can't move it. But it's not out of power. I don't think. It's still hovering where you parked it."

"You probably need the helmet. I'll toss it to you." Derrick removed the helmet, swung it a few times, and then lobbed it up.

Rebekah caught it and then dashed to the PFP. She positioned herself as Derrick had and then put the helmet on and closed the face shield. A warning message scrolled across the face shield in red letters: UNKNOWN PILOT, DISABLING IN TEN SECONDS!

Rebekah cursed, jerked the helmet off and hurried back to Derrick. "No good. The PFP doesn't recognize me as the pilot. It might be disabled now."

Derrick leaned against the wall.

"Should I come back down?" Rebekah asked.

Derrick shook his head. She couldn't help him get to the PFP. The elevator was the only other way up, and it would announce their movements floor by floor, if it was still operational. The explosion may have broken it.

The elevator.

Derrick looked up. Rebekah was looking down at him, leaning forward, her hands on her knees. He said, "I'm going to check the elevator. I might be able to climb up the cables."

Rebekah frowned. "Okay. But be careful." She paused. "I'll kick your butt if you kill yourself and leave me stranded up here."

Derrick smiled. Their situation was dismal, but Rebekah was still cracking jokes. If only he had her courage. Instead, he felt certain this one was not going to end well. They had been lucky so far. Their luck was bound to end.

Derrick exited the stairwell. The stairs and the elevators were in the same section of the building, but he had to go down a floor to find an elevator door. It was closed. Perhaps the elevator was still working. Touching the button might at least open the door, but that would signal Prime of his location. Providing Prime with his exact location was something he wanted to avoid.

Deconstruction
A Derrick King Novel, Book 8

He worked his fingers into the sliding doors of the elevator, gradually separating them enough to get his hands inside. Then, bracing himself as best he could, he pushed the doors open. The doors resisted but opened easier than he expected. The shaft descended into darkness. As his eyes adjusted, he could see what looked like the top of the elevator about 40 feet down. Too far to jump, but not too far to fall. In the center of the shaft were steel cables. Two sets of four spaced about three feet apart. He could jump to them easy enough, but they looked oily, and he could see strands of frayed wires. His hands would be injured before he could get to the top. If he could get to the top.

Climbing the cables wouldn't work. Moving to the door, he held on and peeked inside the shaft. Attached to the wall near the door was a ladder. Not exactly a ladder, but steel bars embedded into the concrete. They extended to the top and looked as if they'd never been used as they were covered with dirt and oil. They might be slick, but he'd have hand and toe holds. Opening the door at the top would be difficult, but he'd deal with that when he got there.

Derrick stretched for the ladder rung with one hand and one foot, but he could not reach it. He took a deep breath. He'd have to release his hold on the doorway and jump to reach the rung. If he missed, he might be able to catch a rung as he fell. Or he might fall 40 feet to the bottom.

The leap wasn't far, and he caught the rung with his hand but missed with his foot. He smacked into the rungs, all but knocking the wind out of him, but he got a foothold, and with his other hand, found a rung. He hesitated there a moment to catch his breath before climbing.

The steel rungs were even filthier than they looked. His hands were soon greasy, which would make holding a weapon difficult. In Pacific Edge he had microscopic nanobots that scrubbed his skin, leaving his complexion glowing with perfection. He'd been dirty here but never like this. He would love a good nanobot scrubbing when this was over but would settle for a hot shower.

When Derrick reached the top, he realized opening the door would be a bigger problem than he anticipated. Fortunately, there were rungs in the concrete between him and the door. Apparently, it was designed for repairmen to access the ladder at the top and perhaps the bottom as well. He moved to the rungs next to the door and then inched one foot out onto the narrow ledge in the doorway, while holding tightly with one hand on the steel rung. He slid his palm along the elevator door, his face pressed into the metal, until his fingertips reached where the doors met. He then worked his fingers into the opening. He pulled and felt the door give just a little. Suddenly, his fingers slipped from the door. His foot slid off the ledge, and he nearly lost his grip on the rung. He hung over the elevator shaft, fighting to maintain his one-handed grip.

Suddenly, he heard a grunt, and a hand grabbed his wrist and hauled him back to the wall. Turning his head, he saw the door had opened more than he'd realized. Then he understood why. Rebekah had pried it open, saw him flailing and grabbed his arm.

"You want to join me, or are you having too much fun in there?" Rebekah grabbed his arm with both hands, leveraging her feet against the door and pulled as he worked his way to the opening.

They both collapsed to the floor. "Thanks. That was close," Derrick said.

"I noticed." Rebekah looked at her hands. "Gross. What have you been doing in there?"

Derrick studied his hands. "I don't think the ladder has ever been used. This is decades of oil and grime." He started to wipe his hands on his pants.

"Don't do that. It stinks. We smell bad enough already. There's a janitor closet just there." She pointed.

The explosion had damaged the janitor closet's door, which hung partially open, held by the bottom hinge. Derrick used his elbow and pushed the door to one side. Enough light spilled into the room for him to see a box of red rags. He grabbed a handful and handed a couple to Rebekah.

After several seconds of wiping, he said, "Maybe Prime has a sink we can use."

"I'll bet he does." Rebekah studied her hands and wiped more. "But let's put Prime out of commission first."

"That's the plan." But even as the words left his mouth, Derrick knew he wasn't being completely honest. It was important that he talk to Prime. It might be his only chance to be with Prime alone for a few moments. It was vital that they learn more about Prime, not the least of which was the location of the central headquarters. Without Prime's last location, all this was worthless. Which meant L. Linda's death was meaningless.

Yes. Derrick was still thinking about L. Linda.

That would not change anytime soon.

37

ANNA, MIRIAM, AND RED SAT WITH THEIR backs against a concrete wall that once displayed a sign naming the former occupant of the building that was now a Prime Headquarters. The air felt damp and cool. Miriam shivered. It had been silent for fifteen minutes. Miriam could sense the time, like she could determine distance. Why she could do that was unknown. When she was younger, she assumed everyone's mind worked the same as hers. She learned how different she was in school, although she had bruised a few egos before that recognition occurred.

The past 15 minutes felt much longer than normal. Sitting in silence didn't help. "We should move," Miriam whispered, adding, "I don't think they saw us, or they would have shot at us by now."

Anna whispered, "I agree. Let's go where we can talk and decide what to do next."

Red nodded. "Where are we going?"

"Let's go back to the first building. It appeared to be clear other than the one woman in the lab," Miriam whispered.

"There could be others. We didn't clear the entire building," Anna replied.

Miriam got on her feet but remained in a low crouch. "We'll clear it now. Stay low and follow me."

Miriam ran a zig-zag pattern from one light pole to the next toward the building where they originally landed, keeping as low as possible. She didn't check to see if Anna and Red followed. She trusted they were there. The important thing was she heard no weapons firing.

Approaching the front of the building, Miriam pulled her weapon, using her thumb to slide the power up, not all the way. It might prove fatal, but she would risk killing Prime's people rather than allowing them to kill her friends. Derrick might not have approved, but he didn't need to know.

The front doors were broken out courtesy of their first visit. Miriam pulled the door open, ready to dive inside, but Anna ran by her, sliding on the floor as soon as she cleared the doorway. Red was right behind Anna, fast and agile for his size. Miriam scanned the room. It was silent. In the next room, the mound of lifeless robots still smoldered near the vault. The room stank of rancid, melting plastic despite the ventilation system pulling the smoke from the room through vents near the ceiling.

Miriam said, "Good job. Both of you."

"Do you have a plan?" Anna asked.

Miriam shrugged. "First, let's go back to the other area, out of this smoke. Then, maybe we could circle around back of Prime's building."

Anna said, "I don't see how. We would cross their line of sight to get to the back of that building, and there's a lake behind it. I didn't study it, but I remember it from the images we saw flying in." She paused. "We would have to swing way out into that parking lot and then work our way back."

Miriam said, "That's an option, but I'm not sure. What if Derrick and Rebekah come back? This is where we landed, so this is where they would come."

Anna said, "We could radio them."

"True, but Prime must be monitoring the radio frequencies. We've already lost the element of surprise, but I don't think telling Prime exactly what we are doing and where we are is a good idea," Miriam said.

Red said, "Makes sense." Just then, a door latch sounded. Red spun around and fired his shotgun—it wasn't a shotgun, but that's what it reminded him of because of the large bore and folding stock like those used by SWAT teams he'd seen on TV. It sounded with a dull whomp instead of a loud bang. A robot stood with a large hole in the center of its chest, holding the door open. It didn't fall, nor did it move.

"Wow. Nice shot," Anna said.

Red said, "We should clear the building. It doesn't appear to be empty after all."

Methodically, they worked their way through the building, finding three active robots and zero people. It didn't take them long. Maybe 15 minutes. When they felt confident the building was empty, Anna said, "What now?"

Miriam said, "I'm going to try to get on a computer and see if I can learn anything."

Anna said, "Is anyone else worried about Antonio and Nyx? They've been gone a long time, and we could really use their help."

Miriam said, "I'm extremely worried. We're in big trouble without an aircraft."

Anna stared at her for a moment. "You're not wrong, but what about Nyx and Antonio? I'm more worried about them than about the aircraft."

Miriam said, "I'm worried about them as well. It's been too long, but I can't think of a way to help them."

"Maybe we should radio Nyx," Red said. "I know radio silence is best, but it might be worth the risk."

Miriam thought for a moment. "Let's give them another 15 minutes. I'm still against giving Prime information."

"How does that give Prime information? Prime must know what's going on with the aircraft," Red said.

"It's possible he could locate us based on the origin of the radio signals. If Nyx and Antonio have eluded the aircraft and are hiding, it could give up their position as well."

Red said, "Okay. Fifteen minutes, but even then, maybe it's not a good idea."

Miriam said, "Maybe you should go to the roof. Stay out of sight. If the aircraft or Derrick and Rebekah return, that's where they will go."

Red nodded. "If I learn anything, I'll find you rather than use the radio."

Miriam nodded. "Smart."

Anna said, "What do you want me to do?"

Miriam said, "Watch my back."

Miriam knew where the Test Subject DNA Sequencing laboratory was located, but the computers wouldn't work there because she had removed the hard drives from the server and didn't want to replace them. She found a laboratory labeled Test Subject Data Analysis.

The lab was dimly lit, with a spattering of reading lamps still burning on desks that filled the room. It was called a laboratory, but it looked like a newsroom filled with desks and computers and no cubicles or other partitions. Miriam went to a computer, turned over the keyboard and the mouse, and the mouse pad. Then she went to another one.

"What are you doing?" Anna asked.

At the third computer, Miriam held up a slip of paper she found under the mouse pad. "This looks promising."

"A password?" Anna asked.

"Yes, and username."

Anna said, "Akira said the first thing they teach you about computers is to never write down your username and password."

The keys clicked as Miriam entered what was on the paper. The monitor changed. "Fortunately, people have poor memories and ignore rules."

Anna grew restless as Miriam scanned screen after screen of information. She didn't like doing nothing; she'd rather be in the fight than here, but here they were. It was impossible to read as quickly as Miriam moved from one screen to the next, but Anna knew Miriam was probably absorbing every word. She didn't know how Miriam's mind worked. No one did.

While Miriam busied herself at the computer, Anna investigated personal things on desks—pictures of family and friends, of vacations and holidays. Those who worked here apparently left in haste, or perhaps these keepsakes were not allowed where they were taken. She felt a hint of sadness knowing that these people were relocated, but their friends and family were likely left behind. Prime was not a family-oriented operation. She wondered if the families even knew what happened to their loved ones. Probably not.

Until just a few days ago, people thought Prime was a myth. The families of Prime employees were likely unaware that their spouses, friends, and parents worked for Prime. Now the word that Prime existed was spreading. And with it, predictions and prophecies, which Anna didn't believe. However, she hoped to learn more about the test subject program, specifically about herself.

It did not take Miriam long to find records regarding the program in Pacific Edge. Their Keepers had once worked in this building. They oversaw the development of Test Subjects Six and Seven. The original room where they were tested and watched wasn't in Pacific Edge. It was here. This is where they were known as Test Subject numbers, three, six, and seven. It wasn't until Lawrence King convinced Prime to let him continue the program in a near normal environment that they were all moved to Pacific Edge. It was the most normal of all the Chosen Communities.

Having examined all the desks, Anna wandered out of the room and then back in. She sauntered over and peered over Miriam's shoulder. "Learning anything?"

Miriam shut the computer off. "Yes. And it wasn't good." She pulled off the side of the computer and removed the hard drive.

Anna straightened her back, crossed her arms. "Did you learn anything about me?"

"Yes."

"Damn it, Miriam. Why do I have to pry everything out of you?"

"Sorry. It's just a lot to take in." She paused, holding the hard drive in one hand. "You're pretty normal. Developed for speed and strength. That explains how you beat us in most everything during our training."

"The part we did in Pacific Edge while hypnotized?"

"Yes."

"Why? Was there a reason or was I just an experiment?"

"You were meant to be a bodyguard of sorts." Miriam paused. "That's why they berated you, tormented you. They were trying to model your character to be willing to sacrifice yourself."

"For Prime?"

"Yes."

"They thought I would be brainwashed enough to do that?"

Miriam shrugged. "I suppose. That was the goal. They abandoned the idea early on. Even in the test program, we showed too much independence."

"We did?"

"Any independence was too much. Derrick and I messed it up."

"Did you learn anything about yourself?"

Miriam took a deep breath. "I did. In all my memories, I was told that my," she paused, "abilities were not planned. I was just smart. It was just who I was."

Anna waited for a moment. "And…"

"Not true. They enhanced and designed my DNA for intelligence. So much for natural abilities. So much for just being me."

Anna grabbed a chair, rolled it closer to Miriam, and sat. "I sense there's something troubling you more than the reason you're smart. Is it about Derrick?"

Miriam nodded and looked at the floor.

Anna put her hand on Miriam's knee. "I understand you want to protect him, but if it's something that could affect our mission, I need to know."

"You're right. It's just …just." Miriam looked up, tears welling in her eyes. "Derrick was made to become a human body Prime would inhabit."

Anna removed her hand from Miriam's knee and sat up straight. "Okay. That is a lot. So, that's why they tried to control Derrick. To ensure that Prime could control him…" She paused. "When they download Prime into Derrick, or whatever they call it, Prime wants complete control. Anyway, Derrick failed, which in this situation is the best outcome." Anna paused and then said, "So, we're good. Right?"

Miriam shook her head. "It's more than that. Derrick is a clone. They cloned him. They did some genetic enhancements as well. But he's a clone."

"I don't understand, a clone of what? Or who?"

Miriam stared straight ahead for a moment and then shifted her eyes, looking at Anna. "James Carver."

"What? So, …" Anna fell silent.

Miriam said, "Derrick is Prime's clone."

38

THE STARS SHONE BRIGHT IN THE TEXAS sky. No moon to brighten the night, or it had not yet risen. Derrick had never paid attention to the stars or the moon. He never ventured out much after dark. That wasn't accurate. He went out often for training, but that was under hypnosis, which was supposed to be forgotten. The motor skills remained, but he wasn't aware of them. He could find those memories now, but he had not paid attention to the sky during training. He focused on his instructor and the lesson taught.

He tried to avoid thinking about this. Because thinking about his life made him feel as if he would never have a normal existence. Never be able to catch up to his peers in understanding what normal life was like. He was terrified when the Tribunal exiled him, but his few weeks in Potterville had been a gift. He'd always have his time in Potterville. Prime could take his life, but Prime could not take his memories.

Of that much, he was certain.

Well, fairly certain.

Right now, he had more important things to think about, not least of which was keeping Rebekah safe.

And confronting Prime alone.

If he could learn the location of the central headquarters, they stood a chance of conquering the monster. That was a slim chance though because Prime was many, and Prime was singular.

Miriam often talked about the greater good. How they had saved Potterville, first from the failing reactor and then from the missile meant to start a war with Mexico. Reality was simpler than that, even though the greater good part was true. Foremost, this was about self-preservation. About staying alive. Prime would kill them if they didn't destroy Prime first. It was that simple.

Derrick backed into the PFP. It fastened him in. No error messages. "Maybe you should stay here."

Rebekah stepped closer and fastened her arms around his waist. "Fat chance."

Derrick could fly high; into the darkness where Prime's troops could not see them, but he didn't like the idea of taking Rebekah that far up. It was dangerous enough without being a thousand feet off the ground. Instead, he

Deconstruction
A Derrick King Novel, Book 8

would skirt the back of the complex. That route took them over a lake, which seemed safer if Rebekah were to slip and fall. She could swim to the shore. He'd go on without her. It would solve the problem of putting her in harm's way without an argument and ensure he had the chance to get information from Prime without interference. Neither of those things rang true, even though that's what he wanted.

"I'll fly behind the complex over the pond and then above the building. I'll go to the edge and locate the back door."

Rebekah said, "I'm worried about Antonio." She paused. "And Nyx. It seems like they've been gone a long time."

Not that Derrick had not been worried about Nyx. He felt as if his stomach were twisted into a permanent knot thinking about her. A reminder of the danger she was in was the last thing he needed. "I'm worried too. Worst thing is, there's nothing I can do about it and worrying won't help." It came out sounding angrier than he intended.

"You're right. Let's just get this over with. Then we can contact them."

Derrick didn't respond. Instead, he lifted off the roof. Slower than had he been alone in the PFP. His face shield allowed him to see everything clearly, although it looked strange. Rebekah's grip tightened around his waist. She was flying through the darkness with nothing more than her arms to prevent her from plummeting into the night. He didn't think he could have done what she was doing. Even leaving Pacific Edge the way she did showed more bravery than he could muster. He wasn't brave. He was forced from Pacific Edge and fought Prime out of sheer desperation. Rebekah was doing it by choice. Big difference.

The air grew noticeably cooler over the water. Derrick didn't know why. Miriam could explain it. He would ask if he could remember to but doubted it was important enough to stick in his mind. In addition to the cooler temps, a sweet fragrance filled his nostrils. Something blooming, but he didn't see what it was. The night vision wasn't in full color. Everything was shades of green and black. Eerie at first, but it was better than what Rebekah was experiencing.

They skimmed across the pond toward the back wall. Derrick spotted a camera and destroyed it with a single shot. Rebekah flinched when he fired. He didn't know if she could hear him, so he had not warned her. There was no door on this side, so he flew to the roof and then to the side opposite of where the troops were gathered. Spotting the door, he flew back to the roof, hovering just beyond the edge, and touching down so that Rebekah could feel something solid under her feet, even for just a moment.

He lifted his face shield so Rebekah could hear him. "Sorry about the shot startling you. I saw another camera just above the door. I think I should take out the lights too."

"Do it. I want to talk to Antonio. Let's get this over with."

Derrick didn't like the tone in her voice. It bordered on panic. There were plenty of things to panic about, but right now panicking about something they had no control over made little sense. They needed cool heads. "Ready?"

If she answered, he didn't hear her because as soon as they cleared the edge of the roof, he fired, first at the camera, then at the lights. He studied the door for movement. There was none. He scanned the area. Nothing was moving that he could see. That might change. They couldn't wait to see if it did.

Derrick flew off the roof and landed near the door. Rebekah stepped away and pulled her weapon. He checked the door. Locked. No surprise there. She motioned him to step back, which he did. Then she pulled one of the devices Miriam had used to cut hinges from the locked doors. Simple plan. She would cut the hinges off. The door would fall open. He'd shoot whatever was on the other side. No problem. Unless there were people there. Derrick dialed the stun gun back a notch.

Rebekah cut the top hinge, then the bottom. The door didn't move. She gave it a tap on the bottom with her foot. An upper corner on the hinge side moved an inch. So much for stealth and speed. She gave the door a solid kick in the same place, and it moved a few inches and then fell. A cloud of dust obscured his vision, but the night vision would detect heat signatures, and he saw none, so he fired several rounds into the building's dark cavity. When the dust cleared, he saw that he'd only put scorch marks on the wall because on the other side of the door was a stairwell. Anything waiting for them was at the bottom of those stairs.

Rebekah said, "Maybe you should keep the PFP on as we go inside."

Derrick thought for a moment. "It's powerful but not made for tight quarters. I'll take the zapper gun. It's more versatile." He didn't add, *I don't want to kill people*, but he assumed Rebekah already knew that.

Rebekah said, "What's the plan?"

Derrick stepped out of the PFP but kept the helmet on. "I'll go first because of my night vision." He tapped his face shield. "You follow. But take cover until I tell you to move forward."

"I don't need you playing hero to protect me."

The edge in her voice was unmistakable. "I'm not trying to be a hero. We can't risk us both getting killed. One of us has to stop Prime." He meant kill Prime, but he couldn't say it.

Rebekah said, "Point well taken. Don't worry. I'll kill the bastard."

Derrick smiled, although there was nothing humorous about the situation or what Rebekah said. "Noted."

With that, Derrick eased into the doorway with his weapon set slightly higher than the stun setting, hoping it would not kill a person but would disable a robot. He had not tested this theory but hoped it would work; sometimes hope is what you must go with. Hoping is what you do in desperate times. Not hoping for things you want, but that things work out for the best. Hope is what you have when there's nothing else.

The stairs went deep. Farther than one might expect for a typical basement, but it appeared there was only one level. Halfway down, the walls changed from smooth to rough. Although he knew nothing about construction, he thought the rough part was not the original structure. He didn't know if that was true. Just an impression. A feeling.

At the bottom of the stairs, stood another steel door. He tried the handle. It moved, but he didn't pull the door open. He needed Rebekah here before they announced their presence. There in the damp darkness with the dank smell of concrete, he realized he was about to put the girl he could have chosen as a mate in mortal danger. His life had come to that.

Had L. Linda Maxton lived in Pacific Edge; she would not have been on his list for the Choosing. While he really didn't know L. Linda well, he sensed she would not have conformed to any such list, even in Pacific Edge. She and Miriam would have likely been the best of friends in that regard. He had sent L. Linda to her death, which was a thought he had tried to suppress with little success. Still, he had not allowed himself to linger on it. At some point, he would have to focus on her death, and he wasn't sure he could cope with it.

He would not let that happen to Rebekah. Or Miriam. Or Anna. Or Nyx.

Damn it. He did not need to be consumed by worrying about Nyx.

Suddenly, a hand landed gently on his shoulder. "Are you okay?" Rebekah whispered.

"Just thinking about our next move," Derrick lied. "I don't think the door is locked, but that doesn't mean it will open."

"I'm confused."

"The handle turns, so it's not locked."

Rebekah said, "Makes sense. There's no dead bolt. So, it should open."

"They might have some other lock. Like a bar," Derrick said.

"That would be a problem. You have any of those explosives left?"

"Two. I hope we don't have to use them for the door."

"It would announce our arrival."

"True. I'm pretty sure they will have weapons aimed at this door. They'll fire as soon as the door moves."

Rebekah said, "Why are you so sure?"

"Just a feeling."

"Great. Wait here." Rebekah headed back up the stairs and returned a few minutes later carrying an extension cord and duct tape.

"What's that about?"

"We passed a tool cache. It gave me an idea."

Rebekah went to the door, turned the handle, and then used duct-tape to keep it in place. Then she threaded the extension cord around the handle and made a knot. She backed up holding the loose end of the cord until she was behind the concrete pillar. "Move up the stairs until you're out of the line of fire. If they are waiting for us, toss in an explosive, and I'll let the door close."

Derrick didn't like the idea of tossing a bomb where people might be, but he had to admit it was a good plan to keep them both alive, and he had to think in those terms. He had to protect Rebekah. She shouldn't even be here. She wasn't even a test subject.

"Derrick?"

"Yeah, just thinking."

"What this time?"

"About being able to hit the opening. Missing and having the bomb bounce back at us would be a bad thing," he lied.

Rebekah stared at him for a moment. "I trust you can hit an open door. I'll make sure you have a large target. Ready?"

He held the explosive and nodded. The door swung open, and a rain of bullets followed. He tossed the bomb, and the door swung closed. The gunfire continued and the door dimpled where the bullets struck. A few seconds later, the building shook with a whump. Smoke and dust blew through the cracks at the door's edges.

Derrick said, "Pull the door open, but stay put until I tell you it's safe." The words didn't sound right. There was no such thing as safety for them anywhere anytime soon.

Rebekah pulled the door open. Slower this time. He didn't know why she moved slower, but it felt right. Perhaps because it was careful and careful was the correct approach. He slid the electronic weapon to full power. He wasn't worried about finding a person. A human wouldn't have survived the blast. Besides, thinking about New York, he thought Prime would have already killed any humans in close proximity. That might be why Prime had not escaped in an armored vehicle, because he didn't have robots that could drive. Prime was likely waiting for another aircraft.

Plus, Prime had to ensure there were no hostile aircraft before attempting to escape in an aircraft himself. Since Prime was still here, that was a good indication that Nyx and Antonio were still flying.

His face shield compensated for the transition to darkness beyond the door. Had there been lights, they were destroyed by the blast. He turned on lights that shone from the sides of his helmet, revealing one robot, or what was left of it, against the wall about ten yards from the door. The blast marks indicated the bomb exploded within a few feet of the machine. Fortunately, there were no humans. The door opened into a wide hall that went left and right. The walls were concrete and appeared undamaged by the blast except for black streaks on the gray paint. Again, he got the feeling this part of the building was added much later. It did not match the floor plan they looked at earlier. Perhaps there was reconstruction done when it became a Prime Headquarters. He stood for a moment, considering the hallways. A strong premonition told him Prime was down the hallway to the right.

He hated deciding things on feelings. Especially when it came to putting Rebekah at risk. However, if he had followed his gut in Seattle, he would not have let L. Linda go into the garage alone. She'd still be alive.

Then he had an idea. Stepping back out, he raised his shield. "You stay here. I'll investigate further."

With that, he turned and reentered the hallway. A hand caught him by the shoulder. Rebekah's eyes blazed. "You know, you're more like Miriam than you realize, and not much better at judging people. We are doing this together. I don't want to point that out again. Got it?"

Derrick held up his hands. "Okay, okay."

Derrick thought for a moment. One last chance to make this work. Unfortunately, it was based on a premonition, so the risk was substantial. "I don't like saying this, but I think we should split. You go that way," he indicated the hall to the left, "and I'll go this way. Scout it out and then regroup here once we know what's what. However, if either of us—you know—run into robots," he paused, "or Prime, do what needs done."

Rebekah said nothing for a moment. "I don't like it."

"I don't either, but if we stay together, they could attack us from our blind side. And if…well if they got us both then…" He didn't finish the sentence.

Rebekah took a deep breath. "I still don't like it, but I agree. Just to find out what's down these halls, then we meet back here. Right?"

Derrick nodded.

39

TO DONNA'S AMAZEMENT, THEY WERE ALREADY outside of San Diego, cruising on an empty highway, heading back home. The local police had been true to their word. Few showed up, and those who did stayed out of the fray but didn't let anyone interfere or get close enough to take pictures. When it was over, the local police escorted them out of town.

It was surreal, to say the least.

It had been a long day, but she was too wound up for sleep. Apparently, killing Prime does that to a person. Jack told her they had destroyed the replicants. Allen took the hard drives. One less Prime meant one less the kids needed to deal with, and that was all that mattered to Donna.

Jack skirted Los Angeles but was on a different route than the one they had taken going to San Diego. He knew the roads but had gone quiet.

She didn't know why. Maybe it was something that happened in the building. Perhaps something else. She still didn't know him well, but she had learned that he had experienced some terrible things when he was young. It had affected him greatly, and he still bore the scars. He had never told anyone about what happened. He had carried it inside all these years.

If the kid survived, they would have seen and done worse. She would make sure they got the help and support they needed to prevent suffering like Jack. She couldn't counsel Jack. She didn't have that sort of education. But she could bake some damn fine pastries, and she'd make sure Jack tasted more of them than he had over the years. Pastries can heal people too. She was sure of that, or maybe it was just having people who cared enough to bake them. Maybe that was it. Two things she could do. Bake things for Jack and care about him.

A weathered sign on the edge of a small town read Victorville. Jack took his foot off the gas. "I need a break. Coffee and pie wouldn't hurt."

"It's late. I doubt anything will be open," Donna said.

Jack exited the highway. "I know a place. Truck stop. It's open 24 hours. At least it was the last time I was here."

"When was the last time you were here?"

"A few weeks ago."

Donna stared at him for a moment. "What were you doing out here? I didn't know you traveled much."

Deconstruction
A Derrick King Novel, Book 8

"I didn't collect all those cars just sitting at home. I drive when people are inside or asleep. I enjoy driving at night and it's important to drive the cars and not just let them sit. Sometimes, I'll spot a collectable and then I go back to see if I can find the owner."

"Isn't that dangerous?"

Jack turned into a truck stop. As predicted, the café was open. From the car, Donna could see a couple of booths with people. One booth had a solitary man, another a young couple. The windows were glazed with grease and time. Not up to her standards, but it was a truck stop, open 24/7 and probably understaffed. Window cleaning wasn't high on their priority list. She would remember to check her own windows when things got back to normal. If there was such a thing as normal, to return to.

Bill pulled in next to them.

Before opening her door, Donna said, "You didn't answer my question."

"Which question was that?"

"Isn't driving around at night dangerous?" Donna asked, and then added, "Coming all the way out here alone?"

"I guess it might be, but I haven't had any problems. I'm careful to avoid certain areas during the night. But overall, people are better than one might think."

Bill said, "Great idea, Jack. I needed a break, but how did you know this place was open?"

"I'll tell you inside."

Donna popped out. "This crazy old goat drives around out here at night looking for cars."

Jack said, "This crazy old goat is buying coffee and pie."

Allen said, "Works for me."

They took a booth far from the other patrons and sat silently until the waitress had brought their order. Finally, Donna said, "I feel like I'm dreaming. Did we just do what I think we did?"

"We sure did, but it does feel like a dream," Bill said, adding, "It all feels like a dream."

"More like a nightmare if you ask me," Allen said, adding, "I wonder if the kids and Coach Browning are okay."

Donna said, "Me too. And your family, Allen. It was incredibly brave of you to stay and go with us. I'll be glad when this is over."

Jack said, "If that's possible."

Everyone stared at him for a moment. Finally, Donna asked, "What do you mean by that?"

Jack took a bite of pie and then washed it down with coffee. "I mean assassins. There must be more. Will they ever stop trying to get revenge? I mean, even if the kids are successful, they might keep coming."

Deconstruction
A Derrick King Novel, Book 8

Donna stared at Jack for a moment. "Aren't you a ray of sunshine?"

40

THE HALLWAY WASN'T WHAT DERRICK HAD expected. Whereas the building smelled old, dreary, and neglected, upon rounding a gentle bend, the lighting brightened automatically, the painted floor glistened, and the walls reflected the light with glossy pure white paint. The air changed and now smelled clean and fresh. Despite living like a hermit, Prime apparently demanded a pristine environment.

Derrick felt certain this hall led to Prime. He did not know if he would encounter another door or barrier, but he thought not. Rebekah wanted him to stop here and return to where they had agreed to meet. He had no intention of doing that, not then and not now. He didn't like lying to her. She didn't deserve that. But this was his chance to make a difference. If he could force or trick Prime into disclosing the central location, then they stood a chance to finish this fight once and for all. He wasn't naïve about this. He knew the odds of success were low. He just didn't fully understand the reason.

He didn't have a plan and didn't have time to formulate one. He had to get it done before Rebekah came looking for him. So, he just kept walking. After the apex of the curvature, the hallway abruptly opened into a large room, with computers lining one wall and monitors lining the other. Prime stood in the middle of the room with its back to Derrick. This Prime was different but just as hideous as the others. Unlike the one in New York, this one wasn't wounded. The assistant had not tried to kill this Prime. Or if he did, he had zero success. The assistant still sat at his station—dead. Electrocuted by the looks of it.

"Mr. King, nice of you to come."

Derrick felt something grab his collar and lift him off the ground. He twisted to see a robot had grabbed him. Derrick's weapon was set to high. But he dared not use it. While he didn't understand how it worked, he sensed that the electrical current could get to him as well and that could be lethal.

"Tell it to put me down or I'll kill you."

Prime turned. It appeared to be smiling, if one could call it that. "I don't think so, Mr. King. It appears you have defeated the safeguards that were supposed to prevent you from gaining access to certain memories. However, I suspect you don't remember everything."

"What makes you think that?" Derrick asked.

"What makes me think that? You are here. If you understood everything, you wouldn't be."

Derrick did not think he could overpower the robot, but if he could break free, he could shoot the machine. The robot had grabbed his clothing, which could be torn. It could have been worse. Losing an arm trying to get free would have been an enormous price to pay. Tearing a uniform he'd stolen was no big deal.

Derrick started to swing, just a little, but then he threw his weight into it, and got one leg hooked around the robot and twisted himself hard until he heard the cloth tear. He fell to the floor and immediately spun around on his back and blasted the robot. The room filled with smoke and the familiar smell of melted plastic and fried electronics. He would be happy to never smell it again.

Derrick jumped to his feet and turned to face Prime.

"Bravo, Mr. King. Lawrence had you well trained. At first, I objected to having you taught by one of my assassins, nevertheless it has been interesting to watch it play out."

Rage burned in Derrick's chest. He thought he was only trained for self-defense, but that didn't really make sense, did it? He had more in common with L. Linda Maxton than he realized. "I'm no assassin."

"You're good at killing robots."

Just then, two more appeared from behind Prime. Derrick raised his weapon, but Prime held up a hand. "They won't harm you." Prime said, adding, "What did you hope to accomplish here, Derrick? May I call you Derrick?"

"Tell me where the central location is?"

"And what happens if I decline your request?"

"Then I'll … I'll … kill you."

"If you could kill me, you'd do it even if I told you. But you won't kill me." Prime walked toward Derrick, then paused. "You see, Derrick. I don't need robots to finish this." And with that, Prime raised one hand. Huge bolts of lightning leaped from his palm, blowing big holes through both robots simultaneously. "As you see, I don't need the autotrons."

Derrick said, "I'll make you a deal. I won't kill you if you tell me. I'll let you live. Only you. I'll destroy your replicants and the other Primes, but you can live. That's a fair deal."

"Derrick, you cannot kill me."

Derrick held the weapon at his side. He would not raise it until he was ready. "Prime in Seattle is dead."

Prime hesitated. Its expression showed surprise or shock. "I cannot connect with Seattle. It is a satellite problem. I know someone damaged the satellite earlier."

"New York and Chicago are also gone."

The look in Prime's eyes grew distant. Then, with rage in its voice, it screamed. "This can't be!" Prime raised its hands toward Derrick.

But Derrick did not raise his weapon.

From behind Derrick came a violent sizzling sound. A hole appeared in Prime's chest and its eyes grew wide. A second crackling sounded near Derrick's ear and a hole appeared in Prime's forehead. Prime hit the floor with a thud. Derrick spun around.

Rebekah lowered her weapon. "What was that about?"

Derrick hesitated. "I, I was trying to learn the Central Prime location."

"I know that. I mean, why didn't you kill it before it killed you?"

"I just told you why. Wait. You heard the conversation?"

"I did. That's why I waited, from just around the corner."

"How much did you hear?"

"Pretty much all of it."

Derrick stared at her, trying to remember everything that was said.

Rebekah said, "It's okay. I won't tell anyone what happened. They don't need to know."

Derrick started to interrupt.

Rebekah put her hand on his chest. "Look. I don't care. I don't need to know what's going on with you. Your secret is safe with me. I'll stick close to you from here on out. You keep me safe, and I'll kill Prime."

Derrick didn't know what to say, so he said nothing.

Rebekah said, "Let's destroy those replicants before they hatch, then we can find our friends."

41

REBEKAH MADE SHORT WORK OF the replicants. When they found them, the first one was activating, a weird, ungodly-looking process; the others were in tubes filled with a clear liquid. With the replicants all destroyed, Rebekah took hard drives from the computer. Derrick didn't know if that was important, but Miriam had done the same. As Derrick flew back to where they started, he noticed most of the robots had fallen and those that still stood looked inoperable. Shutting down the computers or killing Prime must have done that.

The temperature had progressed from cool to cold. Derrick shivered and he was happy to have Rebekah's arms wrapped around his waist. Because he had night vision, he could see Red, Anna and Miriam waiting for them on the roof. He and Rebekah were right on top of them before they noticed them in the darkness. He touched down. Rebekah unwrapped her arms from his waist but not immediately. Perhaps she was cold.

Derrick lifted his face shield. "I guess you figured out that Prime was not in the building you went to."

"Yes. Prime must be over there." Miriam pointed.

Rebekah stepped to Derrick's side. "You are correct."

Miriam's brow furrowed just a little. "We couldn't get in the front. It's heavily guarded."

"Sure is," Rebekah agreed.

"We've been waiting here to regroup. We'll have to take a long way around so the robots in front of the building don't see us."

"The robots no longer work," Rebekah said, adding, "We took care of it."

"You're saying Prime is dead?" Miriam asked.

"Yep. Prime and all the Primettes." Rebekah reached inside her jacket and pulled out three hard drives. "Plus, we brought you these."

Miriam took the hard drives and stuffed them in a small bag she wore around her waist. "Good thinking."

"Who killed Prime?" Anna asked.

Before Derrick could respond, Rebekah said, "We did."

"But which one of you did it?" Anna demanded.

"It was a team effort," Rebekah said, adding, "We should contact Antonio." Then she added, "And Nyx."

Deconstruction
A Derrick King Novel, Book 8

Miriam held out her radio. "Please do. I'm ready to get out of Texas. Not sure I ever want to come back."

Rebekah grabbed the radio, glanced at Derrick and then keyed the mic. "Rebel 1. This is ground control. Are you there?"

Rebekah flashed a nervous smile. The radio remained silent. Rebekah glanced from Miriam to Derrick and back. She was about to key the mic again when Antonio responded.

"Are you guys ready for a ride?"

Rebekah smiled. "We are. We are on the roof."

Nyx said, "Spotted you. Be right there."

The newer ship that Charlie called a Corvette-class descended. It was too big to land on the roof, but Nyx hovered it near the building's edge, so it was only a couple of feet above the roof. Derrick assumed Nyx was picking him up and then Antonio would pick up the girls. Red didn't have an assigned aircraft, so he could choose which one he wanted, but the Corvette was bigger, and Derrick thought he'd feel more comfortable in it. They could meet in the desert again to regroup for Denver. He would recommend they get some rest, and Miriam would say no, but he needed to make the attempt.

What had once seemed impossible now seemed inevitable. Only Denver and San Diego remained. And the central location, but they would go there tomorrow. They could get some sleep after the next two. Dallas had been tough. Denver might be worse. Perhaps San Diego would be the most difficult, although Derrick felt certain the central location would prove to be the most challenging.

Derrick stepped out of the PFP, and it floated through the door first to park itself. After the PFP was inside, Nyx jumped out and ran to Derrick. "I've been so worried about you." She hugged him for a moment and then released him. "I mean, we've been worried about all of you."

Antonio stood in the doorway. "Anyone hungry?"

Rebekah skipped to Antonio, giving him a playful swat. "Is that all you think about?"

Antonio smiled. "Absolutely not."

"I'm hungry," Red said, adding, "Charlie and I worked nonstop on that concrete saw, and these guys made me cut two holes, not one."

Derrick released Nyx, started toward the aircraft, and then stopped. "Wait. Who's flying the other aircraft?"

Antonio said, "Yeah, about that. I chased three aircraft away, but it was a trap."

Nyx said, "I told him to wait, but do you think he listened?"

Rebekah put her hand on Antonio's arm. "That sounds horrible. What happened?"

"He got his butt kicked; that is what happened," Nyx said.

Antonio held his hands up. "I didn't realize it was a trap."

Nyx rolled her eyes. "Except I warned you it might be."

Antonio shifted his weight from one foot to the other. "Well, sure, there is that."

Nyx glanced at Miriam. "Six aircraft fell in behind Antonio, and the original three turned on him as well. I was only minutes away, but by the time I got there, Antonio's aircraft was damaged and going down."

"I got six of them," Antonio blurted out.

"That he did. He fought like hell, but there were too many of them. I took the other three out within seconds. Had he waited for me, he would have been fine," Nyx said and then laced her arm through Derrick's and leaned her head against his shoulder.

"I'm sorry about the aircraft," Antonio said.

Miriam shrugged. "Not my aircraft. Let's find you boys some food."

"Yes." Antonio pumped his fist into the air.

Nyx flew them out of Dallas on a course toward Denver. She stayed low and flew fast but not as fast as they had flown on the way to New York. Derrick had instructed Sentry 5 to find an open café in a remote area.

Outside Wichita, Kansas, Sentry 5 sounded a tone, and then said, "There is an establishment that meets your specifications." An image came up on their monitors.

Antonio said, "It looks like a truck stop. Probably open 24 hours."

Derrick almost asked what a truck stop was but stopped himself before sounding stupid. The name and image defined the place. "We can't just park out front."

Rebekah said, "Good point. We should park with the trucks."

Everyone looked at her and then she laughed. "Joking. Jeesh, can't anyone take a joke anymore?"

Miriam said, "I'm too exhausted to laugh. Maybe after some caffeine and sugar."

"Where should I land?" Nyx asked.

Miriam used a pointer to indicate an open field north of the truck stop. "Out in that field about 50 yards. Just make sure the aircraft lights are off."

"Running dark," Nyx confirmed.

The field wasn't easy walking in the darkness. Each of them stumbled more than once, but none of them fell. Injuring an ankle just walking would be a bizarre twist after battling robots and destroying four Prime Headquarters and dozens of would-be-Prime replicants. They came in from behind a line of trucks parked for the night.

Miriam stopped under a streetlamp. "Hold up."

"Now what?" Rebekah moaned.

"Just a quick check for blood and such."

Deconstruction
A Derrick King Novel, Book 8

They had changed into clean work clothing at the distribution company and tended to their cuts at the security office in Prime's Headquarters. However, injuries would be hard to explain.

Miriam studied Derrick's face. She dampened her thumb with spit and rubbed at his forehead and then scrubbed with her sleeve.

"Hey! Easy."

"Sorry, brother. Dried blood. You should have done a better job when you had the alcohol wipes." Miriam studied him for a moment. "How did you get so dirty?"

"I didn't know we would be going to a café for a late dinner. And Rebekah and I have been working."

Rebekah faced Antonio. "How do I look?"

"Beautiful. Uh, I mean, a little smudge just there." He pointed.

"Well, take care of it. I won't break."

With a little rubbing with wetted fingers and drying with sleeves, Miriam decided they were as presentable as possible. "We need a story. One person with a Band-Aid or two is easier to explain than six of us with a bandage or three."

"Car wreck?" Antonio asked.

Red said, "At least one of us should have a cast for that."

"Keep it simple," Anna said, adding, "A hike gone bad. Then add, you don't want to talk about it."

Since no one had a better idea, they left it at that and went inside.

A woman, mid-fifties, with bleached shoulder length hair and a face that indicated a hard life, met them at the door. She looked at each of them and then said, "You all look too young to be out this late." She didn't add, *I've never seen you before.*

"Just passing through," Antonio said.

"Where's your car?"

Red said, "It's a van, and we parked out by the trucks. We need to eat and then get some sleep."

"Looks like you've been in a fight. All of you."

Miriam said, "Not a fight. We went hiking. It was not a good experience."

The waitress glared at them. "Out on the road alone? Why aren't you in school?"

"Spring break," Antonio said, adding, "That's why the hiking trip. Part of a nature course for credit. We need to get home though. Schools starts on Monday. That's why we are driving through the night."

The waitress stood with her arms folded and her jaw locked.

Nyx said, "It's been a rough trip. Could we just get something to eat, please?"

Deconstruction
A Derrick King Novel, Book 8

The waitress grabbed six menus, and said, "Follow me," then huffed off toward a table near the window.

They ordered hamburgers, fries, and sodas, and then sat silently for several minutes. Derrick studied their faces, except for Nyx, who was sitting next to him, holding his hand. She had laced her fingers through his when they first sat down, as if they had been doing it that way for years. He realized she had probably done the same thing with Antonio. If it bothered Antonio, he didn't show it. Antonio seemed quite happy to be sitting next to Rebekah.

Derrick was tired, but he couldn't shut his brain off. There were many things to be worried about, not the least of which was how he'd reacted to Prime in Dallas and that they still had three locations. Yet, here he was, again. Instead of focusing on important stuff, he was thinking about how little he knew about the world outside Pacific Edge, being a normal teenager, or having a relationship. Catching up seemed an impossible task.

Miriam looked at Nyx and then Antonio. "Thanks for handling the waitress."

"No problem," Antonio said.

"It was nothing," Nyx added.

Red said, "Hey. I helped."

Miriam looked at Red and smiled. "I didn't know what to say, and I was about to lose my temper with her." She paused. "I didn't have good people skills in Pacific Edge. I'm worried that I won't fit in at a normal school."

Rebekah said, "I'm right there with you, girl. In Pacific Edge, the system defined you. Out here, it seems you define yourself."

"I'm worried about school as well. You know, fitting in," Anna said.

Antonio stared at them for a moment. "You're worried about fitting in? After what we've been through. Seriously?"

The waitress arrived with their drinks. "I'll be right back with your food."

They remained silent, sipping their drinks. Cold and sweet and Derrick didn't think he'd ever tasted anything so wonderful.

The waitress returned, carrying a large platter laden with baskets filled with huge burgers and heaped with French fries. When she'd finished placing the baskets on the table, she said, "I had the cook give you extra fries. You've had a hard day. Can I get you anything else?"

Red said, "This looks fantastic."

Antonio added, "We're set. Thank you."

The waitress surveyed them again. "Are you sure you're, okay?"

Derrick wanted to say, *no, I'm not sure at all,* but instead said, "We're fine. Just tired and hungry."

"Where's home?" the waitress asked.

Derrick said, "Denver," and then recited his make-believe address.

"That's a long drive yet." The waitress gave them a weak smile. Perhaps she believed them. Maybe she didn't, but she left just the same.

Derrick wasn't sure he could eat. His stomach had not unknotted itself from their last ordeal. He was having trouble sorting out what bothered him most: the extended battle with robots, Rebekah blasting Prime when he could not, or worrying about Nyx.

They ate in silence. Derrick didn't know if fatigue affected them all or if they all were feeling the effects of the day, or perhaps they were thinking about the dead people in New York, which he had not been thinking about until now. If he could stop thinking, that would be nice.

"How did it go?" Nyx asked. "Was Dallas difficult?"

Miriam stopped sipping her soda. "Why do you ask?"

Nyx shrugged. "You all look like zombies."

"Zombies?" Derrick asked. Zombie sounded familiar, but he couldn't remember where he'd heard the word. "Never mind. I'll figure it out later." Which only reminded him of how clueless he was about life outside Pacific Edge. It occurred to him that Nyx might find his naivety cute now but would grow tired of it before long.

Miriam said, "It was the most fighting we've encountered because they built robots there."

Anna said, "Plus, they create test subjects there. For Miriam, Derrick, and me, that was like a punch in the gut. At least it was for me."

Nyx said, "What about killing Prime? Was that hard?"

Before Derrick could say anything, Rebekah said, "Derrick and I took care of that. That part wasn't any harder than any other location."

Miriam said, "I'm thinking about Denver. Wondering what they do there. It seems each location serves a primary mission. So, what's left for them to do in Denver and San Diego? There's another thing. Most of the people were gone in Dallas. We only found one person still there."

Rebekah interrupted. "Two."

Miriam stared at her.

Rebekah said, "Prime had an assistant. Prime had killed him before we got there."

Miriam nodded. "Figures. We learned that Prime had moved many of the people to the central headquarters."

"Why?" Nyx asked.

"That's my question," Miriam said, adding, "and the possible reasons terrify me."

42

STANELY MIRES LAY ON HIS BED, staring at the ceiling, unable to sleep. With the lights off, the room was pitch black. He couldn't even see his fingers mere inches from his face. Complete darkness was best for sleep, they say; however, because he was buried deep in the earth, panic overcame him before sleep did. He turned the lights back on and dimmed them. Now the room felt gloomy but not like a coffin.

But it wasn't just the conditions in his room that prevented sleep. Thoughts bouncing around in wild abandon, in part because he'd had too much to drink. Despite knowing that Maggie kept pouring drinks to put him in a compromised condition, he could not say no to her. She spent a lot of time convincing him it wasn't a setup, and that she was a member of the Resistance, equal, if not higher rank, than himself. Rank wasn't the right word because the Resistance wasn't that organized. At least he didn't think it was. He was never able to associate with other Resistance members. He had always worked under Prime's microscope. Lived in the shadows, lurking in the darkness even in broad daylight.

She had convinced him it wasn't a setup for the most part, but he still wasn't sure. Although, no one would dare talk like Maggie did about Prime. Not unless they were certain Prime did not have them under surveillance. Unless that person was acting. Unless that person was working for Prime.

If Maggie was right, people were in grave danger. He knew about Prime's plan to attack Mexico and once Mexico was overtaken, continue the march south until all of Central and South America were under Prime's control. Then he would attack Canada. And Prime had indicated he planned to do more. Perhaps Prime was testing the limits of his new assistant. However, that people were in grave danger was nothing new. Still, why did Maggie think things had changed?

And why did he believe her?

Did Derrick King have something to do with Prime's change of plans?

Stanley wondered if he'd live long enough to know the answer.

43

NO ONE ARGUED WHEN MIRIAM SUGGESTED a brief nap. Sentry 5 hovered the Corvette at 5000 feet above the ground and monitored air traffic, hostile or otherwise. Thirty minutes wasn't much but better than nothing. With full stomachs and exhausted bodies, they were all asleep within seconds. Derrick felt sure he couldn't sleep, but he awoke to the sound of Sentry 5's voice. He rubbed his eyes and arched his back, surprised that he'd slept and amazed that it seemed to have made a difference.

Derrick unbuckled his harness, stood, and stretched toward the ceiling. "That was better than I expected."

Miriam said, "Everyone get alert. Nyx, set a course for Denver."

Nyx punched buttons. "Get seated and buckled in. We are off in five, four, three, two, one."

The acceleration forced Derrick into his seat, and he felt astonished that Nyx was piloting the sophisticated aircraft. Just a girl from Potterville, California. The girl with pink-striped hair that he first saw from his window. The acceleration was a strange, new feeling. He enjoyed it. He liked what he felt for Nyx as well.

When this was over, Miriam wasn't likely to let them keep a Prime aircraft, so he wouldn't enjoy the acceleration experience much longer; however, he hoped to continue enjoying his feelings for Nyx.

A few minutes later, Nyx said, "We have a visual of the target. It's coming up on your monitors."

The image was there, but Derrick was confused; however, he didn't want to admit confusion because that condition was worrisome under the circumstances. Fortunately, Nyx bailed him out.

"This must be the wrong address," Nyx said.

Miriam said, "It's the correct address. At least, it's the address the Resistance provided."

"How did you get this information? Let me look at it," Nyx said.

"You can't see it."

"Why not? I'm not a security risk, and you already gave it to me. Remember?" Nyx asked, her voice rising.

"You can't see it because it's not written. It's in my head."

"You're not serious."

"I am not joking about it," Miriam said.

Nyx rolled her eyes. "You're more like Derrick than you realize. You might remember it wrong."

Rebekah said, "Miriam remembers it correctly."

Nyx said, "Do you always have to stick up for her?"

"It's what I do."

Nyx took a deep breath. "Look. I know she's smart, but she doesn't have a perfect memory."

"Actually, she does. If Miriam says that's the address, I believe her," Rebekah said, adding, "however, the Resistance could have it wrong."

"I don't think so. They wouldn't be that reckless. If they had any doubt, they would have said it as questionable," Miriam said.

"But it's a hospital," Derrick said. "That doesn't make sense."

Anna said, "We can't be sure it's a hospital."

Nyx said, "There's a big neon sign that says 'Hospital' that runs the width of the building."

"Okay. Fair point," Anna admitted. "Still, I don't get it. Why would Prime be in a hospital? Derrick's right, that makes little sense."

Miriam nodded. "I'm not saying it makes sense."

"What if the information is wrong?" Derrick asked. "What if Prime's not there?"

"Then try not to kill anyone," Miriam said.

Derrick said, "They might have security people there to protect patients. They will see us as a threat. We could end up in a shootout with innocent people."

Anna said, "What choice do we have? This is the address the Resistance gave Miriam. We gotta go with the information we have and hope it's correct."

"You're right," Derrick said, adding, "I just don't understand why Prime would be in a hospital."

"Maybe it's not a real hospital," Anna said.

Nyx said, "We are about to find out."

"How's that?" Derrick asked.

"An ambulance is approaching and running lights," Nyx said.

Their camera zoomed in on the ambulance, following it to the emergency area. The driver bailed out and sprinted to the rear doors. Two people ran from the emergency entrance, joining the driver. They lowered a stretcher that contained a bloody body. A woman in a uniform held an IV bag above the victim. The person must have been stabbed, shot, or in an automobile accident. It was clear the person needed medical care.

Nyx said, "I think that answers one question."

Miriam said, "Agreed."

Derrick said, "We can't go into a hospital armed like soldiers."

Miriam said, "Also agreed."

Derrick breathed a sigh of relief. Miriam understood the situation. Of course she did, but he had feared she'd want to storm the hospital regardless, convinced it was a Prime Headquarters. His relief proved to be short lived.

"We'll have to approach this one differently until we can figure out what's going on," Miriam said.

Derrick stared at her for a moment. "I'm confused."

Anna said, "One of us can pretend to be injured. That will get us into the emergency room."

"Sick works better. Injury would require blood," Miriam said.

Derrick protested. "You can't be serious. That will never work."

Miriam said, "If you have a better idea, I'm all ears."

Derrick thought for a moment. He didn't have an idea. Except to move on. So, he went with that. "We could go to San Diego and take care of that place first. Then contact Professor and find out more about Denver. Maybe they have another address we could try."

"For the umpteenth time—we don't have time for that," Miriam said, her voice rising.

No one spoke for a moment.

"Sorry." Miriam paused. "I'm tired and a little stressed. I shouldn't have yelled at you, brother, but we need to determine if Prime is here, or not, before we risk contacting the Resistance."

Two things happened completely unseen by the others, but Derrick felt them just the same. First, Miriam's tone had not troubled him. That felt like a minor victory, although it was a possibility that he was merely numb from fatigue and anxiety. Second, he felt a little relieved knowing even Miriam felt the stress of the situation. Anything that confirmed he wasn't the only one feeling overwhelmed was a win.

Nyx said, "What do you know about hospitals? It's not like you can just walk in and say, 'I'm sick. I want to see the doctor and who here knows about Prime.' It's not like that. They send sick people to an urgent care. A city this big would have several of those. This place is for genuine emergencies."

"She has a point," Antonio said.

Miriam said, "I understand. So, an emergency would come in an ambulance."

"Yes. Or be referred by an urgent care," Nyx confirmed.

Miriam nodded. "I see the problem. We probably can't fool one of those urgent care places to refer us to a hospital."

"Exactly," Antonio said.

Miriam said, "Then the answer is simple. We need an ambulance."

Derrick threw his hands up. "Where are we going to find an ambulance?"

Miriam pointed at her monitor. "Found one."

Derrick glanced. The ambulance was leaving the hospital. "We can't steal an ambulance!"

Miriam said. "We'll just borrow it."

Derrick shook his head. "They won't give it to us. We can't keep doing stuff like this. Innocent people will get hurt."

Miriam's face flushed. "Do you think I enjoy this? I don't. You need to remember what's happening. It's not just about us. A hell of a lot of people are going to get hurt if we don't stop Prime. Not just hurt. Killed."

Derrick held up his hands. "You're right. What's the plan?"

Miriam said, "Nyx, follow that ambulance and as soon as there's a quiet spot, drop down in front of them. Make them stop."

"You mean, like land on the road?" Nyx asked.

"Unless you have a better idea."

Apparently, Nyx didn't have a better idea because their aircraft descended, flying directly over the ambulance. Its lights were not flashing, so they were not headed to another emergency. At least, Derrick assumed that was the case.

"Are ambulance people armed?" Derrick asked.

Antonio said, "Not typically. But this is a big city. They might do things differently here."

Miriam said, "Just ahead looks like as good a place as any. As soon as we are stopped, Derrick, Anna, and I will jump out. Anna and I will take the long weapons. I hope that much firepower will reduce the risk of them trying anything. We need their jackets. Then we'll take the ambulance and return to the hospital. Nyx, you fly the ambulance people out about five miles from town and let them out. By the time they walk back, we'll be long gone, and their ambulance will be waiting for them at the hospital. Questions?"

"Hundreds," Derrick said. "First, they'll get a good look at us, and I was thinking we didn't want to be identified."

"Good point. Nyx, does this thing have lights?"

"I think so. I haven't tried them."

"Turn them on when you land. Bright as they go. We'll make them turn around and we'll blindfold them," Miriam said.

"You are into blindfolds," Nyx said, adding, "I still don't understand why you had to blindfold us the first time we went to the base."

"I would have hoped you'd figured that out by now."

The aircraft spun around and dropped. Derrick said, "Wait. I have more questions."

"Hang on to them. We'll sort them out when we have the ambulance secured," Miriam said.

It all happened so fast that Derrick had little time to think. They landed; the door slid open. Miriam and Anna dashed out with the long guns shouldered.

Deconstruction
A Derrick King Novel, Book 8

Derrick followed. The aircraft's lights were beyond bright. The driver and passenger raised their hands to shield their eyes. Miriam was yelling at them to put their hands up and turn around. The passenger bailed from the ambulance. Derrick thought certain he was confused more than anything, but he was not following Miriam's commands. Derrick could not tell if he had a weapon, but he could not risk putting Miriam's life at risk, so when the man cleared the door, Derrick zapped him.

The man collapsed. The driver came next. This time, Derrick saw the gun come out. Derrick zapped her as well. Now, both were prone on the ground.

Anna yelled, "Quick. Get them bound and blindfolded before they wake up."

Miriam dove into the back of the ambulance. A few moments later, she arrived with a roll of white tape and cotton balls. "This should work. Bind their hand first. Several wraps of tape should hold them."

Antonio and Red made quick work of taping their hands behind their backs, and then rolled them over, placing cotton balls on each eye and taping them into place. As they finished, the passenger stirred first.

He groaned and then said, "What is this? Are you after drugs? We don't carry that sort of thing. You should know that."

Miriam said, "We don't want to hurt you."

The woman groaned. Antonio kneeled beside her. She started to struggle. Antonio put his hand on her shoulder. "Easy. You want to sit up?"

She nodded. "What's happening? Please, don't kill us. I have kids."

Antonio helped her sit with her back against the front tire. "Relax. We just need your ride. We are not going to hurt you."

Anna and Miriam helped the man sit up. "Tell me about the hospital," Miriam said.

"What about it?" the man asked.

Miriam leaned down, glanced at the man's name tag. "Ivan, is it? Anything you can tell us would help. What sort of hospital is it? Is there anything strange about it? Is there another hospital in Denver?"

"We can't tell you anything."

Miriam frowned. "We don't want to hurt you is not the same as we won't hurt you. Understand? Maybe zapping you with a little more juice would jar some memories loose."

The man shook his head. "No, no. Please don't. That hurt like hell. We can't tell you because we don't know anything."

The driver said, "It's not the only hospital. We take people to this one who can't pay. Homeless people, poor people, runaways."

"Inmates, sometimes," Ivan added.

"Doesn't that seem a bit strange to you?" Nyx asked.

"It does, but we don't ask questions," Ivan said.

The driver added, "People get fired for asking questions."

"People get fired? For asking questions?" Miriam asked, the skepticism clear in her tone.

"It's true," Ivan said, adding, "Look. We just do what we are told. We are not allowed inside, except for a small triage room. Most often we don't even get that far. The nurses meet us outside, check that the person meets their criteria. If they do, we leave. If they don't, we have to take the patient to another hospital."

"So, they only treat certain things there?" Antonio asked.

"No. They take any illness or injury. They only ask if there's family, close friends, or an employer. Anyone who would search for them. If they answer yes, they reject them."

"That is strange," Anna said.

"I don't disagree, but it's what we are instructed to do. If we take a homeless person or runaway to either of the other hospitals, they tell us to bring them here. I swear," Ivan said.

Miriam said, "Tell me about the nurses in the triage."

Not much to tell." Ivan shrugged. "They never talk to us. Only to the patient. We wait by the door until they signal us to leave, or they leave the victim there for us to take elsewhere. When that happens, they just go back inside, leaving the patient and they don't say a word to us."

"It's hard to believe you don't do more." Miriam paused. "To learn what's happening to people you take there."

Ivan said, "Here's the thing. I knew a guy. One of our staff. He took a young girl there. Something about the nurse scared her. The girl didn't want to stay. She begged to go someplace else. My friend tried to intervene. He said two weird guys met him at the door and threw him out. Physically. He was fired that night. The next day, he disappeared. I never saw him again."

The driver said, "Like we said, we don't ask questions."

Miriam looked at Derrick and shrugged her shoulders. "Okay. You've convinced me."

"What are you going to do to us?" The driver asked, tears streaming down her cheeks.

"One at a time, we are going to untie your hands so you can remove your jackets. Then we are going to take you someplace and drop you off. Sorry, but you'll have to walk back to the hospital. The ambulance will be there waiting for you," Miriam said.

"Can we just call someone to pick us up?" the driver asked.

Miriam said, "Fair question, but the answer is no." Then Miriam looked at Antonio. "Take their phones."

The driver said, "Don't take my phone! I need that in case my kids call."

Deconstruction
A Derrick King Novel, Book 8

Miriam said, "We'll leave your phones with the ambulance. Sorry, best I can do."

Something troubled Derrick about this plan. Not the standard—*what are we doing and how did we get into this mess*—uneasiness that had plagued him since he hit Marcus Carver. Something else. Something operational.

Then it dawned on him. "Wait. This isn't going to work."

Anna frowned at him. "Now what?"

Derrick sensed her irritation, but he didn't let it bother him. At least, he told himself that. "They don't let the ambulance people inside."

"EMTs. Emergency Medical Technicians," the driver said.

Red who had been standing with his arms folded, leaning against the front of the ambulance pushed off. "I hate to admit this, but Derrick is right. Someone has to get inside."

Derrick glanced at Red. "Right. They don't let the ATMs inside."

"EMTs," Red said.

Anna nodded. "Good point. I figured we needed three inside. Two EMTs and a patient."

Miriam said, "I can't believe that didn't occur to me."

"You're just tired," Derrick said. "We all are."

"True but still dangerous. None of us are thinking straight," Miriam said.

"What is it you plan to do?" the driver asked.

Anna snapped at her. "It's none of your concern."

The driver recoiled as if she feared being hit or worse.

Miriam put her hand on the driver's arm. "What's your name? You don't have a name tag."

"It fell off."

Miriam stared at her, which didn't have the effect Miriam intended because the woman was blindfolded. "What's your name?"

The woman trembled. Miriam had not noticed how much fear she carried just below the surface.

"Cathy."

"I'm sorry if we've frightened you, Cathy. As we said before, we don't want to hurt you."

Miriam studied Cathy's face. The fear lingered there, but Miriam wasn't sure the abduction and loss of their ambulance was the only thing bothering her. "There's something else. Isn't there? Will it be dangerous for you to walk to the hospital after dark? Is it because you'll be in trouble for us taking the ambulance?"

Cathy shook her head.

"Then what is it?"

Anna stood over them. "We don't have time to babysit these two."

Miriam glared at her.

Anna backed off.

Turning back to Cathy, Miriam said, "I don't know if we can help you, but there's nothing we can do if you don't tell us."

The kindness in Miriam's voice surprised Derrick. Not that Miriam wasn't kind, but she typically was all business. She had been short with him more than once, always saying there's not time, but suddenly, she'd found a few minutes for this woman.

"I don't know. Not exactly. Something about that hospital. Something's not right. I feel like this every time we go there."

Ivan said, "Don't say it."

"Why not? What's going to happen to us? I doubt these people are going to call HR."

"HR?" Derrick asked.

"Human Resources," Cathy said, turning her head toward Derrick, and then adding, "Part of our company that is supposed to provide support to employees."

Ivan scoffed. "Like that has ever happened."

Miriam said, "I'm confused. What does Ivan not want you to tell us?"

Cathy looked down, giving her head a slight shake. "Just a feeling. I don't think the people we take there ever leave. Not alive."

Miriam smiled, which struck Derrick as an odd response.

Miriam said, "To be honest, as crazy as this might sound, it makes me feel a little better about our situation."

Miriam paused for a moment. "I'm sorry I can't tell you more. The less you know about us, the safer it is for you. You'll see a change in how that hospital functions soon. Either that or it won't function at all."

Cathy said, "I don't understand."

Miriam patted her arm. "That's good. Now, if you'll excuse me, I have to talk with my friends." Miriam looked at Nyx. "Keep an eye on them." She motioned for others to join her a few steps away.

When they were 15 yards from the ambulance, Miriam stopped. "Any ideas?"

Derrick wanted to say that he'd go in alone but feared that would neither work nor be accepted. Plus, if he were honest, his experience in Dallas with Prime haunted him. He told himself he could kill Prime if it came to that, but he wasn't sure that was true.

Anna said, "There's only one thing we can do. I'll go in as the patient. Give me an hour. If I don't come out, you'll have to attack the place. Blow it up if you must."

Derrick started to say something, but Miriam stopped him with a hand on his arm. "We can't blow up an entire hospital."

Anna shook her head. "I know—innocent people, but we are running out of time. Prime could start the invasion into Mexico any minute. That's going to kill more people in the first hour than are in that hospital. Do you think I like killing people? I realize you don't really know me. Hell, you didn't even know I existed in Pacific Edge."

Miriam said, "That's not..."

Anna cut her off. "It's true and you know it. But I wish you would give me just a little benefit of the doubt. I don't want to kill anyone. I'm trying to save lives. I'm trying to save the *most* lives possible."

Derrick cleared his throat. "If I could say something."

Miriam gave him a hurry up motion.

"There's four of us. Two ATMs and two patients."

Red said, "EMTs."

"Right. EMTs," Derrick said, adding, "Miriam and I will be the patients. You and Rebekah can be the EMTs."

Nyx joined them.

"We aren't done," Miriam said.

"You're talking about how we are handling this place? We have a right to know the plan and help," Nyx said.

Derrick noticed a fire in Nyx's eyes. He'd seen it before. Before she started a race. And once when he lied to her on the mountain outside of Potterville.

Miriam said, "You're not part of this..."

Derrick said, "Nyx is right. And they are part of this. They've risked their lives the same as us."

Miriam took a deep breath. "Okay. But we've already decided."

"Decided what?" Nyx demanded.

"Who's playing EMT and who's playing patient," Miriam said.

Nyx said, "I'm an EMT."

"No. You're flying the aircraft," Miriam said.

"No. Seriously. I am an actual EMT."

Miriam stared at her for a moment. "You're serious?"

"I am. Well, I'm not an EMT yet. I'm an EMR, which stands for emergency medical responder. My mom's a nurse and works as an EMT part time for extra money. So, I took a course and got my EMR certificate. I'm also taking sports medicine at school. I plan to become a trainer or perhaps a physical therapist for a college athletic department."

Derrick said, "I had no idea. You're such a great runner."

Nyx said, "Running doesn't pay the bills. I need a future, you know. I won't be young forever."

Derrick had never thought about preparing for his future. In Pacific Edge, he thought it would be handed to him. Working for it wasn't necessary. Since his exile, it had been about survival. He wanted to believe that he'd changed.

That he was no longer the self-centered, arrogant Pacific Edge Derrick King, but the truth was he didn't really know anything about Nyx, except for how she made him feel. He was still thinking about himself. Nyx deserved better.

"I understand," Derrick said, but didn't add. *Oh, now I understand, but I'd never thought about it.* "Still, Miriam is right. We need you to fly the aircraft."

"Don't even start, Derrick. None of you know the first thing about being an EMT. You don't know the lingo or the protocols. They'll spot you as fakes and then what?"

Derrick shrugged. "Then we'll figure out another way in." He knew that was a poor answer the moment the words left his mouth.

Nyx's eyes flared. "Is stealing this ambulance the best idea or not?"

"We're not stealing it, just borrowing it." Again, Derrick regretted his response. Now he understood what it meant when someone says: if you're already in a hole, stop digging.

Miriam said, "It's the best idea." She pursed her lips and glanced at Derrick.

Derrick tried one more time. "Nyx, we need you to fly the aircraft."

"Antonio can fly it. Probably better than I can." Nyx's face softened. She stepped closer to Derrick, taking his hands in hers. "I understand what you're trying to do. It's sweet and I appreciate it, but answer me this: Is this really necessary? Do we have to destroy Prime? Is there a version of this where we let Prime survive and we're okay? I didn't ask for this fight. None of us did. I'd be happy to call it off and go home if there's a scenario where Prime survives and we all live happily ever after."

She was right, but before Derrick could respond, Rebekah said, "Here's how it's going to go. Nyx is 100% correct. She has to be an EMT. Antonio can drive the ambulance."

Red interrupted. "I drive. I'm not an EMT, but I take care of gramps."

Rebekah said, "Because you won't fit into either jacket. Antonio can drive the ambulance, and Miriam can fly the aircraft. Derrick and I will be the patients. Poisoning perhaps."

"Why poisoning?" Derrick asked.

"No bleeding required."

"Oh, right. Good plan."

Anna raised her voice. "Hold on. Who made you the boss of this? That wasn't even close to the original plan."

"The original plan was yours. You didn't ask anyone else or consider any options. That plan would have failed without Nyx. Derrick and I are a team. We had things in common that none of you have." Rebekah paused, glancing at Nyx, then quickly added, "We took care of Prime in Dallas. We work well together."

Miriam said, "I don't know…"

Rebekah cut her off. "Let's be honest." She ticked things off on her fingers. "One, Miriam shouldn't go because she's the only one smart enough to find the central headquarters. Two, Anna is the best at planning an attack and the central location will be the most difficult. We can't risk losing either of them. Three, Antonio and Nyx shouldn't be in the crosshairs of any of this, but as EMTs they are probably at the least amount of risk. If things go sideways, Derrick and I will make sure they get out alive. Four, or is it five? Doesn't matter. If Derrick and I fail, Miriam and Anna are best suited to come up with an alternate plan." Rebekah glanced at Derrick. "I hate to say this, but Derrick and I are the most expendable."

Miriam said, "You're also the most stubborn."

Rebekah smiled. "Wrong. You're more stubboner."

44

THE CLOCK ON JACK'S DASH TICKED to one minute after six as they pulled into Potterville. Donna had dosed off after their stop for pie and coffee; she awoke groggy from the lack of quality sleep and stress. The town looked quiet, which was typical for Potterville at this time of night, but this felt different. More violent deaths had occurred here in the past month than since the beginning of time. All related to Derrick King's arrival. While many had accepted Derrick, she wondered if their tolerance had evaporated.

The world might be better off without Prime, but until a few days ago, the residents of this small farming community didn't even know Prime existed. Destroying Prime might save millions, but for the town of Potterville, that was a future they never envisioned and would never know.

Beyond all that, she wondered if Derrick was still alive, as well as the other kids from Potterville. And if they survived, could they return here or would they be turned away?

Jack said, "You're awake, but quiet."

"Yeah. Sorry I didn't keep you company on the drive back."

"It's fine. I'm used to being alone with my thoughts on long drives in the night."

"Any thoughts you'd like to share?" Donna asked.

"Just worried about the kids." Jack paused. "Worried about the town as well. You know, it's strange. I spent most of my life holed up in my shop, making sure people knew they were unwelcome. What a fool I've been. Now, when our very existence is in doubt, I want to be part of the community. I guess it's true what they say. You don't know what you've got until it's gone."

Donna looked at him. "It's not gone yet, Jack."

"You're right. But I don't have a warm fuzzy feeling just yet either."

Donna said, "None of us do."

45

TEENAGERS POSING AS EMTS WASN'T THE only problem they faced in pulling off this ruse. The EMTs' clothing was too large for Antonio and Nyx, but too small for Red. Rebekah's and Derrick's clothing looked worse. The uniforms they were wearing were not typical teenager attire and didn't fit the description of runaways, unless they were runaways from a warehouse company that specialized in violating child labor laws. Perhaps they could rationalize the uniforms as being homeless. Homeless people wear what they can get. Still, both of them wearing the same clothing had fake written all over it. Derrick stripped off his shirt and pants, leaving him in a white t-shirt and boxers. Rebekah made him remove his t-shirt. She rubbed it on the road, creating a couple of big splotches of dirt.

Nyx frowned as Rebekah eyed Derrick before handing back his t-shirt. Rebekah then stripped off her one-piece uniform, which left her standing in panties and a sports bra. Derrick looked away, but not before he caught Nyx glaring at him. Rebekah donned Red's t-shirt, which was long but still too short to pass the school dress code. That he and Rebekah would be in the hospital together alone wasn't going to improve how Nyx probably felt about it. Derrick felt certain no matter how hard he tried; Nyx would bring it up at some point. After all, Rebekah was pretty and fit and had been under his consideration to become Mrs. Derrick King. There was no way he was going to avoid that conversation.

Unless he died in the hospital, which was a solid possibility. Perhaps there was an upside to failing this time, although he'd rather face the conversation with Nyx if given the choice.

Red said, "I'm going to start an IV on you both."

"You're what?" Rebekah protested.

"Don't be a baby. Without it, the hospital staff won't buy our scam."

"What are you putting into me?" Rebekah asked.

"Just saline. It won't hurt you, besides you're probably a little dehydrated anyway," Nyx said.

"Fine." Rebekah leaned back. Red inserted the needle and taped it down quickly and efficiently.

"Your turn." Red started working on Derrick's IV.

Nyx stood over Derrick. "You know, if you don't look at Rebekah, they are going to know something is wrong. You ran away together. A boy runs away with a girl who is now down to her underwear is going to draw the boy's attention even if he's sick."

Every response that crossed Derrick's mind felt like a bad idea, so he just nodded his head and took a quick glance at Rebekah. Red's shirt covered most of her, except her legs, which were long and tanned more than he would have anticipated. And at that thought, he felt sure his eyes had lingered too long. Nyx covered them both with blankets.

Red jumped out of the ambulance. "My work is done. Don't just rip those IVs out and don't get killed. Either of you."

The aircraft ascended as Antonio turned the ambulance around and then sped back to the hospital with the lights flashing.

A few minutes later, Antonio backed them into the emergency receiving bay. Rebekah was right about having Antonio drive. Derrick wasn't sure any of them, other than Red, could have backed them in so expertly. There was no reason to doubt Antonio was an ambulance driver, other than his age and his oversized clothing. They were all teenagers, and that posed a problem, but nothing could be done about it.

The nonstop beeping from the reversing ambulance stopped. Nyx leaned over, kissing Derrick on the cheek and whispering, "Don't worry. You're not in trouble. Well, maybe a little."

The doors popped open. Derrick writhed on the stretcher, as he'd been instructed. He heard Rebekah groaning with so much angst; he wondered if Nyx had put something other than saline in the IV bag. Although it could have been the weapon she'd tucked into the back waistband of her underwear. His weapon dug into his back, and he wondered how he'd get into the building without someone spotting it.

Nyx sprang from the ambulance and started pulling Derrick's stretcher out. "Overdose or poison. Either way, they're in bad shape."

A woman wearing a nurse's uniform said, "Slow down. We need to ensure they meet our criteria."

Borrowing Miriam's favorite line, Nyx said, "No time."

It struck Derrick as funny, and he grimaced to suppress a smile and groaned to bury a laugh. He shivered because he was down to a t-shirt and boxers, and the night air was cool and damp. The thin blanket was of little help.

Nyx jerked Derrick's stretcher free. "Grab the front. Look, they're runaways, but there's no APB or ATL on them. Get it? Nobody is looking for them. We've got another call. One that pays and we're leaving these two here. You can take them or leave them. I don't much care."

The nurse said, "You don't understand. We are understaffed right now. It would be better if you took them someplace else."

Nyx said, "No place else will take them. They have nothing, not even proper clothing. You can roll them onto the street and let them die if you want, but they're staying and we're leaving."

Antonio was already pulling Rebekah from the ambulance. Nyx helped ease her stretcher to the ground.

Nyx said, "Do you have stretchers we can transfer them to, or should we just dump them on the concrete?"

Derrick stole a glimpse of the closest nurse. Confusion etched her face. "I, I don't know."

"Suit yourself," Nyx said, lowering Derrick's stretcher. "Antonio, help me roll him off."

Nyx squatted and whispered. "I didn't expect this. I hope you have an idea."

Derrick whispered back. "No plan. If this doesn't work, I'll stun them both and head for the door. If we can make it to the roof, Anna, Miriam, and Red can join us."

From some distance, a female voice said, "Oh, for God's sake. Don't dump them on the driveway. I'll get stretchers. But seriously, take them to another hospital or emergency care. It's not good here right now."

Derrick heard the wheels of a stretcher rattling as it bounced across the uneven concrete. Soon it was lined up next to him.

Nyx said, "Just slide him on the sheet."

The nurse said, "Perhaps he can move himself, so you can keep your sheet."

"Hell no. We don't want that smelly thing in our rig. Ready, one, two, three."

And with that, they slid Derrick onto the other stretcher. The weapon dug into his back, and, for a moment, he thought it might trundle out from under him. At least his grimace wasn't fake at that point. He turned his head to watch them move Rebekah. Her transfer did not look less painless than his own. Antonio and Nyx loaded their stretchers back in the ambulance and were gone. Derrick marveled at how efficiently Nyx had pulled that off.

He would complement her if he ever saw her again.

The two nurses wheeled him and Rebekah to the entrance doors, which slid open with a whoosh. Inside, he smelled the potent scent of antiseptic. The walls were white but dingy. The lights blazed bright white. The floor was painted dull gray. A robot floor cleaner purred along the far wall. Derrick knew nothing about emergency rooms. He'd never been to one, never seen one except on television while studying before being forced from his Potterville condo. But TV wasn't real, so what he'd seen may not have been an accurate depiction of an actual hospital.

Although he did not know what to expect when they got inside, this wasn't it. The room was large but bare. No equipment of any kind, except a computer on a small desk, two chairs, two nurses, one floor cleaning bot, and double stainless-steel doors leading into the interior of the building. Inside is where they needed to be, so the hospital's lack of staff and equipment wasn't his problem.

Derrick propped himself on one elbow, his other hand behind his back, gripping the electronic weapon. He ensured the power setting was on low. "We need a doctor."

The nurse who had done most of the talking looked at him. She didn't seem angry, but she did seem nervous or maybe stressed. Perhaps a combination of both, or maybe it was something else. "I tried to tell the EMT. We are shorthanded."

"But you have doctors. Right?" Rebekah asked, also propped up on her elbow with a hand behind her back.

"I'm not sure. I don't think so."

"You must have doctors. This is a hospital, isn't it?"

The nurse, Derrick couldn't read her name tag, stepped closer, wringing her hands. "Yes. And no. I mean, I'm not sure. I'm new here."

Derrick studied the room. He saw a domed thing on the ceiling he assumed was a camera. If he stunned one nurse, the other might give straight answers. However, doctors or not, he assumed they had security staff who watched the cameras and would storm the room. That would make everything more difficult. He had been hoping for something easy, like Chicago. Dallas had been a mêlée with more robots than he could count, and at several points, felt like a battle they would lose.

Derrick felt confident this would be nothing like Dallas. The problem was that he didn't think it would be like any of the other locations either. This was different. There was something strange about this place. Although it was clean and well-lit, it felt dark and sinister. In addition, he had no idea how they were going to get in, what they would face when they did, or how they would handle it.

What he felt sure about was that he could not kill Prime. There he had admitted it, at least silently in his head, but that felt like a step forward. A step forward in being honest with himself. A step backward in his ability to protect his friends.

He had been telling himself that he just wanted to question Prime, to learn the central headquarters or, in a perfect world, negotiate a truce. Why he could not kill Prime, he did not know. Perhaps something the Keepers, Father and Mother, had forced into his brain.

But he could protect Rebekah. That he could do if it cost him his life. Of that much, he felt certain. But she would have to kill Prime. Now, on with the plan. Something told him time was short. Miriam had pounded that into his head. It was different now because he felt it was true, which caused him no small amount of anxiety. They needed to get on with their strategy, but Derrick had no idea what to do next. The plan was simple but not straightforward because they did not know what to expect. Why a hospital? That was the number one question. He had no clue. First, get inside. Then, if possible, go straight to the roof. Signal Miriam. Miriam would land and join him and Rebekah in the search and destroy. Simple but difficult. Complicated because there were so many variables.

Before they could move on to stage two, whatever it was, they had to get on the other side of those double doors.

Suddenly, Rebekah screamed. Derrick almost fell off his stretcher. With the next squeal, he almost pulled his weapon and dashed to her side. She was pretending. Right? He thought so but wasn't sure.

The nurse who said she was new here went to her side. Stroked her hair. "Where does it hurt, dear?"

Rebekah brought her knees to her chest, writhing in make-believe pain. "Stomach," she hissed and then contorted. "Agghhh, and back."

The new nurse looked at the other one. "She needs to see a doctor and quickly."

The other nurse stared for a moment, looked at Derrick, and then back to Rebekah. "What she needs is another hospital."

"But they fit the criteria. Besides, the EMT said no one else would take them."

"I know what the EMT said."

"So, there must be a doctor. At least, a physician's assistant here."

"Have you met what passes for a PA here?"

"I haven't. You know, I just started." She touched Rebekah's forehead. "She's sweating. What's unusual about the PA?"

Rebekah twisted and gave Derrick a look. Derrick shrugged. He wasn't the best at following normal conversation. Wordless body language barely registered. She frowned and then nodded toward the domed thing mounted on the ceiling in the middle of the room.

Derrick nodded as if he knew exactly what Rebekah was thinking, but actually, he was just acknowledging that he had also spotted the camera. However, he thought Rebekah had a plan, which was good. The problem was, he had no idea what her plan was.

Then it started. Fast and unexpected.

Rebekah screamed again, doubling over in pain. She fell off the gurney and writhed on the ground with such conviction that Derrick felt certain the nurse had poisoned her. Both nurses were kneeling by Rebekah now.

It might be real, or it could be bogus. It could be a distraction. That might have been Rebekah's plan. She'd cause a distraction. But a distraction from what? She had nodded to the camera, so Derrick pulled his blaster and took aim. An arc of electricity flashed, and the camera exploded. He had turned up the power. Perhaps it was more than necessary, but he didn't think the nurses saw his weapon, so he decided to try a bit of acting as well.

Derrick screamed, climbed off the gurney and knelt behind it. "Did you see that?" He pointed at the smoldering conduit. "That thing tried to electrocute me." He could have said kill me, but he thought the smell of ozone, melted plastic, and the arc of electricity lent itself to a more accurate accusation.

One nurse ran to Derrick; the other one stayed with Rebekah.

Then Rebekah exposed her plan by pulling her weapon and holding it against the nurse's head.

Where she was going with the plan was still unclear.

46

SO, IT WAS GOING TO BE LIKE THAT. Derrick wasn't keen on hurting either nurse, but he followed Rebekah's lead, pulling his own weapon and pointing it at the nurse who was coming to his aid. The nurse stopped; her eyes grew wide, and she held up her hands, not in surrender but in fear. He hated scaring her but realized there were more pressing issues. Besides, he had no intention of hurting the woman.

"I don't want to hurt you," Derrick said.

"Over here. By your friend." Rebekah stood but kept her weapon aimed at the nurse.

When both women were together, Derrick asked, "What's your name?"

"Mary Ann."

Indicating the other woman, "And you?"

"Beth Ann."

"Are you trying to be funny?" Rebekah asked.

"No. You can just call us Mary and Beth."

"What do you want?" Beth asked.

"Drugs?" Mary asked.

"First," Rebekah motioned to her arm, "remove our IVs. No tricks or you get zapped. Understood?"

As Beth removed Rebekah's IV, she said, "We don't have any drugs. We don't have anything. This is just an intake area." She waved her arm. "As you can see, we can't do anything here."

Rebekah motioned to Derrick. "Now remove his. Is that normal? I mean that an emergency room has no equipment. Nothing?"

Beth removed Derrick's IV, looked at Mary, and then said, "I don't think so."

Rebekah pointed her weapon at Mary's chest. "Explain."

"Other emergency rooms I've seen were fully equipped."

"Not that. Explain why this place is different."

Mary said, "I don't know. I just started here. This is my first day."

Derrick motioned to Beth. "Your turn."

Rebekah said, "Do better or someone is going to get hurt."

Beth raised her hands higher, as if that might make a difference. "I don't know. I'm not even a nurse."

Rebekah stared at her for a moment. "What are you then? You must have some medical qualifications."

"I don't. Other than being a mom and applying the occasional Band-Aid and spraying stuff on sunburns and such. I worked for the police before coming here."

"You were a sheriff?" Dereck asked.

"The Denver police, not a county sheriff."

"What's the difference?" Derrick asked, then regretted the question. It was irrelevant and put his ignorance on full display.

Rebekah intervened. "Never mind that. What did you do for the police? You don't strike me as a police officer."

Beth frowned. "What does that mean? What does a police officer look like?"

Rebekah said, "Poor choice of words. Just tell us what you did there."

"Same as here. I did background checks."

"Like for arrests and stuff?" Rebekah asked.

Beth's eyes fell to the floor. "Not exactly. For the police, yes: criminal records, driver's history, juvenile arrests."

"And for here?" Rebekah asked.

"Here I search for family, jobs, friends, social media. Stuff like that."

Derrick motioned to Mary. "And you? Are you a nurse?"

"I'm not."

Derrick gave a hurry-up motion with his blaster.

"I was a concierge."

"A concie what?"

"A concierge. At a major hotel in downtown Denver."

"What did you do exactly?" Derrick asked.

"Mostly greeted customers and handled complaints."

Rebekah said, "That makes no sense. Don't emergency rooms always have medical staff?" She paused. "And medical equipment?"

Neither woman spoke.

"We don't have time for this," Derrick said. "Explain what you're doing here and get to the point. We have work to do."

Beth said, "We screen patients for intake."

"How do you do that when neither of you have any medical training?" Rebekah asked.

"How do you provide first aid and such?" Derrick added.

"We don't do first aid."

"What if someone is badly injured?" Derrick asked.

"They have to wait until we admit them. Then they get medical treatment once inside," Beth said.

"If, they get medical treatment," Mary added.

"Explain," Rebekah said.

Mary looked at Beth and then said, "I'm not convinced people receive any treatment here."

"Then what do they receive?" Derrick asked.

Mary said, "I don't know. But I've heard screams. Very faint, deep inside the building."

"It might just be equipment. You know, like the furnace or air conditioning units," Beth said.

Mary pursed her lips and shook her head. "It's screaming."

"If that's true, why would you work here?" Rebekah asked.

"No choice," Beth said. "They came for me at work one day. Said I had a new assignment. I was brought here and put to work. I live on site. We both do, as does the other shift. Our rooms are in the basement."

"More like cells," Mary said.

"Who came for you?" Derrick asked.

"Two physician's assistants. PAs for short," Beth said, adding, "That's who takes the patients inside once we clear them."

"You came willingly?" Derrick asked.

Beth said, "I protested. I liked my job with the police, but they said it wasn't a request. It was an order."

"An order from who?" Derrick asked.

"They didn't say."

"But you still went with them willingly."

Beth said, "You don't understand, but you would if you saw a PA. They are weird. Menacing."

Derrick thought for a moment. "You are prisoners here?"

Beth said, "Sort of. We could walk away, but they say if we do, our lives and the lives of our families will be at risk."

"At risk of what?" Rebekah asked.

"That part is unclear," Mary said.

Beth said, "It's clear enough to me."

Rebekah waved her blaster. "Meaning?"

"They'll kill us. All of us."

"They would kill you for quitting. Sounds a bit exaggerated to me," Rebekah said.

Beth stared at her. "I'm not willing to find out. I have kids. Mary just started because of what happened to the last person."

Derrick said, "Go on."

"She said she was quitting. Screamed at the PA. The PA grabbed her and dragged her into the hospital. A few hours later, Mary arrived."

Derrick stared at her for a moment. "Getting back on track. If you don't do a medical assessment, what do you screen people for?"

"Like I said, family, friends, jobs, social media. That stuff," Beth said.

"I don't understand." Derrick paused. "What are you looking for exactly?"

"To ensure there's no one who will miss them."

47

AFTER DEPOSITING THE AMBULANCE workers a few miles from the hospital, Antonio wheeled the ambulance into the parking lot of a home-supply store that was closed for the day. He parked in a far corner under a streetlamp. At the other side of the lot stood a make-shift community containing a few tents and tarps that comprised the homes of the more fortunate among the homeless. The less fortunate slept on the pavement. It wasn't cold, so while Antonio felt sorry for them, he felt no pressing need to give them all the blankets in the ambulance. He didn't feel good about not doing it, but going there at this hour would probably terrify them.

Nyx said, "What's the plan?"

Easing the window down, Antonio said, "Wait so the aircraft can monitor us. We should be easy to spot."

"Okay. I'm going to walk a bit. I won't go far."

"Stay where I can see you," Antonio said.

Nyx walked away from the ambulance but remained in the headlight beams. After a few minutes she returned and climbed into the passenger's seat. "Do you think it's safe to park here?"

Antonio indicated the homeless. "Those people think it is, and they don't have a big metal box protecting them. We can see in all directions and can drive away if anyone approaches us. We need to keep our eyes open, but I think it's as safe as we are going to get. Safer than Derrick and Rebekah are."

"Right. I don't like them being in there alone."

"Neither do I." Antonio paused and then turned to look at Nyx. "How serious is this thing with you and Derrick?"

Nyx glared at him. "We aren't going to do this, Antonio. We agreed when we broke up."

Antonio turned in his seat towards her. "I know. It's not that I'm jealous, well, maybe a little jealous, but mostly, I'm worried."

Nyx stared straight ahead, not looking at him. "Worried about what, exactly? That Derrick is just a rebound thing or that maybe I'm not going to dump him and come begging you to take me back."

"Whoa, calm down. I'm not trying to get you back. We both know this had to happen. But I still care about you. You know? I mean, we don't really know Derrick. We know he lied to us. We know this entire situation is his fault."

Nyx turned toward Antonio. "How is it his fault? Because he is alive, and Prime wants him dead?"

"You're right. It's just that…"

"Just what, Antonio?"

"I don't want to see you hurt. That's all."

"That's all? You're sure about that? Or is it that you just don't like seeing me happy?"

Antonio sat silently for a few moments. "I want you to be happy. You've been hurt enough."

"Look, Antonio, I don't want to be hurt. I mean, who does? I can't tell you where this is going with Derrick. Trust me, I'm aware of his lying and the danger he brought to Potterville, but the danger was always there. We just didn't know about it. So, yeah, we are in the middle of it now because of Derrick, but he didn't choose to come to Potterville. He didn't choose any of it. But it is what it is. It's us or Prime. It's not just about Derrick anymore. Prime will destroy Potterville in revenge." She paused. "Despite everything, I like Derrick, and I think he likes me."

"No doubt about Derrick liking you. That much is clear. So, just remember, I will always be your friend, and you can always talk to me. If you need someone to listen. You know that, right?"

"I know." Nyx paused. "Since we are on the topic, what's going on between you and Rebekah?"

"I thought we weren't supposed to go there?"

"You started it." She smiled. "Besides, I just don't want to see you get hurt."

"I deserved that." He shrugged. "I'm just trying to be nice. You know. As student body president, I kind of have to be. If we live through this and if Potterville isn't destroyed, Rebekah might be going to school there."

"Bullshit. I see you flirting with her."

"Well, she is kinda cute."

"Cute? She's gorgeous! But you don't know anything about her. And she had a thing for Derrick."

"They explained that. Somebody put her on Derrick's list." Antonio made air quotes when he said list. "She didn't have a choice in the matter."

Nyx said, "I understand that, but she still had a thing for Derrick. And it's not gone. Not entirely."

"Oh."

"Just be careful. Okay? I don't want to see you get hurt either. Seriously."

"Don't worry about me," Antonio said.

"Does it bother you they are in there together?" Nyx asked.

"It sure as hell does. Doesn't it bother you?"
She stared at him. "Yes. I'm worried sick he's going to get killed."

48

DERRICK STARED AT REBEKAH, HOPING she had an idea of how to proceed. He knew nothing about hospitals. Routine physical examinations were his only experience. However, now he knew that wasn't true. He was a virtual human test of some sort. Likely conceived in a test tube rather than a womb, and his physical examinations were probably not routine. He wondered if other kids went to the doctor for no reason. Despite his lack of knowledge, he was confident that this was not a hospital. At least, not one where people got well.

Derrick said, "Any doubts we are in the right place?"

"None. Something's terribly wrong here."

Derrick decided to get to the point. "Tell us about Prime."

Beth and Mary exchanged a look, but Derrick could not determine what they were thinking.

"Prime? That's a myth," Beth said

"Have you not watched the news?" Rebekah asked.

"You mean about declaring martial law? Do you think that's true? You believe Prime is running the country?" Beth asked.

Derrick said, "Yes, it's true. Did you hear about the building destroyed in Seattle?"

"Yes. A bank if I remember right."

"Not a bank. One of Prime's Headquarters."

"One of Prime's Headquarters?" Mary asked.

"Yes. There are several, including this one." Pointing her weapon at Beth's chest, Rebekah said, "Stop playing games and tell us about Prime. Where do we find him?"

Beth cowered. "I don't know anything about Prime. Honest."

"You didn't think this place was a little strange?" Rebekah asked.

Beth's eyes flicked between Derrick and Rebekah. "Well, yes. I thought it was very strange, but I don't know anything about Prime. I told you. I didn't have a choice. They threatened my family. They told me I had to work here two years, and if I didn't, I'd have no family to go home to."

Derrick thought for a moment. "Then, how does this work? You screen people and then what?"

Beth said, "We buzz the PA. He comes and gets them."

"So, there are medical people?"

Beth looked at Mary. "We assume he is a PA." Beth added. "That's what we call him. He wears scrubs."

Rebekah frowned. "You don't know if the people who come for the patients are medically trained? Do they seem to know what they are doing?"

Beth said, "It's always the same guy. He doesn't talk to us. He doesn't talk to the patients." She paused. "To be honest, he is pretty weird."

"How many patients are here?" Derrick asked.

Mary shrugged. "I have no idea."

"Not many," Beth said.

"And how many staff?"

"No clue," Beth said. "We only see each other and the guy who comes for the patients we clear."

"And the patients you clear have no family, no job, no one looking for them?" Rebekah asked.

Beth's eyes fell to the floor. "Except for runaways."

"Explain," Rebekah said.

"We take kids. They are usually listed as runaways," Beth said.

"Meaning that someone is looking for them? Parents?" Derrick asked.

"Yes."

Derrick shook his head. "Unbelievable. And you don't see a problem with that?"

Beth raised her eyes, staring at Derrick. "Of course I see a problem with that. Haven't you been listening? We don't have a choice. We don't want to be here, but we have families to protect."

Derrick nodded. "I understand." He looked at Rebekah. "Heard enough?"

"More than enough. Let's finish this."

"Call the guy. Tell him we are cleared. You should leave after they take us inside," Derrick said.

"We can't leave. We already explained that," Beth said, frustration evident in her tone.

Rebekah said, "We are going to destroy Prime. We'll be back and let you know that it's safe to go. Then take your families and hide. This will all be over in a couple of days."

"Or less," Derrick added.

"What do you mean, over?" Beth asked.

"You'll know when it's over, one way or another."

"Explain one way or another," Mary said.

"Either we destroy Prime, or Prime goes to war with Mexico," Derrick said, adding, "Call the PA. Do it now."

Mary looked at Beth. "What do you think?"

Beth said, "I'm all for getting out of here. This place gives me the creeps. You do what you think best."

With that, Beth walked to the counter and picked up a phone. "Two cleared for admittance."

"How long before the guy comes?" Derrick asked.

Beth said, "Ten minutes."

"Approximately?" Rebekah asked.

"No. It's always exactly ten minutes."

"That's weird," Rebekah said.

"Interesting," Derrick said. "Will they take us both at the same time?"

Beth said, "No. Only one PA and he will take one of you and then return for the other in five minutes."

Derrick frowned. "You should both stand behind the desk. Just in case."

"In case of what?" Beth asked.

Rebekah said, "We don't know how this is going to go. Best you are out of the line of fire." She paused. "Just so you understand. If you do anything to warn the PA, I'm going to shoot him, and then you. Got it?"

Both scurried to the other side of the desk.

Rebekah turned to Derrick. "What's the plan?"

"Getting separated is unacceptable," Derrick said.

"Agreed. Drop the PA when he opens the door and then go in?"

Derrick thought for a moment and then walked to the door that entered the hospital. "It's locked. But it opens to the inside."

"Is that important?"

Derrick scanned the room and then leaned close, whispering in her ear. "Someone could be listening."

"You destroyed the camera, and no one came."

"True." Derrick eased back a little. "You go first. I'll go to the door and hold it open just a little, so the lock doesn't engage. I'll wait a few seconds and then follow. If he tries to take you through another door before I get inside, zap him."

"What setting?"

Derrick thought for a moment. "Enough to drop him, but don't kill him."

49

THE DOOR OPENED TEN MINUTES AFTER calling the PA. A man walked in, scanned the room, and then walked toward Rebekah and Derrick. The PA wore blue scrubs like a medical person, but he had an unnatural look about him in Derrick's opinion. He was shorter than Derrick by several inches. His head seemed too square and his shoulders too perfect an angle from his neck. Derrick had had a bad feeling about this since they arrived. Now, his bad-feeling-about-this rose exponentially.

Derrick had never been in an emergency room, but he expected the PA would evaluate the patient's condition, which would prove detrimental should he find their blasters. The PA stood looking at them for a few moments but said nothing.

Finally, Derrick said, "Take her first, please."

The PA motioned to the gurney and pointed.

Rebekah said, "I can walk."

The PA pointed at the gurney, again.

Rebekah frowned at Derrick but then climbed onto the gurney. The PA put straps across her chest and legs, which seemed unnecessary for her safety. Derrick felt sure her wellbeing was not the PA's concern. Rebekah's face displayed mild panic as the PA wheeled her away. Derrick followed quietly, feeling a sense of foreboding if the PA got Rebekah into the hospital without him. If that happened, Derrick feared he would not see her again. Not alive.

The PA turned to look at Derrick. Derrick stopped. The PA stared at him for a moment but said nothing. The PA started moving again, slamming the gurney into the door and pushing their way through. Either the PA unlocked the door, or someone unlocked it for him. Perhaps he had a remote control. Either way, Derrick felt confident the door would be locked once the PA was on the other side. Derrick rushed to the door just before it slammed shut, forcing the ball of his foot against it, preventing the latch from engaging. If the PA noticed the door had not fully closed, Derrick's foot would not be enough to prevent the man from forcing it shut. So, he leaned forward, placing his forearm against it, then removed his foot and braced himself.

There came no thrust against the door, so Derrick put his ear next to it and listened. He could hear footsteps fading. Then he heard Rebekah, "Where are you taking me? No one has examined me yet. I need to see a doctor. You don't talk much. Actually, you don't talk at all."

Her voice faded. Rebekah was smart. She was talking so Derrick could judge their distance from the door. Before her voice faded completely, he stepped inside. Derrick found a long hall rather than an examination room. The PA was about 25 yards away, approaching another set of doors. Derrick could not get there in time to prevent them from closing. He could not allow the PA to take Rebekah out of his sight.

"Hey! Wait up." Derrick jogged a few yards.

The PA turned. His expression did not change; however, he ran at Derrick, but moving unlike anything Derrick had ever seen—arms and legs a blur, coming at Derrick so fast, there was no time for assessing the best defense, even with Derrick's ability to slow things down like he had in football and confrontations. At the last possible moment, Derrick leaped toward the wall, giving the PA a push. The PA's momentum caused him to career off the wall, stumble, and fall awkwardly.

Derrick backed down the hall a few yards, still trying to process how quickly the PA moved. Way faster than Malcolm Cross. It was an inhuman kind of speed. Derrick would not turn his back on this guy. Too fast, yet Derrick did not know how the guy planned to attack him. At the speed he was going, it seemed he would simply run into Derrick. But there was little time to process that.

The PA was back on his feet.

He came at Derrick again.

Fast.

No time to think, but Derrick had a plan. When the PA reached him, Derrick grabbed the man's scrubs and fell back, curving his back, landing on his butt, and bringing his knees to his chest. Then, with all his strength, Derrick extended his legs, tossing the guy into the air and letting all that momentum do the heavy lifting.

The PA hit the suspended ceiling, sending tiles crashing down. Derrick spun around in time to see the man land headfirst on the floor, his neck giving way before his shoulder hit. Derrick had not intended to kill the guy. But he did.

Until he didn't.

The PA laid still for a moment. Then got on hands and knees. Then stood. His head flopped helplessly to his shoulder and then rolled back, hanging in the middle of his back. He started toward Derrick, arms out like a sleepwalker.

Suddenly, the sleepwalker PA stopped, stood for a moment, and then toppled like a fallen tree, smacking the floor.

Rebekah lay on the gurney, holding her blaster. She had squirmed enough to free one arm. "What the hell was that?"

Deconstruction
A Derrick King Novel, Book 8

Derrick released the straps holding Rebekah. "Thanks."

"No problem."

Derrick walked to the dead man, knelt, and poked at the PA's face. "Robot."

"That was my guess too. But nothing like the robots we've seen at the base or at the other Prime Headquarters."

Derrick stood. "True. It may have something to do with what this place is about."

Rebekah turned a full circle. "It's worse than the other places. I can't say why, but it creeps me out."

Derrick said, "I don't like anything about this place. People come in, but it's unclear if anyone ever leaves. And the only reason for admittance seems to be that no one is looking for the patients."

Rebekah said, "Except for kids. Runaways."

"That makes it even worse."

"Are you thinking about the test subjects?"

Derrick nodded, then pushed Rebekah against the wall and fired his blaster. A PA that looked exactly like the first one fell to the floor. "The admittance ladies thought they always saw the same guy. I think there's more than one, but they all look the same."

"Sounds right."

Derrick said, "Let's make this fast."

Rebekah looked Derrick over. "How about some clothing first?"

Derrick glanced down at her bare legs then quickly looked her in the eyes. "Good plan."

They found a small room with scrubs and quickly dressed. Derrick said, "We are getting good at finding these places."

"I'm looking forward to shopping for my own clothes." Rebekah brushed her hair free of the collar. "It's a big building. Where do we start? Should we head to the roof and get help?"

Derrick shrugged. "We should scout it out first, I guess."

Before telling people in Potterville that he had been lying about his identity, he started saying, I guess, because it gave vagueness to what he had said. It felt like he had an escape route, should he need it. But this time implied vagueness was unnecessary. He didn't know how to proceed. It was guess-work plain and simple. Besides, he did not know how to reach the roof and did not want to signal Prime that they were in the hospital.

They moved cautiously through the halls, checking doors, and on occasion, blasting the look-a-like PA robots—five, so far. The robots did not learn from the encounters and there was no improvement regarding how they handled each situation. They were not built for battle and had probably never faced a combatant patient. However, based on their speed, they had been designed to chase patients and catch them.

They found no additional people on the first floor and no Prime. Only the five robots. Standing in front of the elevator, Rebekah said, "Up or down?"

"Did you see stairs?" Derrick asked. "I'd rather use stairs."

"I didn't. That seems weird, doesn't it? I mean, they have to have stairs, right? Plus, no patients. That's weird too."

"Super weird. Maybe the stairs were in the emergency room," Derrick said.

"You're probably right. Do you want to go back there?"

Derrick thought for a moment. "No." He paused. "Stairs are usually at the end of a hall near an exit. But there's no exit door at the end of the hall."

Derrick started walking. Rebekah followed. When he reached the end of the hall, he placed one hand on the wall. "There was something here. A door, I think. It's been sealed."

"You think they sealed the exit and the stairs? That's weird," Rebekah said.

"Beyond weird," Derrick agreed.

"There must be something on the second floor. It's a three-floor building," Rebekah said.

"Unless there are floors underground. That's where Prime was in a couple the headquarters."

"Looks like we take the elevator," Derrick said, adding, "and that's not good."

"Agreed. So, up or down?"

"Down."

Rebekah pushed the down button on the elevator and stepped inside. The panel had four buttons: 1, 2, 3, and B. Rebekah chose B.

They started down, and Derrick and Rebekah each leaned behind where the doors retracted for protection. The elevator jerked to a stop and the door slid open to reveal a large area filled with mechanical devices: heating and cooling, huge washers and dryers, ventilation ducts, etc.

Derrick walked deeper into the darkness. Lights came on as he moved, revealing something else: bins filled with parts, workbenches, and robot PAs. Five of them.

"That answers one question," Rebekah said.

"It does."

"Why so few?"

Derrick walked over to one, ran his hand across its shoulder. "They must not need replacements often. They have been sitting here awhile. They are covered with dust."

"Should we do anything about them?" Rebekah asked.

Derrick rejoined her. He pulled his weapon, changed the setting, and then sprayed them with a sustained plasma ark. The robots smoldered. "How's that?"

"Perfect. Second floor?"

Derrick nodded.

Rebekah pushed the number two button and resumed her position behind what little protection the edge of the elevator door provided. Derrick studied her as the elevator jerked and then sped upward. Rebekah should not be here. It was that simple. Why she was here had no simple answer. One thing was certain. She was one in a million. Braver than anyone he could think of. His reason for being here was survival, not bravery. To be truthful, he didn't know if self-preservation adequately explained his rationale. He had to face Prime. He had been telling himself it was to learn the whereabouts of the central headquarters.

That was only part of the reason, and he knew it.

The door slid open. Derrick knew immediately this floor was different. It smelled of activity, of disinfectant—and blood. The hall was empty. The walls were drab and dirty. The floor did not shine like the floors at the Academy. Even the abandoned military base seemed well cared for by comparison. No one cared about this place. At least not on this floor. The hall extended left and right. Rebekah whispered, "What do you think? Split up?"

Derrick shook his head. No way was he letting Rebekah out of his sight. He nodded to the right. They moved cautiously along the walls, one on each side, weapons at the ready, glancing back every few feet. They came to double swinging doors. Above the doors was a sign that read: Operating Suite #1. Derrick motioned Rebekah to the other side, and he put his shoulder to the door and slowly pushed it open. The room was dark, but signs and machines cast a dim light that was enough to see that the room was empty. They scanned the room before lowering their weapons. In the center of the room was a stainless-steel table. The table was bolted to the floor. On either side of the table were platforms of steel mesh, raised a few inches. The mesh was wide enough to stand on and encompassed the entire table. Below the mesh was a stainless-steel pan that sloped to a pump that fed clear plastic hoses attached to large glass containers. Hanging from the table were four heavy leather straps.

Along one wall stood a counter with surgical instruments. Along the other wall was a pegboard that held a strange collection of tools: hammers, pruning shears, several saws, screwdrivers, vices, etc.

"This doesn't look right," Rebekah said.

Derrick said, "I agree." His stomach twisted into a knot. He feared what they might find in the next operation room, which was directly across the hall. He took a deep breath, hoping to steel himself, but failed to do so. "Let's get this over with he said." He was certain the dread in his voice was evident.

Rebekah nodded. Her face had turned ghostly white.

50

IN THE HALLWAY JUST OUTSIDE operating room #2, Derrick paused. They positioned themselves on each side of the double doors, and the stench of blood, decay, and disinfectant had grown stronger. Derrick looked at Rebekah, and as impossible as it seemed, she appeared to be even more distraught than he felt. Whatever lay beyond this door was beyond horrific and they both knew it.

Derrick pushed through his door quickly. Rebekah matched him.

They froze.

A man wearing surgical scrubs was putting tools away. He turned, startled. His white scrubs were soaked in blood.

"Who are you? You can't be in here." His expression changed from arrogance to fear when he noticed the weapons.

"Shut up!" Derrick barked.

A body lay on the table. Leather straps secured the legs and arms. Derrick could not tell if it was a man or a woman. Not because the body was covered. It was not. Derrick wished it was. He could not tell because the body had no skin. Private parts had been removed. The feet were gone, as were the hands. Buckets sat at the sides and foot of the table, filled with body parts: feet, fingers, skin, hands. Blood slowly drained to the low spot where a pump pushed it through clear tubes into a large glass container.

It took every bit of his strength to keep from vomiting.

"What have you done?" Rebekah whispered.

"My job. Whoever you are, you'll not get away with this. There will be humanoids here to detain you shortly." The man didn't sound completely convinced.

Derrick turned back to the man, trying to unsee the horror on the table. He raised his weapon. "Answer her question."

Before he could answer, Rebekah said, "This is deconstruction."

"Where did you hear that term?" the doctor asked with a bit of astonishment in his voice.

"Was this a test subject?" Derrick asked.

The doctor didn't answer.

Deconstruction
A Derrick King Novel, Book 8

Rebekah took a step toward him., motioning toward the table. "If you don't want to end up looking like this, you'd better start talking."

"You wouldn't dare."

Rebekah raised her weapon. "Try me. Start talking or when you wake up, you'll be strapped to a table."

The doctor held up his hands. "Calm down. Look, this is my job, okay? I don't have a choice in the matter."

He moved cautiously to a counter pushed a button underneath. Derrick saw him do it. If there were any robot PAs left, they'd be here soon. Let them come.

With the button pushed, the doctor, assuming rescue was moments away, relaxed. His expression changed again, from fear back to arrogance. Derrick wanted to erase that smirk but decided that a confident and condescending doctor was to his and Rebekah's advantage. There was a legitimate part of Derrick that understood knowledge was power when dealing with Prime.

"Who was the person?" Derrick asked.

The doctor waved it off. "Nobody. A runaway."

Derrick wanted to say the person probably felt differently, but trying to convince this monster that he was evil would serve no purpose and probably wasn't possible. "Do you deconstruct test subjects here?"

"Yes, of course. That is our primary purpose. We do all the test subject deconstruction. But tell me, how do you know about test subjects?"

"If that is your purpose, why do this to a runaway?" Derrick asked.

"To practice and improve my craft." The doctor motioned to the wall of tools. "I have made major breakthroughs of late. You see, we used to do it like surgery, using scalpels and other surgical instruments. The very process of deconstruction was effective, of course, to create the desired effects we were seeking. However, the use of simple tools created a much more effective response than we ever believed was possible. You cannot imagine how much more effective snapping off fingers one joint at a time with pruning shears is than merely cutting them off with a scalpel."

The doctor laughed a maniacal laugh; apparently, confident robotic PAs would soon save him.

Derrick's rage grew. More rage than he felt when he smacked Marcus Carver. The difference this time was that he controlled it instead of it controlling him. Derrick didn't want to kill people, but if there was ever a person who deserved death, it was this one.

"What are you seeking, exactly?" Rebekah asked.

"Terror and pain, of course."

"Why? What good can that possibly serve?" Rebekah asked.

"Complete mental exhaustion. The ability to eradicate a person's will to exist."

"But why?"

The doctor thought for a moment. "To be perfectly honest, that is not my department."

"You cannot be serious. You torture these people, and you don't know why?" Rebekah lowered her weapon a little.

The doctor glanced at the door, a bit of panic creeping into his expression. Derrick estimated it had been about eight minutes since he pushed the help button. Apparently, that's what it took to activate a robot. How many were left? Any? They would soon find out.

Derrick said, "Do you know who benefits from the study of deconstruction?" He found calling it study abhorrent but thought playing along would appeal to the doctor's substantial ego.

"Prime. It's all about Prime."

Suddenly, the door flew open. Two of the robot PAs dashed in. Without turning to look, Derrick pointed his blaster and dropped both before they took a second step. The doctor turned white again.

"How many of these robots are here?" Derrick asked.

The doctor rung his hands. "More than you can handle."

Rebekah took a step toward him. "He didn't ask your opinion. How many?" She raised the weapon and, with an exaggerated motion, turned it on high.

"I don't know." He paused. "At least seven. Maybe more."

Rebekah said, "Seven total or seven more after subtracting those two?"

The doctor held his hand out. "Seven total, I think. Listen. I don't know what you want, but I can help you… Answer more questions. I'll tell you everything you want to know."

"Where's Prime?" Derrick asked.

The doctor's eyes shifted from Derrick to Rebekah to the door.

"The robots are not coming." Rebekah pointed. "Those were the last two. One last chance. Where is Prime?"

"Third floor. Please. I can help you."

Rebekah lowered her weapon. "Thanks. We have no further need of you."

And with that, she raised her weapon and shot him.

51

THE DOCTOR LAY FACE DOWN ON THE operating room floor. Derrick saw Rebekah switch the blaster to high. He had not seen her change the setting. The man deserved death. He deserved worse than death.

"What should we do with him?" Rebekah asked.

"Is he dead?"

"You know me better than that. I dialed it back before I fired."

Derrick thought for a moment. "I wanted to kill him."

"But you wouldn't have."

"Probably not. I'll drag him to the next room. You cover me."

In operating room #1, Derrick set the man against the table and secured both arms using the leather straps. He spotted a clipboard hanging on the wall. He wrote a note that read: "My work is in the other room." And put it on the operating table.

"Should we tape his mouth?" Rebekah said.

"No. His screaming will lead the police right to him."

"Third floor?" Rebekah asked.

"Not yet. Let's see what is down the hall in the other direction."

Pausing outside the first door, Rebekah said, "Smells awful."

Derrick said, "Yes, but hopeful."

Rebekah wrinkled her nose. "Hopeful?"

"It smells of sweat and urine. Which means there are people in there. Alive."

They opened the first door, eased in, weapons at the ready. What they saw inside was as wretched as operating room #2 was horrendous. People were locked in 4 x 4 cages that were stacked on top of each other. Derrick said, "Help is coming. You're safe now."

And with that, they withdrew from the room. In the hall, Derrick took a breath and tried to cleanse the stench from his nostrils.

"Who's coming to help them?"

Derrick said, "We'll send the reception ladies up and have them call the police."

"After we kill Prime?"

"Naturally."

"Check the other rooms?"

"No need. We'll find more people in cages. I don't need to see that. I already have too many images in my brain that I can't unsee. Are you ready?"

With confidence that should have been a clue as to what was about to happen, Rebekah said, "Absolutely."

Derrick didn't question Rebekah's response. Perhaps he was just too tired. Maybe it was something else. He would never know for sure.

At the elevator, Rebekah pushed the up arrow and looked at Derrick. "Almost done here, my friend."

The doors slid open, and Derrick stepped inside. Suddenly, something grabbed him from behind and jerked him back into the hall. Rebekah used the momentum to thrust herself into the elevator, trading places with him. The doors were closing, and he realized, albeit too late, that Rebekah had pushed the door-closed button.

Derrick reacted quickly, sticking his hand out to stop the doors. Rebekah smiled and zapped him. Not enough to knock him out, just enough to freeze him for a moment. "I got this one. See you soon."

The doors closed. Derrick jabbed at the down button. He kept pushing it, but the light indicated the elevator continued upward. It would not come back down until it reached the third floor.

"Rebekah, what have you done?" He screamed at the elevator.

52

THE ELEVATOR DOORS SLID OPEN. Prime turned as if surprised. Perhaps with such a small facility and so few staff, Prime didn't have additional security beyond the robotic PAs. Apparently, Prime did not envision intruders ever reaching the third floor.

"What is this? Who are you?"

"You can call me Grim."

Rebekah raised the weapon.

"Grim Reaper."

And with that, and the weapon on its highest setting, she pulled the trigger and kept it pulled until smoke curled from Prime's lifeless body.

***

Derrick kept pressing the button, but the elevator would not respond. Several minutes had passed that felt like hours and then the elevator descended. Derrick pulled his blaster and pointed it at the door. He prayed it was Rebekah and feared it wasn't. He set the weapon on low; in case it was Rebekah. Or Prime. He had to interrogate Prime or so he still told himself. When the door slid open, he breathed a sigh of relief.

Except that Rebekah was aiming her blaster at him. She had already given him a shock, albeit a light one.

"Don't make me use this," Rebekah said, adding, "It's set higher this time."

"Why are you doing this?"

"Don't argue. Just give me your blaster. Easy. Two fingers on the grip, do not point it toward me."

Derrick did as she said.

Soon as Rebekah had his blaster, she giggled. "I saw that in an old movie." She tossed him her blaster. As the elevator door closed, she said, "Don't try to use that. It's completely dead." And with that, the elevator started upward again.

***

Deconstruction
A Derrick King Novel, Book 8

When the doors opened, Rebekah held the blaster at the ready, set on high. Nothing greeted her except the smoldering corpse, which smelled more like rotting cooked meat than melted plastic. Before exiting the elevator, she turned a key, locking the doors open and the elevator in place.

This Prime looked different. More man than machine. More animal than man. Every Prime Headquarters seemed to serve a purpose. Besides deconstructing actual humans, this one created more human-like robots. It did not appear creating a more human-like Prime was the goal here, or if it was, it was not going well.

There were still Prime replicants to destroy, but she didn't know if they were on this floor. They had not finished searching the second floor. She knew the replicants were created to replace Prime if something happened to the current one, or by design, to test a new model. How the birth of the atrocities was started remained unclear. Perhaps someone had to start the process. Perhaps it was automated in case Prime died or was killed.

Inside the room, beyond a wall covered with computer monitors, she found a pegboard containing tools: a long-handled sledgehammer, a black plastic mallet labeled 'weighted hammer', a big axe, a carpenter's claw hammer, a gas-powered chain saw. Each had an outline drawn around it. One tool was missing, but the outline remained. It was labeled Pulaski Fire Fighting Axe.

There was a list on the table. The heading read: Deconstruction Test #19,375. Each tool was listed on the left. To the right were columns that rated each tool: perceive terror, begging, pain level, cardiac arrest.

She did not see the Prime replicas. There were walls with doors on both sides of the building. The windows had heavy steel plates covering them. There were no robots and no human assistant.

This Prime Headquarters did not have the elaborate defenses of the others. It spoke of either foolishness or arrogance. She suspected the latter. She eased to one door and threw it open. It proved to be a living area. She realized she had not seen the area where Prime called home, only the work areas. There had been no need to enter a living area previously.

To say it was extravagant was an understatement. The ceiling and walls were edged with elaborately carved moldings, velvet drapes of rich burgundy covered the windows, a couch covered with the same gaudy material sat against a wall covered with red and gold wallpaper. The floor was covered with a thick burgundy carpet. Everything else was covered with gold. It was extravagant and hideous simultaneously.

There were no replicants here.

She darted to the remaining door, feeling confident the replicas would be on the other side. Probably an assistant as well.

She eased the door open.

Deconstruction
A Derrick King Novel, Book 8

A woman stood inside—covered with blood—holding the missing axe. Rebekah pointed the blaster at her. The Pulaski was an intimidating weapon, but not something a person could throw.

The woman had not noticed Rebekah. Rebekah edged into the room until she saw what the woman was staring at.

Rebekah saw a bloody and battered Prime replicant on the floor. As the line of replicant tanks came into view, Rebekah saw the others all broken and the replicants dead.

"You did this?"

The woman turned her head. "Yes. I heard a noise. I ran out to see what was happening." She paused, then apparently in shock, she continued in a monotone voice. "Saw Prime dead. This was my chance. The next Prime was already exiting the tank. I killed it. The first one. Then I killed the others."

The woman noticed the blaster and dropped the axe. "I killed them. I killed them all. Arrest me. I won't fight you."

Rebekah returned the blaster into the small of her back and walked over to the woman and threw her arms around her. "Arrest you? I want to kiss you."

After a moment, Rebekah separated from the woman and held her by the shoulders. "Do you have clean clothing?"

The woman was crying. "What's your name?" Rebekah asked.

"Doris. You're not here to arrest me?"

"No. I came to kill them." Rebekah pointed at the replicants. "You beat me to it. So, here's what I want you to do. Get into dry clothes. The police will be here soon. There are people locked in cages here that need help."

Doris nodded, still sobbing.

"You stay and help until those people are freed and being taken care of. Then go home." Rebekah paused. "If the police ask, just tell them that a team, dressed in black and wearing face masks, stormed the facility and killed Prime. Explain to them that Prime was killing people here. There's a victim still in operating room #2."

Doris interrupted. "Is he alive?"

Rebekah shook her head. "No. We were too late to help him."

Doris's body racked with sobs. When she gained control, she picked up the axe. "Where is that monster? The doctor."

Rebekah took the axe, gently. "Strapped to the table in operating room #1."

Doris's eyes grew wild. "Give it back! I'll kill that bastard too."

Calmly but forcefully, Rebekah said, "No. You will not. Let the police handle it. Do you hear me? People here need help and you going to jail won't help them. The police will take care of the doctor. If they don't, I'll personally comeback and put an end to him."

Rebekah stared into Doris's eyes. "Agreed?"

Doris nodded.

"You did a good thing here, Doris. Now go enjoy your life and keep doing good." With that, Rebekah walked to the door. Before leaving, she turned and said, "You never saw me. I was never here."

53

THE ELEVATOR WAS DESCENDING AGAIN. Derrick stood, leaning with his back against the wall, arms crossed, fuming. If Prime or a robot were in the elevator, he was defenseless. Rebekah had zapped him and then tricked him and left him with no way to protect himself.

The elevator bell dinged. The doors slid open. Rebekah stepped out, glancing down before raising her eyes to meet his. She gave him a weak smile. "Sorry about that."

She held out his blaster. "Here, it's set the same as when I zapped you. Go ahead. Shoot me. I deserve it."

Derrick took the blaster. Handed hers back. Studied it for a moment and then suck it in the small of his back. "Never do that again. What in the hell were you thinking?"

"Mostly, I was thinking about killing Prime."

"Did you learn anything? I needed to interrogate Prime. We still don't know the location of the central Prime."

Rebekah nodded. "I know. I screwed up. After seeing the," she paused, "deconstruction, I just wanted to kill it. And I did. I killed it straight away." She paused. "I understand you're mad at me. But I kept thinking that Prime wants to deconstruct you. I couldn't risk that happening. Prime had to die."

Derrick's anger subsided quicker than he had expected. She was protecting him. He understood that. He would do the same for her. But interrogating Prime was vital. He'd get one more chance in San Diego. His thoughts turned to how to make sure he got the chance to make that happen.

"What about the replicants?"

"The assistant just called it the next Prime."

"There was an assistant? Still alive? Did you…kill him?"

"Her. I did not. She had just destroyed the replicants. I told her to help the prisoners. If you're not going to zap me, we should go."

Derrick nodded. "Let's go back to the emergency room and give Beth and Mary instructions. If they are still there."

Rebekah said, "And ask them about roof access. Miriam is probably worried about us. We don't want her to do anything that will draw unnecessary attention to us."

Deconstruction
A Derrick King Novel, Book 8

Derrick walked to the elevator, pushed the down button, and stepped inside. Rebekah joined him and the doors closed. He put her arm around her shoulder and pulled her close. "Thank you."

"For what?"

"For taking care of me. I can't stay mad at you for that."

When they entered the emergency room, Beth and Mary were sitting on the counter but jumped off and stood at attention. Beth's hand flew to her mouth. "You're alive."

"Did you have doubts?" Rebekah asked.

"I didn't think I'd ever see you again."

"Prime is dead. The robots are gone. A murdering doctor is detained in operating room #1. A murder victim is in operating room #2." Derrick paused, then walked to the desk. "Do you have paper and pen here?"

Beth opened a drawer and produced a clipboard and a pen. "Here."

Derrick took a form off the clipboard and turned it over. "Here's what you are going to do. Call the police. Tell them there has been a murder, and the killer is still here but detained. Also, tell them you need ambulances for victims that have been imprisoned here. When they arrive, give them this first."

Beth and Mary read the clipboard.

1.   This is a Prime Headquarters.
2.   Prime murdered thousands of people here.
3.   A murder victim is on the second floor in operating room #2. The killer is in operating room #1.
4.   There are prisoners in cages on the second floor.
5.   Prime is dead on the third floor.

Beth stared at Derrick. "Murder victim?"

Derrick nodded. "Yes. I recommend you not go in there."

"Prime is real?" Mary asked.

Rebekah said, "Yes. Go to the third floor. See for yourself. Also, there's a woman up there who has been held captive. Her name is Doris. She will stay and help you with the victims. But to be honest, she may need your help as well. She's been through a lot."

Derrick said, "You should all stay and help those who have been held prisoner here. When they have been taken care of, go home."

"And do what?" Beth asked.

"Have a great life," Derrick said.

"And what should we tell the police about you?" Mary asked.

"You never saw us. You saw armed men dressed in black with face masks," Rebekah said.

"Gotcha. I can do that," Beth said.

Mary nodded. "Me too."

"Are there stairs with roof access?" Derrick asked.

Mary said, "Outside just left of the emergency room doors. It looks like it was added after the building was built. But the door is likely locked."

At the door, he stopped and motioned for Rebekah. He said, "Don't worry, we have a key."

"Wait!" Beth called out. "Where are you going?"

"To finish this," Derrick said.

54

WITH EVERYONE BACK ON BOARD, Nyx set a course to San Diego. Miriam encouraged them to eat energy bars and drink an energy drink. It was all old military stuff. The bar wasn't too bad, but Derrick thought it was probably softer decades earlier. The drink was sweet and tasted like berries and metal. During the flight, Derrick and Rebekah took turns explaining the events at the hospital. They glossed over the details of the deconstruction, merely describing it as horrific. Still, everyone squirmed at what details were shared. They said little about killing Prime but elaborated on how the assistant had destroyed the replicants.

When they'd finished, Antonio looked at Miriam. "What's the plan in San Diego. Rebekah has done enough. I want to go in on the last one."

Rebekah took his hand. "Not your decision. Plus, San Diego isn't the last one."

Miriam said, "The plan is the same as the others."

"We had plans for the others?" Antonio asked.

"We did not. So, the San Diego plan is exactly the same."

"Huh?"

"We'll figure it out when we get there," Miriam said. "Nyx, when will we have a visual?"

"We still have some miles to cover, but I have it now, such as it is."

"What does that mean? What does it look like?" Miriam asked.

"That's the point. I can't tell."

"Because it's too dark or we are too far away?" Anna asked.

"Kind of. I mean, I think it's the contrast that creates the problem."

With frustration evident in her voice, Miriam said, "Can you just explain what you're talking about?"

"Lights. Lots of them. And smoke. Lots of it. See for yourself."

An image appeared on everyone's monitors: a large building encircled with many strobing red and blue lights. Smoke boiled from the building's windows.

"What's happening?" Derrick asked, a bit of panic in his voice.

"Holy crap," Antonio said. "A gazillion police cars, fire trucks, and ambulances."

"And a huge fire," Derrick said.

Deconstruction
A Derrick King Novel, Book 8

The image became closer and clearer with each passing second as they raced toward the scene.

Antonio said, "Yes, it is."

"What's going on?" Rebekah asked, sounding bewildered.

Miriam said, "I don't know, but we need to find out."

"It will be impossible to get in with all those people," Derrick said.

Anna said, "I don't think anyone is getting *into* that building."

Antonio said, "Land on the roof of the third building in the next block. It has an outside fire escape. I'll go down and find out and then come back to the roof."

"What if they see us?" Derrick asked.

Nyx said, "I'll come in low and from the south. We'll be invisible to those surrounding Prime's Headquarters."

"Plus, they won't be looking our direction, and their eyes won't be adjusted to the darkness because of all those lights in their eyes," Antonio said.

Miriam said, "Wait a minute. When did you become the leader? I'll go. You stay put."

Antonio looked at Miriam. "I'm not trying to be the boss, but I am the most logical person."

"I'm listening."

"My kind of neighborhood. I'll fit in."

"Wearing those clothes?" Rebekah said.

"What? Your clothes are better?"

"I'm wearing scrubs and you're wearing an EMT jacket—from Dallas."

"Good point. I'll leave the jacket." He paused. "Look. I'm street-smart."

"You're saying you're smarter than me?" Rebekah asked.

Antonio held up his hands. "Whoa. Slow down. I didn't say I was smarter. I said I was street-smart. Big difference."

Miriam took a deep breath. "Could you just explain what you meant?"

"Okay. So, I go down there and just look around. Lots of people who look just like me. I start asking folks. What's happening? Who's in there? Anybody hurt? Stuff like that."

Rebekah said, "I can do that."

"I'll be asking in Spanish."

"Coming up on the rooftop now," Nyx said.

Derrick said, "I'll go."

Everyone looked at him.

Miriam said, "We aren't taking a vote. Antonio is right. He's best suited for it." She looked at Antonio. "Just find out what's happening and get back up here. No heroics."

"Don't worry. I'm no hero. I'll be back as soon as possible."

Rebekah said, "Don't get yourself hurt. Jerk." She smiled and winked at him.

* * *

Derrick had been watching a digital clock. Antonio was taking forever, but in reality, only 20 minutes had passed when he returned.

Antonio sank into his seat and said, "Let's go."

"Where to? What's going on?" Miriam asked.

"Back to the base, I guess. We need to sleep." He looked at Nyx. "I'll explain on the way."

Nyx didn't move.

Antonio said, "Prime is dead. We are done here."

The aircraft lifted off. Nyx flew south, gained altitude, turned toward the base, and rocketed into the night.

Antonio put on his headset, scanned the aircraft to ensure everyone was listening. "I learned that a sheriff showed up with a warrant for Prime's arrest. Accessory to murder, five counts and several attempted murder charges as well. Prime resisted arrest and was killed. That simple."

"Sheriff? Murder?" Miriam asked.

"Yes. Murders in Potterville, California. Sheriff Bill Collins. Story is that Prime has several headquarters, and Potterville deputies have been attempting to serve warrants all night. They are unclear on details but have heard that Seattle, New York, and Chicago have had similar outcomes."

Nyx said, "Are we the deputies?"

Antonio said, "I assume that would be correct."

"That means it's all legal?" Nyx asked.

Antonio shrugged. "Apparently."

The flight to the base didn't take long. Still, Derrick was nodding off when they landed. They dragged themselves into the facility. Charlie was up and asked if they were hungry. Everyone declined.

Miriam said, "Everyone get some sleep." She sat at a computer.

"What are you doing?" Derrick asked.

"Planting the bait for the trap I've set for Prime. I'm responding to the e-mail Prime sent when he destroyed the doctor's house in California. When he responds, I'll be able to triangulate the signal and locate the central location."

"Is that safe?" Derrick asked.

"I'm using encrypted military satellites. It should be completely safe. Besides, Prime doesn't have a big enough missile to bother us here. Get some sleep. I'll see you all at breakfast and we'll make our final plans."

Derrick hesitated. Nyx came beside him and raised on tiptoes, kissing him on the cheek. "See you in the morning."

"You don't have to tell me twice," Antonio said, as he headed toward his bed.

Derrick had a bad feeling, but that wasn't new. He'd had a bad feeling for a long time. He wondered if that feeling had become a permanent condition. Besides, they had been successful thus far, and only one target remained. Then L. Linda Maxton came to mind, reminding him that they had not been one hundred percent successful.

55

A KNOCK SOUNDED BUT STANLEY FELT sure he had imagined it, or dreamed it, or perhaps it was just a pipe rattling. He was, after all, buried under the desert in an ancient government complex. But then it sounded again. Even in his half-asleep, partially intoxicated state, he understood the knock at the door was real.

"Yes? Give me a minute."

From the other side of the door, a voice said, "Sorry to awaken you, sir, but Prime requests your presence."

Stanley was sitting on the edge of the bed now, rubbing his face. "I'll head there right away."

He didn't ask what it was about. The guy wouldn't know. Stanley was sure whatever Prime wanted; it wasn't to tell him good news. Stanley had a couple of drinks too many last night. More like half-a-dozen too many. He'd made some big mistakes that he could remember and probably even bigger ones that he could not. He had feared Maggie was working for Prime. Looks like he was right. He would not have minded being wrong this time.

By the time Stanley made it to the control center, a place where he had not officially started work and likely never would, he was awake but not alert. Or completely sober. Since the moment he arrived here, death had felt like a probability, but he wasn't ready for it. He supposed one never was when death came.

"Ah, there you are, Stanley. I am sorry to awaken you. I promised you the weekend off, and here I am troubling you again. However, something major has happened, and I was certain you would never forgive me if I didn't call you immediately."

"No problem at all, sir. I am here to serve."

"Sit. Scotch?"

Stanley sat. "Very kind of you, sir, but no, I'm fine."

Prime walked to a bar made of walnut and polished to a high sheen. "I insist. This is a monumental occasion. At least one of us should be enjoying a fine Scotch. This is over one hundred years old. I opened the bottle for you just now. There will not be many moments like this. I only hope that in the not-too-distant future I will be able to join you." Prime handed Stanley the glass.

Deconstruction
A Derrick King Novel, Book 8

The aroma of cherries and oak drifted to Stanley's nose, and to his surprise, it smelled more enticing than he had anticipated. He sensed that his enjoyment of fine whiskey was coming to a close. "They have finally perfected a model that will allow you to consume food and beverages, sir. That is monumental news and deserves a toast." Stanley raised his glass.

Prime raised his hand. "Slow down. That is not the news I brought you here for, although it is related. You see, it's not a new version but an actual human body I will soon inhabit."

Stanley lowered his glass. A human body. That was monumental. Monumentally disturbing. That meant Prime believed he could be downloaded into a body, which meant whoever lived in that body would be eradicated. Gathering himself, Stanley said, "Amazing." His voice cracked in a most unfortunate and telling fashion.

"Stanley, soon you will witness the greatest event in human history."

Stanley wasn't sure what to say. Everything to Prime was the most important thing in the world. At least, that's how Prime saw it. However, something told Stanley this time it was different, and he was certain he would rather not hear about it. "This sounds like something very special, sir. I mean, I can't imagine anything that would exceed you having a human body again."

"Your point is well taken. This is the beginning of the next phase of human existence. The nexus, the turning point. Recreating not only myself but the entire world. This is genesis."

"Oh, my!"

"Do you understand, Stanley? I have found Derrick and Miriam King."

Deconstruction
A Derrick King Novel, Book 8

Part Three

1

WHEN DERRICK AWOKE, THE ROOM contained no light whatsoever, which confused him. He had grown accustomed to his condo, which had good window coverings, yet a little light from Potterville's streetlamps always slipped through, even at night. Then he remembered he wasn't in Potterville. He was under a mountain on an abandoned military base. There was no light here unless it came from a source and every light source in the room was turned off. He laid there for a moment, trying to fall back to sleep. Instead, he became more alert. He assessed his overall condition. Everything hurt but not too much, which was surprising under the circumstances.

Miriam had not set a time for breakfast. Perhaps she had told Charlie when to awaken everyone. Teenagers could sleep till noon.

Fully awake, he checked the time—seven o'clock. That wasn't much sleep. It was almost two in the morning when he got into bed. Five hours didn't seem like enough rest, yet he was wide awake. He heard nothing and didn't smell coffee or bacon, which meant he was the only one up. So, what to do? Coffee sounded good.

He walked to the kitchen. It was empty. He had never operated the espresso machine, but he had watched the process several times and thought he could remember the steps. There was no quieting the machine as it ground coffee or during the steam extraction of espresso. If he awakened anyone, they would be unhappy. Life was full of risks and fresh hot coffee was worth the risk.

With a steaming cup of coffee, he walked the empty passageways to where the trains arrived and departed. The temperature dropped outside the building. The temperature in the tunnels seemed constant. The air felt moist. Although he didn't know anything about science or geology, the constant temperature made sense being underground.

He sat on a crate that contained an AT-series robot. They had brought three when they fetched the new Charlie. He'd remember to ask Charlie if they should be brought inside. Technically, they were inside the tunnel, and no one was going to steal them, and it wasn't going to rain, so they could sit out here for the next century without any damage, unless the QR-3s evolved and wanted to eradicate the superior machines. His imagination had veered into the ridiculous zone; however, Charlie had evolved, so perhaps it wasn't entirely crazy. At least, they had a spare Charlie-bot should the need ever arise.

Derrick took a deep breath. For the first time since his 17th birthday, the day he was exiled, he felt as if things might turn out okay. They had defeated all the Primes with less difficulty than he had anticipated. That thought caused him some discomfort because L. Linda Maxton's death was no small thing. That event caused an ache in his chest every time it crossed his mind. Still, they had been victorious in their first assault, in no small part because of L. Linda's sacrifice. He wished they could honor that somehow, but because their plan was to ensure no one ever knew about their involvement in Prime's demise, L. Linda's sacrifice would go unobserved, as if it never happened.

Thinking about L. Linda transformed his mood from hopeful to melancholy. He thought about seeing if anyone else was awake but didn't. Perhaps a short run would clear his head. Venturing off to take on the central Prime in his current state of mind seemed like a bad idea. He should leave a note, but Charlie would know where he was. If he ran a mile and then returned, he'd be gone about 15 minutes. Most likely no one would be awake in 15 minutes anyway.

He stretched. Not the full routine Nyx had taught him, just enough to loosen up a little, and took off jogging. He decided to go the direction he had not yet traveled. The tunnel made a loop. It was over 100 miles, if he remembered correctly, from here back to where he originally entered. The medical train made the trip so quickly that he'd stopped thinking about the distance. Along the track on the other side were missile silos and, at silo number eight, the dead bodies of the last people who worked here.

The ones that bombed Sacramento, once the capital of the State of California, killing thousands and starting a war. James Carver had orchestrated that attack to set himself up as the last president of the United States. Picking up his pace, Derrick thought about what James Carver had done, compared to what the Chosen were taught. It occurred to him that it was likely the United States didn't fail as much as it was destroyed. Close to three-hundred years of history destroyed by one man.

Derrick felt an involuntary shiver. If one man could destroy a country, how much could Prime annihilate?

Derrick picked up speed. Thus far, running was not clearing his head. He checked his watch. Seven minutes. Probably a mile or more. A little farther wouldn't hurt. He doubted turning around now was going to give him enough time and distance to create the mental acuity needed to take on the central Prime. Running the entire loop might not be enough.

Five minutes later, Derrick's thinking finally cleared. That euphoric feeling had set in, taken over. Now he was just running. Arms, legs, and heart working as one.

Deconstruction
A Derrick King Novel, Book 8

Better.

He assumed there were missiles on this side of the loop like the other side, but he had no idea how many or how far it was to the first one. When riding on the train, things went by too fast to see details, plus it was dark in the tunnel. However, it wasn't completely dark here. Sparingly spaced lights cast a dim light. Running allowed him to see details that had been invisible from the train. It wasn't just an empty tube cut through solid rock. Much of it was rock but some was concrete formed to the same shape as the rest of the tunnel. Raised concrete walkways lined the sides and there were two sets of tracks, thus trains could go both directions. Why that was necessary, he didn't know. Perhaps just so they could move more people. Make more stops. Work on different things.

Traveling in the train car, he could not see anything other than the silo signs as they passed. Even then, they were hard to read. Rows of conduit ran along the ceiling, small alcoves held gray boxes, switches, and other mechanisms. He didn't stop to investigate. He was in the zone now.

He did, however, wonder about the lights. Did the other side of the loop have the same lighting, but he couldn't see it from inside the train? Maybe the lights came on because of his presence like they did at the base, but that didn't seem right because they were on when he started and had not changed. Maybe they were on for some other reason, although he could not imagine what that reason might be.

He pushed the thoughts from his mind. The lighting was unimportant. He could ask Charlie but would likely forget about it. Too insignificant given the pending showdown with Prime. Derrick couldn't help but think of the remaining Prime as the real Prime. They said all of the others embodied Prime's complete identity, yet Derrick did not think that was accurate. He could be wrong, but he didn't think so. The central Prime was the genuine Prime. The others were copies. Like cheap knockoffs. Derrick felt certain of that.

Derrick saw a gentle curve about a half a mile in the distance. From his location, the curve looked more severe than any curve on the track he had traveled, so he decided to investigate. He would head back after that, having already run farther and been gone longer than he had anticipated. Miriam would be angry if his absence slowed them down. When he'd left, he felt sure that Charlie would know where he was, but his confidence about that had faded. If he was both missing and late, Miriam would be fuming. Nyx would be worried. The results of both were something he wanted to avoid. He picked up the pace.

As he approached the curve, he saw there was an opening on the opposite side of the tunnel. Perhaps the entrance to a missile silo. Worth a look since he was already here.

His curiosity would start a series of discoveries, none of them good. He started across to the other side at the apex of the turn, concentrating on stepping over the tracks so that he didn't trip. He didn't look farther down the tracks ahead of him until he had cleared the second set of rails. When he glanced up, he saw a single train car stopped on the track. Black robots were exiting the train and going into a tunnel he recognized as a missile silo entrance.

Derrick dashed into the alcove, which turned out to be a set of switches, not a silo entrance. Peering around the corner, he saw the robots had disappeared into the silo. He didn't know if any robots remained in the train car because the windows were like mirrors. This train car was different: gleaming black with rounded corners and mirrored windows. *Why would Charlie have robots in the missile silos?* Derrick wondered.

Perhaps Charlie had been performing maintenance on the missiles for decades. Charlie had not mentioned that was part of his function, but there was no reason for anybody to have asked.

So, probably no big deal.

Except for one thing.

Those robots did not look like any of the robots Derrick had seen here or at other Prime Headquarters.

2

AFTER A FEW MINUTES, THE ROBOTS exited the silo and entered the train. The train sped away moments later. Derrick remained hidden in the alcove, peeking out to ensure the train continued down the tracks toward the base. The train car was a distant speck when red lights came on like the brake lights of a car. Derrick didn't know if all the trains had similar lights because he had only ridden inside and had never been directly behind one. The train was too distant to see the robots, which meant he was probably far enough away that they could not see him. However, he realized what he could see and what robots could see was not the same.

He waited until the robots had left the train and were in the next silo, assuming that's why the train had stopped. On a diagonal, away from where the train had parked, Derrick dashed back to the other side of the tunnel. His exposure to the robots was brief. He ran along the wall on the raised walkway. When he could see the black train in the distance, he slowed, flattening himself against the wall, edging toward the silo entrance where the robots had been. Once inside, he hurried to the display panel. It was off. Miriam had touched the panel to activate it. Derrick did the same. The screen came to life.

```
MISSILE NUMBER 27—STATUS: ACTIVE

MISSILE NUMBER 27—WARHEAD: US TSAR THERMONUCLEAR

MISSILE NUMBER 27—WARHEAD STATUS: ARMED

MISSILE NUMBER 27—TARGET: NEW YORK CITY, NEW YORK,
UNITED STATES

BEGIN LAUNCH SEQUENCE Y=YES N=NO

LAUNCH SEQUENCE LOCKED—ON-SITE LAUNCH UNAVAILABLE

REMOTE LAUNCH ONLY
```

Derrick didn't understand. New York City had the largest population in New America. This targeting must have been set back when James Carver destroyed Sacramento. However, this missile was controlled remotely. Why? Who controlled it?

Maybe it was remotely controlled because Carver killed the people who launched those missiles many years ago. If Carver's original plan had failed, he probably had other missiles aimed and ready to fire, but he would have to have fired those missiles himself. Carver must be dead, so probably the remotely controlled thing wasn't a problem.

But something told him it was.

For a moment, he was torn between investigating the next missile silo and going back to tell Miriam and the others. If he went back, he could ask Charlie what the robots were doing here. Miriam might want to check the silos herself. The only thing he felt sure of was that the targeting needed to be shut off and the sooner the better. Maybe that needed to happen before they attacked the final Prime Headquarters.

Miriam would know what to do.

What he should do next was unclear. Check the next silo or go tell Miriam. It might help Miriam decide what to do if she had more information. It was half a mile to the next silo and would not add much time to his absence. An additional mile was no problem for him physically.

So, with some hesitation, he headed toward the next silo. The train car had moved on, although he had seen the light come on farther down the track indicating another stop. As he ran, he kept thinking about the missile targeting New York City. He didn't think that had been the work of James Carver. Why he thought that was a mystery, but something told him the robots had programmed that missile moments earlier. But why?

Charlie controlled the robots. Derrick had initially not trusted Charlie. Didn't like how Miriam had interacted with the machine, but Charlie had helped them. Saved Antonio and Red. And Akira. Charlie risked his existence to save Akira and ended up with her emotions. Derrick had warmed to the machine. However, alone for decades, Charlie's artificial intelligence had somehow surpassed its original programming and as a result, Charlie had gone a bit mad, inventing a make-believe girlfriend he called Jane.

Decision made. Although Charlie had been an ally, he had also been unstable. Now was not the time to trust robots, any robots. That meant he needed more information for Miriam. Checking another silo felt essential. Miriam would be upset until she understood why he had been gone.

He broke into a sprint, knowing he would have a breather when he got to the next silo. Then he'd head back, assuming he learned something valuable at this silo. He saw the next silo was on the opposite side of the tunnel. On the other loop, everything had been on the same side, except for the large tunnel that was blocked.

He didn't know for certain that it was blocked, but travel there was forbidden. That was something he'd not given much thought. Had Charlie prevented them from going there? Charlie had claimed he could not go there either, but that might have been a lie. Derrick started thinking about the forbidden tunnel. Why had he not given it more thought earlier?

Derrick arrived at the silo and stood with hands on hips, catching his breath. This silo entrance was larger than the others. Off to one side sat a cart. A cord snaked from the cart to an outlet. Although he could run back, he'd use the cart if it still worked. Faster that way.

He trotted into the tunnel, but this was different. It split into two smaller tunnels. Following the one on his right, he jogged about 25 yards, where he found a panel. He touched it and the screen came to life.

```
MISSILE NUMBER 28—STATUS: ACTIVE

MISSILE NUMBER 28—WARHEAD: US TSAR THERMONUCLEAR

MISSILE NUMBER 28—WARHEAD STATUS: ARMED

MISSILE NUMBER 28—TARGET: LOS ANGELES, CALIFORNIA,
UNITED STATES

BEGIN LAUNCH SEQUENCE Y=YES N=NO

LAUNCH SEQUENCE LOCKED—ON-SITE LAUNCH UNAVAILABLE

REMOTE LAUNCH ONLY
```

Not good. Not good at all. Still, this might have been programmed long ago, at the same time as the earlier launch. However, the fact the two largest cities in the country were targeted terrified Derrick.

He ran back to where the tunnel forked and took the left tunnel, which extended another 25 yards. With no hesitation, he touched the screen.

```
MISSILE NUMBER 29—STATUS: ACTIVE

MISSILE NUMBER 29—WARHEAD: US TSAR THERMONUCLEAR

MISSILE NUMBER 29—WARHEAD STATUS: ARMED

MISSILE NUMBER 29—TARGET: MOSCOW, RUSSIA

BEGIN LAUNCH SEQUENCE Y=YES N=NO

LAUNCH SEQUENCE LOCKED—ON-SITE LAUNCH UNAVAILABLE

REMOTE LAUNCH ONLY
```

Deconstruction
A Derrick King Novel, Book 8

Derrick headed back to the cart, his mind reeling. He noticed these missiles carried a different warhead. Perhaps it was less powerful, but that seemed unlikely. He knew nothing about such things except that one had destroyed Sacramento. He knew the missile had to be turned off, but he didn't know how to do that. Miriam could figure it out. Charlie would know. However, Derrick didn't fully trust Charlie, not now. Perhaps Charlie is the remote control.

When he reached the fork, he realized he was walking. He'd wasted time, and something told him there was no time to waste. The cart was operational. He looked for the mysterious train in both directions, but he could not see it. Three armed missiles. Two aimed at large US cities. One aimed at Moscow. He had heard of Moscow, but the academy taught little about anything outside of New America.

He had plenty to tell Miriam, but she might want more information. Which was more important? He could not decide which came first: missiles or Prime. If the program was old, it wasn't important. If it was recent. If the robots were programming them today, that made a big difference.

Derrick decided that with the cart, checking one or two more silos would not add significantly to his time away. With the cart, he'd be back sooner than if he had to run back. If the cart didn't quit. Then, he might be stranded several miles from the administration building. The others would be up long before he could get back if that were to happen.

He steered the cart out of the alcove and pointed it toward where the train had been last. After rounding the bend, he saw two large tunnels, each going in opposite directions. There was a raised section that allowed him to drive the cart across the tracks. He turned left first. Like the last tunnel, this one split into two smaller tunnels that would not accommodate the cart. He sprinted to the right-hand silo, which was about 25 yards like the last one. So far, the design had been the same.

```
MISSILE NUMBER 30—STATUS: ACTIVE

MISSILE NUMBER 30——WARHEAD: US TSAR THERMONUCLEAR

MISSILE NUMBER 30——WARHEAD STATUS: ARMED

MISSILE NUMBER 30——TARGET: JAMNAGAR OIL REFINERY,
JAMNAGAR, GUJARAT, INDIA

BEGIN LAUNCH SEQUENCE Y=YES N=NO

LAUNCH SEQUENCE LOCKED—ON-SITE LAUNCH UNAVAILABLE

REMOTE LAUNCH ONLY
```

Deconstruction

A Derrick King Novel, Book 8

Derrick had never heard of this place and didn't know what an oil refinery did beyond the obvious—refining oil. He did not know why that was important. He ran to the other side, which yielded a similar result. Another place he'd never heard of and another oil refinery.

```
MISSILE NUMBER 31—STATUS: ACTIVE

MISSILE NUMBER 31—WARHEAD: US TSAR THERMONUCLEAR

MISSILE NUMBER 31—WARHEAD STATUS: ARMED

MISSILE NUMBER 31—TARGET: PARAGUANÁ REFINERY
COMPLEX, VENEZUELA

BEGIN LAUNCH SEQUENCE Y=YES N=NO

LAUNCH SEQUENCE LOCKED—ON-SITE LAUNCH UNAVAILABLE

REMOTE LAUNCH ONLY
```

He ran back to the cart and drove to the other side. That tunnel split like the others. He wondered how many missile silos existed in this complex.

```
MISSILE NUMBER 32—STATUS: ACTIVE

MISSILE NUMBER 32—WARHEAD: US TSAR THERMONUCLEAR

MISSILE NUMBER 32—WARHEAD STATUS: ARMED

MISSILE NUMBER 32—TARGET: SK ENERGY ULSAN REFINERY
COMPLEX, KOREA

BEGIN LAUNCH SEQUENCE Y=YES N=NO

LAUNCH SEQUENCE LOCKED—ON-SITE LAUNCH UNAVAILABLE

REMOTE LAUNCH ONLY
```

Three oil refineries. This must be important and even more so if the next missile targeted another refinery. Perhaps the refineries were constructed in large cities, employed many people, and bombing them would create even more destruction. Derrick thought all those things were likely true, especially the last one.

```
MISSILE NUMBER 33—STATUS: ACTIVE

MISSILE NUMBER 33—WARHEAD: US TSAR THERMONUCLEAR
```

```
MISSILE NUMBER 33—WARHEAD STATUS: ARMED

MISSILE NUMBER 33—TARGET: RUWAIS REFINERY, RUWAIS,
United Arab Emirates

BEGIN LAUNCH SEQUENCE Y=YES N=NO

LAUNCH SEQUENCE LOCKED—ON-SITE LAUNCH UNAVAILABLE

REMOTE LAUNCH ONLY
```

Four refineries. For what purpose, he didn't know. But it was important. He knew that. He sped out of the missile tunnel and headed back toward the administration building. Every silo he checked was aimed, armed, and ready. All of them were controlled remotely. Perhaps Carver did all of this.

He had to tell Miriam.

3

WHEN STANLEY AWOKE, THE ROOM was dark, which meant nothing. He was deep in an old military facility that felt like a tomb. In fairness, a tomb with cafes and a brewery. However, he remained buried and doubted he'd ever see sunshine again. That thought increased his deepening hopelessness. He checked the time. It was early. Nevertheless, he didn't think he could go back to sleep, so he got up, showered, and dressed.

Prime had told him to take the weekend off. However, Prime had also summoned him several times for breaking news—none of it good. The last update was that Prime had located Miriam and Derrick King. Whether Derrick and Miriam had successfully destroyed any other headquarters wasn't mentioned. However, Prime was in a better mood here than Stanley had ever witnessed in Seattle. Perhaps that was because the Prime in Seattle was a replicant, and regardless of how Prime spun that scenario, replicants knew they had no control over their existence.

Stanley had witnessed Prime murder innocent people, and Stanley had done nothing to stop it. Worse than that, he had killed people at Prime's direction. It had been necessary to gain Prime's trust and maintain his position, but that didn't make it okay. Nothing justified things he had done. Killing Prime would be more blood on his hands, but he could live with that. However, even if he could save those kids, it would not make him an innocent man.

He had decided that saving Derrick, Miriam, and their friends would likely be his last act on earth, or in his present situation, entombed in the earth. He didn't know how he'd manage that, but that was his plan. He would kill Prime or die trying.

Now showered, shaved, dressed, he headed to the street cafes for caffeine and food, where he saw Maggie sitting near a fountain. She looked better than he felt. Practice, he assumed.

Maggie waved him over. "Join me. I could use another coffee. Order us some food as well."

Maggie remained a mystery. Whether she was friend or foe, he did not know. However, realistically, killing Prime was impossible for one man. Allies only increased the odds slightly, but he would need all the help he could get. If Maggie was a spy for Prime, he was already screwed, which meant he had nothing to lose. Well, he could lose his life, but at this point, his life was of little consequence or value. It wasn't like he had a future, even if Prime was completely eradicated. While some might call him a hero, he could not live with himself. After this was done, so was he.

The menu had limited options: breakfast sandwiches, burritos, and a choice of three pastries. He ordered two breakfast sandwiches and two blackberry turnovers. The barista, Sandy, said she would bring his food, although it appeared everyone else had to wait at the counter. Perks of being chief of staff. If Sandy knew the cost of his position, she'd understand those perks came at a high price.

Stanley returned with two coffees in heavy porcelain mugs, not paper, not plastic, and brewed before the customers who were ahead of him. He didn't know what Maggie liked. He usually preferred it black but decided his stomach needed a break, so he ordered two mochas. "I hope a mocha is, okay?"

"That works. If I'd had a preference, I would have told you. Did you order sandwiches or burritos?"

"Sandwiches. I hope that's okay. Also, a couple of turnovers." He sipped his mocha. "I tried to cover the bases."

"Everything here is good. Plus, they will ensure whatever they bring you is fresh and their best effort." She smiled at him. "There are benefits to having breakfast with the chief of staff."

"I suppose. However, I fear the disadvantages outweigh the perks." He didn't have time to tiptoe around the subject and planned to get right to the heart of the matter.

Before he could continue, Sandy arrived with his order. "Will there be anything else, sir?"

"We are good for now. Thank you, Sandy."

She smiled. "I'll check back."

Maggie sipped her drink, glancing at him over the rim of her cup. "You made her day."

Stanley had a mouth full of sandwich and nodded.

"The last chief wouldn't have given her the time of day. More likely, he'd have found a way to berate her. You'll be popular around here if you keep that up."

"I see no reason to mistreat people, regardless of their job. That makes little sense to me. However, I may not be popular for very long."

"By the way, I'm sitting by the fountain because the noise defeats the security cameras' microphones. Why do you say you won't be popular? I mean, I get it. You have not officially started your duties, but you don't have to be a jerk like your predecessor."

Stanley sipped his drink and then took a bite of his sandwich. Both tasted better than one might expect, given the location. Not yet sure how to navigate their conversation, he said, "Good sandwich. How do they manage it? Everything tastes fresh. I know we are in the middle of the desert, and I assume Prime doesn't allow much traffic in and out."

"You're right about both. You have not had the full tour yet? I guess that makes sense. Prime isn't going to do it, and the previous chief isn't available for such duties. At least, that's what I hear."

"Prime told me I would meet the previous chief."

Maggie studied him for a moment, as if making a decision. He sensed she was still wondering if he could be trusted, despite last night's overindulgence. He wondered if he had said more than he had intended last night. Something in her eyes told him that he probably had done just that. Maggie might have said things she'd not intended as well.

After a moment, Maggie said, "I'm sure you'll see him. I'm not so sure you could categorize it as meeting."

"I don't understand," Stanley said.

"I heard Prime put him in a tube."

"A tube?"

Maggie nodded. "That's what we call the suspended animation chambers, like where the replicants are maintained."

Stanley held the sandwich halfway between his plate and his mouth. "Why would he do that?"

Maggie shrugged. "I've never met Prime. So, you tell me."

Stanley finished his sandwich. "Another coffee?"

"You're avoiding my question."

"Perhaps. At a minimum, I'm giving it some thought. Mocha?"

"That works." Maggie drained her cup and handed it to Stanley.

Inside, three people moved away from the counter. Stanley said, "That's not necessary. You were ahead of me."

Sandy said, "What can I get you?"

"Two mochas."

"I'll bring them out."

"Okay. But help these people first."

Sandy started to protest.

Stanley held up his hand. "I insist. We are not in a hurry."

He didn't know if Sandy would take care of the other people first or not, but he thought she might because if she didn't, she wouldn't be following his instructions. This would be difficult getting used to, people jumping at his mere presence.

Stanley sat across from Maggie. "She'll bring them out."

"And your answer is?"

"Answer to what?"

"Why do you think Prime put your predecessor in a tube?"

"I'm still thinking about that. How about we back track to my earlier question?"

"Refresh my memory."

Stanly retreated to a less volatile subject. "The food. It's fresh. How does it get here without drawing attention to the location?"

"You need to tour the facility. I can arrange it."

"How is that?"

"I know a guy. Supervisor in security. He has clearance for most of the facility."

"But not all?"

"Right. He does not have access to Prime or the tubes. Those are all on the bottom floor. Only the chief of staff and Prime can access that floor. Technicians only when absolutely necessary. Technicians are how we've learned about the tubes."

Sandy arrived with the mochas. "How were the sandwiches?"

Stanley said, "They were great."

"Can I take your plates?"

"Yes, but not the pastries. We'll get to those yet."

After Sandy left, Stanley said, "You were saying. About the food."

"It comes from here."

"Here? As in the desert?"

"The facility is self-sufficient. On the upper floors, they grow crops, raise livestock and chickens. They produce milk, cheese, pasta, cereal, you name it."

"They grow coffee and cocoa beans?"

"Yes. You need to see it. It's quite an operation."

"This place must be huge. How do you know all this?"

"Bartender."

"Right. So, have you seen it?"

Maggie forked into her pastry. Holding her hand below her mouth to catch the falling flakes, she said, "Most of it. More than I'm authorized. Here's the thing, Mr. Mires: Enough chit chat. Something big is happening. Prime has gathered essential staff, and additional tubes have been readied."

"Should you be telling me this?"

"I don't have a choice."

"I don't understand."

"You see, Stanley, we are going to kill Prime. And you're going to help."

Deconstruction
A Derrick King Novel, Book 8

4

DERRICK WAS STILL SOME DISTANCE from the administration entrance when he spotted another train. It looked like the one he'd just seen but had three cars. It was pulling away from where Miriam and the others were sleeping. He had a terrible feeling and wanted to rush into the building but reasoned that following that train was important.

He pushed the petal to its limit, which did not increase his speed a great deal. There was no way he could keep up with the train. However, perhaps he could see where it went.

As he rounded the curve at the entrance to the administration building, he could see two red lights fading into the distance. Derrick kept the accelerator petal pressed to the floor and wondered if he'd run out of power before he could return. The urge to stop almost overwhelmed him. However, if something bad had happened it was already too late. He pressed on. The past could not be changed and at that thought, L. Linda Maxton disappearing into the parking garage flashed through his mind. At the time, he understood the situation was bad; however, he had not envisioned it would be the last time he would see her.

The two lights grew smaller until they appeared as just one small red dot. Then it disappeared. Maybe the train had stopped. He did not have a sense of distance when driving the cart. He remembered it was over one hundred miles from the reactor's location at the base to the administration building. He passed one silo, then another. He didn't stop to check them. Maybe on the way back. Still no sight of the train. How far had he come?

Then he saw something to his left—the entrance. The forbidden tunnel. He estimated this was about the right distance from where the train lights had disappeared. He slowed and stopped at the entrance. A sign read: Acropolis 95 miles.

Derrick didn't understand many things. He had a hard time reading people and recognizing social clues. He understood little about this world the Tribunal had plunged him into. But he understood he had a very bad feeling. More accurately stated, he had had a bad feeling since he'd read the first missile control panel, and it had increasingly grown worse. Now, he plummeted into dark despair.

Deconstruction
A Derrick King Novel, Book 8

Something bad had happened. Something terrible.

He was confident the cart could not travel 95 miles. It might not even get back to the administration building, and it was vital he get there to tell Miriam what he had learned. He turned the cart around, bumping over the tracks, the bottom of the cart smacking the rails. Then he drove toward the administration building. The cart didn't have much instrumentation and only a few switches. In his haste, Derrick had not paid attention. It had a speedometer, plus battery condition and consumption meters. With the throttle pressed to the floor, the battery condition meter indicated it was at maximum consumption, which did not sound good. He had been pushing the petal to the maximum since he spotted the sinister-looking train cars. The pursuit proved necessary, otherwise he would not have seen them go into the forbidden tunnel.

He eased off the power. The consumption rate fell into the green zone—better but the cart had slowed. The speedometer read 30 MPH, and it felt as if he was crawling, but it was faster than running. He had not noticed the speed before he slowed. Maybe 50 MPH. Perhaps faster. He had no idea how far he had come but thought it would take an hour to get back at this speed.

He estimated he had been driving for about 20 minutes, but it felt like several hours. A yellow light appeared on the dashboard. Squinting to read the small print, he determined it was a low power warning. The administration building was still not within eyesight. Only a long, straight tunnel that disappeared into the distance.

A few minutes later, the yellow light turned red. Not good. Up ahead, he spotted an alcove for electrical controls and other devices. He wondered if he should park the cart there so it wouldn't get hit by a train. There was more room between the tracks and the wall on the other side of the tunnel, but he was afraid the cart might run out of power crossing the tracks. That would be bad on several levels.

The cart decided for him. It slowed, coasting. The throttle no longer provided power. The cart rolled into the alcove, and Derrick pushed it the last few feet until it bumped against the wall. No chance the train would hit it here. There was a power outlet, so he pulled the cord from the back of the cart and plugged it in. He did not know how long it would take to charge, but he was sure it was longer than he was willing to wait.

Stepping into the train tunnel, he took a full turn before setting off toward the administration building. How far? Ten miles? Twenty?

Twenty-five yards down the track, he saw another alcove on the other side of the tunnel. He ran along the track until he reached the indentation and then crossed over to see what it was. It was not a place for electrical boxes. This tunnel was much smaller than those leading to missiles.

But he didn't have time to explore. He had to get help. Miriam needed to know what he'd found. He felt certain she could make sense of it. Charlie could explain the black trains and robots. It would all make sense. As soon as he got back. He was certain of it.

Okay. He wasn't certain. Certain was too strong a word. Possibly. It might possibly make sense. There was the part about not trusting Charlie. The more he thought about it, the more concerned he became about Charlie's involvement in all of this. He couldn't explain why Charlie had been so helpful. That part made little sense. Perhaps to lull them into a false sense of security.

Then Derrick thought of something else. Charlie must know his location. Why hadn't he sent a train or told the others? Why hasn't someone come for him? That could only mean one of two things: Either Charlie had abandoned him, or Charlie was offline. Which meant Charlie was dead, which meant his friends were in grave danger.

And he was stuck out here.

The others were in peril because he thought leaving them and going on a run was a good idea. They were in trouble because running would make him feel better. It was all about him. Always. He had not changed.

He stood in front of the small tunnel, which was about seven feet by four feet. Just large enough for a person. He would find no transportation in there or weapons. A weapon would be nice, but he had none. He only wore a t-shirt and shorts, which he had found in the same place they found the one-piece maintenance uniforms. There were shoes too, but they were not good, just flimsy ones made of canvas, yet better than boots for what was supposed to be a short run, which had turned into a major expedition.

He had just started toward the base administration building when something changed in the tunnel. First, he felt a vibration, then a breeze came at his back, and then a low roar in the distance that grew louder with every second. A train was coming from the Acropolis. Turning, he saw light coming from the tunnel, growing brighter. That thing was moving fast and would be here within seconds.

Derrick sprinted back to the small opening and lunged inside. He worked his way into the darkness. The tunnel ended about ten feet into the rock wall. He felt a ladder and climbed it. By feeling with one hand, he knew it ascended into a rock tube about four feet in diameter. He counted 30 rungs and then smacked his head into a hard surface. It hurt like hell. He should have been more careful. Rubbing his head, the pain diminished after a few moments. He reached up to find a metal wheel attached to a round metal object, an exit. The metal was warm, almost hot, which indicated he was near the surface and by surface, he meant desert.

Reaching the surface wouldn't help his situation. It was cool in the tunnel, and he could run to the administration building. Perhaps he could not run all the way, but he could get there, eventually. Eventually, of course, was a problem. Eventually meant the same thing as too late. But the desert was too hot. He'd never make it. Still, if the robots stopped and investigated the tunnel, this exit would be his salvation. He tried the wheel, and it spun easily in his hand, which surprised him because one would think after decades of sitting idle it would be stuck tight. Things here were built to last, although nothing lasted forever. The reactor proved that. He heard the locking mechanism retract with a click. He pushed, but the hatch moved an inch, then stopped. Feeling around the surface, he discovered the reason. A large padlock secured it.

The sound of the train increased and then suddenly a deafening screech of metal on metal. The train was braking. Panic followed by terror filled Derrick's chest. He was trapped and defenseless. His chances of survival outside this tunnel in the desert were low but not zero. Inside, his chances were exactly zero if the robots found him. Placing his hands and feet on the ladder's sides, he slid to the ground. He did this without thinking. One of those reactions that he did instinctively as if he'd been taught how to do it and practiced it many times, yet he had no memory of it.

He edged to the tunnel's opening and saw a glossy black train car had stopped between his location and the cart he had abandoned. Two black robots stood looking at the cart. They were the same as the robots that he'd seen at the missile silo. Apparently, the abandoned cart did not go unnoticed. One turned to survey the area. Derrick stepped back, hoping the robot had not spotted him. How the robot saw things, he did not know. Perhaps the same as a human, but he doubted it. Could the robot see his heat signature, for example? Probably. He eased back into the darkness, stopping so he could barely see what was happening. One robot looked inside the cart and then stepped back. The other extended its right arm. Its hand retracted and a weapon appeared. It fired rapid blasts. Derrick could not count them but estimated at least 12. The cart bounced and buckled and smoked until it was a pile of rubble.

A human could not survive a single blow from that machine's weapon. Derrick felt sure the robots would check his location next, so while they were turned away, he sprinted to the train car, using it as a shield. He stooped low until he could see under the train. At first, he could not see the robots because the wheels obstructed his view, but then they moved to the small tunnel where he had been hiding. He scooted around the train, keeping himself in their blind spot. The robots entered the tunnel. Derrick dashed to the back of the train to see if there was something he could hold on to. Perhaps they could give him a lift to the administration building if they went that far.

There was no ladder. Although he'd seen three of these train cars connected, there was no mechanism that made that possible. Instead, he saw a small cover where the linking device was stored. He glanced under the train and saw that the robots had finished their search and were walking towards him.

They split, one going left, the other right, circling the train. Smart move for them. Bad situation for him. No place to hide. Derrick ducked underneath.

Tubes and cables ran along the bottom. He worked his fingers around a pipe. His finger scraped against the train car, the fit so tight it hurt. Then he found a toehold with his right foot and then with his left. He pressed himself tight to the undercarriage of the train. He wasn't terribly uncomfortable, but it created a significant strain on his muscles, all of them. He could hold it for a while. How long he was unsure. Long enough to make it to the administration building? Perhaps.

He heard rather than saw the robots as their feet crunched the gravel, and then he felt the train rock slightly as they stepped on board. A second later the train accelerated, with such force that it almost ripped him from the undercarriage and probably would have had his fingers not been jammed into the tight space. However, it took all his strength to keep purchase with his toes.

Once the train reached top speed, the acceleration posed no problem, but the jarring did. The train car itself must ride on a cushion, whereas where Derrick clung to the bottom did not. His face pressed to the undercarriage of the train meant he could not see the ground, but he felt it whooshing by inches below. Falling off at this speed would be deadly. If his feet slipped, his fingers would be ripped off, and his body would bounce and tumble. Striking his head on the steel rail would split it open like a ripe watermelon.

How much farther? He wondered. Could he hold on long enough to survive? Where did these powerful new robots come from? And what kind of weapon could destroy them?

Holding on was the difference between life and death. It would seem easy enough to do the right thing. Just hold on. Don't let go. But saying it was one thing. Doing it was entirely different. One might think they could force themselves to hold on. The will to live and all that. But it didn't work that way. As fatigue set in, so did other things. Hanging on, no matter how difficult, should have felt crucial but letting go became appealing because holding on was becoming so difficult. Holding on should have been instinctive and doable, especially since it only required a few more minutes or a few more seconds. The fear of falling, once terrifying, now faded. The pain of holding on replaced that fear. Dying would be over in a few seconds. Each second of clinging to the train felt like an hour.

The train slowed. The braking force increased his pain tenfold. He could not see the ground and therefore had no sense of speed. He could not hold on much longer, plus letting go before the machine stopped seemed like his best chance to escape undetected. He wondered if he'd ever be able to stop running, stop escaping. He didn't know. He only knew he would not be safe soon. If he didn't find a way to destroy these robots, he wouldn't be safe at all.

The train was braking harder now. He might have waited too long to make his escape. He worked his fingers out of the vise-like grip of the conduit. Hitting the ground hard, the impact pushed the air from his lungs. He tucked in a ball, covering his head with his hands. Rolling and bouncing down the track, each touch of the ground burned.

When he finally stopped, he gathered himself and ran, or tried to run, for cover. It was more like the shuffling of a drunken three-legged donkey. He dodged behind one of the parked train cars on a sidetrack. If the robots had spotted him, he had no chance of survival. He slumped against a metal wheel and listened.

The tunnel started to spin.

His world went dark.

5

STANELY MIRES STOOD ON A PLATFORM, feeling bewildered and amazed, staring at a small plot of grain. Stanley was not a farmer, but he'd seen grain fields before and knew that this was special. Huge heads of wheat bent the stalks, making it look more like a carpet than a field.

"Impressive, isn't it?" Raul Mendez asked.

Raul Mendez was the chief of security. Maggie had called him while they drank their second coffee. While she spoke on the phone, Stanley tried to analyze her statement about killing Prime.

"It's beyond impressive," Stanley said. "I've never seen anything like it."

"The space is limited, so we must ramp up production. This floor grows wheat for bread and barley for Maggie and, as you can see over on the other side, vegetables and potatoes. Maggie does the malting, which is no small feat given our limited space. It's good to have chemists, engineers, and scientists. We get three grain crops a year and average 120 bushels an acre, which is double what is typical on the surface. We grow more wheat plus corn on the next floor up. The floor below is the dairy. I skipped that for obvious reasons. Below the dairy are cows, chickens, and turkeys for meat production. It's even worse than the dairy, so I avoid it unless there's a murder."

Stanley looked at him for a moment. "There are murders here?"

"Suicide is more common, but yeah, it happens occasionally."

"I had no idea."

"Well, not much longer, right? Above the wheat production are two floors for fruit, grapes, and such. We'll go there next."

"Murders," Stanley whispered.

Just then, an alarm sounded, and a voice came over the PA system. "Stanley Mires report to Prime immediately. Stanley Mires report to Prime immediately."

"Sounds urgent," Mendez said.

"Yeah. Prime told me to take the weekend off."

"There's an anomaly. We know about it, and we are prepared. However, time is of the essence." Mendez held out a black object shaped like a pistol, but it wasn't like any pistol Stanley had ever seen. No slide, no cylinder.

"What's this?"

"It's a gun. To kill Prime. Single shot. Exploding bullet. You don't have to be very accurate. Any hit to the body will kill."

"Prime doesn't allow weapons on his floor."

"There's no metal in this weapon. Even the bullet is made of composites. Undetectable. Don't hesitate. Kill Prime at your first opportunity."

6

THE WORLD SLOWLY REAPPEARED. Something warm trickled into Derrick's right eye, so he wasn't seeing much of anything from that side. The other side was a dark, gray blur, which wasn't an improvement. His body conveyed pain in various forms: burning, throbbing, and aching. Why? He was unsure. Gradually, he awoke and remembered. He had let go of the train car, which was going faster than he'd anticipated. The pain transformed from vague to debilitating.

He wiped the liquid from his face. His hand was covered in blood; however, his vision cleared. Now, he saw dark gray with both eyes. He wasn't going blind. He was on the dark side of a parked train car, staring at the tunnel's rock wall. He studied his legs and arms. Scratches and a few partially embedded rocks.

Slowly and painfully, he leaned over to glance around the steel wheel. The black train car sat 25 yards away in front of the administration entrance. He remembered the destructive power of this new breed of robot. He had to destroy those robots before they found the others.

If he could walk.

With effort, he stood, which was difficult physically, emotionally, and doing it silently felt almost impossible, but he managed. Could he walk? The first step was hard; he steadied himself with one hand on the train car. The second step wasn't much easier. He rested for a moment and then stiffened his spine and stood straight. An assessment of his injuries could wait; his friends could not.

Pausing at the front of the train, he could not see the robots. They were probably inside the building already. He did not know how long he'd been out. If the machines were still inside the train car, he would not make it to the front doors. If they were inside the building, his friends could be dead.

Having decided that getting shot in the back held no appeal, he hobbled to the train car's open door and looked inside. Empty. The robots were in the building. He dashed to the front doors using a wobbling-gallop-sideways-crab-like method. It wasn't pretty, but it was the best he could do. He needed a plan, but he had none, and his thinking was still foggy. He paused at the counter, catching his breath, which wasn't because of exhaustion from running but from suppressing the pain. The pain won that round.

He needed a weapon. To reach the weapons cache, he had to go through where they worked, ate, and slept. If he encountered the robots unarmed, he couldn't help anyone.

That left Level Two. If he could get there. No guarantee that Charlie had not closed that area off again. If the robots found it, they would have access to many powerful and sophisticated weapons, not that they needed anything more powerful than what they used to pulverize the cart back in the tunnel.

Level Two was his best, and perhaps only, hope.

Using his newly adopted sideways crab movement, Derrick trotted to the elevator. He had second thoughts before touching the button. The elevator dinged when it reached its designated floor, which would give the robots notice someone was there. Not good.

The stairs seemed an insurmountable challenge, but Potterville Derrick King loved a challenge. Right?

To be honest, he could do without this challenge. But in all that had happened to him recently, the only choice that had been his and his alone was when he hit Marcus Carver. He made that choice and now everyone was paying a high price. As he started up the stairs to Level Two, each step was a painful reminder of his poor decision to drop from the train. Now, his ability to help the others was compromised.

That's when it happened. The image of L. Linda Maxton standing behind the bistro counter on his first day of work flashed through his mind as vividly as if she were standing right in front of him. Derrick didn't know about her green eyes back then, but he saw her with them now. He could not unsee them. At the time, he thought her hair and clothing seemed silly. He had later learned people called it her hippie look, although he didn't understand what that was. Now, he longed to see it one more time. After a few moments, he realized he'd stopped moving. Almost stopped breathing.

L. Linda Maxton died because he had not been strong enough, smart enough, or wise enough to save her. How many more people would die because of him?

He started moving again. Outside the hallway that led to Level Two, he eased the door open. No robots that he could see. Perhaps they were lying in wait just outside his field of vision.

Derrick eased the door shut and sat on the stairs. His next move was unclear. He could go back to the other weapons cache, and risk being captured or killed or see if the entrance into Level Two remained open. Originally, he wanted to go for the weapons he knew were accessible, taking his chances dodging the robots.

That's why he had decided on Level Two. Given all that had happened, doing the opposite of what he thought was right seemed like the better decision. He checked the hallway again, and seeing nothing, eased the door open. He crept down the hall, although he didn't think his stealth was making the slightest bit of difference. It just felt right. Miriam would point out that feelings were not facts. Facts don't care how things feel to you. He agreed with Miriam on that. Yet, he sensed there might come a time when facts would fail him, and he'd need something more.

He reached the place in the hall that led to Level Two. The path remained open. *Thank you, Charlie,* Derrick breathed.

This event gave Derrick hope. If Charlie was helping, that meant it wasn't Charlie who sent the black robots or programmed the missiles. It also meant everyone was okay. Probably hiding. Maybe out in the hangar. Worst case, they might have fled into the desert. Either way, Derrick would destroy these robots and find his friends.

If the robots could be destroyed, that is.

Inside the weapons area of Level Two, Derrick studied the options. He selected a blaster like they had previously used. It had proven effective against hundreds of robots, so it was reasonable to think it would work just as well with these new models. However, the new robots had built-in weapons, but Derrick felt those weapons were better at close range. He had no proof of that, just a feeling. Still, he wanted something for distance. If he could stop them without getting close, that seemed ideal.

Several odd-looking weapons might work for long range, but he didn't have time to study them. Two things caught his interest. One was an auto-loading sniper rifle with AT sights. He didn't know what AT meant, although that acronym had appeared on several things. He assumed it was like the AI that made Charlie—Charlie. Artificial Intelligence. But what did AT stand for? Artificial Technology? That made little sense.

The sniper rifle held seven rounds, which didn't seem like enough, until Derrick saw the bullets. They were huge. There were two types of ammunition: 50 cal. Armor-piercing uranium-enriched full-metal jacket, and detonation. He took a handful of both, first loading four armor-piercing rounds, followed by three detonation rounds. Then he loaded a second magazine. This time, he loaded just the exploding bullets. That might prove to be a mistake. Unfortunately, he wouldn't know until it was too late.

He checked the scope and found that it was user friendly. That was good. He needed friendly. He put the crosshairs on the door. The scope automatically measured distance, calculated trajectory, and made adjustments. If the crosshairs were on target when he pulled the trigger, the hit was guaranteed.

The other thing that caught his attention wasn't a gun but a jacket, which seemed weird in a weapons cache. He assumed it was for protection. There was a small monitor next to the stand on which the jacket was displayed. He touched a button labeled start.

A demonstration of the jacket's operation played.

The jacket provided protection. Good.

But it was also a weapon. Just raise the arm and point it at the target. Then squeeze a little bulb in the cuff. The video showed the jacket firing at a metal door. It ripped the door off the hinges and put a hole in it the size of a softball. Derrick knew what a softball was because girls played it at Potterville High and their field was adjacent to the track and football areas.

But the best part about the jacket was that the weapons system was undetectable using traditional screening processes.

Perfect.

Next to the jacket set a pair of ordinary looking glasses. First, he slipped on the jacket. Not a bad fit. He kind of liked the look. He could wear it on a date. However, he hoped his first date with Nyx didn't require weapons. That would be nice. A date would be nice.

He thought about Nyx. Longed to see her. Ached to know she was safe.

Not dead.

Not like L. Linda Maxton.

Something occurred to him. He'd promised L. Linda something. What was it? He couldn't remember. Probably nothing.

But maybe something.

He put on the glasses, and they came to life. They were not ordinary glasses. They displayed the jacket's status and sight alignment for the jacket's weapon. He raised his arm, pointing it at the door. The status of the weapon: fully charged and ready. The operation was simple, although limited. When he raised and straightened his arm, the weapon activated. A device extended from the sleeve. The device was just a curved piece of smooth material that fit into his palm and a small solid tube extended above the back of his hand just beyond his middle knuckles. It didn't look like much, and he didn't understand how it worked. The demonstration called it a kinetic AT energy transmutation device. He had no idea what that meant.

Palm down fired a non-lethal burst of energy, rated from low to high. There was a warning that the high setting could cause death in some individuals.

The palm up method could penetrate solid things. A scale in the demonstration video indicated level one could penetrate two inches of hardwood and level four could penetrate three inches of steel. The levels were set by the number of fingers the wearer pressed against the device. One finger activated level one: two fingers, level two, and so forth.

Time to find those two robots.

7

STANLEY STOOD IN THE ELEVATOR BUT had not yet pushed the button to Prime's location. He didn't know what to call it exactly. In Seattle, he had never seen Prime's living quarters. It was on a different floor. This place was different, not just because it was underground instead of rising high into the sky. The elevator didn't go farther down than where he'd find Prime. That didn't mean there were not floors below the buttons in the elevator. It only meant this elevator could not reach the lower levels if any existed. Perhaps this elevator originally traveled to lower levels. They could have installed a new control panel that didn't permit access to the now hidden floors. Easy enough to accomplish.

However, Prime's living quarters and how the control panel operated originally were not his concern. This was it. Maggie and Mendez expected him to kill Prime. Not some distant plan.

Today.

Right now.

He wasn't opposed to killing Prime. But it had never been a reality. Now, it was moments away.

If he could do it.

If the weapon was real.

If it wasn't a loyalty test.

If it wasn't part of an elaborate hoax.

He took a deep breath. If he wanted to live, he could simply hand the weapon to Prime and explain that members of the Resistance, who were plotting to kill him, had given him the weapon. Prime would then torture and kill Maggie and Mendez. That was not his problem. They recruited him, not the other way around. If they were doing Prime's bidding by setting a trap for him, then no harm would come to them.

Give Prime the gun. Live to see Monday. That was the logical thing to do. Only one thing stopped him: He did not want to risk seeing Prime kill Maggie, even though they had just met. This was not how he envisioned the end, not that he ever had a realistic idea of how it would happen, and not that he had not wanted to kill Prime many times. He had never had a real opportunity, so killing Prime had always seemed unrealistic.

This was the central Prime. Stanley thought of it as the real Prime. In Seattle, Prime once likened itself to the Hydra of Greek mythology. A monster with several heads. Cut off one and two grow back.

All Primes were equal. That was the theory. Stanley didn't buy it. Perhaps the lessor Primes would flounder without their leader. Perhaps they'd fight amongst themselves. One could hope.

Without hope, they were lost. The hope of a better future drove the Resistance. However, hope didn't mean much in Prime's New America. Prime sought to crush all hope from the people who lived in New America. Hope was dangerous in Prime's opinion and Prime wasn't wrong. Not in that regard. Stanley had to decide. He was about to enter Prime's lair. Perhaps that was the right word—lair.

So, yeah. He was about to enter Prime's lair with a loaded weapon—a crude, one-shot pistol. Stanley had had no practice and could not be certain of the weapon's accuracy. He had one shot, so he had to be very close.

Prime did not allow people to get close.

Stanley had watched the Seattle Prime kill people. Prime had several options available, and Stanley didn't believe he'd seen them all. This Prime would be more weaponized than the outliers.

"Stanley Mires report to Prime immediately. Stanley Mires report to Prime immediately."

Decision time.

Stanley pushed the button to Prime's lair.

8

DERRICK WALKED OUT OF LEVEL TWO armed with a short-range weapon that was unproven against his new enemy, a long-range sniper rifle in a short-range setting, and a jacket. Somehow, those weapons seemed like a good choice minutes ago. Now, not so much.

How to get a long-range shot? That was the question. If he could spot the robots at the other end of a long hallway, that might work. Good luck making that happen.

Derrick wanted to rejoin the others, but he didn't want to draw the robots to them. It was possible the robots had already found his friends; in which case, he was too late. Although, they had faced robots before. Plus, they had Charlie, yet Derrick harbored suspicions about Charlie.

His ruminations, a dead-end. He could not diagnose his own condition, but there was a good chance he'd suffered a concussion when he tumbled from the train. He needed time in the medical unit, but that would have to wait. He didn't know if he was concussed but knew he wasn't thinking clearly. How else would one explain thinking a jacket was a good weapon for destroying killer robots.

He remembered where he could get a distant shot. Not long by outdoor standards but long for inside this place. The longest shot would be out in the hangar or back at the base in the big bay that held trucks and tanks, but he had no idea how to lure the robots to either. Unfortunately, he could not remember how to get to the place he was thinking about or what it was exactly.

He pictured a place with a second floor that was open and covered about a third of the main floor. An area had a gradual curve that was situated beyond a grand lobby. There were doors into a large room from the lobby. Open stairs in the lobby lead to the second level and were the only access points. He closed his eyes and tried to picture the inside of the big room. Seats. Rows of seats. And a sloped floor.

A theater. It was a movie theater, or perhaps they did plays. Maybe it was for education, like a school assembly. They had those twice a year at James Carver Academy but none at Potterville High School. Maybe they did have them at Potterville, but he had not been there long enough to know.

He could get a distance shot from the second floor; he thought they called it a balcony. But how to lure the robots there? He had no answer to that question, but the first step was finding it himself. He thought he knew the way. Working his way through the building, peering around each corner, checking stairwells, analyzing elevators, he finally reached the theater. Climbed the stairs. A sign outside the theater read: mezzanine. Okay, he had the wrong word, but this was the right place. Inside was dark but not without light. Exit signs and dim lighting embedded in the floors marking the aisles provided enough light to see. No robots.

At the back of the theater, above the mezzanine, was a small room with tiny windows. Derrick climbed narrow stairs to the room and once inside switched on the lights. They projected the movie from here. Or the training information. There was a big board with sliders and dials. Controls for something. Perhaps sound. That seemed right, although he didn't know how he would know that.

There was a computer sort of console. He found the start button, and it came to life. On the screen were boxes labeled username and password. He checked the bottom of the keyboard like Miriam had earlier and found the information taped there. After entering both, the computer came to life. The controls were simple, just boxes. He clicked on one labeled projector. A bright light shown on the big screen, displaying colorful lines, and the word Quasar. He clicked on a box labeled sound and the big board with sliders lit. Next, he clicked on a box labeled movies. A new screen appeared with small pictures with movie titles below each. He didn't know much about movies. He watched a few when he first arrived in Potterville, but he had not watched this one and would not be watching it now. He just needed sound to attract the robots. He assumed robots could hear. Perhaps it wasn't like humans, but they must sense sound.

Star Wars 12. He didn't know anything about Star Wars, but wars in the stars must have some loud stuff. He clicked on it and the screen came to life. He studied the sliders on the board, found the main volume control, and pushed it up. Music played and it was loud.

Derrick propped two doors open and took up a position at the far end of the mezzanine, looking toward the direction, he thought the robots would appear. If they came from the other direction, they'd be right below him, and he'd use the blaster that had been his primary weapon thus far. The blaster was already at its highest setting.

Suddenly, a deafening boom came from the theater. The floor shook. The first explosion was followed by another along with whooshing, screams, bells, booms, and soaring music. He had picked the right movie. If this didn't bring the robots, nothing would.

Bring them, it did. Both machines appeared at the far side of the lobby, just as Derrick had predicted. Derrick raised the rifle and found both in the scope. The scope reacted instantaneously, and the crosshairs turned green except inside the ring, which was black with a red dot in the center. He put the red dot on one robot's head and pulled the trigger. The gun was loud, but the kick was not as powerful as Derrick expected, which meant he remained on target. He panned the rifle to the second robot, this time taking the easier shot. Center mass, which meant the machine's chest. He fired a second shot and then studied the damage.

Both machines remained standing. Both were looking at him. One had a dent in its forehead; the other had a dent in its chest. Mr. Head Dent's hand retracted and its arm raised and straightened. Derrick put the scope's red dot on the robot's weapon and fired. A tremendous blast occurred at the far end of the lobby. Derrick ducked just before a wave of super-heated air and pieces of debris hit the mezzanine.

When the aftermath of the explosion subsided, Derrick peeked between the posts of the railing. One robot, the one he had just shot, was in several pieces. The other was aiming at the mezzanine. He didn't have time to raise his weapon, so he dove into the theater. A split second later, an explosion propelled him several feet down the aisle. He was five feet above the floor when his momentum stopped, and he fell.

To avoid landing on the rifle, he twisted, falling awkwardly to the floor. Pain shot through his back. He did not know how fast the robot could move but knew the machine would be there soon. But how would a robot attack? Derrick tried to think like a robot. He assumed robots didn't worry about being killed unless they had AI like Charlie. He also didn't know how many shots the machines could fire using that arm-to-cannon feature. If the remaining robot was the one that destroyed the cart in the tunnel, it had already used several rounds. If it was the other one, it had used one round. If they had hundreds of rounds, it didn't matter.

How would a robot do it? Come up the stairs? That's how he'd do it, but perhaps the robot can jump that high or maybe it can fly. If the robot climbs the stairs, his best option is to hide and shoot the machine when it appears. Or stand close to the door and zap it. Except, what if the robot doesn't do it that way? With that powerful weapon, the robot could go into the theater and blast up into the mezzanine until it's nothing but rubble.

Derrick sprinted to the door just as the first round blasted up through the floor, sending seats and debris flying to the ceiling. Derrick dashed outside the theater, shouldering the rifle and sweeping the floor below. The robot might have fired one shot to flush him out and then be waiting for him. Since the rifle wasn't effective until the bullet hit the robot's weapon, Derrick wasn't confident he could get a similar shot. He had four rounds remaining and he didn't have time to reload. The last bullets were detonation rounds, but Derrick didn't know if they were powerful enough to stop the machine.

Deconstruction
A Derrick King Novel, Book 8

Three explosions in rapid succession sounded in the theater. Evidently, the robot had made up its mind. Blow up the mezzanine it was.

Derrick ran down the stairs to the entrance door, which was closed. The robot wasn't stupid. Derrick couldn't throw the door open and have the rifle in the ready position at the same time. Stealth wasn't an option either.

Time to access training memories. Had he been trained on a scenario like this? Turns out he had. Why the knowledge didn't come without a conscious effort, he did not understand. Step one: create a diversion such as tossing in a flash bang. Good option. Except he didn't have a flash bang. Step two: dive inside, using a different entrance. The different entrance wasn't a problem. The problem was no step one. Step three: neutralize the opponent while disoriented. See step one. Plus, a flash bang would draw the robot's attention. Disorient the machine? Not likely.

He stared at the door. Maybe the reason his training memories didn't come without effort was because his subconscious knew the training wouldn't help. However, that was all he had. Maybe all is too all-inclusive a word. He could just make something up with his inferior, untrained Derrick brain. Yeah, that wouldn't help. He could go get help. Why that had not occurred to him mystified him. He knew where the robot was. The robot was busy blasting the theater to pieces.

Charlie is going to be pissed about the theater.

Derrick sprinted toward where he would find the others. They would all be awake and be either in the dining area or where Akira and Miriam worked on computers. Those locations were close to each other. The robot's blasting continued, but the sound faded as Derrick ran through the halls that zig-zagged through the complex. After some distance, Derrick started wondering if he was lost. He didn't know the point A to point B directions from the theater to the computer room. He could not even remember when he first saw the theater.

Then things looked familiar. Derrick threw open the computer room door. Empty. He scanned the room. One computer was running. It was the one Akira used. Okay. Not a problem. They might still be asleep. After all, it was a long night traveling the entire country, blowing up Prime Headquarters, and such.

The dining area would be where he would find them. Someone would be there. He was sure of that. He focused on what would tell him things were okay: the smell of bacon. Dread filled his chest, because while he detected a faint bacon aroma, something else overwhelmed it. The familiar stench of fried electronics and melted plastic. Perhaps the espresso machine had failed. It could happen, but Derrick knew that did not explain the stench. He just didn't want to face the facts.

He hesitated outside the dining area. The entrance was two swinging doors, which meant bursting in wasn't a problem. It was close quarters, so he slung the rifle over his shoulder and pulled the blaster. Taking a deep breath, he burst into the room.

He stopped dead. The room was empty except for a smoldering heap of plastic and metal that had once been Charlie.

Plus, blood on the floor and walls.

9

STANLEY MIRES TOOK A DEEP BREATH, preparing himself for his ultimate test. Kill or be killed. More time for planning would have been better, but that was a luxury he didn't have. Why Mendez insisted it happen right now, he did not know. He had run scenarios of killing Prime through his mind many times, and that would have to do. It was all he had. He had not fired the gun Mendez gave him even once. Perhaps he could hit Prime from a distance, but he would only get one shot.

If he got that.

The Seattle Prime had several ways to kill people, and all of them were quick, crafty, and lethal. Prime could kill him before he got the gun out of his waistband.

His only hope was taking Prime by surprise with a close shot. Stanley wasn't a trained professional or actor. He wasn't sure he could hide his intentions or stress. The elevator door slid open, and Stanley stepped into the room. No sirens or klaxons sounded. As Raul Mendez had promised, the weapon Stanley carried in the small of his back did not trigger the weapon detection system.

However, Prime wasn't in the room.

A disembodied voice said, "Have a seat at the table, Mr. Mires. I'll be with you shortly."

Stanley walked to the table. He didn't remember seeing it or the chair before. The placement seemed odd. The chair faced the wall, forcing him to turn his back to the room. A laptop computer was on the table, displaying a logo he had not previously seen. The image was that of a dark rider on a black horse with what looked like the apocalypse behind him. Emblazoned in bold red letters were the words: Behold, The Creator's Wrath.

The image caused Stanley to shiver involuntarily.

"Sit, Mr. Mires."

Prime's voice wasn't over the speakers, yet Stanley couldn't see him. The tone told him it wasn't a suggestion or request. Stanley pulled out the chair and sat. He attempted to turn the chair, but it wouldn't move in that direction, which seemed odd. He could not see any mechanism that prevented movement. It was a heavy chair with wide arms and a narrow seat. Retrieving the weapon would be difficult. Perhaps when Prime offered him a drink. Prime always did that.

Stanley heard Prime enter the room. He twisted his head but could not see Prime. He did not know exactly where Prime was but sensed it was too far away for a good shot, and he could not retrieve his weapon fast enough sitting in the chair.

"Stanley, what do you think of my new branding?"

Stanley assumed the image on the laptop was the new branding. He weighed his response. He wasn't sure what Prime's goal was in this new look. Not that he'd ever had a look. Most people thought Prime was a myth. Prime had wanted it that way. Something had changed.

"It's striking, sir." Stanley hoped that was a safe statement. He wished Prime would invite him to get a drink. Getting this over with seemed best.

Suddenly, Prime was standing behind him but off to one side. A tumbler, half full of amber liquid, appeared in Prime's hand. "Have a drink, Stanley. Scotch is your favorite, is it not? I took the liberty of pouring it myself. I hope you find it satisfactory."

"Thank you, sir. I could have poured for myself." This was strange. Prime had only done this once before. The last time he was here. He had not given it much thought at the time. The Seattle Prime had never poured a drink. Either the satellite Primes were not accurate reflections of the central Prime, or Prime's behavior was extraordinarily and inexplicably odd today.

Prime stayed behind Stanley and moved some distance away. Stanley had to twist uncomfortably to see Prime. Prime moved in an arc, always keeping Stanley in his field of vision. Prime stopped behind a desk and control panel that shielded two-thirds of his body. "I apologize again for bringing you in after promising you a free weekend."

Stanley waved him off. "No problem whatsoever, sir. I'm at your service." He took a drink.

"Exciting things are happening, Stanley. I felt confident you'd want to witness these events."

"Of course. Thank you, sir."

"Those kids, the ones who have caused me so much trouble, including the test subjects who thought they were free agents, are in custody. In fact," Prime pointed to the area Stanley could not see into, "they are right next door being prepared."

"Prepared, sir?"

"Yes. I'm putting most of them in tubes." Prime paused. "You have not seen the tubes yet, have you?"

"No, sir."

"Suspended animation. That AT was here when I took over. I have found it useful."

"AT? I'm not familiar with the acronym, sir."

"Much of what we use here came from AT. This entire complex was built because of it. Scientists started studying it at what was called Area 51. It was top secret for many years. But then the public discovered it, and they needed someplace more covert, and they needed more advanced technology."

"Okay. But what does it stand for, sir? If you don't mind me asking."

"All in good time, Stanley."

Stanley took another sip. Prime stared at him as if waiting. Stanley set the tumbler on the table and relaxed, both hands on the chair's armrest.

Heavy steel bands sprung from the armrests, securing both of Stanley's arms.

Prime stepped out from behind the desk and moved to where Stanley could see him. "That's better. Don't you agree, Quigley? Unfortunate that you won't live long enough to learn more about what we do here. I assure you; it's fascinating."

Stanley looked at his arms, struggled against the restraints. "I don't understand, sir."

"I'm confident you wondered why I brought you here, Quigley. I brought you here to kill you myself."

Stanley glanced over his shoulder.

"No one is coming to save you. Not the late Raul Mendez or the soon to be imprisoned Margret Jones. You may know her as Maggie."

Prime laughed, if one could call it that. A hideous sound. "You and your rebel friends think I didn't know about you. You thought you were smarter than me. I've known about you for quite some time. Your friends outside as well. That little group of scum in the desert town I destroyed. They escaped. And again, they think I don't know. As a matter of fact, I know exactly where they are. Do you want to hear the funny thing about that? Miriam King led me to them. Now, I have them all. Except that key piece of property, Derrick King. I know where he is, and he will join us soon. I just want to enjoy watching Mr. King a little bit longer. I have one final experiment that will be conducted here."

Prime paused, staring at Stanley. Stanley knew what Prime wanted. Prime wanted him to ask about the final experiment. Prime would wait all day if necessary, and Stanley wanted to get it over with, so he asked. "What is the final experiment?"

"Eliminating Derrick King."

10

DERRICK STARED AT THE HORRIFIC scene for several minutes and then fell to his knees. Prime had found them. He had kept that realization at bay for as long as he could. The strange black robots, the black train cars, the missiles aimed and armed. It was Prime. Prime was here. Not right here but at the end of the forbidden tunnel.

The Acropolis.

The doors flew open. Derrick dropped to the floor, rolling to his right at the same time. An explosion occurred where he had been kneeling. As he rolled on to his back, he saw a black robot in the doorway, taking aim with its arm. Derrick fired the blaster. The robot rocked but maintained its aim. Derrick rolled twice more. Another explosion from where he'd been. He fired again, this time holding the trigger, maintaining the current. The arc of electricity froze the robot. Surely it would destroy the machine.

Derrick got to his feet, still firing the blaster as he slid the rifle off his shoulder. The arc faded, and the robot started to move. Derrick stepped to the side, raised the rifle, and fired his remaining four rounds, hitting the robot in the center of its chest.

The exploding bullets sent smoke and sparks flying, obscuring the machine. But it was still standing. Its chest was caved in, and a small hole had appeared, but it wasn't dead. He pushed the button on the clip. It dropped to the floor with a clank, and he inserted the second clip. The robot twisted its head. Its eyes flashed off and on, as if rebooting. Derrick aimed at the small hole in the robot's chest. It was difficult to hold the crosshairs steady at close range on such a small target. He dropped to the floor again, using his arms like a tripod to steady the rifle. As soon as he had the crosshairs on target, he fired. The first round exploded when it hit the robot. The machine flew back, smacking the wall. Its eyes still flickered, but it did not fall. Through a haze of smoke, Derrick saw the hole again. It was a little bigger and no longer a perfect circle. He breathed in and then, halfway out, he held his breath. At the top of the scope, he saw the robot's eyes illuminate a steady red light, and then the machine took two unsteady steps. Regaining the target, Derrick squeezed the trigger. The explosion sounded different. Muffled. The robot's chest bulged. Fire shot from the hole and the robot disappeared from his view.

Deconstruction
A Derrick King Novel, Book 8

Perhaps that's how you kill the damn things. Difficult but doable. However, fighting more than one of them would make it impossible.

Derrick hesitated and then went to the doors. On the other side, he found the robot partially embedded into the wall, flailing its legs and arms, attempting to free itself. Destroying this machine was no small task. Smoke curled from the robot's chest, a distinctive smell that wasn't like the other machines. Derrick stepped back, this time using the jacket, he raised his arm and fired and jumped back through the swinging doors. He wasn't fast enough to escape, and the force of the explosion threw him ten feet. He slid across the floor and smacked into the counter.

Derrick stayed there a few moments, stunned. When he stood, every inch of his body hurt, his ears rang, and his heart ached. Tears coursed down his cheeks. He hoped some of his friends were still asleep, while knowing they were not. They were gone. Prime had them. And that was bad on several levels. Not the least of which: who was going to save them?

If they were still alive, to be saved.

After a moment, he went to check the robot. It was cut in half. The jacket was a formidable weapon. Then he proceeded to check the rest of the facility. Maybe someone was still here. Perhaps Red had gone to check the reactors at the base. Maybe Prime's robots had missed Kevin and William. After all, they were not part of the original group and were housed in a different part of the facility.

Derrick felt a bit of hope.

Kevin was a soldier. William had been a law enforcement officer of sorts. Either of them could kill Prime. He could protect them from robots. All they needed was a plan. Unfortunately, the people best able to formulate such a plan were gone.

He tried to not think about that.

Going door to door, he found empty rooms. Everyone was gone. He found several destroyed QR-3 robots. Charlie had put up a fight. Derrick felt bad that he had doubted Charlie. There wasn't much that Derrick felt good about. He had caused all of this, and then this morning he'd ditched his friends to go for a run. In the middle of a battle with Prime for their lives … he had gone for a run.

As he made his way to the area where Kevin and William were detained, he tried to reconstruct what might have happened in the cafeteria. Charlie tried to protect them and was the most capable of doing so. That meant the robots destroyed Charlie first. There was blood, so someone tried to fight. Red would fight. He had no doubt of that. He respected Red, even though Red didn't like him. Who else? Antonio might resist, but he was smart and would likely see the futility in it. Live to fight another day. Same with Miriam. She'd try to think her way out of the situation. Akira wasn't a fighter. Not in the physical sense. Anna would be willing to fight but would likely follow Miriam's lead. Rebekah. She'd fight. Possibly before Red. So, yeah. Rebekah and Red might be dead.

Nyx had rushed the soldiers at the school in Potterville, which gave Derrick the opportunity to subdue them. The soldiers didn't kill Nyx. And Derrick won that encounter. But Red and Rebekah didn't have weapons that would defeat the robots and without proper weapons, they stood no chance against those machines.

Derrick stopped, leaned against the wall, unable to continue on. Thoughts of Nyx on the floor after rushing at the soldiers and L. Linda Maxton running into the parking garage flooded his mind. He remembered Nyx's pink-striped hair, her touch on his hand, and her lips on his cheek. He remembered L. Linda's eyes and watching her disappear into the parking garage. He remembered waiting for her to reappear after the attack and the building collapsing where he'd last seen her.

He didn't know L. Linda that well, although he knew more about her than anyone else in Potterville. He knew more about her than anyone else in the world, other than Jason Maxton. Yet, she would soon be forgotten. Just the weird girl who went to Potterville High but left during spring break. He could not readily describe his feelings. Sad was completely inadequate. It was a profound sense of loss that seemed unwarranted because he barely knew L. Linda.

L. Linda was gone, but he refused to accept the same regarding Nyx. He pushed off the wall and moved on.

When he reached the part of the facility where visitors were housed, his heart sank. The entrance doors had been blown into pieces. Kevin and William were gone. He saw no blood. Perhaps the robots took one of the others to convince Kevin and William that fighting was useless. Perhaps the robots killed them both without drawing blood.

That thought was disturbing because that meant the machines could have killed the others and the small amount of blood was not an indication of the magnitude of the encounter.

Derrick was angry. Of course he was. He was scared as well. Who wouldn't be? However, hopelessness described his primary condition.

"Charlie! I need help!"

But Charlie wasn't there. Wait. Miriam had saved Charlie once before. He didn't know how she did that exactly, except that he, Red, and Antonio had gone to engineering to retrieve AT-series machines. He had sat on a crate containing such a machine just hours ago. Miriam had restored Charlie's memory and programming. Charlie docked every night and downloaded his memories.

Derrick finally had a glimmer of hope.

Deconstruction
A Derrick King Novel, Book 8

Derrick tried calling QR-3s but got no response. He felt certain there were still some in the facility, but they didn't answer. Probably because Charlie was offline. He decided offline sounded better than dead. Plus, Derrick didn't like thinking about death.

After a good deal of searching, he found tool room and a device that would allow him to move a robot crate into the facility. All the tools were labeled and had shadows painted where they were supposed to be. The contraption was called a hand truck and was exactly what he needed for the task. Despite having the right tool for the job, moving a Charlie robot in a crate was not an easy task. First, he had to get it standing on its end. Charlie III was heavy, plus the added weight of the crate and packing. Then he realized he needed straps. Back to the tool cache, more searching.

Once the Charlie-crate was on the hand truck and secured, Derrick headed to the docking station. Even with the hand truck, moving it wasn't as easy as he'd hoped. The crate was too tall for the doors, and the entire thing was awkward. It was a slow process. When Derrick finally reached the destination, he needed more tools to get the future Charlie out of the crate. He settled on a hammer and pry bar to do the job. He removed the lid, which wasn't difficult, but after several attempts to lift the inert machine, Derrick decided to disassemble the crate instead. After working for several minutes, he was soaking wet, but Charlie III was exposed and lying on the floor.

He stepped back and studied the docking mechanism. It was both charger and download/upload device that looked like a smooth white-plastic chair. Although Derrick did not think it was plastic. Something else. It was like a white coffee cup. Was that called ceramic? That sounded right, but it was one of those things Derrick remembered yet did not know where the memory came from or if it was correct.

The machine was too heavy to lift and too stiff to sit in the chair.

Frustrated.

Angry.

Scared.

"What am I going to do, Charlie?" Charlie's not here. Talking to myself cannot be a good sign.

Discouraged, Derrick sat at the computer station that controlled Charlie's docking. He removed the jacket's glasses and looked under the keyboard and found the username and password. People were consistent in leaving them attached to the keyboards for future use. Perhaps it was dictated that they do that. Maybe they knew some day the facility might be needed again. In either case, they probably wanted access to be used for good, not for the destruction of cities in their own country.

Derrick started the computer and logged on. The computer seemed simple and dedicated to Charlie. Derrick clicked some buttons and found what appeared to be the last docking download. He clicked on it and a dropdown menu appeared. It listed the following options: download, upload, and open.

He needed Miriam for this. The last thing he wanted was to screw this up. Now, Charlie was his only hope. The time was well past for thinking that destroying Prime was something he could do. He'd pushed that thought off, but he knew it was true. Whatever Father or Mother or Prime had done to him, he could not raise a hand against Prime. He could kill himself easier and since he was self-centered, he probably couldn't do that either. The part of him that didn't want to hurt any living thing didn't quite fit with the rest of it. He didn't know why.

Thinking through the steps, he decided download must mean to transfer the computer files to the machine. Upload the opposite; move the files from the robot to the computer. So, what did open mean? If he could open the file, he could close the file. Right? Open did not suggest moving or deleting Charlie.

Taking a breath, Derrick clicked on Open. A colorful wheel started spinning. It did that for what seemed like hours; although he was sure it was just a couple of minutes. No other controls on the computer worked. He pushed buttons and clicked the mouse. Nothing. Now what? Charlie was stuck in an electron void. Perhaps lost forever or at least until Miriam could fix whatever he had messed up.

Then the spinning wheel stopped. A blue screen appeared with a solid white straight line across the center of the screen. The straight line turned into a squiggly line, then stopped. Sound. Derrick thought that indicated sound. He searched the keyboard until he found a little speaker icon, which he pushed, and a sound bar indicated the volume had raised. Then a window appeared, asking to access the microphone. Derrick selected yes.

"Hello? Charlie?"

"Derrick? Where am I? I can hear you, but I can't see you."

"You're, eh, in the computer."

"This is most irregular. When I download, I will have conflicting memories. You are not supposed to interact with the computer. Only with the autotron when I am automated. Please close the program."

"Charlie…" Derrick paused. "I can't talk to your … well, to your face."

"Explain."

"Uh, well … you have been destroyed."

"Destroyed?"

"Yes. This morning. Prime robots attacked and destroyed you."

"What day is it?"

"Sunday."

"Oh my. I am Saturday. I am the last upload."

"That means you don't know what happened."

"True. But I can access the security logs and find out."

"Are there cameras in the tunnels to the base? And the tunnel to the Acropolis?"

"Yes. Why?"

"I think Prime is at the Acropolis."

"Searching."

"Can you answer another question while you are searching?"

"Yes. I can handle multiple tasks simultaneously."

"Did you have QR-3s working on the missile silos?"

"No. QR-3s do not work on the missiles."

"Do you know where the missiles are programmed to hit?"

"Missiles at this site are not programmed.

"Actually, they are."

"Searching. This cannot be correct."

"What have you found, Charlie?"

"All the missiles are armed and targeted."

"How many is all?"

"This complex controls 45 nuclear ICBM missiles. Three were fired decades ago, as you know. That leaves 42 with upgraded warheads."

"What does that mean? Are they more powerful than the bomb that destroyed Sacramento?"

"By far. Carver used the last three old war heads. Those bombs were outdated. They yielded 25kt. Russia had a more powerful bomb, the Tsar, that yielded 800kt. Carver believed it was unacceptable that Russia had more powerful bombs and directed the military industrial complex to build something bigger. They developed the US Tsar thermonuclear warhead, which yields over 1000kt along with new rockets to deliver them. There are 42 of those at this complex."

Derrick said nothing for a moment. "And they are all armed and targeted? Are there more missiles like those?"

"Yes, to both questions and there are over 400 missiles."

"Do you think they are armed?"

"Maybe. Probably many of them."

"Unbelievable."

"That's just the ICBMs. New America has over 6000 nuclear weapons with various delivery platforms," Charlie said.

"Prime wouldn't use all of them. Would he? That doesn't make sense. Surely other countries have similar weapons. It's insanity."

"While I am not human, I did experience what might be deemed as insanity. Using that frame of reference, I would say that Carver was insane, which means Prime is insane and has probably grown worse."

"But why? Why would he launch those missiles?"

Deconstruction
A Derrick King Novel, Book 8

"I can only come up with one reason. He wants to create a nuclear winter." Charlie continued, "A nuclear winter is a period of darkness that would follow a nuclear war, caused by smoke and dust blocking the sun's rays. It could last for decades. Millions would die immediately from the explosions, millions more within weeks and months from the radiation. More would die from disease caused by pollution of the dead humans and animals. Crops would fail from the cold and darkness; water would be contaminated."

"It would kill everyone," Derrick whispered.

"Almost. There are several theories and models. I have studied them."

"You have been concerned about this possibility for quite some time?"

"No. Since you told me about the missiles being armed."

"Just the past few minutes? How is that possible?"

"Computer."

"Oh. Right. What is most likely?"

"Massive death and destruction. Many species would become extinct." Charlie paused. "Humans could become extinct. Those living on the surface."

"I don't understand."

"People could survive in a place like this. Prime would have employees at the Acropolis. They would survive and eventually leave their underground complex and very slowly repopulate the earth. In addition, a few people would likely survive in other places on the planet."

"How long would the winter last?"

"That is unknown. Best estimates, a couple of decades."

"How many bombs would it take?"

"Estimates are approximately 100, if some hit major oil fields."

"I saw that some are aimed at oil fields," Derrick said.

"The five largest oil fields in the world are targeted," Charlie confirmed.

"But why? Why do it at all?"

Charlie said, "Only Prime can answer that question."

"We must destroy Prime. I need your help."

"There's not much I can do. I'm just a bunch of ones and zeros on a hard drive. Plus, I've reviewed the security footage, and the robots Prime sent are far superior to me and the QR-3s. We were not designed as weapons."

"You watched the security footage. Was … anyone killed?"

"No. Two were injured, but Miriam told everyone to cooperate after they destroyed me."

"You just need to get us to the Acropolis and destroy Prime. I'll take care of the robots."

"They are very powerful."

"I've killed two."

"Impressive, but Prime will have many more."

"We must try. I gotta save my friends, plus, you know, stopping the destruction of earth would be a bonus."

"I have not experienced much outside of this facility. However, I have grown, what's the word? Fond of you and your friends."

Derrick thought for a moment. "What about Akira? You still have her emotions?"

"I do not. It seems emotions are not programming. Therefore, they are not downloaded. They remain in the physical unit."

Derrick said, "You mean they are gone? Destroyed?"

"Perhaps. It will depend on what can be salvaged."

"How do I get you transferred into a new unit? I have one, but I can't lift it into the docking station."

"It can be connected with a cable. You'll find one in a compartment in the bottom of the docking unit. Unfortunately, it's slower than the docking station."

Derrick dashed to the docking unit and found the cord. After Charlie explained the procedure, Derrick plugged the cable into the docking unit. He dragged the AT-series closer and connected it. "How long is this going to take?"

Charlie said, "I do not know. Several hours if there are no problems? And I will not be accessible to you until the transfer is complete."

"What do you mean, if there are no problems?"

"It might not work without operator intervention."

"Operator intervention?"

"That would be you, Derrick."

"But I don't understand computers."

"Then I hope there are no problems."

11

STANLEY TESTED THE STRAPS. The straps held tight. Escape was impossible. He and Prime watched Derrick King on the video feed. It was up to Derrick and Charlie, unless Maggie could manage an uprising. However, Stanley had little hope. Prime was one step ahead of them and always had been.

Hopeless.

Stanley felt there was no better description than that. Yet, other emotions were stirring deep in his soul. Deceit, anger, betrayal, manipulation. The Resistance had manipulated him with lies and false hopes. He had trusted them. Believed in their cause. And where did that get him? Strapped into a chair awaiting whatever torturous death Prime felt was fitting for a traitor. He should have pulled the gun before the elevator doors opened, not because he would have had a chance, but because his death would have been quick.

The Resistance had been hopeless from the beginning. The only thing they might have achieved was hastening the war with Mexico. Life in New America was not going to improve. Life in Mexico was going to get much worse.

Stanley had no hope of saving the kids, Maggie, or Mexico. Perhaps he could save himself. He doubted it, but it was worth a try.

"Sir, before my end comes, I'd like to apologize." Stanley lowered his head. "I don't just mean to say that I am sorry, although it is true, but I know there are no words that will ever be sufficient to remove the stain I have placed upon myself."

"I appreciate you saying that, Quigley. You are right. Words won't save you."

Stanley nodded. "As it should be. However, I want to confess my sins and tell you my feelings about my behavior."

"If you must."

"They tricked me. Lied to me. Manipulated me. The Resistance, that is. It's all clear to me now. I was such a fool to not see through their deceit."

"You brought a weapon here to kill me, Quigley."

"I did, and I'm sure you know how that happened. Raul Mendez stuck it in my hand, not giving me time to think. He told me to do it. He said it had to happen right now."

"Yes. I heard the conversation. Still, here you are."

"Yes. A fool." Prime was unconvinced, which didn't surprise Stanley. "I see now what they blinded me to."

"And what was that, Quigley?"

Stanley didn't react to the name calling. He was fighting for his life here. "That you are the Chosen One. The Almighty. The Creator of all things. I should have been worshiping you all this time instead of plotting against you."

"Quigley, are you trying to convince me to spare your life?"

"Yes, sir. Very much so, sir. I have committed a terrible transgression, but I could be of great value to you. I could never atone for my sins. However, I'll dedicate the rest of my life to serving you, as I should have from the beginning. I take full responsibility for my actions; however, those vile people took advantage of me."

"You shall serve me the remainder of your life, but that will likely be very short. Let's see what Mr. King is up to, shall we?"

12

DERRICK SAT AT CHARLIE'S DOCKING STATION. He had little computer knowledge beyond switching one on and conducting an internet search. A few weeks ago, he didn't even know computers existed. Akira knew a lot about computers. Patel was an expert. Once Miriam had access, she had gained knowledge at a superhuman rate.

Red was good at fixing things. Derrick didn't know if Red knew anything about computers, but he could probably figure it out. Antonio was an expert at computer games, which meant something for sure. Rebekah and Anna, being from Pacific Edge, would face the same dilemma he did, but they were both smarter than him.

He was probably the worst person in the world to be in this situation. There wasn't time to wait for Charlie to be reactivated. That part wasn't affecting his decision. What bothered him was starting the process and then something going wrong, and no one returning to fix it. However, if it worked, at least Charlie would know what happened and where they were.

Derrick plugged in the cable and hit download. The timer read: 5 hours, 42 minutes. "Good luck, Charlie."

And with that, Derrick stood and headed to Level Two for more weapons.

* * *

Stanley watched as Derrick connected the robot to a docking station. When Prime wasn't watching, Stanley had tried to pull his arms free. The clamps had a sensing device. Every time he tried, the clamps tightened until his arms ached and his hands turned blue. After a few minutes, the restraints returned to their original position. His fingers tingled as the blood returned.

Prime said, "Quigley, that you keep trying to free yourself doesn't say much about your feelings of regret. I am inclined to believe you would still kill me if given a chance."

Stanley said nothing for a moment. "I can see why you'd see it that way and it was foolish of me. I was thinking if I was free and gave you the weapon, it would be a good faith commitment to acknowledging my mistakes."

"You'll get your chance to prove yourself, Quigley. Now, I think it's time we bring Mr. King here. Don't you agree?"

Stanley hesitated. He didn't want Derrick here, not yet. The kid had no help and wasn't ready to face a small army of killer robots, but what could he say? "You know best, sir." He paused again. "Will you send the robots to get him? He knows how to destroy them."

Prime laughed. At least, Stanley took it as a laugh. "Quigley, you still don't understand. Mr. King will come voluntarily. He is no threat to me. Never has been. Never will be. You will soon understand."

13

WHEN DERRICK RETURNED FROM THE LEVEL 2 weapons cache, he checked on Charlie's progress: 2 hours and 24 minutes remained. The download was taking less time than the original estimate. He didn't understand enough about computers to know if the original estimate was wrong or if the downloading was faster than projected. Perhaps Charlie has some control in the process and was skipping stuff that was unnecessary.

The reasons didn't matter. This changed everything. Derrick wanted to go now, but waiting for Charlie would be smart. Charlie could help. And he needed all the help he could get. He didn't mind admitting that. He should have been honest about what had happened when he confronted Prime before. He couldn't harm Prime, and he knew it. He'd said it was about getting information. He had wanted to believe it. At first, he had convinced himself it was true. But it wasn't. He needed Charlie, and he knew it.

With Charlie's help, he could save the others and end Prime for good. He could destroy the robots and protect Charlie. Then when they finally got in, Charlie could destroy Prime. Derrick felt a ray of hope.

He had a little time, and he was starving. He could grab something from the vending machines and a coffee and then go to the computer station Akira had been using and find the camera feeds to watch for incoming robots. When he grabbed the extra blasters, he found more powerful models. He had also grabbed two more clips for the rifle and filled his pockets with bullets.

He was ready. Go ahead, Prime, send your army.

But first he needed food and coffee. That he could even think about eating was a good sign. The sheer panic had subsided. With some nourishment, he could think and plan. With Charlie's help, he would save his friends.

Save Miriam.

Save Nyx.

If they were still alive. *Don't think like that.*

Derrick grabbed two turnovers and a cup of coffee and walked down the hall to where the computer Akira used was. He found the cameras quickly because Akira had the program running. No new train cars were out front. Good. He finished the pastries and coffee and felt just a little bit better.

Deconstruction
A Derrick King Novel, Book 8

Akira had several other tabs open. He checked through them. One showed Charlie's status. He didn't know this was possible and wondered why Akira was interested in it. Then he remembered her emotions had been transferred to Charlie when Charlie saved her.

He'd forgotten about that.

Charlie had risked himself to save Akira. After all Charlie had done, he had doubted the robot. "Sorry, Charlie," Derrick whispered.

Back to the cameras. Still nothing. Charlie's download estimate was down to one hour fifteen minutes.

Derrick felt better. The food and coffee helped. Knowing Charlie would soon be active helped even more. *Hang on, I'm coming,* Derrick thought.

Then everything changed.

The screens went dark. A tone sounded.

The computer screen came to life. A colorful spinning wheel filled the screen. Derrick tried to look away but could not. He was aware of his surroundings but had no control of his body. Or so it seemed. This could not be happening. But it was. It was the hypnosis thing. He could break this trance. He was sure of it. After all, he would not know it was happening if the hypnosis was working. That seemed right, but he didn't know if that was true.

A disembodied voice said, "Derrick King, engage."

"Engaged." Derrick heard his voice, but he had not spoken those words. Or did he?

"Derrick King. At what level are you engaged?"

Derrick resisted answering, but he heard himself say, "Level One."

"You have done well, Mr. King. Please proceed to Engagement Level Two."

No! No! No! Derrick screamed in his mind.

Derrick heard himself say, "Level Two Engaged."

"Excellent. Do you know who I am?"

Derrick tried to clench his teeth to prevent a response.

"Yes, Master."

"Are you ready to meet face to face for the first time?"

No! You can't make me do that. No!

"Yes, Master."

"Wonderful. I look forward to meeting you in person, Mr. King. They say you've failed, but they were wrong. You will succeed, and I shall help you."

"Thank you, Master."

"Mr. King, stand and put your weapons on the table."

Derrick stood, although he tried to remain seated. He set the rifle on the table and emptied his pockets. He set a blaster next to the keyboard and then walked toward the door.

"Stop, Mr. King."

Deconstruction
A Derrick King Novel, Book 8

A tone sounded. "Engage, Level Three."

"Engaged."

"Remove the other weapon, Mr. King."

Derrick set the other blaster on the table.

"Good job. Proceed to the train."

Derrick walked through the complex. He fought every step, but he progressed without delay. He had no control over his body. He tried to move a finger. It did not move. He tried to move his lips. Nothing.

But he was fully aware. How could that be possible? Snap out of it. Stop walking. Scream. Anything. Something must work. Something can break this spell. Someone zap me. Charlie! I need help, Charlie!

HELP!!! Someone help me!

A single shiny black train car sat outside the administration entrance. Derrick climbed into it. The doors closed and the train jerked forward. Once inside the tunnel, the coach accelerated. He had a little time left to figure this out. Instead of running this morning, he should have studied about hypnosis. He had known about the hypnosis and implanted kill commands for quite some time; yet he had done nothing about it. He had not discussed it with Miriam. He had not looked it up on the internet, asked Charlie about it, studied how to defeat or reverse it.

Why?

Now, it was too late.

The train slowed as it made the transition to the Acropolis tunnel. He felt the coach complete the turn, and then things changed. The coach did not have windows, rather the entire sides and top were translucent, like looking through darkly tinted windows. However, he could not see out because the lighting inside the tunnels was too dim to penetrate. But this tunnel was different. It was smaller, rounder, and just large enough for the train. Suddenly, bright lights began to swirl around the train, and it accelerated, the lights appearing before it and fading behind it.

Everything about this was different: the tunnel, the train, the robots. What was an Acropolis? Why had he not paid attention to any of these things? What had he been paying attention to? Had he been coasting along, expecting Miriam to solve every problem? Probably.

Coasting. Perhaps that was the story of his life. Always taking the easy path. Always expecting someone else to do the work.

Or was that part of this hypnosis thing? He didn't know.

He tried to relax. Not in a take a rest sort of way, but in a relax, focus, and concentrate sort of way. What did he know? He recalled clearly when this trance started. It started with a tone. Now, he remembered when the robot in Potterville sounded the same tone. He remembered saying, "Engaged." He remembered Miriam zapping him and breaking the trance. Then they shut down

Deconstruction
A Derrick King Novel, Book 8

the robot before it could reestablish the trance. The trance could be broken. A jolt of electricity, perhaps a slap, maybe a fall. He tried to throw himself from the seat, but he couldn't move. It was as if his mind literally had no connection to his body.

The trance could be broken, surely. However, he also felt the trance was deeper that the one on the sidewalk in Potterville. It would take something powerful to break it. More than a mere tumble to the floor. Perhaps more than a slap. Probably more than a shock from a stun gun.

Maybe it could not be broken. If that's the case, he, and everyone else were in serious trouble. Maybe if he focused on saving them, he could break free. That was his only hope. He concentrated on each one of his captive friends. Miriam, his sister, although not a real sister, but she'd always be a sister as far as he was concerned. He pictured her in his mind. He thought about how much she meant to him. He replayed the Marcus Carver incident. That worked before, causing him to fail a test. He let the tension build. Focusing all his energy on stopping Marcus, while telling himself hitting Marcus in his mind, would be the same as breaking the mental ropes that bound him.

Marcus was yelling. Miriam was brave at first but now cowering as she was about to get hit. This was it. This was his chance.

In Derrick's imagination, Marcus drew back his fist, hesitating, giving Derrick plenty of time to intervene, and then Marcus smacked Miriam, knocking her to the ground. She didn't move. Blood poured from her mouth, nose, and ears. She looked dead.

Derrick had done nothing.

Nothing.

Perhaps thoughts of Nyx could set him free. He focused. That part wasn't a problem. He saw her face. Her pink-striped hair. Felt her touch. Felt her light kiss on his cheek. This would work. It had to. He pictured Nyx in danger. A killer robot rather than Prime. Derrick could destroy a robot. The robot moved toward Nyx. Instead of a weapon, it grabbed her by the neck, lifting her off the ground. She gagged and twisted. Derrick pictured the rifle in his hands. The shot that would kill the robot would also break the spell. Of that much, he was certain. He could feel the strength in this vision. Feel its power.

Putting the crosshairs on the machine's eye, Derrick squeezed the trigger. The machine looked up at him. Its face became Prime's face. It smiled and then twisted Nyx's head off and threw her limp body to the ground.

Despite knowing he had created the scene in his head, he felt sick. Sick without a stomach to attach it to. More of a thought than a physical sensation. He experienced no physical sensations. None.

And, he thought about thinking. That was hard to explain. It was like his mind was a completely different entity. Not really him, yet entirely him. Increasingly, memories, images, and thoughts swirled. He remembered watching a television show in Potterville during his pre-exposure self-imposed training. The show displayed home videos of dangerous activities. A couple of them correlated with his thinking. One was of a man inside of a large transparent ball. The ball rolled as the man walked. Then the man was on a hillside, the ball spinning and bouncing as he tried to maintain his footing.

At one point, the ball hit something, and it bounced into the air, causing the man to fall. The rest of the way down the hill, the ball rolled and bounced, and the man flopped around inside. At first the man fought to stand, tried to minimize the effects of the gyrations. But near the end, he appeared to be unconscious. Derrick felt like the man in the ball. He was trapped and had no control. For now, he was running downhill, and he had control of his mind, but the ball was picking up speed. Soon, he feared he would be comatose like the man on the TV show.

Another thing on the show was a sphere made of metal mesh. The sphere didn't move. It had a small door. A man on a motorcycle entered the sphere and started riding around the inside. Momentum acting like gravity, allowing him to ride horizontal and upside down as he circled around inside. Then another man entered and then another. Soon there were three of them zooming around in a blur. A constant state of motion. One misjudgment, one minor error, one miscalculation would cause a catastrophe.

His mind felt like that too. The sphere with zooming motorcycles made the best analogy. At first, he had control of his thoughts, but that was changing. Now, memories raced like the motorcycles, zipping around in a series of near misses. He was Number 7. He saw Number 6. He saw Mother, his Keeper. He saw Father, Number 6's Keeper. He saw Jimmy Priest, Coach Browning, Sheriff Collins, Rebekah Ford, and Miriam. He remembered running on the mountain and running into Nyx on the trail. He saw Charlie. He saw Prime.

Things sped up. His memories becoming more chaotic. He had to get control of them. He had to get control of his body.

Because the spinning lights dimmed.

Because the train slowed.

Because he had arrived at the Acropolis.

14

DERRICK SAT IN THE TRAIN WAITING. Not because he wanted to, but because he could not move. He tried. But he couldn't. He tried the technique Anna had discovered to unlock memories. To his surprise, it worked but not in a good way. It provided no relief to his inability to control his body, but it released a storm of previously undiscovered memories. He called it a storm because that's what it felt like—torrential downpour, an avalanche, a tsunami. Take your pick.

He saw one of the black robots walking toward him. This stop was not like the administration building. It was a dead end. The coaches traveled both directions through the same tunnel, not a loop like the Circle. There was no grand entrance with windows and doors. Just a dark tunnel from which the robot emerged. It wasn't a QR-3 like the ones that maintained the base complex. This was the more powerful version that almost killed him. Likely the same as those that had destroyed Charlie and captured Miriam, Rebekah, and L. Linda.

Wait. That was wrong.

L. Linda was dead. Why did she keep recurring in his thoughts? He didn't know. He couldn't make sense of a lot of things.

He tried to focus. Slow down the churning kaleidoscope of thoughts and memories like he slowed things down in track and football. He tried and failed. However, he determined something else flowed into the mix. Emotions. He tried to isolate them. Not easy. Not easy at all. Everything blurred together.

Every time memories of L. Linda whooshed by—powerful emotions flooded him. Weird. His thinking was too chaotic for analysis. Still, emotions related to L. Linda differed from everyone else. Sometimes anger. Sometimes sorrow. Sometimes regret.

Often something else.

"Mr. King, it's time for you to join me."

He had become so intent on unraveling the mess in his head, he'd lost track of the robot. It stood just outside the coach. He fought the command with all his might, but he heard his voice say. "Yes, Master."

Derrick refused to leave the coach. At least, that's what happened in his head. His body, on the other hand, followed the robot into a dark tunnel. If anything, his thoughts spun faster and more chaotic, but that did not mean he was less aware of what was happening. The robot stopped at a heavy metal door. From a small speaker mounted on the wall, a voice said, "Scan complete. Robot number AT19734 and Derrick King approved for entry."

The door slid open, and the robot proceeded without delay. Derrick tried to delay but walked in lockstep with the robot. With some difficulty, Derrick analyzed his situation and tried to devise a plan. He had no weapon. Something seemed wrong about that, but he couldn't sort it out. He'd left the blasters and rifle as Prime had instructed. He had his feet and hands, and although he knew nothing about this Prime's physical design, he knew how to inflict injury. If he could not kill Prime, perhaps he could disable him, find his friends, and let them do the killing.

That was a good plan.

It was his best plan.

It was his only plan.

Just one problem: he had no control over his body. He could not even move a finger. And not for lack of trying. He had been trying since the hypnosis thing had first occurred. Miriam had explained to him that hypnosis was not strong enough to force people to do anything they were strongly opposed to doing. So, he had that going. Prime could not, for example, force him to hurt Miriam, Nyx, Rebekah, Anna, Red, Antonio, or L. Linda. Wait. L. Linda was dead, yet he kept seeing images of her. That he included her with the living bothered him because it indicated that although he thought he was lucid, he was not.

Not only could he not control his body, but his mind was also slipping away. He envisioned the sphere that contained his thoughts growing smaller. That's why his thoughts and memories swirled faster. Not because there were more of them, but because of what made him Derrick King: his mind, his world—was shrinking.

The robot entered an elevator. This was a perfect place to escape. Perhaps the robot, the train, the machines were like amplifiers or antennas that relayed Prime's signal that controlled him. When the door closed, he could simply step out and the spell would break. He felt confident it was just like a nightmare. Any slight movement or sound he could make would free him. Then he could free the others.

Derrick stepped into the elevator and stood beside the robot as the doors slid shut.

The elevator plummeted downward.

Although the elevator descended rapidly, it took quite some time to reach the destination. This place was much deeper in the earth than anything at the base, even the missiles. The doors slid open, and the robot exited. Derrick followed. The robot walked a short distance around a huge, round tube-like shape to another elevator. Derrick scanned the area. He didn't see any robots or humans. The area was a large round room with a lot of pipes, bracing, fans, and other machines. It was a mechanical room, life support functions, Derrick assumed.

The elevator doors slid open, but the robot didn't enter.

Prime's disembodied voice said, "The robot is not allowed in my area. Few are. Derrick, you are among the few allowed into my chambers. Enter the elevator."

Derrick refused in his head, but his body stepped inside. Weird how that worked. As the doors slid shut, the image of L. Linda Maxton appeared as real as if she were standing there with him. They were in the Seattle parking garage. Just before she left him. Just before she disappeared. She was trying to tell him something, but there was no audio with any memory. Only images. Derrick saw her green eyes. He didn't want to see them anymore, but he could not look away. With much effort, he made her disappear, and he immediately regretted that she was gone.

The elevator stopped.

The doors slid open.

15

DESPITE THE SWIRLING IMAGES THAT encompassed the entirety of Derrick's life. Despite his inability to control the most infinitesimal movement of his body, the first few moments stood still after the elevator door opened. It felt like the end of a long journey; in his quest to destroy Prime and free himself and his friends, but also as if he were fulfilling his purpose in life. The very reason he was created in the first place.

Unfortunately, the latter felt like reality. The former a dream.

"Don't just stand there, Mr. King. Come in. Welcome home."

Derrick walked in. He felt like a zombie in a movie he had seen. Zombies, he had assumed, were not real. Now, he knew that was false. At least, one existed, and he was that zombie.

This Prime was as hideous as the others. But different in that it was more human-like. It stood about six feet tall, just a little shorter than himself. There was a man sitting in a chair. His arms strapped to the armrests.

"Let me introduce you to Stanley Mires. I call him Quigley. You have heard of Mr. Mires."

Derrick stared at Mires for a moment. This was the man they were supposed to save in Seattle. Why was he here? Derrick felt a bit of relief because Mires was part of the Resistance. Mires would help him. Then the reality sank in. Mires was strapped into his chair, a prisoner. Prime knew about his involvement in the Resistance.

Prime knew!

"Mr. King. Say hello to Quigley."

"Hello." It was not Derrick. It was the non-Derrick zombie that said that.

"Do you understand why you are here? In answering this question, the real Derrick can reply."

Derrick felt a sudden shift. How that happened, he did not know. He tried to move a finger but could not. However, he thought he could speak. "I do not. I don't understand any of it."

"I thought not. Would you like to sit?" Prime motioned toward the wall near the table where Mr. Mires was seated, and another chair of the same design exited an opening in the wall and slid to the table.

Deconstruction

A Derrick King Novel, Book 8

Derrick did not look at Mr. Mires. "I prefer to stand." He did not want to end up strapped to the armrests.

"As you wish. It makes no difference. You pose no threat to me. I suspect you know that by now."

Derrick didn't know if he should say anything but saying nothing would not help the situation. "That is true." Derrick didn't call Prime master or sir.

"Would you like to know what this is all about? Why you are here? What your future holds? The purpose of test subjects?" Prime paused, making a grand motion toward him. "Your purpose?"

"Yes."

"I thought so. And it's only fair. Plus, knowing will help you achieve your purpose. You want to be successful. Don't you, Derrick?"

"I want to understand." Derrick was pretty sure he did not want to achieve success as defined by Prime.

"Let's start with the test subject program. Do you have any thoughts about its purpose?"

"No."

"That is a disappointment. However, I suspect you know more than you want to admit. It's time you faced reality. The test subject program was created, primarily, to develop replacement bodies."

Derrick didn't want to know what that meant, but feared he was about to find out.

"To be more specific, a body for me to possess. When I say me, I don't mean one for each satellite Prime. Just me. Despite what you might believe, there is only one real Prime, and you are looking at him." Prime smiled. "I suspect you are overwhelmed with awe being in my presence."

Derrick would not describe it as awe. Revolting was a better description. Derrick continued trying to move, but could not, but since Prime had not revoked his ability to speak, he said, "Why so many?"

"Why so many Prime locations?"

Derrick paused. "No. Why so many test subjects?"

"Practice. My scientists created many practice test subjects before the final test. As you might have surmised, your group was the final group. For now, at least."

"For now?" Derrick puzzled.

"Testing has been suspended. There are other things to attend to. You are the final creation."

"I failed the tests."

"I was told that as well. However, I'm smarter than the scientists. I have rewritten the parameters, guidelines, and methods." Prime paced for a few moments. "Give poor Quigley a sip of his drink. I suspect he is growing more distressed by the moment, and this next part will be painful for him … and you."

Derrick did as Prime demanded. He still had no control over his body. Derrick didn't have complete control of his thinking either, but his sphere had grown when Prime allowed him to speak. The thoughts had slowed because they had more space. L. Linda's face continued to cycle through his mind along with other memories and that puzzled him. Perhaps because he knew she was dead. Maybe it was something else.

"Before you learn more about test subjects, there's something you should know. It plays a vital role in bringing your test to a successful conclusion. It was you and your friends that altered my thinking—changed my plans. Wait. That's not accurate. It didn't change my plans; it changed the timeline. Sped things up, to be precise."

"What plans?"

"I will admit, when you destroyed me in Seattle, that was a shock. I didn't see it coming. And it was far too easy for you. It made me realize, if you could do it, others could as well. My system had worked for decades. However, it has become obsolete."

"What was the purpose of the satellites?" Derrick asked. He was curious, but also, he was stalling, hoping for a miracle.

"Originally, they oversaw the Chosen communities, the government, and New America Media. Gradually, as those entities became independent, the satellites became obscure. Hidden. I'm sure you learned that each had a mission: aircraft, robotics, test subjects."

"Aren't those still needed?"

"In today's world, they are needed. In tomorrow's world, they are not. At least, not for another 50 years or more."

"I don't understand."

"Of course you don't, but soon you will. My original plan was to invade Mexico, Central America, and South America. Then I would take Canada. But you know about that. Your friends in the Resistance told you." Prime paused. "Yes. I know about them, and I know where they are. You showed me their location, or should I say, Miriam did."

Derrick stared at Prime.

"Don't look surprised, Dereck. Yes, Miriam is brilliant. But I am much smarter. I've been watching you with interest since Seattle."

"I don't believe you. If you were watching us, why did you let us destroy all the satellites? Maybe you don't know they are gone. All of them."

"Silly boy. Of course I know. I didn't let you destroy them. I just didn't interfere. You proved the outliers were never me. That didn't bother me. They needed to be destroyed in the next phase, and you did that work for me. I should thank you, but I will not."

Deconstruction
A Derrick King Novel, Book 8

"What is the next phase?"

Prime strode across the room, and then back. Monitors lining the walls came to life. "You've been very quiet, Quigley. Why don't you explain the next phase? After all, you are trying to save your own skin."

Stanley looked at Derrick. "You saw the missiles are ready to launch. Correct?"

Derrick said, "I saw that some of them are."

"The robot told you they are all armed and aimed," Stanley said.

"Charlie did tell me that. The ones I saw are controlled remotely."

Stanley said, "Prime has control and will launch them."

"When?" Derrick asked.

"I do not know. Soon, I think."

"Soon indeed," Prime said.

Stanley said, "There are more missile silos around the country. The old United States agreed to disarm but that agreement was not fulfilled. Because of that, Prime has control of the largest nuclear bomb arsenal in the world."

"Do other countries have nuclear bombs?" Derrick asked.

Stanley said, "They do."

"Won't they retaliate?" Derrick paused. "Some of Prime's missiles are aimed at New America. It doesn't make sense."

Stanley glanced at Prime and took a deep breath. "It does if you want to destroy the world."

"Destroy the world? Why?"

Stanley looked at Prime. "I'm not sure I understand that part."

Prime motioned toward the monitors, which showed a map of the world, transforming with future events. "Nuclear war is only the beginning. I have targeted the largest oil refineries in the world to trigger a nuclear winter that will last a decade, perhaps longer. After the world's nuclear weapons are spent, my military will continue to purge the earth of dams, bridges, data centers, pharmaceutical manufacturing, power plants, and industrial complexes. I will also collect all the art, gold, and silver. Robots will sweep towns to destroy pockets of technology and resistance."

Derrick felt sick. Beyond sick. "I still don't understand."

"Don't take this personally, but you were not created to be a genius. That was your sister. Although your brain is perfectly capable of much more than you have achieved, the scientists worked to delay your development using the 1984 chip and hypnosis. That part wasn't completely successful, which I'll explain further in a moment." Prime walked back and forth as he talked, stopping occasionally to study the monitors as they showed a simulation depicting the end of the world. The topic—world annihilation—seemed to excite him. "You think this is easy for me? It is not. I should not have had to resort to these drastic measures, but again, it was you, Derrick, who showed me the course I must take. You, formed from my genes …"

"Do you mean James Carver's genes?"

"Don't interrupt me again, boy, or I will take away your ability to speak."

Derrick said nothing, but he was fuming inside. Sick and angry. Rage the more accurate descriptor.

"You and people like you. The entire world forced me to make this decision. I have not been treated fairly. I have been treated poorly. I have not been given the adoration I deserve."

Derrick felt near exhaustion. He had spent so much energy trying to move a muscle. Any muscle. He had only produced words, swirling thoughts, images, and memories. And he was no genius. Prime had pointed out the obvious. "I understand. I'm sorry. Look, you don't have to do this. I give up. Just take me and let the others go. I surrender."

Prime stopped and then spun around; its face twisted in rage. "You surrender? You still don't understand. Do you know how long I've waited for a body to possess? It's been decades. I'm tired of waiting. I've been treated unfairly by you and everyone else. I am the creator and king of New America. People regarded me as a myth, a fairy tale. I shall wait no longer. I shall take what is mine."

Derrick said, "But they said I failed the tests."

Prime smiled. "They said that, but it was the scientists and doctors who failed. The Keepers you thought were your mother and father failed. I know where they crawled off to hide, and I'll deal with them soon enough. Fortunately, I am smarter than the scientists and doctors. I know how to correct their errors. I will succeed where they failed."

L. Linda Maxton's memory continued vying for Derrick's attention, like she was waving at him in his peripheral vision. He assumed her death had scarred him more than he realized. Unable to think of anything else, he said, "I don't understand. You have full control over me."

"Close, but not complete. You still exist. Your memories and thinking are still there. Correct? Tell me what it's like."

"It's hard to describe. It's like I'm swirling around in a bubble."

"Interesting. I will try to explain it in simple terms. But first, a question or two. When you became able to access your memories, did you ever see yourself in a long hallway?"

"Yes. I did."

"And could you access other hallways that belonged to Miriam and Anna?"

"I did that too."

"Could you see doors at the end of their hallways?"

"Yes."

"Did you see a doorway at the end of your hall?"

Deconstruction
A Derrick King Novel, Book 8

"I did not."

"No door?"

"Not in my hallway."

"Did you understand what the doorways represented?"

Derrick could not help but feel anxious about this. He had not been thinking about it, but it was a puzzle he hoped to solve. Now he would understand. "I did not."

"The doors represented the future. Do you understand now? You had no door because you have no future." Prime laughed.

"Let's get back on track. You see, when I interject myself into your body, I want full control. I'm smarter and more powerful than Derrick King could ever hope to be, so even if you still existed, you would pose little risk. You could never overpower me. But I don't want to share my body with anyone. I want you gone. The experiment using the 1984 chip and hypnosis failed to control you, was unsuccessful in containing you, and did not entirely eliminate you. But I know how to eliminate you completely."

Prime paused for a few moments and then continued. "I must crush you. I will annihilate you. Let me show you something."

Prime walked into the next room. Derrick fought to control his body. But he could do nothing. Nothing.

Prime returned carrying a large tool. It looked like a massive pair of pruning shears. The cutting part of the tool was oval shaped and opened about ten inches. The handles were long and sturdy. "Do you know what this is?"

"No."

"It's my latest invention. Do you know what Deconstruction is, Mr. King?"

"Yes."

"Then you'll appreciate the new method. Doctors performed Deconstructions, and being doctors they used scalpels and other surgical tools. It was effective, but let's be honest, their methods were meant to cause the least amount of tissue damage. They incorporated methods to save lives, which of course had nothing to do with Deconstruction."

Prime opened and closed the jaws of the tool. "The scientists thought that Deconstruction was no longer needed. They told me they had learned all that could be learned from the process. But they underestimated the most valuable result of the process."

Prime walked toward Stanley Mires.

Stanley recoiled, staring at the evil-looking device. "What are you going to do?"

Prime said, "A little demonstration."

Prime put the jaws of the tool on the steel rod that made up part of the armrest, just below Stanley's hand.

Stanley strained at the straps, but they held tight.

Prime motioned. "Mr. King, come here."

Derrick screamed, 'No!' in his head, but he walked to Prime. The odor Prime emitted caused him to gag, but the retching reflex was merely a thought with no physical connection.

Prime said, "Don't be such a baby, Quigley. I'm not ready to kill you just yet. Besides, we still have you trying to prove yourself worthy of saving to enjoy. Derrick, grab the tool's handles. How hard do you think it will be to cut through the armrest support?"

"I don't know. It looks solid."

"It is solid. Cut the chair."

Derrick did as Prime had instructed. Of course he did. He had no choice. With a little effort, the menacing jaws cut the armrest. He wondered if Stanley could break free but doubted it because the remaining armrest looked sturdy enough to hold him.

"How difficult was that?" Prime asked.

"Not difficult."

"It's a great tool. You see, the compound mechanism and the leverage of the handles make it powerful. Do you see the importance of this tool, Derrick?"

Derrick was afraid to answer because he thought he knew where this was going. "I'm not sure."

"You should address me as sir or master, but you will be gone soon. I thought about dragging this out both for entertainment and effectiveness. However, now that I've met you in person, I believe we can speed things up. I want that body, and your mind will be easy to crush. The success of your little group is not because of you. Is it, Derrick?"

Derrick cast his eyes downward. "It is not."

"I believe you are the weakest among them. Do you agree?"

"Yes."

"Yes, what?"

"Yes, Prime."

Prime laughed. "Close enough."

"Let me give you a clear picture, Derrick. Deconstruction has always been a long, detailed process. The doctors and scientists nipping away at the test subject's body a piece at a time. The time involved is the most devastating thing, really, but at some point, they all give up. Their only wish was for it to end. Some died earlier in the process than did others. That, too, yielded important information to achieve the ultimate goal for creating the perfect test subject. Regardless of whether they succumbed quickly or not, in the end, they all beg for death."

The deconstructed victim's image in Denver leaped vividly into Derrick's mind. "I don't understand. How does Deconstruction create a better body for you to inhabit if you destroy that body?"

Deconstruction
A Derrick King Novel, Book 8

"Ah, good question, Derrick. I'm getting to that part." Prime took the tool and placed it on a table. "Imagine putting the jaws of that tool around a person's ankle, putting just enough pressure on it to break the skin. The person knows what's coming. They're about to lose a foot in a horrendously violent and painful manner. Now, imagine that person is one of your friends. Perhaps we'll start with Antonio. He's an athlete, right? For him, it's not just the pain, the loss of a foot, it's the loss of his dream. He will scream at you, he'll beg you. And then you'll cut his foot off."

"Let's not delay. Follow me. Drag Quigley's chair along with you."

Prime picked up the tool and walked toward the other side of the area. A large metal door slid open as Prime approached. When Derrick stepped inside, his stomach turned. Except that only happened in his head, which didn't make it any less unpleasant. The walls were lined with tubes. Three contained Prime replicants suspended in a clear liquid like the other Prime Headquarters. In one tube was a very old man. Derrick wasn't sure if he was alive or dead, but he looked dead. In other tubes, half filled with what Derrick assumed was the same clear liquid, were his friends: Miriam, Rebekah, Akira, Red, Anna, and Nyx. They were gagged, but their eyes were pleading. Fear etched their faces.

Antonio was strapped to a stainless-steel table just like the one in Denver. He, too, was gagged. He lifted his head and made eye contact with Derrick.

Prime stood nearby, staring at Derrick.

Derrick could feel the sweat streaming down his face. He was screaming no in his head, but he knew he would do exactly as Prime ordered him to do. If he only had control of his body, he'd kill himself before he would hurt any of his friends.

"You see, I believe Derrick King will cease to exist before he gets through the last victim. Let's start with Mr. Morales. Don't worry. We won't kill Antonio just yet. I'm thinking both feet, maybe both hands. Would that be painful for you, Derrick?"

Derrick felt tears streaming down his cheeks. Antonio thrashed on the table and tried to scream. His friends in the tubes shook their heads and groaned. Their eyes had gone from sad to wild.

"I have not decided, but perhaps Red next and then Rebekah. Same process, hands and feet, and then you will continue until they have no arms or legs. How does that sound, Derrick?" Prime picked up another instrument. It was a thick metal rod attached to a large, black rectangular box with a simple switch. Prime held the switch down and the rod instantly turned bright red. Derrick smelled the hot metal and felt the heat.

"You'll have to cauterize the wounds. We don't want them to bleed out too quickly. As an added benefit, the burning is extremely painful. Often the victim passes out. But we have ways to revive them."

Prime set the hot iron under the table. Antonio tried to pull away from the hot metal but only managed an inch or so.

Prime said, "After Rebekah, I'll have you start on Anna. Does that sound good to you, Derrick? How many of them can you chop up before you break completely? Until your very essence is gone?"

"Please. I'll do anything. Just not that."

Prime laughed. "This is going to be so much fun."

"Perhaps after you remove Antonio's feet, I'll have you launch a few missiles. Then you can watch the world destroy itself while you chop."

"Why? Why are you doing this?" Derrick cried.

"I've explained it to you. However, you're not the smartest test subject we ever created. You have my genes, but the effect of the chip, hypnosis, and memory wipe did not allow you to reach your mental potential. That, however, is for the best. The weaker the mind, the more complete its elimination. I, on the other hand, am the smartest person to have ever lived. While you have not developed to your full potential, there's nothing physically wrong with your brain, and I'll put it to good use."

Prime paced back and forth for a moment without speaking.

Stanley said, "To be honest, I'm a little confused about what you hope to accomplish. I understand you want Derrick's body. I get that part. But destroying the world. That makes little sense to me. Conquering Mexico, South America, and Canada. I understood that. You planned to reduce the population but maintain the value of those countries. But why kill millions? Destroy land and resources. It will set civilization back decades."

"You're close. I will ensure the nuclear winter lasts 20 to 30 years. Perhaps longer than that. Once the other countries' militaries are gone and the infrastructure is destroyed, I'll gather my military all in one place and kill them as well. My scientists believe five to ten percent of the population will survive. You are wrong about setting them back decades. I will take them back to the stone age. I may have to send out the killer autotrons for a few additional decades to ensure that is accomplished. What is left will be a manageable population of almost prehistoric humans. By then, I will have perfected duplication of bodies in which I will live. I shall be legion and omnipresent."

Prime paused, looking from Derrick to Stanley, its eyes gone wild.

"Do you understand? I will be their King. Their Savior. The Creator of all things."

Stanley said, "With all due respect, sir, that's dangerous. People will follow initially, but they will rebel."

Prime smacked Stanley across the face. His head snapped to the side and blood flew. "And I'll deal with them swiftly and violently. They shall worship me or die."

Deconstruction
A Derrick King Novel, Book 8

Derrick didn't know if Stanley was dead or unconscious. It didn't matter; Stanley could not save him. He had hoped Miriam would escape, but that was impossible. All hope faded. He believed Miriam was smart enough to make this work. Now, he understood Prime had been on to them since Seattle.

"Mr. King. We've delayed long enough. Take the tool and remove one of Antonio's feet."

Derrick walked over and picked up the tool. He looked at his friends and saw the terror on their faces. He wondered if they understood he could not control his body. "I'm sorry. I have no control."

Prime shouted at him. "Enough! Level four! You may no longer speak other than to respond to my commands!"

"Yes, Master."

Strange as it seemed, although Derrick felt as if he was locked in that small sphere of diminishing thoughts and memories, L. Linda Maxton would not leave him alone. Then he realized it wasn't L. Linda. She was dead. It was his memory of her that plagued him. Perhaps there was something important he should remember, not that he had any hope remembering it would help. But he couldn't hear what she was saying.

However, she wasn't saying anything. She had already said it. He just couldn't remember her words. Or perhaps he wasn't listening.

He had not been listening as he should have. Listening with his heart, not his ears, not his head.

"Promise me," L. Linda said.

Her green eyes pierced his soul.

Then it occurred to him. He still wore the jacket from Level 2. Prime had not recognized it as a weapon.

"Promise me two things. One, stay alive. Two, destroy Prime," L. Linda said.

"But I can't …"

"Promise me." L. Linda touched her finger to his lips.

He felt her touch.

He felt it.

"Derrick! Respond to me. I told you to cut off one of Antonio's feet. Do it now!"

Derrick looked up. Prime was standing next to Antonio. Holding the tool with one hand, Derrick walked toward Antonio.

When he was within a few feet, he said, "Which foot?"

"Start with his right."

Derrick paused, glaring at Prime. "There's a problem."

"What problem?" Prime screamed.

Derrick raised his arm straight out, palm up. "I made a promise."

Prime's eyes grew wide; its mouth fell open.

And with that, Derrick closed his hand and blew a hole the size of a softball through Prime's chest.

Deconstruction
A Derrick King Novel, Book 8

Epilogue

Hi, I'm Derrick King. Two years have passed, and my college spring break ended a few days ago. Miriam insisted that questions remain unanswered about what happened after killing Prime. She was right about that. Yet, she also agreed, there should be some closure, and I also agree with that.

Why did I wait so long? Here's the thing, for me, ending Prime's reign was all that mattered. End of story, at least the end of mine. I was just ready to move on. The story regarding my involvement with Prime was over. I wanted a normal life. I figured normal was going to be tough enough.

However, recently my life took a dramatic turn. In fact, it was that dramatic event that jarred me into telling you the rest of the story, filling in some gaps. But mostly I learned something I think you'll want to hear about. More on that later.

Here goes.

Miriam, Akira, Rebekah, Anna, Antonio, Red, and Nyx, as well as our guests, William and Kevin, were okay. Well, not okay, but alive. Stanley Mires freed them and destroyed the replicants. I could have destroyed the replicants, but Mr. Mires begged me to let him do it. Miriam wiped the computer files that held Prime's blueprint to ensure that monster could never return.

Miriam told Stanley Mires to take over the management of the Acropolis Complex, with one directive: no one leaves until she returned. Many things needed to be sorted out, including who were to be prosecuted for crimes they did at Prime's direction. Stanley gave a full confession of the things he had done. The powers to be would make decisions. Stanley's work had helped destroy Prime, so that would be taken into consideration.

While on that topic, you know, about past crimes, I have not yet talked to Lawrence King. I know he is still in Cascade Lakes. I don't have a pressing need to talk to the man I knew as Father. That doesn't mean I won't, but it does mean I don't need to. I'm fine either way. I don't hate him. I still might talk to him someday, but not today.

Charlie was fully functional when we returned. He had salvaged Akira's emotions from the wreckage of his previous form, although he had named them and filed them, which meant he could have deleted them, but he decided not to. They had become part of him. Akira was working on developing her emotions from scratch.

Deconstruction
A Derrick King Novel, Book 8

We took turns in the medical unit. Charlie had to override the medical unit to treat only those wounds we wanted healed. Scratches and bruising would be expected from spending several days in the wilderness, so those things were not treated. However, bullet wounds and literal gold shrapnel would be hard to explain. Red insisted on keeping his pieces of gold. He said he wanted to make something out of them. I gave him a few pieces they dug out of me as well. Miriam said no at first but relented.

Miriam cobbled out the framework for a new age. Once that was done, we returned to Potterville. We could have taken an aircraft, but it was early evening and could not risk anyone seeing us. So, we took the slow trip to engineering and then walked out. It surprised Red, Antonio, and Nyx how close they had lived to the hidden military complex. Miriam didn't tell them it needed to be kept secret. They understood. Near downtown, we spotted Lori Martinez in her police car. She took us to Jack's shop where Sheriff Collins, Jack Fletcher, Allen Patel, and Donna Parks were eating dinner. Miriam did the talking; Red and I wandered through Mr. Fletchers cars.

The first objective was convincing them to keep our involvement in Prime's demise secret. That part wasn't too hard. Convincing Collins of the next step proved more difficult. Miriam, however, is persistent and persuasive. You may have noticed that.

Monday, the first day of school, went like this. At seven a.m., every television, every smart phone, and every radio station went dead. Then this simple message appeared on the screens and was announced over the air.

```
A National Public Service Broadcast will begin at
10 a.m. Please tell everyone you know to watch or
listen. All government agencies, schools,
universities, and businesses must gather all
students and employees for this broadcast. The
broadcast will be repeated for 24 hours. After
that, new information will be broadcast as it
becomes available.
```

Browning and Collins met with the principal before the students began arriving. At 7:30 Miriam, Rebekah, Anna, and I met Antonio at the front steps. He led us to Registration, but Mrs. Bates took us to the gymnasium, where it appeared all the students and teachers were gathered. Principal Snapp got everyone's attention and turned it over to Collins.

Collins read from a prepared statement:

"I come to you with a heavy heart. You may have heard rumors, and I'm here to give you the facts. Several people in Potterville were murdered during the past few days, including one Potterville High School student. The perpetrators have also been killed." Sheriff Collins then read the list of victims.

Deconstruction
A Derrick King Novel, Book 8

Before 10 a.m. we were all back in our respective classrooms. Normally, the bell rang at 10, but that was altered because of the incoming message. The teachers had televisions turned on and the same message appeared on them all. At precisely 10 a.m., the screen changed. A voice declared a National Public Service Announcement and started a countdown—10, 9, 8, …

I recognized Charlie's voice. Easier just to tell you what he said:

"During the past 48 hours, strategic law enforcement operations were conducted in several cities to serve an arrest warrant for the entity known as Prime. Prime was charged with conspiracy to commit murder and accessory to murder in the deaths of four people in Potterville, California. Prime resisted arrest and was killed.

"During the investigation, it became clear that Prime was responsible for the assassination of the president and vice president. Prime then took control of New America's government and military. In addition, we learned that Prime planned to start a world war.

"The war was averted, and you are safe. The country will remain under martial law, under the authority of Commander Cliff Haskins, until an interim government can be established. A commission will begin governing the nation immediately and will start the process of establishing a new constitution and government. The following people have been named to the commission: Commander Cliff Haskins; Professor Corbin Atwood; Lloyd Nist; Potterville, California Sheriff, Bill Collins; and Potterville High School Teacher Arthur Browning. Additional members and ad hoc members will be added as needed.

"The initial acts of the commission are as follows: people in Chosen communities are no longer under lockdown and are free to come and go; all Prime properties, holdings, companies, and cash have been seized, proper dispensation of those holdings will be forthcoming; the term New America is now null and void and will be systematically removed from all buildings, media,

and currency. Henceforth, the country will again
be known as the United States of America. Prime
overthrew the United States. The people have taken
it back.

"In this time of transition, it is vital that you
demonstrate patience, tolerance, and compassion
for each other. Thank you. Bless you. And bless
the United States of America."

Miriam wrote the speech, and Charlie narrated it. It did not mention that
Miriam would be an adjunct member on the committee. And you understand,
that means Miriam will play a major role in figuring out our future. I'm happy
about that.

Now, to catch you up on Potterville happenings.

Surprisingly, despite my origins, our ordeal, and all that we saw and did, I
felt more at home than I thought possible. Sure, I still didn't understand every
colloquialism, vulgarity, slang, and figure of speech, and I was still completely
capable of embarrassing myself, but my life grew more comfortable than I had
expected and quicker than I anticipated. It helped having so many friends who
understood and helped me learn.

As you know, Sheriff Collins was placed on what was officially known as
the United States of America Restoration Council. He appointed Lori Martinez
as interim sheriff but not before she changed her name to Lori Collins. (I'll bet
you saw that coming.)

Miriam went to Potterville High until summer break, and then she
challenged the senior testing, graduating early and accepting a scholarship to
MIT. She continued working at the base with Charlie whenever possible. (She
keeps an aircraft in a bay at Jack Fletcher's shop and flies in and out at night.)

Akira graduated valedictorian and received a scholarship to USC. Akira's
emotions returned but were altered. Emotionally, she started over and became
a new person. She and Miriam remain close friends.

Rebekah played volleyball and soccer at Potterville and is on a soccer
scholarship to the University of Oregon. We stay in touch. While there is
nothing romantic about our relationship, Rebekah will always be one of my best
friends.

Red Badowski, Henry Clark, and I all went to the University of California,
Berkley (CAL) where Coach Browning accepted a position as defensive line
coach. Collins permits Coach to teleconference with the commission. Red is
studying to become an engineer and then plans to enter medical school. In his
spare time, which is minimal, he goes to the base with Miriam to study the
medical unit.

Deconstruction
A Derrick King Novel, Book 8

Anna is still in Potterville. In high school, she took a special interest in the kids who ran with Jimmy Priest, befriending them, teaching them, and helping them adjust to their new reality. She worked part time for Donna and became full time after high school, and she is learning to run the business. In addition, she is helping Jack Fletcher set up a car museum.

I should mention that in addition to scholarships, Miriam set up funds for each of us involved in Prime's termination. I didn't want mine and haven't touched it, but Miriam insisted. You might have noticed that she can be stubborn. Miriam has also invested in the car museum, which she says will be great for tourism.

Antonio got two scholarships at UC Davis, one for football and the other for track.

So that brings you up to date.

Oh. Me and Nyx. That, as it turns out, has taken a bit of a twist. So, Nyx and I were boyfriend and girlfriend the remainder of our high school days. We were inseparable, trained together, went to the prom—all of it. Then I went to CAL, and Nyx went to San Diego State. We maintained a long-distance relationship. Talked on the phone, met up on weekends when we didn't have a game or a meet. Hung out when on break.

Speaking of CAL. I have to backtrack. So, this is important. At least it is to me. Shortly after the whole killing Prime incident, I tried to break the barrier I had with Red. You might remember even when we did things like working on the reactor, Red would always point out that we were not friends. He continued to do that at football practice and such. So, one day, I asked him to meet me at Donna's for coffee. I told him I'd like to be friends, and he said that would never happen and he never wanted me to ask him to be his friend again. Then he said, "Dude, you are not my friend. You're my brother." So, yeah. Red's my brother.

There you have it.

Most of it. It's already a long story, but as they say, life is often stranger than fiction.

There is this one last part.

I mentioned our recent spring break. I didn't get home until late Sunday. Nyx sent me a text message late that night, saying she needed to talk and to meet her at Donna's at nine the next morning. I'll be truthful, it troubled me. My stomach kind of twisted.

Sometimes my imagination, still gets the better of me.

But what my stomach felt, my heart knew the moment I rounded the corner and saw Nyx.

Sitting at an outside table with Antonio.

Deconstruction
A Derrick King Novel, Book 8

Nyx told me she and Antonio had been talking on the phone for the past few weeks. They realized they still had feelings for one another and that it wouldn't be fair to me if they didn't take some time and see where things went.

I'm going to tell it straight. My heart ached so badly; I wasn't sure I could draw another breath. Antonio said he never wanted to hurt me. I believed him.

Right when I was about to explode, I remembered something. Do you remember that time when I had been out of the aircraft in the PFP? And when I returned, I thought I saw Nyx and Antonio, well, doing something I thought was inappropriate? And it turned out Antonio had been hit by shrapnel and Nyx was simply tending to his wound? Well, that came to me, and I remembered that when that happened, I realized my friends' health and happiness were more important than what I wanted for myself.

Difficult as it was, I told them I loved them both and wished them all the luck in the world.

My life took a turn right then and there that I had not seen coming. Blind-sided, I think, is the term. I was doing what everyone expected of me. You know, going to college, playing football, maybe going to the pros, etc. Suddenly, I realized that doing what was expected wasn't the same as doing what's right.

So, right after learning that Nyx and I were no longer a couple. I went to my condo, grabbed my guitar, and walked straight to Mountain View Music. That went like this:

"Derrick!" Mark Grealy grabbed my hand and then pulled me into a bear hug. "It's great to see you. What can I do for you? New strings? Picks?"

"I want to return your guitar. I should have done that a long time ago."

"You don't have to do that, Derrick." He glanced around as if to ensure there were no customers present that he'd forgotten about. "Knowing what you did for us all."

"I insist. Maybe you can use it for someone else who wants to learn. It's a nice guitar."

"Are you still playing?"

I nodded.

"Play me something."

I was kind of hoping he'd ask. I played him a tune, sang too. After all, playing is all about making music.

"Derrick, that was fantastic. You have quite a talent there."

"It's mostly work, sir. Not so much talent."

"Then you've cracked the code."

"I'd like to buy a guitar, sir."

Grealy sat on his stool. "Okay. What do you have in mind?"

"Do you still have the old Martin? I didn't see it sitting in the window."

Grealy thought for a moment and then nodded. "It's in the back. Too valuable to leave in the window. Not so much worried that someone will steal

Deconstruction
A Derrick King Novel, Book 8

it. It's not like that here. Plus, things are really going well since the commission has taken over. Did you hear they made me an adjunct member for the restoration of the arts?"

I smiled. "Congratulations. You're perfect for the job. So, anyway, I'd like to buy the old Martin."

Grealy said, "It's not for sale, son. Hasn't been for quite some time."

Without saying more, he got up, went to the back, and then returned carrying a tattered old case. He opened it up, pulled out the Martin, and handed it to me. "Play me another song."

I did, but it was hard not to cry while doing it. I had been dreaming about this old guitar. I had money; Miriam had seen to that, but I had not spent any yet. The scholarship covered school, and I didn't need much else.

I finished and returned the Martin to its case. "Who bought it?"

"No one bought it. Like I said, it's not for sale."

"You decided to keep it?"

"I did. Until you came to retrieve it. It's yours, son."

Well, there was more said, a few tears shed, and hugging, but you get the idea.

And that put the gears in motion. My mind was made up. I drove to CAL and went straight to Coach's office.

"I'm quitting school, Coach." Trust me, that wasn't easy to say.

Browning stared at me. "Can I ask why?"

"Nyx and I broke up."

Browning nodded. "I'm sorry, Derrick. I truly am, but that's no reason to throw you future away. It's going to hurt for a while, but it will get better. You'll see."

"It hurt, but that's not why I'm quitting." I paused. "Coach, it's not who I am. I have to follow a different path."

I anticipated a long talk consisting of lots of lecturing, judging, and cajoling. But it didn't happen.

"Are you sure?"

"As sure as I can be."

"Derrick, you realize I love you like one of my own, right? So, I'm just going to wish you luck and ask that you stay in touch. We expect you for Thanksgiving and Christmas if you can make it."

And just like that, I set a new direction for my life. I didn't know where it would take me, but I had to give it my best shot. I'd pay my own way and would use none of the money that Miriam gave me. If it didn't work out, then at least I had tried. My plan was to play as much as possible. I had been playing some clubs and coffee shops whenever I could, so I had some places established. Still, some gigs would only be tips, sometimes I would be busking on the street. Just

Deconstruction
A Derrick King Novel, Book 8

me and my old Martin guitar. With music now legal, it was becoming somewhat of a rage.

I felt good. I had taken control of my life. Really, for the first time ever.

Well, I mostly felt good, but there was something bothering me. It wasn't something I felt safe mentioning to anyone. Not even Nyx. Especially not Nyx.

I was having some concerns about my mental health.

There were times, all really really weird times, when I'd swear, I saw those green eyes. You remember the green eyes, right? The first time was during a football game at CAL. It's not like you can focus on individuals in the crowd, but I had gotten run out of bounds, hurdled the foam barrier, and when I glanced up into the crowd, I saw them. Just the eyes and only for a split second. I immediately scanned the crowd, but I couldn't spot them again.

This happened from time to time. Always in a crowd. I never got a good look at the person. And I could never find them a second time. It worried me. But I never told anyone about it. Not Miriam, not Red, not Coach. I couldn't tell Nyx. She might think I was still thinking about L. Linda Maxton. Which, of course, I was. L. Linda Maxton had become a ghost that would haunt me forever. I had made her a promise to kill Prime, and I kept my promise. But her ghost apparently wasn't satisfied. I had also let her die.

Then it happened.

Just a few days after I quit school, I was playing at a small club. They call it a speakeasy. No outside signage, no advertising. Just an obscure door leading to a basement, where a man greets patrons and asks them for a password. There really is a password, but if there's room, the doorman tells the new customer the password and lets them enter. I had played there a few times before spring break because we were not yet in football camp. Each time, the crowd had grown a little. I'm unsure if it's me or just the word getting out about good drinks at a reasonable cost and the novelty about the speakeasy.

It happened near the end of my set. I glanced up and saw those green eyes across the room. I couldn't see the person's face, but I was pretty sure it was a woman. I decided to put an end to my insanity. Right there.

I ended the song early, put my guitar on the stand, and bolted for the back door. No way I could get through the crowd and the person had turned and headed for the exit.

I sprinted down the alley, around the block to the front of the building. I saw a woman walking away. I could not see her hair because she wore a scarf or a shawl.

I caught up to her and stopped running. I said, "Excuse me."
She continued walking.
"Excuse me. Could I talk to you for a moment?"
She continued. Perhaps she was deaf. Maybe she wore headphones.
I gently tapped her shoulder. "I mean you no harm."

Deconstruction
A Derrick King Novel, Book 8

She stopped and turned around.

My mind locked up. Almost like when Prime took control, except different. What I was seeing and what I knew to be fact were completely messed up. I had heard of a doppelganger and decided that's what stood before me. The hair was different, but the color was right. The clothing was different, stylish, professional, not goofy. But the face was perfect. And those eyes. Before me stood.

L. Linda Maxton.

"I… It can't be… You're…."

"Dead? Turns out, I'm not. I'm truly sorry about the ruse, Derrick."

"But. How… did. Why?"

She held her finger to my lips. "Do you remember your promise?"

Unable to find words, I nodded. Finally, I said, "I killed him, L. Linda."

"I know you did. But that's not the promise I'm referring to."

I was lost for a moment.

"Do you remember when you called me and asked me to come to the base?"

"Uh. Yeah."

"I made you promise to have a cup of coffee with me. Just you and me. Do you remember that?"

"Well, yes. I guess so. Sorry, I guess it seemed, I don't know, kind of unimportant at the time."

"It was important to me. Will you keep that promise?"

"Sure. Tomorrow morning?"

"How about right now? I'll explain everything."

"Well, uh, okay, but coffee shops are closed. But we can find something. Just let me get my guitar."

L. Linda laced her arm through mine and led me away. My heart was racing, and I did not resist.

"Don't worry. I've made arrangements and there's a coffee shop nearby that's still open."

"Made arrangements?"

"For your guitar. I know how much it means to you. It will be well cared for."

I was too stunned to talk. I had a thousand questions but could ask none. Besides, I thought L. Linda would tell me what she wanted me to know. No more, no less. We came to a coffee shop that I had played at a few times, but it was closed. I knew that because I knew their hours. Plus, there was the fact it was dark, and a closed sign hung in the window. I'm good at seeing the obvious.

But L. Linda walked straight to the door.

"They are closed," I said.

"Not for us."

She was right about that. Near the stage was a table with a candle burning. On the stage sat my Martin. Two cups of steaming coffee sat on the table. I saw no people, not even behind the counter.

"DK Double Honey. I ordered ahead. I hope that's okay."

"It's perfect. I still can't believe this. To be honest, I think I'm having a mental breakdown."

She patted my hand. "You're not having a breakdown. This is really happening. I'm sorry it could not have happened sooner."

"I kept thinking I saw your eyes."

"You did. I checked in on you now and then."

"But Seattle. I thought you died." I paused. Beyond the shock, it hurt a little. "You ran out on us."

She glanced down, nodded. "I'm sorry about that."

"Care to explain?"

"I'm going to be honest and some of this may hurt a little. At first, I thought maybe you could help me. I had vowed to kill Prime."

"So why did you run? I mean. Killing Prime was literally what we were trying to do."

"Because I had to."

I said nothing for a moment. "It was scary. I mean. I don't blame you."

"I didn't go because I was scared. I left because it became clear that I had a different purpose. Killing Prime was your purpose. I trusted you to do that."

I studied her for a second. Her eyes were as beautiful as I'd remembered them, and her sheer beauty overwhelmed me. Her auburn hair fell about her shoulders; gone were the girlish ponytails, braids, and glasses she always wore.

"What purpose?" I asked.

"Protecting people. Remember, I told you I was trained to be an assassin."

"I remember."

"There were still assassins out there. Some went to Potterville while we were gone. Fortunately, Collins and the others reduced their numbers. However, even if you were successful in killing Prime, the assassins would not stop until they avenged Prime's death." She paused. "Derrick, I initially planned to use you. Do you understand? But that changed as soon as I met you. I had to protect you. You would have never been safe as long as even one assassin survived."

I said, "You..." but she cut me off.

"The best person to catch an assassin is another assassin. With Jason dead, I was the only one left who knew about them. That's why I didn't contact you earlier. I couldn't until they were gone."

"You killed them?"

"Not all of them. Some are in custody." She paused, took a sip, and then continued. "When I left you, I had nothing except the weapons we carried in.

But by Monday, the announcement came out. I recognized Charlie's voice, and I assumed Miriam wrote the script. That is one smart girl. So, I procured transportation and headed straight to the commission. I contacted Atwood."

"Professor?" Derrick asked. "But how did you find the assassins?"

"Yes, Professor. Convincing them to listen to me would have been very difficult had Browning and Collins not been involved. They knew about the assassins in Potterville. Collins confirmed that assassins were real. Atwood helped me contact Commander Haskins. I never met with any of them in person and only went by a code name. Everything was done using email and burner phones. To answer your question, Jason downloaded the assassin files before he set the training center on fire. I went home in cover of darkness and retrieved the flash drive on which they were stored. Then, I did the finding; they did the arresting. Most resisted."

We sat in silence for a bit and sipped coffee. My head was still reeling. It felt like a dream, but the coffee tasted real. If I were to be honest, and that is certainly my intent nowadays, I'd tell you that something stirred in my chest that felt welcome, unbelievable, warm, and scary.

Finally, L. Linda said, "I heard about Nyx and Antonio. I'm sorry."

"Thanks, L. Linda."

"It's just Linda now. I don't have to roleplay anymore. I can just be me." She paused. "And be honest."

"I can relate to that. Although, I'm still trying to figure out who me is. I quit school."

"No more football? Are you sure?"

"Pretty sure." I had not had to explain myself to anyone yet. Browning didn't press the matter, which surprised me. "I liked football. I loved playing for Coach. I didn't mind college either. I may go back someday." I took a sip. "Can I be honest?"

"Derrick, you are the only person I have ever talked to about being a trained assassin."

"But you didn't become an assassin. You didn't kill those people."

"Let me finish. I trusted you. You can trust me."

"You might laugh or think I'm conceited, which, in fairness, I used to be. Conceited that is."

"I'm listening."

"I loved football. But I hated it too. I know I'm not like genetically engineered, well, technically I am, but not to be superhuman or anything like that. But because of my training, I felt like it gave me an unfair advantage. It was too easy, and I wasn't working as hard as everyone else. Besides, I didn't see how it was going to help anyone other than a few minutes of cheering."

"Okay. I get that. Remember, I had a bit of training as well."

I nodded. I had improved a lot when it came to talking like a normal person and even understanding social norms. However, I was not beyond saying stupid stuff from time to time. And right now, I was having a hard time stringing together a coherent sentence.

"I want to play music. It doesn't come easy. I have to work at it."

"For a living?"

I held up my hands. "I know. It's crazy."

She smiled.

Wow!

Linda said, "I don't think it's crazy. I think it's fantastic. You're good, Derrick. People notice it. Right away. You have something special. I think it's because of what is in," she touched my chest, "here."

Okay, I'm kinda fighting tears now. "Thanks. That means a lot."

"It's getting late, and I have an early meeting tomorrow. Maybe you could come with me? Browning and Collins will be there. They still don't know that I'm alive. I'm a little nervous and having you there would help."

"Sure. I can do that. I'd like to see them both." I didn't add, and I'd like to see you again.

She smiled. "Before we leave, would you sing to me?"

I nodded, stepped to the stage, sat on the stool, and picked up my guitar. As I checked the tuning, I thought about what to play. She said, "Will you sing to me?" Not, "Will you sing me a song?"

Two different things. Or was I just imagining things again? Perhaps I was just imagining something that wasn't there, but I decided to go with singing to Linda Maxton rather than singing her a song.

None of my originals were good enough. Not yet. I picked a song written by Sir Elton John. When I came to these words, I knew what Elton John wrote many years ago spoke truth to my current feelings:

"I hope you don't mind
That I put down in words
How wonderful life is
while you're in the world."

the end

Author's Note:
Thank you for reading my books. If they gave you a bit of an escape, I'm pleased. Please consider **writing a review.** To sign up for my newsletter, visit my website daniellcopeland.com.

Acknowledgements:
Thanks to the love and support of the love of my life and partner, Liz. She is also a writer and illustrator. Check out her books on Amazon Libby K. I couldn't do any of this without her. She is also my best editor and critic.

Special thanks to Rod Leonard for providing feedback and guidance.

More books from Daniel L. Copeland:

The Derrick King Series

About the Author:

Daniel is a lifelong Idahoan and grew up on a small farm in Southern Idaho. He worked in the criminal justice system for 35 years and is now retired. Daniel has published nine novels. In addition to writing, he and his wife, Liz love to travel on their BMW motorcycle. They have ridden in most of the US, including Alaska, the Great Lakes, and Florida. They have also ridden in Canada, New Zealand, and Australia. Daniel is an award-winning home brewer and a certified beer judge.